IVANHOE

SIR WALTER SCOTT

In Two Volumes
Volume I

With a Preface by
MALCOLM ELWIN

DISTRIBUTED BY
HERON BOOKS

CONTENTS

PREFACE

"The charm of Ivanhoe *is addressed," wrote the weighty Walter Bagehot, "to that kind of boyish fancy which idolises meadiaeval society as the 'fighting time'." Victorian and Edwardian schoolmasters agreed with him that "a martial society, where men fought hand to hand on good horses with large lances, in peace for pleasure, and in war for business, seems the very ideal of perfection to a bold and simply fanciful boy." Consequently* Ivanhoe *became a "set book" in Eng. Lit. at schools.*

This was very well before the 1914 war, when Kipling's jingoism was the fashion and wars were fought by professional armies on remote imperial frontiers. I myself found Ivanhoe *a happy contrast with chemistry, geometry, and Caesar's repetitive habit of going into winter quarters, and went to the school library to find* Quentin Durward *and* The Talisman *for myself. But the scientists have since robbed war of its ancient glamour, and a friend who was at school in the 1930s tells me, "I was put off Scott by having to read* Ivanhoe *at school."*

That the popularity of Ivanhoe *might prove damaging to Scott's reputation was foreseen by Lockhart, who wrote, "I believe that no reader who is capable of thoroughly comprehending the author's Scotch character and Scotch dialogue will ever place even* Ivanhoe, *as a work of genius, on the same level with* Waverley, Guy Mannering, *or* The

PREFACE

Heart of Midlothian." *Even earlier Hazlitt (in* The Spirit of the Age, *1825) gave only passing mention to "the fine old English romance of* Ivanhoe" *before concentrating his attention on "the Scotch novels." At the turn of the century Professor* W. H. *Hudson related how he re-read all the Waverley Novels chronologically in preparation for his study,* Sir Walter Scott *(1901), and "*Ivanhoe *was the first I came to that left me with a distinct feeling of disappointment. I remembered it as rapid, passionate, full of breathless incident, and of enthralling interest; I found it a superb piece of stucco-work, melodramatic and wholly unreal."*

The judgment is not unjust. In Ivanhoe *the hero and heroine deserve all that Bagehot syas in disparagement of Scott's heroes and heroines: Wilfred of* Ivanhoe *has "little personality," with no such problems of divided loyalties as perturb Morton in* Old Mortality *or the Smith in* The Fair Maid of Perth; *the Lady Rowena is "good-looking, and well-dressed (according to the old fashion), and sensible" — though she has scant claims to the last quality, shows little spirit, and dissolves into tears on the only occasion when faced with serious trouble. There are no comic characters of the stature of Bailie Jarvie in* Rob Roy *or Dalgetty in* A Legend of Montrose; *the best in* Ivanhoe *are the gallant, irrepressible jester Wamba and brawling, brawny, gluttonous Friar Tuck. There are no such subtle studies of historical figures as Claverhouse in* Old Mortality *or Louis XI in* Quentin Durward; *King Richard defies probability in returning incognito from the Crusades to fraternise with his oppressed subjects — if, as Bagehot says, he is "the traditional Richard," it is because the popularity*

PREFACE

of Ivanhoe *imposed Scott's conception upon the Victorian historians.*

Having been read by all Macaulay'x schoolboys, Ivanhoe *lends credence to Bagehot's charge that Scott was unconcerned with "the searching and abstract intellect," to V. S. Pritchett's that his heroes and heroines are too often "wooden idealisations, projections of our more refined, sixteen-year-old wishes," to E. M. Forster's superficial assertion that "Scott is not interested in reasons... to make one thing happen after another is his only serious aim."*

Well, when all is said, the master storyteller does "make one thing happen after another." In Ivanhoe *one vivid scene after another is brilliantly conjured from the hat of the magician's imagination: the reception of the Normans at the Saxon feast, the tournament at Ashby, the Black Knight's comic reception by the hermit, the siege of Front-de-Boeuf's castle and his haunted death, Rebecca's trial by the Templars and the suspense of awaiting her champion, the king's rescue by the forest outlaws, the sensational death of Bois-Guilbert when he has Ivanhoe at his mercy. John Buchan fairly calls it "a pageant so far-flung and glittering that, in spite of its artificiality, it captivates the fancy."*

The English have always loved pageantry; they have never been generous patrons of thought and art. At the time Ivanhoe *was written, they had lately driven Byron, Shelley, and Landor into exile. A shrewd observer of humanity, Scott may not have been unmindful of these national characteristics in making "an experiment on a subject purely English." He is unafraid to confess (Chapter XL) that he is using personalities from the "penny-histories of Robin Hood"—which apparently existed in his days, as*

XI

PREFACE

in the familiar yellow wrappers sold for a penny before 1914. He forgets only Little John till too late to make use of him, so mentions him as "absent on an expedition" to the Scottish border.

In his notes to the collected edition he ably defends himself against those academics who impugned his accuracy in historical detail, and acknowledges his faults. Some eight years after Ivanhoe, *in refusing Ballantyne's request that Oliver Proudfute in* The Fair Maid of Perth *should be spared from assassination, he reminded him that "the resurrection of Athelstane was a botch." He acknowledges his readers' indignation at the sad departure of the noble Rebecca, so much more deserving of a heroine's reward than the vapid Rowena. Such indignation inspired Thackeray to write his satirical sequel to the novel,* Rebecca and Rowena, *in which Rowena after marriage continually taunts Ivanhoe about his "flirtation" when "you were locked up with the Jewess in the tower." Some of Scott's solemn critics will find most of their points anticipated in* Rebecca and Rowena!

As to "thought", there is surely food for it in the revelation of sinister power possessed by the masonic order of Templar Knights and in the study of Isaac the Jew. We see the brutal persecution of the Jews, but also how they invited resentment by their insistence on nationality and their abuse of the power of money; Isaac's counting of Gurth's cash in Chapter X has the same comic effect as Figaro's counting in Rossini's opera, The Barber of Seville. *But nobody can accuse Scott of anti-semitism, since Rebecca is shown so far above the Saxon princess in nobility of character.*

PREFACE

At first it was intended to publish Ivanhoe *pseudonymously—hence the dedicatory epistle by "Laurence Templeton"—but the publisher Constable decided against dispensing with the selling impetus of the legend, "By the Author of* Waverley." *"Almost the whole" of* Ivanhoe *was dictated, as Scott was still suffering from the "stomach cramps" which caused his resorting to dictation of* The Bride of Lammermoor *and* A Legend of Montrose. *The first volume was "very nearly finished" by 19th July 1819; the book was completed by 10th November, and published in three volumes at ten shillings a volume on 18th December 1819. Twelve thousand copies of this edition were sold, for, says Lockhart, "Ivanhoe was received throughout England with a more clamorous delight than any of the* Scotch novels *had been."*

However critics may carp, they cannot deny to Scott a shrewd sense of his market. If there is less "thought" than in the Scotch novels, the "art" of the master is abundantly evident. As a tale of action, Ivanhoe *is a masterpiece of melodrama—an exposition of consummate skill in the art of storytelling.*

MALCOLM ELWIN.

IVANHOE

A ROMANCE

Now fitted the halter, now traversed the cart,
And often took leave,—but seemed loath to depart !*

PRIOR.

* The motto alludes to the Author returning to the stage repeatedly after having taken leave.

INTRODUCTION

THE Author of the Waverley Novels had hitherto
proceeded in an unabated course of popularity, and
might, in his peculiar district of literature, have
been termed *L'Enfant Gâté* of success. It was
plain, however, that frequent publication must
finally wear out the public favour, unless some
mode could be devised to give an appearance
of novelty to subsequent productions. Scottish
manners, Scottish dialect, and Scottish characters
of note, being those with which the author was
most intimately and familiarly acquainted, were
the groundwork upon which he had hitherto relied
for giving effect to his narrative. It was, however, obvious, that this kind of interest must in
the end occasion a degree of sameness and repeti-
tion, if exclusively resorted to, and that the reader
was likely at length to adopt the language of
Edwin, in Parnell's Tale :—

> ' " Reverse the spell," he cries,
> " And let it fairly now suffice,
>   The gambol has been shown." '

Nothing can be more dangerous for the fame

of a professor of the fine arts, than to permit (if he can possibly prevent it) the character of a mannerist to be attached to him, or that he should be supposed capable of success only in a particular and limited style. The public are, in general, very ready to adopt the opinion, that he who has pleased them in one peculiar mode of composition, is, by means of that very talent, rendered incapable of venturing upon other subjects. The effect of this disinclination, on the part of the public, towards the artificers of their pleasures, when they attempt to enlarge their means of amusing, may be seen in the censures usually passed by vulgar criticism upon actors or artists who venture to change the character of their efforts, that, in so doing, they may enlarge the scale of their art.

There is some justice in this opinion, as there always is in such as attain general currency. It may often happen on the stage, that an actor, by possessing in a pre-eminent degree the external qualities necessary to give effect to comedy, may be deprived of the right to aspire to tragic excellence; and in painting or literary composition, an artist or poet may be master exclusively of modes of thought, and powers of expression, which confine him to a single course of subjects. But much more frequently the same capacity which carries a man to popularity in one department will obtain for him success in another, and that must be more particularly the case in literary composition, than either in acting or painting, because the adventurer in that department is not impeded in his exertions by any peculiarity of features, or conformation of person, proper for particular parts, or, by any peculiar mechanical habits of using the pencil, limited to a particular class of subjects.

Whether this reasoning be correct or otherwise, the present author felt, that, in confining himself to subjects purely Scottish, he was not only likely to weary out the indulgence of his readers, but also greatly to limit his own power of affording them pleasure. In a highly polished country, where so much genius is monthly employed in catering for public amusement, a fresh topic, such as he had himself had the happiness to light upon, is the untasted spring of the desert ;—

> ' Men bless their stars and call it luxury.'

But when men and horses, cattle, camels, and dromedaries, have poached the spring into mud, it becomes loathsome to those who at first drank of it with rapture ; and he who had the merit of discovering it, if he would preserve his reputation with the tribe, must display his talent by a fresh discovery of untasted fountains.

If the author, who finds himself limited to a particular class of subjects, endeavours to sustain his reputation by striving to add a novelty of attraction to themes of the same character which have been formerly successful under his management, there are manifest reasons why, after a certain point, he is likely to fail. If the mine be not wrought out, the strength and capacity of the miner become necessarily exhausted. If he closely imitates the narratives which, he has before rendered successful, he is doomed to 'wonder that they please no more.' If he struggles to take a different view of the same class of subjects, he speedily discovers that what is obvious, graceful, and natural, has been exhausted; and, in order to obtain the indispensable charm of novelty, he is forced upon caricature, and, to avoid being trite, must become extravagant.

It is not, perhaps, necessary to enumerate so many reasons why the author of the Scottish Novels, as they were then exclusively termed, should be desirous to make an experiment on a subject purely English. It was his purpose, at the same time, to have rendered the experiment as complete as possible, by bringing the intended work before the public as the effort of a new candidate for their favour, in order that no degree of prejudice, whether favourable or the reverse, might attach to it, as a new production of the Author of Waverley; but this intention was afterwards departed from, for reasons to be hereafter mentioned.

The period of the narrative adopted was the reign of Richard I., not only as abounding with characters whose very names were sure to attract general attention, but as affording a striking contrast betwixt the Saxons, by whom the soil was cultivated, and the Normans, who still reigned in it as conquerors, reluctant to mix with the vanquished, or acknowledge themselves of the same stock. The idea of this contrast was taken from the ingenious and unfortunate Logan's tragedy of Runnamede, in which, about the same period of history, the author had seen the Saxon and Norman barons opposed to each other on different sides of the stage. He does not recollect that there was any attempt to contrast the two races in their habits and sentiments; and indeed it was obvious, that history was violated by introducing the Saxons still existing as a high-minded and martial race of nobles.

They did, however, survive as a people, and some of the ancient Saxon families possessed wealth and power, although they were exceptions to the humble condition of the race in

general. It seemed to the author, that the existence of the two races in the same country, the
vanquished distinguished by their plain, homely,
blunt manners, and the free spirit infused by
their ancient institutions and laws; the victors,
by the high spirit of military fame, personal adventure, and whatever could distinguish them as
the Flower of Chivalry, might, intermixed with
other characters belonging to the same time and
country, interest the reader by the contrast, if the
author should not fail on his part.

Scotland, however, had been of late used so
exclusively as the scene of what is called Historical Romance, that the preliminary letter of Mr.
Laurence Templeton became in some measure
necessary. To this, as to an Introduction, the
reader is referred, as expressing the author's purpose and opinions in undertaking this species of
composition, under the necessary reservation, that
he is far from thinking he has attained the point
at which he aimed.

It is scarcely necessary to add, that there was
no idea or wish to pass off the supposed Mr.
Templeton as a real person. But a kind of continuation of the Tales of My Landlord had been
recently attempted by a stranger, and it was supposed this Dedicatory Epistle might pass for
some imitation of the same kind, and thus putting

enquirers upon a false scent, induce them to believe they had before them the work of some new candidate for their favour.

After a considerable part of the work had been finished and printed, the Publishers, who pretended to discern in it a germ of popularity, remonstrated strenuously against its appearing as an absolutely anonymous production, and contended that it should have the advantage of being announced as by the Author of Waverley. The author did not make any obstinate opposition, for he began to be of opinion with Dr. Wheeler, in Miss Edgeworth's excellent tale of 'Manœuvring,' that 'Trick upon Trick' might be too much for the patience of an indulgent public, and might be reasonably considered as trifling with their favour.

The book, therefore, appeared as an avowed continuation of the Waverley Novels; and it would be ungrateful not to acknowledge, that it met with the same favourable reception as its predecessors.

Such annotations as may be useful to assist the reader in comprehending the characters of the Jew, the Templar, the Captain of the mercenaries, or Free Companions, as they were called, and others proper to the period, are added, but with a sparing hand, since sufficient information on these subjects is to be found in general history.

An incident in the tale, which had the good fortune to find favour in the eyes of many readers, is more directly borrowed from the stores of old romance. I mean the meeting of the King with Friar Tuck at the cell of that buxom hermit. The general tone of the story belongs to all ranks and all countries, which emulate each other in describing the rambles of a disguised sovereign, who, going in search of information or amusement, into the lower ranks of life, meets with adventures diverting to the reader or hearer, from the contrast betwixt the monarch's outward appearance, and his real character. The Eastern tale-teller has for his theme the disguised expeditions of Haroun Alraschid with his faithful attendants, Mesrour and Giafar, through the midnight streets of Bagdad; and Scottish tradition dwells upon the similar exploits of James v., distinguished during such excursions by the travelling name of the Good-man of Ballengeigh, as the Commander of the Faithful, when he desired to be incognito, was known by that of Il Bondocani. The French minstrels are not silent on so popular a theme. There must have been a Norman original of the Scottish metrical romance of Rauf Colziar, in which Charlemagne is introduced as the unknown guest of a charcoal-man.* It seems to have been the original of other poems of the kind.

In merry England there is no end of popular ballads on this theme. The poem of John the Reeve, or Steward, mentioned by Bishop Percy, in the Reliques of English Poetry,† is said to have turned on such an incident; and we have besides, the King and the Tanner of Tamworth, the King and the Miller of Mansfield, and others on the same topic. But the peculiar tale of this nature to which the author of Ivanhoe has to acknowledge an obligation, is more ancient by two centuries than any of these last mentioned.

It was first communicated to the public in that curious record of ancient literature, which has been accumulated by the combined exertions of Sir Egerton Brydges and Mr. Hazlewood, in the periodical work entitled the British Bibliographer. From thence it has been transferred by the Reverend Charles Henry Hartshorne, M.A., editor of a very curious volume, entitled 'Ancient Metrical Tales, printed chiefly from original sources, 1829.' Mr. Hartshorne gives no other authority for the

---

* This very curious poem, long a *desideratum* in Scottish literature, and given up as irrecoverably lost, was lately brought to light by the researches of Dr. Irvine of the Advocates' Library, and has been re-printed by Mr. David Laing, Edinburgh.

† Vol. ii. p. 167.

present fragment, except the article in the Bibliographer, where it is entitled the Kyng and the
Hermite. A short abstract of its contents will
show its similarity to the meeting of King Richard
and Friar Tuck.

King Edward (we are not told which among the
monarchs of that name, but, from his temper and
habits, we may suppose Edward IV.) sets forth with
his court to a gallant hunting-match in Sherwood
Forest, in which, as is not unusual for princes in
romance, he falls in with a deer of extraordinary
size and swiftness, and pursues it closely, till he has
outstripped his whole retinue, tired out hounds
and horse, and finds himself alone under the gloom
of an extensive forest, upon which night is descending. Under the apprehensions natural to a situation so uncomfortable, the king recollects that he
has heard how poor men, when apprehensive of
a bad night's lodging, pray to Saint Julian, who,
in the Romish calendar, stands Quarter-Master-
General to all forlorn travellers that render him
due homage. Edward puts up his orisons accordingly, and by the guidance, doubtless, of the good
Saint, reaches a small path, conducting him to a
chapel in the forest, having a hermit's cell in its
close vicinity. The King hears the reverend man,
with a companion of his solitude, telling his beads
within, and meekly requests of him quarters for

the night. ' I have no accommodation for such a lord as ye be,' said the Hermit. ' I live here in the wilderness upon roots and rinds, and may not receive into my dwelling even the poorest wretch that lives, unless it were to save his life.' The King enquires the way to the next town, and, understanding it is by a road which he cannot find without difficulty, even if he had daylight to befriend him, he declares, that with or without the Hermit's consent, he is determined to be his guest that night. He is admitted accordingly, not without a hint from the Recluse, that were he himself out of his priestly weeds, he would care little for his threats of using violence, and that he gives way to him not out of intimidation, but simply to avoid scandal.

The King is admitted into the cell—two bundles of straw are shaken down for his accommodation, and he comforts himself that he is now under shelter, and that

' A night will soon be gone.

Other wants, however, arise. The guest becomes clamorous for supper, observing,

' For certainly, as I you say,
I ne had never so sorry a day,
That I ne had a merry night.'

But this · indication of his taste for good cheer, joined to the annunciation of his being a follower

of the Court, who had lost himself at the great
hunting-match, cannot induce the niggard Hermit
to produce better fare than bread and cheese, for
which his guest showed little appetite; and 'thin
drink,' which was even less acceptable. At length
the King presses his host on a point to which he
had more than once alluded, without obtaining a
satisfactory reply:

> 'Then said the King, "by Godys grace,
>   Thou wert in a merry place,
>   To shoot should thou lere;
>   When the foresters go to rest,
>   Sometyme thou might have of the best,
>   All of the wild deer;
>   I wold hold it for no scathe,
>   Though thou hadst bow and arrows baith,
>   Althoff thou best a Frere."'

The Hermit, in return, expresses his apprehension
that his guest means to drag him into some confession of offence against the forest laws, which,
being betrayed to the King, might cost him his
life. Edward answers by fresh assurances of
secrecy, and again urges on him the necessity of
procuring some venison. The Hermit replies, by
once more insisting on the duties incumbent upon
him as a churchman, and continues to affirm himself free from all such breaches of order :—

> ' Many day I have here been,
>   And flesh-meat I eat never,
>   But milk of the kye;

IVANHOE

Warm thee well, and go to sleep,
And I will lap thee with my cope,
    Softly to lye.'

It would seem that the manuscript is here imperfect, for we do not find the reasons which finally induce the curtal Friar to amend the King's cheer. But acknowledging his guest to be such a 'good fellow' as has seldom graced his board, the holy man at length produces the best his cell affords. Two candles are placed on a table, white bread and baked pasties are displayed by the light, besides choice of venison, both salt and fresh, from which they select collops. 'I might have eaten my bread dry,' said the King, 'had I not pressed thee on the score of archery, but now have I dined like a prince—if we had but drink enow.'

This too is afforded by the hospitable anchorite, who dispatches an assistant to fetch a pot of four gallons from a secret corner near his bed, and the whole three set in to serious drinking. This amusement is superintended by the Friar, according to the recurrence of certain fustian words, to be repeated by every compotator in turn before he drank—a species of High Jinks, as it were, by which they regulated their potations, as toasts were given in later times. The one toper says *fusty bandias*, to which the other is obliged to

reply, *strike pantnere*, and the Friar passes many
jests on the King's want of memory, who sometimes forgets the words of action. The night is
spent in this jolly pastime. Before his departure
in the morning, the King invites his reverend host
to Court, promises, at least, to requite his hospitality, and expresses himself much pleased with
his entertainment. The jolly Hermit at length
agrees to venture thither, and to enquire for Jack
Fletcher, which is the name assumed by the King.
After the Hermit has shown Edward some feats
of archery, the joyous pair separate. The King
rides home, and rejoins his retinue. As the
romance is imperfect, we are not acquainted how
the discovery takes place; but it is probably much
in the same manner as in other narratives turning
on the same subject, where the host, apprehensive
of death for having trespassed on the respect due
to his Sovereign, while incognito, is agreeably
surprised by receiving honours and reward.

In Mr. Hartshorne's collection, there is a
romance on the same foundation, called King
Edward and the Shepherd,* which, considered as

---

* Like the Hermit, the Shepherd makes havock amongst the King's
game; but by means of a sling, not of a bow; like the Hermit, too,
he has his peculiar phrases of compotation, the sign and countersign
being Passelodion and Berafriend. One can scarce conceive what
humour our ancestors found in this species of gibberish; but

'I warrant it proved an excuse for the glass.'

illustrating manners, is still more curious than the King and the Hermit; but it is foreign to the present purpose. The reader has here the original legend from which the incident in the romance is derived; and the identifying the irregular Eremite with the Friar Tuck of Robin Hood's story, was an obvious expedient.

The name of Ivanhoe was suggested by an old rhyme. All novelists have had occasion at some time or other to wish with Falstaff, that they knew where a commodity of good names was to be had. On such an occasion the author chanced to call to memory a rhyme recording three names of the manors forfeited by the ancestor of the celebrated Hampden, for striking the Black Prince a blow with his racket, when they quarrelled at tennis;—

> 'Tring, Wing, and Ivanhoe,
> For striking of a blow,
> Hampden did forego,
> And glad he could escape so.'

The word suited the author's purpose in two material respects,—for, first, it had an ancient English sound; and secondly, it conveyed no indication whatever of the nature of the story. He presumes to hold this last quality to be of no small importance. What is called a taking title, serves the direct interest of the bookseller or publisher, who by this means sometimes sells an edition while it is yet passing the press. But if the author permits an over degree of attention to be drawn to his work ere it has appeared, he places himself in the embarrassing condition of having excited a degree of expectation which, if he proves unable to satisfy, is an error fatal to his literary reputation. Besides, when we meet such a title as the Gunpowder Plot, or any other connected with general history, each reader, before he has seen the book, has formed to himself some particular idea of the sort of manner in which the story is to be conducted, and the nature of the amusement which he is to derive from it. In this he is probably disappointed, and in that case may be naturally disposed to visit upon the author or the work, the unpleasant feelings thus excited. In such a case the literary adventurer is censured, not for having missed the mark at which he himself aimed, but for not having shot off his shaft in a direction he never thought of.

On the footing of unreserved communication which the Author has established with the reader, he may here add the trifling circumstance, that a roll of Norman warriors, occurring in the Auchinleck Manuscript, gave him the formidable name of Front-de-Bœuf.

Ivanhoe was highly successful upon its appearance, and may be said to have procured for its author the freedom of the Rules, since he has ever since been permitted to exercise his powers of fictitious composition in England, as well as Scotland.

The character of the fair Jewess found so much favour in the eyes of some fair readers, that the writer was censured, because, when arranging the fates of the characters of the drama, he had not assigned the hand of Wilfred to Rebecca, rather than the less interesting Rowena. But, not to mention that the prejudices of the age rendered such an union almost impossible, the author may, in passing, observe, that he thinks a character of a highly virtuous and lofty stamp, is degraded rather than exalted by an attempt to reward virtue with temporal prosperity. Such is not the recompense which Providence has deemed worthy of suffering merit, and it is a dangerous and fatal doctrine to teach young persons, the most common readers of romance, that rectitude of conduct and of principle are either naturally allied with, or adequately rewarded by, the gratification of our passions, or attainment of our wishes. In a word, if a virtuous and self-denied character is dismissed with temporal wealth, greatness, rank, or the indulgence of such a rashly formed or ill-assorted passion as that of Rebecca for Ivanhoe, the reader will be apt to say, verily Virtue has had its reward. But a glance on the great picture of life will show, that the duties of self-denial, and the sacrifice of passion to principle, are seldom thus remunerated; and that the internal consciousness of their high-minded discharge of duty, produces on their own reflections a more adequate recompense, in the form of that peace which the world cannot give or take away.

ABBOTSFORD,
1st September, 1830.

DEDICATORY EPISTLE

TO

THE REV. DR. DRYASDUST, F.A.S.
Residing in the Castle-Gate, York.

MUCH ESTEEMED AND DEAR SIR,

It is scarcely necessary to mention the various and concurring reasons which induce me to place your name at the head of the following work. Yet the chief of these reasons may perhaps be refuted by the imperfections of the performance. Could I have hoped to render it worthy of your patronage, the public would at once have seen the propriety of inscribing a work designed to illustrate the domestic antiquities of England, and particularly of our Saxon forefathers, to the learned author of the Essays upon the Horn of King Ulphus, and on the Lands bestowed by him upon the patrimony of St. Peter. I am conscious, however, that the slight, unsatisfactory, and trivial manner, in which the result of my antiquarian researches has been recorded in the following pages, takes the work from under that class which bears the proud motto, *Detur digniori.* On the contrary, I fear I shall incur the censure of presumption in placing the venerable name of Dr. Jonas Dryasdust at the head of a publication, which the more grave antiquary will perhaps class with the idle novels and romances of the day. I am anxious to vindicate myself from such a charge; for although I might trust to your friendship for an apology in your eyes, yet I would not willingly stand convicted in those of the public of so grave a crime, as my fears lead me to anticipate my being charged with.

I must therefore remind you, that when we first talked over together that class of productions, in one of which the private and family affairs of your learned northern friend, Mr. Oldbuck of Monkbarns, were so unjustifiably exposed to the public, some discussion occurred between us concerning the cause of the popularity these works have attained in this idle age, which, whatever other merit they possess, must be admitted to be hastily written, and in violation of every rule assigned to the epopeia. It seemed then to be your opinion, that the charm lay entirely in the art with which the unknown author had availed himself, like a second M'Pherson, of the antiquarian stores which lay scattered around him, supplying his own indolence or poverty of invention, by the incidents which had actually taken place in his country at no distant period, by introducing real characters, and scarcely suppressing real names. It was not above sixty or seventy years, you observed, since the whole north of Scotland was under a state of government nearly as simple and as patriarchal as those of our good allies the Mohawks and Iroquois. Admitting that the author cannot himself be supposed to have witnessed those times, he must have lived, you observed, among persons who had acted and suffered in them; and even within these thirty years, such an infinite change has taken place in the manners of Scotland, that men look back upon the habits of society proper to their immediate ancestors, as we do on those of the reign of Queen Anne, or even the period of the Revolution. Having thus materials of every kind lying strewed around him, there was little, you observed, to embarrass the author, but the difficulty of choice. It was no wonder, therefore, that, having begun to work a mine so plentiful, he should have derived from his works fully more credit and profit than the facility of his labours merited.

Admitting (as I could not deny) the general truth of these conclusions, I cannot but think it strange that no attempt has been made to excite an interest for the traditions and manners of Old England, similar to that which has been obtained in behalf of those of our poorer and less celebrated neighbours. The Kendal green, though its date is more ancient, ought surely to be as dear to our feelings, as the variegated tartans of the north. The name of Robin Hood, if duly conjured with, should raise a spirit as soon as that of Rob Roy; and the patriots of England deserve no less their renown in our modern circles, than the Bruces and Wallaces of Caledonia. If the scenery of the south be less romantic and sublime than that of the northern mountains, it must be allowed to possess in the same proportion superior softness and beauty; and upon the whole, we feel ourselves entitled to exclaim with the patriotic Syrian—'Are not Pharphar and Abana, rivers of Damascus, better than all the rivers of Israel?'

Your objections to such an attempt, my dear Doctor, were, you may remember, two-fold. You insisted upon the advantages which the Scotsman possessed, from the very recent existence of that state of society in which his scene was to be laid. Many now alive, you remarked, well remembered persons who had not only seen the celebrated Roy M'Gregor, but had feasted, and even fought with

him. All those minute circumstances belonging
to private life and domestic character, all that gives
verisimilitude to a narrative, and individuality to
the persons introduced, is still known and remembered in Scotland; whereas in England, civilisation
has been so long complete, that our ideas of our
ancestors are only to be gleaned from musty records
and chronicles, the authors of which seem perversely
to have conspired to suppress in their narratives all
interesting details, in order to find room for flowers
of monkish eloquence, or trite reflections upon
morals. To match an English and a Scottish
author in the rival task of embodying and reviving the traditions of their respective countries,
would be, you alleged, in the highest degree
unequal and unjust. The Scottish magician, you
said, was, like Lucan's witch, at liberty to walk
over the recent field of battle, and to select for
the subject of resuscitation by his sorceries, a body
whose limbs had recently quivered with existence,
and whose throat had but just uttered the last
note of agony. Such a subject even the powerful
Erictho was compelled to select, as alone capable
of being reanimated even by *her* potent magic—

> ——gelidas leto scrutata medullas,
> Pulmonis rigidi stantes sine vulnere fibras
> Invenit, et vocem defuncto in corpore quærit.

The English author, on the other hand, without

supposing him less of a conjuror than the Northern
Warlock, can, you observed, only have the liberty
of selecting his subject amidst the dust of antiquity,
where nothing was to be found but dry, sapless,
mouldering, and disjointed bones, such as those
which filled the valley of Jehoshaphat. You expressed, besides, your apprehension, that the un-
patriotic prejudices of my countrymen would not
allow fair play to such a work as that of which
I endeavoured to demonstrate the probable success.
And this, you said, was not entirely owing to the
more general prejudice in favour of that which is
foreign, but that it rested partly upon improba-
bilities, arising out of the circumstances in which
the English reader is placed. If you describe to
him a set of wild manners, and a state of primitive
society existing in the Highlands of Scotland, he
is much disposed to acquiesce in the truth of what
is asserted. And reason good. If he be of the
ordinary class of readers, he has either never seen
those remote districts at all, or he has wandered
through those desolate regions in the course of a
summer tour, eating bad dinners, sleeping on truckle
beds, stalking from desolation to desolation, and
fully prepared to believe the strangest things that
could be told him of a people, wild and extravagant enough to be attached to scenery so extraordinary. But the same worthy person, when

placed in his own snug parlour, and surrounded by all the comforts of an Englishman's fireside, is not half so much disposed to believe that his own ancestors led a very different life from himself; that the shattered tower, which now forms a vista from his window, once held a baron who would have hung him up at his own door without any form of trial; that the hinds, by whom his little pet-farm is managed, a few centuries ago would have been his slaves; and that the complete influence of feudal tyranny once extended over the neighbouring village, where the attorney is now a man of more importance than the lord of the manor.

While I own the force of these objections, I must confess, at the same time, that they do not appear to me to be altogether insurmountable. The scantiness of materials is indeed a formidable difficulty; but no one knows better than Dr. Dryasdust, that to those deeply read in antiquity, hints concerning the private life of our ancestors lie scattered through the pages of our various historians, bearing, indeed, a slender proportion to the other matters of which they treat, but still, when collected together, sufficient to throw considerable light upon the *vie privée* of our forefathers; indeed, I am convinced, that however I myself may fail in the ensuing attempt, yet, with more labour in collecting, or more skill in using, the materials within his reach, illustrated as they have been by the labours of Dr. Henry, of the late Mr. Strutt, and, above all, of Mr. Sharon Turner, an abler hand would have been successful; and therefore I protest, beforehand, against any argument which may be founded on the failure of the present experiment.

On the other hand, I have already said, that if any thing like a true picture of old English manners could be drawn, I would trust to the good-nature and good sense of my countrymen for insuring its favourable reception.

Having thus replied, to the best of my power, to the first class of your objections, or at least having shown my resolution to overleap the barriers which your prudence has raised, I will be brief in noticing that which is more peculiar to myself. It seemed to be your opinion, that the very office of an antiquary, employed in grave, and, as the vulgar will sometimes allege, in toilsome and minute research, must be considered as incapacitating him from successfully compounding a tale of this sort. But permit me to say, my dear Doctor, that this objection is rather formal than substantial. It is true, that such slight compositions might not suit the severer genius of our friend Mr. Oldbuck. Yet Horace Walpole wrote a goblin tale which has thrilled through many a bosom; and George Ellis could transfer all the playful fascination of a humour, as delightful as it was uncommon, into his Abridgement of the Ancient Metrical Romances. So that, however I may have occasion to rue my present audacity, I have at least the most respectable precedents in my favour.

Still the severer antiquary may think, that, by thus intermingling fiction with truth, I am polluting the well of history with modern inventions, and impressing upon the rising generation false ideas of the age which I describe. I cannot but in some sense admit the force of this reasoning, which I yet hope to traverse by the following considerations.

It is true, that I neither can, nor do pretend, to the observation of complete accuracy, even in matters of outward costume, much less in the more important points of language and manners. But the same motive which prevents my writing the dialogue of the piece in Anglo-Saxon or in Norman-French, and which prohibits my sending forth to the public this essay printed with the types of Caxton or Wynken de Worde, prevents my attempting to confine myself within the limits of the period in which my story is laid. It is necessary, for exciting interest of any kind, that the subject assumed should be, as it were, translated into the manners, as well as the language, of the age we live in. No fascination has ever been attached to Oriental literature, equal to that produced by Mr. Galland's first translation of the Arabian Tales; in which, retaining on the one hand the splendour of Eastern costume, and on the other the wildness of Eastern fiction, he mixed these with just so much ordinary feeling and expression, as rendered them interesting and intelligible, while he abridged the long-winded narratives, curtailed the monotonous reflections, and rejected the endless repetitions of the Arabian original. The tales, therefore, though less purely Oriental than in their first concoction, were eminently better fitted for the European market, and obtained an unrivalled degree of public favour, which they certainly would never have gained had not the manners and style been in some degree familiarized to the feelings and habits of the Western reader.

In point of justice, therefore, to the multitudes who will, I trust, devour this book with avidity, I have so far explained our ancient manners in modern language, and so far detailed the characters and sentiments of my persons, that the modern reader will not find himself, I should hope, much trammelled by the repulsive dryness of mere antiquity. In this, I respectfully contend, I have in no respect exceeded the fair license due to the author of a fictitious composition. The late ingenious Mr. Strutt, in his romance of Queenhoo - Hall,* acted upon another principle; and in distinguishing between what was ancient and modern, forgot, as it appears to me, that extensive neutral ground, the large proportion, that is, of manners and sentiments which are common to us and to our ancestors, having been handed down unaltered from them to us, or which, arising out of the principles of our common nature, must have existed alike in either state of society. In this manner, a man of talent, and of great antiquarian erudition, limited the popularity of his work, by excluding from it every thing which was not sufficiently obsolete to be altogether forgotten and unintelligible.

The license which I would here vindicate, is so necessary to the execution of my plan, that I will crave your patience while I illustrate my argument a little farther.

He who first opens Chaucer, or any other ancient poet, is so much struck with the obsolete spelling, multiplied consonants, and antiquated appearance of the language, that he is apt to lay the work down in despair, as encrusted too deep with the rust of antiquity, to permit his judging of its merits or

---

* The author had revised this posthumous work of Mr. Strutt. See General Preface to the present edition, Waverley, i. p. liv.

tasting its beauties. But if some intelligent and accomplished friend points out to him, that the difficulties by which he is startled are more in appearance than reality, if, by reading aloud to him, or by reducing the ordinary words to the modern orthography, he satisfies his proselyte that only about one-tenth part of the words employed are in fact obsolete, the novice may be easily persuaded to approach the 'well of English undefiled,' with the certainty that a slender degree of patience will enable him to enjoy both the humour and the pathos with which old Geoffrey delighted the age of Cressy and of Poictiers.

To pursue this a little farther. If our neophyte, strong in the new-born love of antiquity, were to undertake to imitate what he had learnt to admire, it must be allowed he would act very injudiciously, if he were to select from the Glossary the obsolete words which it contains, and employ those exclusively of all phrases and vocables retained in modern days. This was the error of the unfortunate Chatterton. In order to give his language the appearance of antiquity, he rejected every word that was modern, and produced a dialect entirely different from any that had ever been spoken in Great Britain. He who would imitate an ancient language with success, must attend rather to its grammatical character, turn of expression, and mode of arrangement, than labour to collect extraordinary and antiquated terms, which, as I have already averred, do not in ancient authors approach the number of words still in use, though perhaps somewhat altered in sense and spelling, in the proportion of one to ten.

What I have applied to language, is still more justly applicable to sentiments and manners. The passions, the sources from which these must spring in all their modifications, are generally the same in all ranks and conditions, all countries and ages; and it follows, as a matter of course, that the opinions, habits of thinking, and actions, however influenced by the peculiar state of society, must still, upon the whole, bear a strong resemblance to each other. Our ancestors were not more distinct from us, surely, than Jews are from Christians; they had ' eyes, hands, organs, dimensions, senses, affections, passions'; were 'fed with the same food, hurt with the same weapons, subject to the same diseases, warmed and cooled by the same winter and summer,' as ourselves. The tenor, therefore, of their affections and feelings, must have borne the same general proportion to our own.

It follows, therefore, that of the materials which an author has to use in a romance, or fictitious composition, such as I have ventured to attempt, he will find that a great proportion, both of language and manners, is as proper to the present time as to those in which he has laid his time of action. The freedom of choice which this allows him, is therefore much greater, and the difficulty of his task much more diminished, than at first appears. To take an illustration from a sister art, the antiquarian details may be said to represent the peculiar features of a landscape under delineation of the pencil. His feudal tower must arise in due majesty; the figures which he introduces must have the costume and character of their age; the piece must represent the peculiar features of the scene which he has chosen for his subject, with all its appropriate elevation of rock, or precipitate descent of cataract. His general colouring, too, must be copied from Nature: The sky must be clouded or serene, according to the climate, and the general tints must be those which prevail in a natural landscape. So far the painter is bound down by the rules of his art, to a precise imitation of the features of Nature; but it is not required that he should descend to copy all her more minute features, or represent with absolute exactness the very herbs, flowers, and trees, with which the spot is decorated. These, as well as all the more minute points of light and shadow, are attributes proper to scenery in general, natural to each situation, and subject to the artist's disposal, as his taste or pleasure may dictate.

XLVIII

DEDICATORY EPISTLE

It is true, that this license is confined in either case within legitimate bounds. The painter must introduce no ornament inconsistent with the climate or country of his landscape ; he must not plant cypress trees upon Inch-Merrin, or Scottish firs among the ruins of Persepolis ; and the author lies under a corresponding restraint. However far he may venture in a more full detail of passions and feelings, than is to be found in the ancient compositions which he imitates, he must introduce nothing inconsistent with the manners of the age ; his knights, squires, grooms, and yeomen, may be more fully drawn than in the hard, dry delineations of an ancient illuminated manuscript, but the character and costume of the age must remain inviolate ; they must be the same figures, drawn by a better pencil, or, to speak more modestly, executed in an age when the principles of art were better understood. His language must not be exclusively obsolete and unintelligible ; but he should admit, if possible, no word or turn of phraseology betraying an origin directly modern. It is one thing to make use of the language and sentiments which are common to ourselves and our forefathers, and it is another to invest them with the sentiments and dialect exclusively proper to their descendants.

This, my dear friend, I have found the most difficult part of my task ; and, to speak frankly, I hardly expect to satisfy your less partial judgment, and more extensive knowledge of such subjects, since I have hardly been able to please my own.

I am conscious that I shall be found still more faulty in the tone of keeping and costume, by those who may be disposed rigidly to examine my Tale, with reference to the manners of the exact period in which my actors flourished: It may be, that I have introduced little which can positively be termed modern; but, on the other hand, it is extremely probable that I may have confused the manners of two or three centuries, and introduced, during the reign of Richard the First, circumstances appropriated to a period either considerably earlier, or a good deal later than that era. It is my comfort, that errors of this kind will escape the general class of readers, and that I may share in the ill-deserved applause of those architects, who, in their modern Gothic, do not hesitate to introduce, without rule or method, ornaments proper to different styles and to different periods of the art. Those whose extensive researches have given them the means of judging my backslidings with more severity, will probably be lenient in proportion to their knowledge of the difficulty of my task. My honest and neglected friend, Ingulphus, has furnished me with many a valuable hint, but the light afforded by the Monk of Croydon, and

DEDICATORY EPISTLE

Geoffrey de Vinsauff, is dimmed by such a con-
glomeration of uninteresting and unintelligible
matter, that we gladly fly for relief to the delightful
pages of the gallant Froissart, although he flourished
at a period so much more remote from the date
of my history. If, therefore, my dear friend, you
have generosity enough to pardon the presumptuous
attempt, to frame for myself a minstrel coronet,
partly out of the pearls of pure antiquity, and
partly from the Bristol stones and paste, with
which I have endeavoured to imitate them, I am
convinced your opinion of the difficulty of the
task will reconcile you to the imperfect manner
of its execution.

Of my materials I have but little to say: They
may be chiefly found in the singular Anglo-Norman
MS., which Sir Arthur Wardour preserves with
such jealous care in the third drawer of his oaken
cabinet, scarcely allowing any one to touch it, and
being himself not able to read one syllable of its
contents. I should never have got his consent,
on my visit to Scotland, to read in those precious
pages for so many hours, had I not promised to
designate it by some emphatic mode of printing, as
The Wardour Manuscript; giving it, thereby,
an individuality as important as the Bannatyne MS.,
the Auchinleck MS., and any other monument of
the patience of a Gothic scrivener. I have sent,

for your private consideration, a list of the contents of this curious piece, which I shall perhaps subjoin, with your approbation, to the third volume of my Tale, in case the printer's devil should continue impatient for copy, when the whole of my narrative has been imposed.

Adieu, my dear friend; I have said enough to explain, if not to vindicate, the attempt which I have made, and which, in spite of your doubts, and my own incapacity, I am still willing to believe has not been altogether made in vain.

I hope you are now well recovered from your spring fit of the gout, and shall be happy if the advice of your learned physician should recommend a tour to these parts. Several curiosities have been lately dug up near the wall, as well as at the ancient station of Habitancum. Talking of the latter, I suppose you have long since heard the news, that a sulky churlish boor has destroyed the ancient statue, or rather bas-relief, popularly called Robin of Redesdale. It seems Robin's fame attracted more visitants than was consistent with the growth of the heather, upon a moor worth a shilling an acre. Reverend as you write yourself, be revengeful for once, and pray with me that he may be visited with such a fit of the stone, as if he had all the fragments of poor Robin in that region of his viscera where the disease holds its seat. Tell this not in Gath, lest the Scots rejoice that they have at length found a parallel instance among their neighbours, to that barbarous deed which demolished Arthur's Oven. But there is no end to lamentation, when we betake ourselves to such subjects. My respectful compliments attend Miss Dryasdust; I endeavoured to match the spectacles agreeable to her commission, during my late journey to London, and hope she has received them safe, and found them satisfactory. I send this by the blind carrier, so that probably it may be some time upon its journey.* The last news which I hear from Edinburgh is, that the gentleman who fills the situation of Secretary to the Society of Antiquaries of Scotland,† is the best amateur

---

* This anticipation proved but too true, as my learned correspondent did not receive my letter until a twelvemonth after it was written. I mention this circumstance, that a gentleman attached to the cause of learning, who now holds the principal control of the post-office, may consider whether by some mitigation of the present enormous rates, some favour might not be shown to the correspondents of the principal Literary and Antiquarian Societies. I understand, indeed, that this experiment was once tried, but that the mail-coach having broke down under the weight of packages addressed to members of the Society of Antiquaries, it was relinquished as a hazardous experiment. Surely, however, it would be possible to build these vehicles in a form more substantial, stronger in the perch, and broader in the wheels, so as to support the weight of Antiquarian learning; when, if they should be found to travel more slowly, they would be not the less agreeable to quiet travellers like myself.—L. T.

† Mr. Skene of Rubislaw is here intimated, to whose taste and skill the author is indebted for a series of etchings, exhibiting the various localities alluded to in these novels.

draftsman in that kingdom, and that much is expected from his skill and zeal in delineating those specimens of national antiquity, which are either mouldering under the slow touch of time, or swept away by modern taste, with the same besom of destruction which John Knox used at the Reformation. Once more adieu ; *vale tandem, non immemor mei.* Believe me to be,

Reverend, and very dear Sir,

Your most faithful humble Servant,

LAURENCE TEMPLETON.

TOPPINGWOLD, NEAR EGREMONT, }
CUMBERLAND, *Nov.* 17, 1817. }

IVANHOE

I

CHAPTER I

Thus communed these; while to their lowly dome,
The full-fed swine return'd with evening home;
Compell'd, reluctant, to the several sties,
With din obstreperous, and ungrateful cries.

POPE'S ODYSSEY.

IN that pleasant district of merry England which is watered by the river Don, there extended in ancient times a large forest, covering the greater part of the beautiful hills and valleys which lie between Sheffield and the pleasant town of Doncaster. The remains of this extensive wood are still to be seen at the noble seats of Wentworth, of Warncliffe Park, and around Rotherham. Here haunted of yore the fabulous Dragon of Wantley; here were fought many of the most desperate battles during the Civil Wars of the Roses; and here also flourished in ancient times those bands of gallant outlaws, whose deeds have been rendered so popular in English song.

Such being our chief scene, the date of our story refers to a period towards the end of the reign of Richard i., when his return from his long captivity had become an event rather wished than hoped for by his despairing subjects, who were in the meantime subjected to every species of subordinate oppression. The nobles, whose power had become exorbitant during the reign of Stephen, and whom the prudence of Henry the Second had scarce reduced into some degree of subjection to the crown, had now resumed their ancient license in its utmost extent; despising the feeble interference of the English Council of State, fortifying their castles, increasing the number of their dependants, reducing all around them to a state of vassalage, and striving by every means in their power, to place themselves each at the head of such forces as might enable him to make a figure in the national convulsions which appeared to be impending.

The situation of the inferior gentry, or Franklins, as they were called, who, by the law and spirit of the English constitution, were entitled to hold themselves independent of feudal tyranny, became now unusually precarious. If, as was most generally the case, they placed themselves under the protection of any of the petty kings in their vicinity, accepted of feudal offices in his household, or bound them-selves, by mutual treaties of alliance and protection, to support him in his enterprises, they might indeed purchase temporary repose; but it must be with the sacrifice of that independence which was so dear to every English bosom, and at the certain hazard of being involved as a party in whatever rash expedition the ambition of their protector might lead him to undertake. On the other hand, such

4

and so multiplied were the means of vexation and oppression possessed by the great Barons, that they never wanted the pretext, and seldom the will, to harass and pursue, even to the very edge of destruction, any of their less powerful neighbours, who attempted to separate themselves from their authority, and to trust for their protection, during the dangers of the times, to their own inoffensive conduct, and to the laws of the land.

A circumstance which greatly tended to enhance the tyranny of the nobility, and the sufferings of the inferior classes, arose from the consequences of the Conquest by Duke William of Normandy. Four generations had not sufficed to blend the hostile blood of the Normans and Anglo-Saxons, or to unite, by common language and mutual interests, two hostile races, one of which still felt the elation of triumph, while the other groaned under all the consequences of defeat. The power had been completely placed in the hands of the Norman nobility, by the event of the battle of Hastings, and it had been used, as our histories assure us, with no moderate hand. The whole race of Saxon princes and nobles had been extirpated or disinherited, with few or no exceptions; nor were the numbers great who possessed land in the country of their fathers, even as proprietors of the second, or of yet inferior classes. The royal policy had long been to weaken, by every means, legal or illegal, the strength of a part of the population which was justly considered as nourishing the most inveterate antipathy to their victor. All the monarchs of the Norman race had shown the most marked predilection for their Norman subjects; the laws of the chase, and many others equally unknown to the milder and more free spirit of the Saxon constitution, had been fixed upon the necks of the subjugated inhabitants, to add weight, as it were, to the feudal chains with which they were loaded. At court, and in the castles of the great nobles, where the pomp and state of a court was emulated, Norman-French was the only language employed; in courts of law, the pleadings and judgments were delivered in the same tongue. In short, French was the language of honour, of chivalry, and even of justice, while the far more manly and expressive Anglo-Saxon was abandoned to the use of rustics and hinds, who knew no other. Still, however, the necessary intercourse between the lords of the soil, and those oppressed inferior beings by whom that soil was cultivated, occasioned the gradual formation of a dialect, compounded betwixt the French and the Anglo-Saxon, in which they could render themselves mutually intelligible to each other; and from this necessity arose by degrees the structure of our present English language, in which the speech of the victors and the vanquished have been so happily blended together; and which has since been so richly improved by importations from the classical languages, and from those spoken by the southern nations of Europe.

This state of things I have thought it necessary to premise for the information of the general reader, who might be apt to forget that, although no great historical events, such as war or insurrection, mark the existence of the Anglo-Saxons as a separate people subsequent to the reign of William the Second; yet the great national distinctions betwixt them and their conquerors, the recollection of what they had formerly been, and to what they were now reduced, continued down to the reign of Edward the Third, to keep open the wounds which the Conquest had inflicted, and to maintain a line of separation betwixt the descendants of the victor Normans and the vanquished Saxons.

The sun was setting upon one of the rich grassy glades of that forest, which we have mentioned in the beginning of the chapter. Hundreds of broad-headed, short-stemmed, wide-branched oaks, which had witnessed perhaps the stately march of the Roman soldiery, flung their gnarled arms over a thick carpet of the most delicious green sward; in some places they were intermingled with beeches, hollies, and copsewood of various descriptions, so closely as totally to intercept the level beams of the sinking sun; in others they receded from each other, forming those long sweeping vistas, in the intricacy of which the eye delights to lose itself, while imagination considers them as the paths to yet wilder scenes of silvan solitude. Here the red rays of the sun shot a broken and discoloured light, that partially hung upon the shattered boughs and mossy trunks of the trees, and there they illuminated in brilliant patches the portions of turf to which they made their way. A considerable open space, in the midst of this glade, seemed formerly to have been dedicated to the rites of Druidical superstition; for, on the summit of a hillock, so regular as to seem artificial, there still remained part of a circle of rough unhewn stones, of large dimensions. Seven stood upright; the rest had been dislodged from their places, probably by the zeal of some convert to Christianity, and lay, some prostrate near their former site, and others on the side of the hill. One large stone only had found its way to the bottom, and in stopping the course of a small brook, which glided smoothly round the foot of the eminence, gave, by its opposition, a feeble voice of murmur to the placid and elsewhere silent streamlet.

The human figures which completed this land-scape, were in number two, partaking, in their dress and appearance, of that wild and rustic character, which belonged to the woodlands of the West-Riding of Yorkshire at that early period. The eldest of these men had a stern, savage, and wild aspect. His garment was of the simplest form imaginable, being a close jacket with sleeves, com-posed of the tanned skin of some animal, on which the hair had been originally left, but which had been worn off in so many places, that it would have been difficult to distinguish from the patches that remained, to what creature the fur had be-longed. This primeval vestment reached from the throat to the knees, and served at once all the usual purposes of body - clothing; there was no wider opening at the collar, than was necessary to admit the passage of the head, from which it may be inferred, that it was put on by slipping it over the head and shoulders, in the manner of a modern shirt, or ancient hauberk. Sandals, bound with thongs made of boar's hide, protected the feet, and a roll of thin leather was twined artificially round the legs, and, ascending above the calf, left the knees bare, like those of a Scottish Highlander. To make the jacket sit yet more close to the body, it was gathered at the middle by a broad leathern belt, secured by a brass buckle; to one side of which was attached a sort of scrip, and to the other a ram's horn, accoutred with a mouthpiece, for the purpose of blowing. In the same belt was stuck one of those long, broad, sharp-pointed, and two-edged knives, with a buck's-horn handle, which were fabricated in the neighbourhood, and bore even at this early period the name of a Sheffield whittle. The man had no covering upon his head, which was only defended by his own thick hair, matted and twisted together, and scorched by the influence of the sun into a rusty dark-red colour, forming a contrast with the overgrown beard upon his cheeks, which was rather of a yellow or amber hue. One part of his dress only remains, but it is too remarkable to be suppressed; it was a brass ring, resembling a dog's collar, but without any opening, and soldered fast round his neck, so loose as to form no impediment to his breathing, yet so tight as to be incapable of being removed, except-ing by the use of the file. On this singular gorget was engraved, in Saxon characters, an inscription of the following purport:—' Gurth, the son of Beo-wulph, is the born thrall of Cedric of Rotherwood.'

IVANHOE

Beside the swine-herd, for such was Gurth's occupation, was seated, upon one of the fallen Druidical monuments, a person about ten years younger in appearance, and whose dress, though resembling his companion's in form, was of better materials, and of a more fantastic appearance. His jacket had been stained of a bright purple hue, upon which there had been some attempt to paint grotesque ornaments in different colours. To the jacket he added a short cloak, which scarcely reached half way down his thigh; it was of crimson cloth, though a good deal soiled, lined with bright yellow; and as he could transfer it from one shoulder to the other, or at his pleasure draw it all around him, its width, contrasted with its want of longitude, formed a fantastic piece of drapery. He had thin silver bracelets upon his arms, and on his neck a collar of the same metal, bearing the inscription, ' Wamba, the son of Witless, is the thrall of Cedric of Rotherwood.' This personage had the same sort of sandals with his companion, but instead of the roll of leather thong, his legs were cased in a sort of gaiters, of which one was red and the other yellow. He was provided also with a cap, having around it more than one bell, about the size of those attached to hawks, which jingled as he turned his head to one side or other; and as he seldom remained a minute in the same posture, the sound might be considered as incessant. Around the edge of this cap was a stiff bandeau of leather, cut at the top into open work, resembling a coronet, while a prolonged bag arose from within it, and

fell down on one shoulder like an old-fashioned
night-cap, or a jelly-bag, or the head-gear of a
modern hussar. It was to this part of the cap that
the bells were attached; which circumstance, as
well as the shape of his head-dress, and his own
half-crazed, half-cunning expression of countenance,
sufficiently pointed him out as belonging to the
race of domestic clowns or jesters, maintained in
the houses of the wealthy, to help away the
tedium of those lingering hours which they were
obliged to spend within doors. He bore, like his
companion, a scrip, attached to his belt, but had
neither horn nor knife, being probably considered
as belonging to a class whom it was esteemed dangerous to intrust with edge-tools. In place of these,
he was equipped with a sword of lath, resembling
that with which Harlequin operates his wonders
upon the modern stage.

The outward appearance of these two men formed
scarce a stronger contrast than their look and
demeanour. That of the serf, or bondsman, was
sad and sullen; his aspect was bent on the ground
with an appearance of deep dejection, which might
be almost construed into apathy, had not the fire
which occasionally sparkled in his red eye manifested that there slumbered, under the appearance
of sullen despondency, a sense of oppression, and a
disposition to resistance. The looks of Wamba, on
the other hand, indicated, as usual with his class,
a sort of vacant curiosity, and fidgety impatience
of any posture of repose, together with the utmost
self-satisfaction respecting his own situation, and

the appearance which he made. The dialogue which they maintained between them was carried on in Anglo-Saxon, which, as we said before, was universally spoken by the inferior classes, excepting the Norman soldiers, and the immediate personal dependants of the great feudal nobles. But to give their conversation in the original would convey but little information to the modern reader, for whose benefit we beg to offer the following translation :—

'The curse of St. Withold upon these infernal porkers!' said the swine-herd, after blowing his horn obstreperously, to collect together the scattered herd of swine, which, answering his call with notes equally melodious, made, however, no haste to remove themselves from the luxurious banquet of beech-mast and acorns on which they had fattened, or to forsake the marshy banks of the rivulet, where several of them, half plunged in mud, lay stretched at their ease, altogether regardless of the voice of their keeper. 'The curse of St. Withold upon them and upon me!' said Gurth; 'if the two-legged wolf snap not up some of them ere night-fall, I am no true man. Here, Fangs! Fangs!' he ejaculated at the top of his voice to a ragged wolfish-looking dog, a sort of lurcher, half mastiff, half greyhound, which ran limping about as if with the purpose of seconding his master in collecting the refractory grunters; but which, in fact, from mis-apprehension of the swine-herd's signals, ignorance of his own duty, or malice prepense, only drove them hither and thither, and increased the evil which he seemed to design to remedy. 'A devil draw the teeth of him,' said Gurth, 'and the mother of mischief confound the Ranger of the forest, that cuts the foreclaws off our dogs, and makes them unfit for their trade!* Wamba, up and help me an thou beest a man; take a turn round the back o' the hill to gain the wind on them; and when thou 'st got the weather-gage, thou mayst drive them before thee as gently as so many innocent lambs.'

'Truly,' said Wamba, without stirring from the spot, 'I have consulted my legs upon this matter, and they are altogether of opinion, that to carry my gay garments through these sloughs, would be an act of unfriendship to my sovereign person and royal wardrobe; wherefore, Gurth, I advise thee to call off Fangs, and leave the herd to their destiny, which, whether they meet with bands of travelling soldiers, or of outlaws, or of wandering pilgrims, can be little else than to be converted into Normans before morning, to thy no small ease and comfort.'

'The swine turned Normans to my comfort!' quoth Gurth; 'expound that to me, Wamba, for my brain is too dull, and my mind too vexed, to read riddles.'

'Why, how call you those grunting brutes running about on their four legs?' demanded Wamba.

'Swine, fool, swine,' said the herd, 'every fool knows that.'

'And swine is good Saxon,' said the Jester;

---

* See Note A.   The Ranger of the Forest, that cuts the fore-claws off our dogs.

13

'but how call you the sow when she is flayed, and drawn, and quartered, and hung up by the heels, like a traitor?'

'Pork,' answered the swine-herd.

'I am very glad every fool knows that too,' said Wamba, 'and pork, I think, is good Norman-French; and so when the brute lives, and is in the charge of a Saxon slave, she goes by her Saxon name; but becomes a Norman, and is called pork, when she is carried to the Castle-hall to feast among the nobles; what dost thou think of this, friend Gurth, ha?'

'It is but too true doctrine, friend Wamba, however it got into thy fool's pate.'

'Nay, I can tell you more,' said Wamba, in the same tone; 'there is old Alderman Ox continues to hold his Saxon epithet, while he is under the charge of serfs and bondsmen such as thou, but becomes Beef, a fiery French gallant, when he arrives before the worshipful jaws that are destined to consume him. Mynheer Calf, too, becomes Monsieur de Veau in the like manner; he is Saxon when he requires tendance, and takes a Norman name when he becomes matter of enjoyment.'

'By St. Dunstan,' answered Gurth, 'thou speakest but sad truths; little is left to us but the air we breathe, and that appears to have been reserved with much hesitation, solely for the purpose of enabling us to endure the tasks they lay upon our shoulders. The finest and the fattest is for their board; the loveliest is for their couch; the best and bravest supply their foreign masters with soldiers, and whiten distant lands with their bones, leaving few here who have either will or the power to protect the unfortunate Saxon. God's blessing on our master Cedric, he hath done the work of a man in standing in the gap; but Reginald Front-de-Bœuf is coming down to this country in person, and we shall soon see how little Cedric's trouble will avail him.——Here, here,' he exclaimed again, raising his voice, 'So ho! so ho! well done, Fangs! thou hast them all before thee now, and bring'st them on bravely, lad.'

'Gurth,' said the Jester, 'I know thou thinkest me a fool, or thou wouldst not be so rash in putting thy head into my mouth. One word to Reginald Front-de-Bœuf, or Philip de Malvoisin, that thou hast spoken treason against the Norman, —and thou art but a cast-away swineherd,—thou wouldst waver on one of these trees as a terror to all evil speakers against dignities.'

'Dog, thou wouldst not betray me,' said Gurth, 'after having led me on to speak so much at disadvantage?'

'Betray thee!' answered the Jester; 'no, that were the trick of a wise man; a fool cannot half so well help himself—but soft, whom have we here?' he said, listening to the trampling of several horses which became then audible.

'Never mind whom,' answered Gurth, who had now got his herd before him, and with the aid of Fangs, was driving them down one of the long dim vistas which we have endeavoured to describe.

'Nay, but I must see the riders,' answered

Wamba; 'perhaps they are come from Fairy-land
with a message from King Oberon.'

'A murrain take thee,' rejoined the swine-herd;
'wilt thou talk of such things, while a terrible
storm of thunder and lightning is raging within a
few miles of us? Hark, how the thunder rumbles!
and for summer rain, I never saw such broad downright flat drops fall out of the clouds; the oaks, too,
notwithstanding the calm weather, sob and creak
with their great boughs as if announcing a tempest.
Thou canst play the rational if thou wilt; credit
me for once, and let us home ere the storm begins
to rage, for the night will be fearful.'

Wamba seemed to feel the force of this appeal,
and accompanied his companion, who began his
journey after catching up a long quarter-staff which
lay upon the grass beside him. This second Eumæus
strode hastily down the forest glade, driving before
him, with the assistance of Fangs, the whole herd
of his inharmonious charge.

CHAPTER II

A Monk there was, a fayre for the maistrie,
An outrider that loved venerie;
A manly man, to be an Abbot able,
Full many a daintie horse had he in stable:
And whan he rode, men might his bridle hear
Gingeling in a whistling wind as clear,
And eke as loud, as doth the chapell bell,
There as this lord was keeper of the cell.

CHAUCER.

NOTWITHSTANDING the occasional exhortation and chiding of his companion, the noise of the horsemen's feet continuing to approach, Wamba could not be prevented from lingering occasionally on the road, upon every pretence which occurred; now catching from the hazel a cluster of half-ripe nuts, and now turning his head to leer after a cottage maiden who crossed their path. The horsemen, therefore, soon overtook them on the road.

Their numbers amounted to ten men, of whom the two who rode foremost seemed to be persons of considerable importance, and the others their attendants. It was not difficult to ascertain the condition and character of one of these personages. He was obviously an ecclesiastic of high rank; his dress was that of a Cistercian Monk, but composed of materials much finer than those which the rule of that order admitted. His mantle and hood were of the best Flanders cloth, and fell in ample, and not ungraceful folds, around a handsome, though somewhat corpulent person. His countenance bore as little the marks of self-denial, as his habit indicated contempt of worldly splendour. His features might have been called good, had there not lurked under the pent-house of his eye, that sly epicurean twinkle which indicates the cautious voluptuary. In other respects, his profession and situation had taught him a ready command over his countenance, which he could contract at pleasure into solemnity, although its natural expression was that of good-humoured social indulgence. In defiance of conventual rules, and the edicts of popes and councils, the sleeves of this dignitary were lined and turned up with rich furs, his mantle secured at the throat with a golden clasp, and the whole dress proper to his order as much refined upon and ornamented, as that of a quaker beauty of the present day, who, while she retains the garb and costume of her sect, continues to give to its simplicity, by the choice of materials and the mode of disposing them, a certain air of coquettish attraction, savouring but too much of the vanities of the world.

This worthy churchman rode upon a well-fed ambling mule, whose furniture was highly decorated, and whose bridle, according to the fashion of the day, was ornamented with silver bells. In his seat he had nothing of the awkwardness of the convent, but displayed the easy and habitual grace of a well-trained horseman. Indeed, it seemed that so humble a conveyance as a mule, in however good case, and however well broken to a pleasant and accommodating amble, was only used by the gallant monk for travelling on the road. A lay brother, one of those who followed in the train, had, for his use on other occasions, one of the most handsome Spanish jennets ever bred in Andalusia, which merchants used at that time to import, with great trouble and risk, for the use of persons of wealth and distinction. The saddle and housings of this superb palfrey were covered by a long foot-cloth, which reached nearly to the ground, and on which were richly embroidered, mitres, crosses, and other ecclesiastical emblems. Another lay brother led a sumpter mule, loaded probably with his superior's baggage ; and two monks of his own order, of inferior station, rode together in the rear, laughing and conversing with each other, without taking much notice of the other members of the cavalcade.

The companion of the church dignitary was a man past forty, thin, strong, tall, and muscular; an athletic figure, which long fatigue and constant exercise seemed to have left none of the softer part of the human form, having reduced the whole to brawn, bones, and sinews, which had sustained a thousand toils, and were ready to dare a thousand more. His head was covered with a scarlet cap, faced with fur—of that kind which the French call *mortier*, from its resemblance to the shape of an inverted mortar. His countenance was therefore fully displayed, and its expression was calculated to impress a degree of awe, if not of fear, upon strangers. High features, naturally strong and powerfully expressive, had been burnt almost into Negro blackness by constant exposure to the tropical sun, and might, in their ordinary state, be said to slumber after the storm of passion had passed away; but the projection of the veins of the forehead, the readiness with which the upper lip and its thick black moustaches quivered upon the slightest emotion, plainly intimated that the tempest might be again and easily awakened. His keen, piercing, dark eyes, told in every glance a history of difficulties subdued, and dangers dared, and seemed to challenge opposition to his wishes, for the pleasure of sweeping it from his road by a determined exertion of courage and of will; a deep scar on his brow gave additional sternness to his countenance, and a sinister expression to one of his eyes, which had been slightly injured on the same occasion, and of which the vision, though perfect, was in a slight and partial degree distorted.

The upper dress of this personage resembled that of his companion in shape, being a long monastic mantle; but the colour, being scarlet, showed that he did not belong to any of the four regular orders of monks. On the right shoulder of the mantle there was cut, in white cloth, a cross of a peculiar form. This upper robe concealed what at first view seemed rather inconsistent with its form, a shirt, namely, of linked mail, with sleeves and gloves of the same, curiously plaited and interwoven, as flexible to the body as those

which are now wrought in the stocking-loom, out
of less obdurate materials. The fore-part of his
thighs, where the folds of his mantle permitted them
to be seen, were also covered with linked mail; the
knees and feet were defended by splints, or thin
plates of steel, ingeniously jointed upon each other;
and mail hose, reaching from the ankle to the knee,
effectually protected the legs, and completed the
rider's defensive armour. In his girdle he wore a
long and double-edged dagger, which was the only
offensive weapon about his person.

He rode, not a mule, like his companion, but a
strong hackney for the road, to save his gallant war-
horse, which a squire led behind, fully accoutred
for battle, with a chamfrom or plaited head-piece
upon his head, having a short spike projecting from
the front. On one side of the saddle hung a short
battle-axe, richly inlaid with Damascene carving;
on the other the rider's plumed head-piece and hood
of mail, with a long two-handed sword, used by the
chivalry of the period. A second squire held aloft
his master's lance, from the extremity of which
fluttered a small banderole, or streamer, bearing a
cross of the same form with that embroidered upon
his cloak. He also carried his small triangular
shield, broad enough at the top to protect the
breast, and from thence diminishing to a point. It
was covered with a scarlet cloth, which prevented
the device from being seen.

These two squires were followed by two attendants, whose dark visages, white turbans, and the
Oriental form of their garments, showed them to

be natives of some distant Eastern country.* The whole appearance of this warrior and his retinue was wild and outlandish; the dress of his squires was gorgeous, and his Eastern attendants wore silver collars round their throats, and bracelets of the same metal upon their swarthy legs and arms, of which the latter were naked from the elbow, and the former from mid-leg to ankle. Silk and embroidery distinguished their dresses, and marked the wealth and importance of their master; forming, at the same time, a striking contrast with the martial simplicity of his own attire. They were armed with crooked sabres, having the hilt and baldric inlaid with gold, and matched with Turkish daggers of yet more costly workmanship. Each of them bore at his saddle-bow a bundle of darts or javelins, about four feet in length, having sharp steel heads, a weapon much in use among the Saracens, and of which the memory is yet preserved in the martial exercise called *El Jerrid*, still practised in the Eastern countries.

The steeds of these attendants were in appearance as foreign as their riders. They were of Saracen origin, and consequently of Arabian descent; and their fine slender limbs, small fetlocks, thin manes, and easy springy motion, formed a marked contrast with the large-jointed heavy horses, of which the race was cultivated in Flanders and in Normandy, for mounting the men-at-arms of the period in all the panoply of plate and mail;

---

* See Note B. Negro Slaves.

and which, placed by the side of those Eastern coursers, might have passed for a personification of substance and of shadow.

The singular appearance of this cavalcade not only attracted the curiosity of Wamba, but excited even that of his less volatile companion. The monk he instantly knew to be the Prior of Jorvaulx Abbey, well known for many miles around as a lover of the chase, of the banquet, and, if fame did him not wrong, of other worldly pleasures still more inconsistent with his monastic vows.

Yet so loose were the ideas of the times respecting the conduct of the clergy, whether secular or regular, that the Prior Aymer maintained a fair character in the neighbourhood of his abbey. His free and jovial temper, and the readiness with which he granted absolution from all ordinary delinquencies, rendered him a favourite among the nobility and principal gentry, to several of whom he was allied by birth, being of a distinguished Norman family. The ladies, in particular, were not disposed to scan too nicely the morals of a man who was a professed admirer of their sex, and who possessed many means of dispelling the ennui which was too apt to intrude upon the halls and bowers of an ancient feudal castle. The Prior mingled in the sports of the field with more than due eagerness, and was allowed to possess the best-trained hawks, and the fleetest greyhounds in the North Riding; circumstances which strongly recommended him to the youthful gentry. With the old, he had another part to play, which, when needful, he could sustain with great decorum. His knowledge of books, however superficial, was sufficient to impress upon their ignorance respect for his supposed learning; and the gravity of his deportment and language, with the high tone which he exerted in setting forth the authority of the church and of the priesthood, impressed them no less with an opinion of his sanctity. Even the common people, the severest critics of the conduct of their betters, had commiseration with the follies of Prior Aymer. He was generous; and charity, as it is well known, covereth a multitude of sins, in another sense than that in which it is said to do so in Scripture. The revenues of the monastery, of which a large part was at his disposal, while they gave him the means of supplying his own very considerable expenses, afforded also those largesses which he bestowed among the peasantry, and with which he frequently relieved the distresses of the oppressed. If Prior Aymer rode hard in the chase, or remained long at the banquet,—if Prior Aymer was seen, at the early peep of dawn, to enter the postern of the abbey, as he glided home from some rendezvous which had occupied the hours of darkness, men only shrugged up their shoulders, and reconciled themselves to his irregularities, by recollecting that the same were practised by many of his brethren who had no redeeming qualities whatsoever to atone for them. Prior Aymer, therefore, and his character, were well known to our Saxon serfs, who made their rude obeisance, and received his ' *benedicite, mes filz,*' in return.

But the singular appearance of his companion and his attendants, arrested their attention and excited their wonder, and they could scarcely attend to the Prior of Jorvaulx' question, when he demanded if they knew of any place of harbourage in the vicinity; so much were they surprised at the half monastic, half military appearance of the swarthy stranger, and at the uncouth dress and arms of his Eastern attendants. It is probable, too, that the language in which the benediction was conferred, and the information asked, sounded ungracious, though not probably unintelligible, in the ears of the Saxon peasants.

'I asked you, my children,' said the Prior, raising his voice, and using the lingua Franca, or mixed language, in which the Norman and Saxon races conversed with each other, 'if there be in this neighbourhood any good man, who, for the love of God, and devotion to Mother Church, will give two of her humblest servants, with their train, a night's hospitality and refreshment?'

This he spoke with a tone of conscious importance, which formed a strong contrast to the modest terms which he thought it proper to employ.

'Two of the humblest servants of Mother Church!' repeated Wamba to himself,—but, fool as he was, taking care not to make his observation audible; 'I should like to see her seneschals, her chief butlers, and her other principal domestics!'

After this internal commentary on the Prior's speech, he raised his eyes, and replied to the question which had been put.

'If the reverend fathers,' he said, 'loved good cheer and soft lodging, few miles of riding would carry them to the Priory of Brinxworth, where their quality could not but secure them the most honourable reception; or if they preferred spending a penitential evening, they might turn down yonder wild glade, which would bring them to the hermitage of Copmanhurst, where a pious anchoret would make them sharers for the night of the shelter of his roof and the benefit of his prayers.'

The Prior shook his head at both proposals.

'Mine honest friend,' said he, 'if the jangling of thy bells had not dizzied thine understanding, thou mightst know *Clericus clericum non decimat*; that is to say, we churchmen do not exhaust each other's hospitality, but rather require that of the laity, giving them thus an opportunity to serve God in honouring and relieving his appointed servants.'

'It is true,' replied Wamba, 'that I, being but an ass, am, nevertheless, honoured to bear the bells as well as your reverence's mule; notwithstanding, I did conceive that the charity of Mother Church and her servants might be said, with other charity, to begin at home.'

'A truce to thine insolence, fellow,' said the armed rider, breaking in on his prattle with a high and stern voice, 'and tell us, if thou canst, the road to——How call'd you your Franklin, Prior Aymer?'

'Cedric,' answered the Prior; 'Cedric the Saxon. ——Tell me, good fellow, are we near his dwelling, and can you show us the road?'

'The road will be uneasy to find,' answered Gurth, who broke silence for the first time, 'and the family of Cedric retire early to rest.'

'Tush, tell not me, fellow,' said the military rider; ''tis easy for them to arise and supply the wants of travellers such as we are, who will not stoop to beg the hospitality which we have a right to command.'

'I know not,' said Gurth, sullenly, 'if I should show the way to my master's house, to those who demand as a right, the shelter which most are fain to ask as a favour.'

'Do you dispute with me, slave!' said the soldier; and, setting spurs to his horse, he caused him make a demivolte across the path, raising at the same time the riding rod which he held in his hand, with a purpose of chastising what he considered as the insolence of the peasant.

Gurth darted at him a savage and revengeful scowl, and with a fierce, yet hesitating motion, laid his hand on the haft of his knife; but the interference of Prior Aymer, who pushed his mule betwixt his companion and the swineherd, prevented the meditated violence.

'Nay, by St. Mary, brother Brian, you must not think you are now in Palestine, predominating over heathen Turks and infidel Saracens; we islanders love not blows, save those of holy Church, who chasteneth whom she loveth.—Tell me, good fellow,' said he to Wamba, and seconded his speech by a small piece of silver coin, 'the way to Cedric the Saxon's; you cannot be ignorant of it, and it is your duty to direct the wanderer even when his character is less sanctified than ours.'

'In truth, venerable father,' answered the Jester, 'the Saracen head of your right reverend companion has frightened out of mine the way home—I am not sure I shall get there to-night myself.'

'Tush,' said the Abbot, 'thou canst tell us if thou wilt. This reverend brother has been all his life engaged in fighting among the Saracens for the recovery of the Holy Sepulchre; he is of the order of Knights Templars, whom you may have heard of; he is half a monk, half a soldier.'

'If he is but half a monk,' said the Jester, 'he should not be wholly unreasonable with those whom he meets upon the road, even if they should be in no hurry to answer questions that no way concern them.'

'I forgive thy wit,' replied the Abbot, 'on condition thou wilt show me the way to Cedric's mansion.'

'Well, then,' answered Wamba, 'your reverences must hold on this path till you come to a sunken cross, of which scarce a cubit's length remains above ground; then take the path to the left, for there are four which meet at Sunken Cross, and I trust your reverences will obtain shelter before the storm comes on.'

The Abbot thanked his sage adviser; and the cavalcade, setting spurs to their horses, rode on as men do who wish to reach their inn before the bursting of a night-storm. As their horses' hoofs died away, Gurth said to his companion, 'If they follow thy wise direction, the reverend fathers will hardly reach Rotherwood this night.'

'No,' said the Jester, grinning, 'but they may reach Sheffield if they have good luck, and that is as fit a place for them. I am not so bad a woodsman as to show the dog where the deer lies, if I have no mind he should chase him.'

'Thou art right,' said Gurth; 'it were ill that Aymer saw the Lady Rowena; and it were worse, it may be, for Cedric to quarrel, as is most likely he would, with this military monk. But, like good servants, let us hear and see, and say nothing.'

We return to the riders, who had soon left the bondsmen far behind them, and who maintained the following conversation in the Norman-French language, usually employed by the superior classes, with the exception of the few who were still inclined to boast their Saxon descent.

'What mean these fellows by their capricious insolence?' said the Templar to the Benedictine, 'and why did you prevent me from chastising it?'

'Marry, brother Brian,' replied the Prior, 'touching the one of them, it were hard for me to render a reason for a fool speaking according to his folly; and the other churl is of that savage, fierce, intractable race, some of whom, as I have often told you, are still to be found among the descendants of the conquered Saxons, and whose supreme pleasure it is to testify, by all means in their power, their aversion to their conquerors.'

'I would soon have beat him into courtesy,'

observed Brian; 'I am accustomed to deal with such spirits: Our Turkish captives are as fierce and intractable as Odin himself could have been; yet two months in my household, under the management of my master of the slaves, has made them humble, submissive, serviceable, and observant of your will. Marry, sir, you must beware of the poison and the dagger; for they use either with free will when you give them the slightest opportunity.'

'Ay, but,' answered Prior Aymer, 'every land has its own manners and fashions; and, besides that beating this fellow could procure us no information respecting the road to Cedric's house, it would have been sure to have established a quarrel betwixt you and him had we found our way thither. Remember what I told you; this wealthy Franklin is proud, fierce, jealous, and irritable; a withstander of the nobility, and even of his neighbours, Reginald Front-de-Bœuf, and Philip Malvoisin, who are no babes to strive with. He stands up so sternly for the privileges of his race, and is so proud of his uninterrupted descent from Hereward, a renowned champion of the Heptarchy, that he is universally called Cedric the Saxon; and makes a boast of his belonging to a people from whom many others endeavour to hide their descent, lest they should encounter a share of the *vae victis*, or severities imposed upon the vanquished.'

'Prior Aymer,' said the Templar, 'you are a man of gallantry, learned in the study of beauty, and as expert as a troubadóur in all matters concerning the arrets of love; but I shall expect much beauty in this celebrated Rowena, to counterbalance the self-denial and forbearance which I must exert, if I am to court the favour of such a seditious churl as you have described her father Cedric.'

'Cedric is not her father,' replied the Prior, 'and is but of remote relation; she is descended from higher blood than even he pretends to, and is but distantly connected with him by birth. Her guardian, however, he is, self-constituted as I believe; but his ward is as dear to him as if she were his own child. Of her beauty you shall soon be judge; and if the purity of her complexion, and the majestic, yet soft expression of a mild blue eye, do not chase from your memory the black-tressed girls of Palestine, ay, or the houris of old Mahound's paradise, I am an infidel, and no true son of the church.'

'Should your boasted beauty,' said the Templar, 'be weighed in the balance and found wanting, you know our wager?'

'My gold collar,' answered the Prior, 'against ten buts of Chian wine;—they are mine as securely as if they were already in the convent vaults, under the key of old Dennis the cellarer.'

'And I am myself to be judge,' said the Templar, 'and am only to be convicted on my own admission, that I have seen no maiden so beautiful since Pentecost was a twelvemonth. Ran it not so?—Prior, your collar is in danger; I will wear it over my gorget in the lists of Ashby-de-la-Zouche.'

' Win it fairly,' said the Prior, ' and wear it
as ye will; I will trust your giving true response,
on your word as a knight and as a churchman.
Yet, brother, take my advice, and file your tongue
to a little more courtesy than your habits of predominating over infidel captives and Eastern bondsmen have accustomed you. Cedric the Saxon, if
offended,—and he is noway slack in taking offence,
—is a man who, without respect to your knight-
hood, my high office, or the sanctity of either,
would clear his house of us, and send us to lodge
with the larks, though the hour were midnight.
And be careful how you look on Rowena, whom
he cherishes with the most jealous care; an he take
the least alarm in that quarter we are but lost men.
It is said he banished his only son from his family
for lifting his eyes in the way of affection towards
this beauty, who may be worshipped, it seems, at
a distance, but is not to be approached with other
thoughts than such as we bring to the shrine of the
Blessed Virgin.'

' Well, you have said enough,' answered the
Templar; ' I will for a night put on the needful
restraint, and deport me as meekly as a maiden;
but as for the fear of his expelling us by violence,
myself and squires, with Hamlet and Abdalla, will
warrant you against that disgrace. Doubt not
that we shall be strong enough to make good our
quarters.'

' We must not let it come so far,' answered the
Prior; ' but here is the clown's sunken cross, and
the night is so dark that we can hardly see which

of the roads we are to follow. He bid us turn, I think, to the left.'

'To the right,' said Brian, 'to the best of my remembrance.'

'To the left, certainly, the left; I remember his pointing with his wooden sword.'

'Ay, but he held his sword in his left hand, and so pointed across his body with it,' said the Templar.

Each maintained his opinion with sufficient obstinacy, as is usual in all such cases; the attendants were appealed to, but they had not been near enough to hear Wamba's directions. At length Brian remarked, what had at first escaped him in the twilight: 'Here is some one either asleep, or lying dead at the foot of this cross—Hugo, stir him with the but-end of thy lance.'

This was no sooner done than the figure arose, exclaiming in good French, 'Whosoever thou art, it is discourteous in you to disturb my thoughts.'

'We did but wish to ask you,' said the Prior, 'the road to Rotherwood, the abode of Cedric the Saxon.'

'I myself am bound thither,' replied the stranger; 'and if I had a horse, I would be your guide, for the way is somewhat intricate, though perfectly well known to me.'

'Thou shalt have both thanks and reward, my friend,' said the Prior, 'if thou wilt bring us to Cedric's in safety.'

And he caused one of his attendants to mount his own led horse, and give that upon which he had

hitherto ridden to the stranger, who was to serve
for a guide.

Their conductor pursued an opposite road from
that which Wamba had recommended, for the
purpose of misleading them. The path soon led
deeper into the woodland, and crossed more than
one brook, the approach to which was rendered
perilous by the marshes through which it flowed;
but the stranger seemed to know, as if by instinct,
the soundest ground and the safest points of passage;
and by dint of caution and attention, brought the
party safely into a wilder avenue than any they had
yet seen ; and, pointing to a large low irregular
building at the upper extremity, he said to the
Prior, ' Yonder is Rotherwood, the dwelling of
Cedric the Saxon.'

This was a joyful intimation to Aymer, whose
nerves were none of the strongest, and who had
suffered such agitation and alarm in the course of
passing through the dangerous bogs, that he had
not yet had the curiosity to ask his guide a single
question. Finding himself now at his ease and
near shelter, his curiosity began to awake, and he
demanded of the guide who and what he was.

' A Palmer, just returned from the Holy Land,'
was the answer.

' You had better have tarried there to fight
for the recovery of the Holy Sepulchre,' said the
Templar.

' True, Reverend Sir Knight,' answered the
Palmer, to whom the appearance of the Templar
seemed perfectly familiar; ' but when those who

are under oath to recover the holy city, are found travelling at such a distance from the scene of their duties, can you wonder that a peaceful peasant like me should decline the task which they have abandoned ? '

The Templar would have made an angry reply, but was interrupted by the Prior, who again expressed his astonishment, that their guide, after such long absence, should be so perfectly acquainted with the passes of the forest.

' I was born a native of these parts,' answered their guide, and as he made the reply they stood before the mansion of Cedric ;—a low irregular building, containing several court-yards or enclosures, extending over a considerable space of ground, and which, though its size argued the inhabitant to be a person of wealth, differed entirely from the tall, turreted, and castellated buildings in which the Norman nobility resided, and which had become the universal style of architecture throughout England.

Rotherwood was not, however, without defences ; no habitation, in that disturbed period, could have been so, without the risk of being plundered and burnt before the next morning. A deep fosse, or ditch, was drawn round the whole building, and filled with water from a neighbouring stream. A double stockade, or palisade, composed of pointed beams, which the adjacent forest supplied, defended the outer and inner bank of the trench. There was an entrance from the west through the outer stockade, which communicated by a drawbridge, with a similar opening in the interior defences. Some precautions had been taken to place these entrances under the protection of projecting angles, by which they might be flanked in case of need by archers or slingers.

Before this entrance the Templar wound his horn loudly; for the rain, which had long threatened, began now to descend with great violence.

CHAPTER III

Then (sad relief!) from the bleak coast that hears
The German Ocean roar, deep-blooming, strong,
And yellow-hair'd, the blue-eyed Saxon came.

THOMSON'S LIBERTY.

IN a hall, the height of which was greatly dispro-
portioned to its extreme length and width, a long
oaken table, formed of planks rough-hewn from
the forest, and which had scarcely received any
polish, stood ready prepared for the evening meal
of Cedric the Saxon. The roof, composed of
beams and rafters, had nothing to divide the apartment from the sky excepting the planking and
thatch ; there was a huge fireplace at either end
of the hall, but as the chimneys were constructed
in a very clumsy manner, at least as much of the
smoke found its way into the apartment as escaped
by the proper vent. The constant vapour which
this occasioned, had polished the rafters and beams
of the low-browed hall, by encrusting them with
a black varnish of soot. On the sides of the apartment hung implements of war and of the chase,
and there were at each corner folding doors,
which gave access to other parts of the extensive
building.

The other appointments of the mansion partook

37

of the rude simplicity of the Saxon period, which Cedric piqued himself upon maintaining. The floor was composed of earth mixed with lime, trodden into a hard substance, such as is often employed in flooring our modern barns. For about one quarter of the length of the apartment, the floor was raised by a step, and this space, which was called the dais, was occupied only by the principal members of the family, and visitors of distinction. For this purpose, a table richly covered with scarlet cloth was placed transversely across the platform, from the middle of which ran the longer and lower board, at which the domestics and inferior persons fed, down towards the bottom of the hall. The whole resembled the form of the letter T, or some of those ancient dinner-tables, which, arranged on the same principles, may be still seen in the antique Colleges of Oxford or Cambridge. Massive chairs and settles of carved oak were placed upon the dais, and over these seats and the more elevated table was fastened a canopy of cloth, which served in some degree to protect the dignitaries who occupied that distinguished station from the weather, and especially from the rain, which in some places found its way through the ill-constructed roof.

The walls of this upper end of the hall, as far as the dais extended, were covered with hangings or curtains, and upon the floor there was a carpet, both of which were adorned with some attempts at tapestry, or embroidery, executed with brilliant or rather gaudy colouring. Over the lower range of table, the roof, as we have noticed, had no covering; the rough plastered walls were left bare, and the rude earthen floor was uncarpeted; the board was uncovered by a cloth, and rude massive benches supplied the place of chairs.

In the centre of the upper table, were placed two chairs more elevated than the rest, for the master and mistress of the family, who presided over the scene of hospitality, and from doing so derived their Saxon title of honour, which signifies 'the Dividers of Bread.'

To each of these chairs was added a footstool, curiously carved and inlaid with ivory, which mark of distinction was peculiar to them. One of these seats was at present occupied by Cedric the Saxon, who, though but in rank a thane, or, as the Normans called him, a Franklin, felt, at the delay of his evening meal, an irritable impatience, which might have become an alderman, whether of ancient or of modern times.

It appeared, indeed, from the countenance of this proprietor, that he was of a frank, but hasty and choleric temper. He was not above the middle stature, but broad-shouldered, long-armed, and powerfully made, like one accustomed to endure the fatigue of war or of the chase; his face was broad, with large blue eyes, open and frank features, fine teeth, and a well-formed head, altogether expressive of that sort of good-humour which often lodges with a sudden and hasty temper. Pride and jealousy there was in his eye, for his life had been spent in asserting rights which were constantly liable to invasion; and the prompt, fiery, and resolute disposition of the man, had been kept constantly upon the alert by the circumstances of his situation. His long yellow hair was equally divided on the top of his head and upon his brow, and combed down on each side to the length of his shoulders; it had but little tendency to grey, although Cedric was approaching to his sixtieth year.

His dress was a tunic of forest green, furred at the throat and cuffs with what was called minever; a kind of fur inferior in quality to ermine, and formed, it is believed, of the skin of the grey squirrel. This doublet hung unbuttoned over a close dress of scarlet which sate tight to his body; he had breeches of the same, but they did not reach below the lower part of the thigh, leaving the knee exposed. His feet had sandals of the same fashion with the peasants, but of finer materials, and secured in the front with golden clasps. He had bracelets of gold upon his arms, and a broad collar of the same precious metal around his neck. About his waist he wore a richly-studded belt, in which was stuck a short straight two-edged sword, with a sharp point, so disposed as to hang almost perpendicularly by his side. Behind his seat was hung a scarlet cloth cloak lined with fur, and a cap of the same materials richly embroidered, which completed the dress of the opulent landholder when he chose to go forth. A short boar-spear, with a broad and bright steel head, also reclined against the back of his chair, which served him, when he walked abroad, for the purposes of a staff or of a weapon, as chance might require.

Several domestics, whose dress held various proportions betwixt the richness of their master's, and the coarse and simple attire of Gurth the swineherd, watched the looks and waited the commands of the Saxon dignitary. Two or three servants of a superior order stood behind their master upon the dais; the rest occupied the lower part of the hall. Other attendants there were of a different description; two or three large and shaggy greyhounds, such as were then employed in hunting the stag and wolf; as many slow-hounds of a large bony breed, with thick necks, large heads, and long ears; and one or two of the smaller dogs, now called terriers, which waited with impatience the arrival of the supper; but, with the sagacious knowledge of physiognomy peculiar to their race, forbore to intrude upon the moody silence of their master, apprehensive probably of a small white truncheon which lay by Cedric's trencher, for the purpose of repelling the advances of his four-legged dependants. One grisly old wolf-dog alone, with the liberty of an indulged favourite, had planted himself close by the chair of state, and occasionally ventured to solicit notice by putting his large hairy head upon his master's knee, or pushing his nose into his hand. Even he was repelled by the stern command, 'Down, Balder, down! I am not in the humour for foolery.'

In fact, Cedric, as we have observed, was in no

very placid state of mind. The Lady Rowena, who had been absent to attend an evening mass at a distant church, had but just returned, and was changing her garments, which had been wetted by the storm. There were as yet no tidings of Gurth and his charge, which should long since have been driven home from the forest; and such was the insecurity of the period, as to render it probable that the delay might be explained by some depredation of the outlaws, with whom the adjacent forest abounded, or by the violence of some neighbouring baron, whose consciousness of strength made him equally negligent of the laws of property. The matter was of consequence, for great part of the domestic wealth of the Saxon proprietors consisted in numerous herds of swine, especially in forest-land, where those animals easily found their food.

Besides these subjects of anxiety, the Saxon thane was impatient for the presence of his favourite clown Wamba, whose jests, such as they were, served for a sort of seasoning to his evening meal, and to the deep draughts of ale and wine with which he was in the habit of accompanying it. Add to all this, Cedric had fasted since noon, and his usual supper hour was long past, a cause of irritation common to country squires, both in ancient and modern times. His displeasure was expressed in broken sentences, partly muttered to himself, partly addressed to the domestics who stood around; and particularly to his cupbearer, who offered him from time to time, as a sedative, a silver goblet filled with wine—'Why tarries the Lady Rowena?'

'She is but changing her head-gear,' replied a female attendant, with as much confidence as the favourite lady's-maid usually answers the master of a modern family; 'you would not wish her to sit down to the banquet in her hood and kirtle? and no lady within the shire can be quicker in arraying herself than my mistress.'

This undeniable argument produced a sort of acquiescent umph! on the part of the Saxon, with the addition, 'I wish her devotion may choose fair weather for the next visit to St. John's Kirk;— but what, in the name of ten devils,' continued he, turning to the cupbearer, and raising his voice as if happy to have found a channel into which he might divert his indignation without fear or control —'what, in the name of ten devils, keeps Gurth so long a-field? I suppose we shall have an evil account of the herd; he was wont to be a faithful and cautious drudge, and I had destined him for something better; perchance I might even have made him one of my warders.'*

Oswald the cupbearer modestly suggested, 'that it was scarce an hour since the tolling of the curfew'; an ill-chosen apology, since it turned upon a topic so harsh to Saxon ears.

'The foul fiend,' exclaimed Cedric, 'take the

---

* The original has *Cnichts*, by which the Saxons seem to have designated a class of military attendants, sometimes free, sometimes bondsmen, but always ranking above an ordinary domestic, whether in the royal household or in those of the aldermen and thanes. But the term cnicht, now spelt knight, having been received into the English language as equivalent to the Norman word chevalier, I have avoided using it in its more ancient sense, to prevent confusion.—L. T.

curfew-bell, and the tyrannical bastard by whom it was devised, and the heartless slave who names it with a Saxon tongue to a Saxon ear! The curfew!' he added, pausing, 'ay, the curfew; which compels true men to extinguish their lights, that thieves and robbers may work their deeds in darkness!—Ay, the curfew;— Reginald Front-de-Bœuf and Philip de Malvoisin know the use of the curfew as well as William the Bastard himself, or e'er a Norman adventurer that fought at Hastings. I shall hear, I guess, that my property has been swept off to save from starving the hungry banditti, whom they cannot support but by theft and robbery. My faithful slave is murdered, and my goods are taken for a prey—and Wamba—where is Wamba? Said not some one he had gone forth with Gurth?'

Oswald replied in the affirmative.

'Ay? why, this is better and better! he is carried off too, the Saxon fool, to serve the Norman lord. Fools are we all indeed that serve them, and fitter subjects for their scorn and laughter, than if we were born with but half our wits. But I will be avenged,' he added, starting from his chair in impatience at the supposed injury, and catching hold of his boar-spear; 'I will go with my complaint to the great council; I have friends, I have followers—man to man will I appeal the Norman to the lists; let him come in his plate and his mail, and all that can render cowardice bold; I have sent such a javelin as this through a stronger fence than three of their war-shields!—Haply they think me old; but they shall find, alone and childless as I am, the blood of Hereward is in the veins of Cedric. —Ah, Wilfred, Wilfred!' he exclaimed in a lower tone, 'couldst thou have ruled thine unreasonable passion, thy father had not been left in his age like the solitary oak that throws out its shattered and unprotected branches against the full sweep of the tempest!' The reflection seemed to conjure into sadness his irritated feelings. Replacing his javelin, he resumed his seat, bent his looks downward, and appeared to be absorbed in melancholy reflection.

From his musing, Cedric was suddenly awakened by the blast of a horn, which was replied to by the clamorous yells and barking of all the dogs in the hall, and some twenty or thirty which were quartered in other parts of the building. It cost some exercise of the white truncheon, well seconded by the exertions of the domestics, to silence this canine clamour.

'To the gate, knaves!' said the Saxon, hastily, as soon as the tumult was so much appeased that the dependants could hear his voice. 'See what tidings that horn tells us of—to announce, I ween, some hership* and robbery which has been done upon my lands.'

Returning in less than three minutes, a warder announced, 'that the Prior Aymer of Jorvaulx, and the good knight Brian de Bois-Guilbert, commander of the valiant and venerable order of Knights Templars, with a small retinue, requested hospitality and lodging for the night, being on their

---

* Pillage.

way to a tournament which was to be held not far from Ashby-de-la-Zouche, on the second day from the present.'

'Aymer, the Prior Aymer? Brian de Bois-Guilbert?'—muttered Cedric; 'Normans both;— but Norman or Saxon, the hospitality of Rother-wood must not be impeached; they are welcome, since they have chosen to halt — more welcome would they have been to have ridden further on their way—But it were unworthy to murmur for a night's lodging and a night's food; in the quality of guests, at least, even Normans must suppress their insolence.—Go, Hundebert,' he added, to a sort of major-domo who stood behind him with a white wand; 'take six of the attendants, and intro-duce the strangers to the guests' lodging. Look after their horses and mules, and see their train lack nothing. Let them have change of vestments if they require it, and fire, and water to wash, and wine and ale; and bid the cooks add what they hastily can to our evening meal; and let it be put on the board when those strangers are ready to share it. Say to them, Hundebert, that Cedric would himself bid them welcome, but he is under a vow never to step more than three steps from the dais of his own hall to meet any who shares not the blood of Saxon royalty. Begone! see them care-fully tended; let them not say in their pride, the Saxon churl has shown at once his poverty and his avarice.'

The major-domo departed with several attendants, to execute his master's commands. 'The Prior

Aymer!' repeated Cedric, looking to Oswald,
'the brother, if I mistake not, of Giles de
Mauleverer, now lord of Middleham?'

Oswald made a respectful sign of assent. 'His
brother sits in the seat, and usurps the patrimony,
of a better race, the race of Ulfgar of Middleham;
but what Norman lord doth not the same? This
Prior is, they say, a free and jovial priest, who
loves the wine-cup and the bugle-horn better than
bell and book: Good; let him come, he shall be
welcome. How named ye the Templar?'

'Brian de Bois-Guilbert.'

'Bois-Guilbert,' said Cedric, still in the musing,
half-arguing tone, which the habit of living among
dependants had accustomed him to employ, and
which resembled a man who talks to himself rather
than to those around him—'Bois-Guilbert? that
name has been spread wide both for good and
evil. They say he is valiant as the bravest of
his order; but stained with their usual vices,
pride, arrogance, cruelty, and voluptuousness; a
hard-hearted man, who knows neither fear of
earth, nor awe of heaven. So say the few warriors
who have returned from Palestine.—Well; it is
but for one night; he shall be welcome too.
—Oswald, broach the oldest wine-cask; place the
best mead, the mightiest ale, the richest morat,
the most sparkling cider, the most odoriferous
pigments, upon the board; fill the largest horns *

---

* These were drinks used by the Saxons, as we are informed by
Mr. Turner: Morat was made of honey flavoured with the juice of

— Templars and Abbots love good wines and good measure. — Elgitha, let thy Lady Rowena know we shall not this night expect her in the hall, unless such be her especial pleasure.'

'But it will be her especial pleasure,' answered Elgitha, with great readiness, 'for she is ever desirous to hear the latest news from Palestine.'

Cedric darted at the forward damsel a glance of hasty resentment; but Rowena, and whatever belonged to her, were privileged and secure from his anger. He only replied, 'Silence, maiden; thy tongue outruns thy discretion. Say my message to thy mistress, and let her do her pleasure. Here, at least, the descendant of Alfred still reigns a princess.' Elgitha left the apartment.

'Palestine!' repeated the Saxon; 'Palestine! how many ears are turned to the tales which dissolute crusaders, or hypocritical pilgrims, bring from that fatal land! I too might ask—I too might enquire—I too might listen with a beating heart to fables which the wily strollers devise to cheat us into hospitality—but no—The son who has disobeyed me is no longer mine; nor will I concern myself more for his fate than for that of the most worthless among the millions that ever shaped the cross on their shoulder, rushed into excess and blood-guiltiness, and called it an accomplishment of the will of God.'

He knit his brows, and fixed his eyes for an

---

mulberries; Pigment was a sweet and rich liquor, composed of wine highly spiced, and sweetened also with honey; the other liquors need no explanation.—L. T.

instant on the ground; as he raised them, the folding doors at the bottom of the hall were cast wide, and, preceded by the major-domo with his wand, and four domestics bearing blazing torches, the guests of the evening entered the apartment.

CHAPTER IV

With sheep and shaggy goats the porkers bled,
And the proud steer was on the marble spread;
With fire prepared, they deal the morsels round,
Wine rosy bright the brimming goblets crown'd.
*   *   *   *   *   *
Disposed apart, Ulysses shares the treat;
A trivet table and ignobler seat,
The Prince assigns——

Odyssey, Book 21.

The Prior Aymer had taken the opportunity
afforded him, of changing his riding robe for one
of yet more costly materials, over which he wore a
cope curiously embroidered. Besides the massive
golden signet ring, which marked his ecclesiastical
dignity, his fingers, though contrary to the canon,
were loaded with precious gems; his sandals were
of the finest leather which was imported from
Spain; his beard trimmed to as small dimensions as his order would possibly permit, and his
shaven crown concealed by a scarlet cap richly
embroidered.

The appearance of the Knight Templar was also
changed; and, though less studiously bedecked with
ornament, his dress was as rich, and his appearance
far more commanding, than that of his companion.
He had exchanged his shirt of mail for an under

tunic of dark purple silk, garnished with furs, over which flowed his long robe of spotless white, in ample folds. The eight-pointed cross of his order was cut on the shoulder of his mantle in black velvet. The high cap no longer invested his brows, which were only shaded by short and thick curled hair of a raven blackness, corresponding to his unusually swart complexion. Nothing could be more gracefully majestic than his step and manner, had they not been marked by a predominant air of haughtiness, easily acquired by the exercise of unresisted authority.

These two dignified persons were followed by their respective attendants, and at a more humble distance by their guide, whose figure had nothing more remarkable than it derived from the usual weeds of a pilgrim. A cloak or mantle of coarse black serge, enveloped his whole body. It was in shape something like the cloak of a modern hussar, having similar flaps for covering the arms, and was called a *Sclaveyn*, or *Sclavonian*. Coarse sandals, bound with thongs, on his bare feet; a broad and shadowy hat, with cockle-shells stitched on its brim, and a long staff shod with iron, to the upper end of which was attached a branch of palm, completed the palmer's attire. He followed modestly the last of the train which entered the hall, and, observing that the lower table scarce afforded room sufficient for the domestics of Cedric and the retinue of his guests, he withdrew to a settle placed beside and almost under one of the large chimneys, and seemed to employ himself in drying his garments, until the retreat of some one should make room at the board, or the hospitality of the steward should supply him with refreshments in the place he had chosen apart.

Cedric rose to receive his guests with an air of dignified hospitality, and, descending from the dais, or elevated part of his hall, made three steps towards them, and then awaited their approach.

'I grieve,' he said, 'reverend Prior, that my vow binds me to advance no farther upon this floor of my fathers, even to receive such guests as you, and this valiant Knight of the Holy Temple. But my steward has expounded to you the cause of my seeming discourtesy. Let me also pray, that you will excuse my speaking to you in my native language, and that you will reply in the same if your knowledge of it permits; if not, I sufficiently understand Norman to follow your meaning.'

'Vows,' said the Abbot, 'must be unloosed, worthy Franklin, or permit me rather to say, worthy Thane, though the title is antiquated. Vows are the knots which tie us to Heaven—they are the cords which bind the sacrifice to the horns of the altar,—and are therefore,—as I said before,—to be unloosened and discharged, unless our holy Mother Church shall pronounce the contrary. And respecting language, I willingly hold communication in that spoken by my respected grandmother, Hilda of Middleham, who died in odour of sanctity, little short, if we may presume to say so, of her glorious namesake, the blessed Saint Hilda of Whitby, God be gracious to her soul!'

IVANHOE

When the Prior had ceased what he meant as a
conciliatory harangue, his companion said briefly
and emphatically, 'I speak ever French, the
language of King Richard and his nobles; but I
understand English sufficiently to communicate
with the natives of the country.'

Cedric darted at the speaker one of those hasty
and impatient glances, which comparisons between
the two rival nations seldom failed to call forth;
but, recollecting the duties of hospitality, he suppressed further show of resentment, and, motion-
ing with his hand, caused his guests to assume two
seats a little lower than his own, but placed close
beside him, and gave a signal that the evening meal
should be placed upon the board.

While the attendants hastened to obey Cedric's
commands, his eye distinguished Gurth the swineherd, who, with his companion Wamba, had just
entered the hall. 'Send these loitering knaves up
hither,' said the Saxon, impatiently. And when
the culprits came before the dais,—'How comes
it, villains! that you have loitered abroad so late
as this? Hast thou brought home thy charge,
sirrah Gurth, or hast thou left them to robbers
and marauders?'

'The herd is safe, so please ye,' said Gurth.

'But it does not please me, thou knave,' said
Cedric, 'that I should be made to suppose otherwise for two hours, and sit here devising vengeance
against my neighbours for wrongs they have not
done me. I tell thee, shackles and the prison-house
shall punish the next offence of this kind.'

Gurth, knowing his master's irritable temper, attempted no exculpation; but the Jester, who could presume upon Cedric's tolerance, by virtue of his privileges as a fool, replied for them both: 'In troth, uncle Cedric, you are neither wise nor reasonable to-night.'

'How, sir?' said his master; 'you shall to the porter's lodge, and taste of the discipline there, if you give your foolery such license.'

'First let your wisdom tell me,' said Wamba, 'is it just and reasonable to punish one person for the fault of another?'

'Certainly not, fool,' answered Cedric.

'Then why should you shackle poor Gurth, uncle, for the fault of his dog Fangs? for I dare be sworn we lost not a minute, by the way, when we had got our herd together, which Fangs did not manage until we heard the vesper-bell.'

'Then hang up Fangs,' said Cedric, turning hastily towards the swineherd, 'if the fault is his, and get thee another dog.'

'Under favour, uncle,' said the Jester, 'that were still somewhat on the bow-hand of fair justice; for it was no fault of Fangs that he was lame and could not gather the herd, but the fault of those that struck off two of his fore-claws, an operation for which, if the poor fellow had been consulted, he would scarce have given his voice.'

'And who dared to lame an animal which belonged to my bondsman?' said the Saxon, kindling in wrath.

'Marry, that did old Hubert,' said Wamba,

'Sir Philip de Malvoisin's keeper of the chase. He caught Fangs strolling in the forest, and said he chased the deer contrary to his master's right, as warden of the walk.'

'The foul fiend take Malvoisin,' answered the Saxon, 'and his keeper both! I will teach them that the wood was disforested in terms of the great Forest Charter. But enough of this. Go to, knave, go to thy place—and thou, Gurth, get thee another dog, and should the keeper dare to touch it, I will mar his archery; the curse of a coward on my head, if I strike not off the forefinger of his right hand!—he shall draw bowstring no more.—I crave your pardon, my worthy guests. I am beset here with neighbours that match your infidels, Sir Knight, in Holy Land. But your homely fare is before you; feed, and let welcome make amends for hard fare.'

The feast, however, which was spread upon the board, needed no apologies from the lord of the mansion. Swine's flesh, dressed in several modes, appeared on the lower part of the board, as also that of fowls, deer, goats, and hares, and various kinds of fish, together with huge loaves and cakes of bread, and sundry confections made of fruits and honey. The smaller sorts of wild-fowl, of which there was abundance, were not served up in platters, but brought in upon small wooden spits or broaches, and offered by the pages and domestics who bore them, to each guest in succession, who cut from them such a portion as he pleased. Beside each person of rank was placed a goblet of silver;

the lower board was accommodated with large drinking-horns.

When the repast was about to commence, the major-domo, or steward, suddenly raising his wand, said aloud, — 'Forbear! — Place for the Lady Rowena.' A side-door at the upper end of the hall now opened behind the banquet table, and Rowena, followed by four female attendants, entered the apartment. Cedric, though surprised, and perhaps not altogether agreeably so, at his ward appearing in public on this occasion, hastened to meet her, and to conduct her, with respectful ceremony, to the elevated seat at his own right hand, appropriated to the lady of the mansion. All stood up to receive her; and, replying to their courtesy by a mute gesture of salutation, she moved gracefully forward to assume her place at the board. Ere she had time to do so, the Templar whispered to the Prior, 'I shall wear no collar of gold of yours at the tournament. The Chian wine is your own.'

'Said I not so?' answered the Prior; 'but check your raptures, the Franklin observes you.'

Unheeding this remonstrance, and accustomed only to act upon the immediate impulse of his own wishes, Brian de Bois-Guilbert kept his eyes riveted on the Saxon beauty, more striking perhaps to his imagination, because differing widely from those of the Eastern sultanas.

Formed in the best proportions of her sex, Rowena was tall in stature, yet not so much so as to attract observation on account of superior height. Her complexion was exquisitely fair, but the noble

cast of her head and features prevented the insipidity
which sometimes attaches to fair beauties. Her clear
blue eye, which sate enshrined beneath a graceful
eyebrow of brown sufficiently marked to give expression to the forehead, seemed capable to kindle
as well as melt, to command as well as to beseech.
If mildness were the more natural expression of
such a combination of features, it was plain, that
in the present instance, the exercise of habitual
superiority, and the reception of general homage,
had given to the Saxòn lady a loftier character,
which mingled with and qualified that bestowed
by nature. Her profuse hair, of a colour betwixt
brown and flaxen, was arranged in a fanciful and
graceful manner in numerous ringlets, to form which
art had probably aided nature. These locks were
braided with gems, and, being worn at full length,
intimated the noble birth and free-born condition
of the maiden. A golden chain, to which was attached a small reliquary of the same metal, hung
round her neck. She wore bracelets on her arms,
which were bare. Her dress was an under-gown
and kirtle of pale sea-green silk, over which hung
a long loose robe, which reached to the ground,
having very wide sleeves, which came down, however, very little below the elbow. This robe was
crimson, and manufactured out of the very finest
wool. A veil of silk, interwoven with gold, was
attached to the upper part of it, which could be,
at the wearer's pleasure, either drawn over the face
and bosom after the Spanish fashion, or disposed
as a sort of drapery round the shoulders.

IVANHOE

When Rowena perceived the Knight Templar's eyes bent on her with an ardour, that, compared with the dark caverns under which they moved, gave them the effect of lighted charcoal, she drew with dignity the veil around her face, as an intimation that the determined freedom of his glance was disagreeable. Cedric saw the motion and its cause. 'Sir Templar,' said he, 'the cheeks of our Saxon maidens have seen too little of the sun to enable them to bear the fixed glance of a crusader.'

'If I have offended,' replied Sir Brian, 'I crave your pardon,—that is, I crave the Lady Rowena's pardon,—for my humility will carry me no lower.'

'The Lady Rowena,' said the Prior, 'has punished us all, in chastising the boldness of my friend. Let me hope she will be less cruel to the splendid train which are to meet at the tournament.'

'Our going thither,' said Cedric, 'is uncertain. I love not these vanities, which were unknown to my fathers when England was free.'

'Let us hope, nevertheless,' said the Prior, 'our company may determine you to travel thitherward; when the roads are so unsafe, the escort of Sir Brian de Bois-Guilbert is not to be despised.'

'Sir Prior,' answered the Saxon, 'wheresoever I have travelled in this land, I have hitherto found myself, with the assistance of my good sword and faithful followers, in no respect needful of other aid. At present, if we indeed journey to Ashby-de-la-Zouche, we do so with my noble neighbour and countryman Athelstane of Coningsburgh, and with such a train as would set outlaws and feudal enemies at defiance.——I drink to you, Sir Prior, in this cup of wine, which I trust your taste will approve, and I thank you for your courtesy. Should you be so rigid in adhering to monastic rule,' he added, ' as to prefer your acid preparation of milk, I hope you will not strain courtesy to do me reason.'

' Nay,' said the Priest, laughing, ' it is only in our abbey that we confine ourselves to the *lac dulce* or the *lac acidum* either. Conversing with the world, we use the world's fashions, and therefore I answer your pledge in this honest wine, and leave the weaker liquor to my lay-brother.'

' And I,' said the Templar, filling his goblet, ' drink wassail to the fair Rowena; for since her namesake introduced the word into England, has never been one more worthy of such a tribute. By my faith, I could pardon the unhappy Vortigern, had he half the cause that we now witness, for making shipwreck of his honour and his kingdom.'

' I will spare your courtesy, Sir Knight,' said Rowena with dignity, and without unveiling herself; ' or rather I will tax it so far as to require of you the latest news from Palestine, a theme more agreeable to our English ears than the compliments which your French breeding teaches.'

' I have little of importance to say, lady,' answered Sir Brian de Bois-Guilbert, ' excepting the confirmed tidings of a truce with Saladin.'

He was interrupted by Wamba, who had taken his appropriated seat upon a chair, the back of which was decorated with two ass's ears, and which was placed about two steps behind that of his master, who, from time to time, supplied him with victuals from his own trencher; a favour, however, which the Jester shared with the favourite dogs, of whom, as we have already noticed, there were several in attendance. Here sat Wamba, with a small table before him, his heels tucked up against the bar of the chair, his cheeks sucked up so as to make his jaws resemble a pair of nut-crackers, and his eyes half-shut, yet watching with alertness every opportunity to exercise his licensed foolery.

'These truces with the infidels,' he exclaimed, without caring how suddenly he interrupted the stately Templar, 'make an old man of me!'

'Go to, knave, how so?' said Cedric, his features prepared to receive favourably the expected jest.

'Because,' answered Wamba, 'I remember three of them in my day, each of which was to endure for the course of fifty years; so that, by computation, I must be at least a hundred and fifty years old.'

'I will warrant you against dying of old age, however,' said the Templar, who now recognised his friend of the forest; 'I will assure you from all deaths but a violent one, if you give such directions to wayfarers, as you did this night to the Prior and me.'

'How, sirrah!' said Cedric, 'misdirect travellers? We must have you whipt; you are at least as much rogue as fool.'

'I pray thee, uncle,' answered the Jester, 'let my folly, for once, protect my roguery. I did but make a mistake between my right hand and my left; and he might have pardoned a greater, who took a fool for his counsellor and guide.'

Conversation was here interrupted by the entrance of the porter's page, who announced that there was a stranger at the gate, imploring admittance and hospitality.

'Admit him,' said Cedric, 'be he who or what he may;—a night like that which roars without, compels even wild animals to herd with tame, and to seek the protection of man, their mortal foe, rather than perish by the elements. Let his wants be ministered to with all care—look to it, Oswald.'

And the steward left the banqueting hall to see the commands of his patron obeyed.

CHAPTER V

*Hath not a Jew eyes ? Hath not a Jew hands, organs, dimensions,
senses, affections, passions ? Fed with the same food, hurt with the
same weapons, subject to the same diseases, healed by the same means,
warmed and cooled by the same winter and summer, as a Christian is ?*

MERCHANT OF VENICE.

OSWALD, returning, whispered into the ear of his
master, 'It is a Jew, who calls himself Isaac of
York; is it fit I should marshal him into the
hall?'

'Let Gurth do thine office, Oswald,' said Wamba
with his usual effrontery; 'the swineherd will be
a fit usher to the Jew.'

'St. Mary,' said the Abbot, crossing himself,
'an unbelieving Jew, and admitted into this
presence!'

'A dog Jew,' echoed the Templar, 'to approach
a defender of the Holy Sepulchre?'

'By my faith,' said Wamba, 'it would seem the
Templars love the Jews' inheritance better than
they do their company.'

'Peace, my worthy guests,' said Cedric; 'my
hospitality must not be bounded by your dislikes.
If Heaven bore with the whole nation of stiff-
necked unbelievers for more years than a layman
can number, we may endure the presence of one

Jew for a few hours. But I constrain no man to converse or to feed with him.—Let him have a board and a morsel apart,—unless,' he said smiling, ' these turban'd strangers will admit his society.'

' Sir Franklin,' answered the Templar, ' my Saracen slaves are true Moslems, and scorn as much as any Christian to hold intercourse with a Jew.'

' Now, in faith,' said Wamba, ' I cannot see that the worshippers of Mahound and Termagaunt have so greatly the advantage over the people once chosen of Heaven.'

' He shall sit with thee, Wamba,' said Cedric; ' the fool and the knave will be well met.'

' The fool,' answered Wamba, raising the relics of a gammon of bacon, ' will take care to erect a bulwark against the knave.'

' Hush,' said Cedric, ' for here he comes.'

Introduced with little ceremony, and advancing with fear and hesitation, and many a bow of deep humility, a tall thin old man, who, however, had lost by the habit of stooping much of his actual height, approached the lower end of the board. His features, keen and regular, with an aquiline nose, and piercing black eyes; his high and wrinkled forehead, and long grey hair and beard, would have been considered as handsome, had they not been the marks of a physiognomy peculiar to a race, which, during those dark ages, was alike detested by the credulous and prejudiced vulgar, and persecuted by the greedy and rapacious nobility, and who, perhaps, owing to that very hatred and persecution, had adopted a national character, in which there was much, to say the least, mean and unamiable.

The Jew's dress, which appeared to have suffered considerably from the storm, was a plain russet cloak of many folds, covering a dark purple tunic. He had large boots lined with fur, and a belt around his waist, which sustained a small knife, together with a case for writing materials, but no weapon. He wore a high square yellow cap of a peculiar fashion, assigned to his nation to distinguish them from Christians, and which he doffed with great humility at the door of the hall.

The reception of this person in the hall of Cedric the Saxon, was such as might have satisfied the most prejudiced enemy of the tribes of Israel. Cedric himself coldly nodded in answer to the Jew's repeated salutations, and signed to him to take place at the lower end of the table, where, however, no one offered to make room for him. On the contrary, as he passed along the file, casting a timid supplicating glance, and turning towards each of those who occupied the lower end of the board, the Saxon domestics squared their shoulders, and continued to devour their supper with great perseverance, paying not the least attention to the wants of the new guest. The attendants of the Abbot crossed themselves, with looks of pious horror, and the very heathen Saracens, as Isaac drew near them, curled up their whiskers with indignation, and laid their hands on their poniards, as if ready to rid themselves by the most desperate means from the apprehended contamination of his nearer approach.

Probably the same motives which induced Cedric to open his hall to this son of a rejected people, would have made him insist on his attendants receiving Isaac with more courtesy. But the Abbot had, at this moment, engaged him in a most interesting discussion on the breed and character of his favourite hounds, which he would not have interrupted for matters of much greater importance than that of a Jew going to bed supperless. While Isaac thus stood an outcast in the present society, like his people among the nations, looking in vain for welcome or resting-place, the pilgrim who sat by the chimney took compassion upon him, and resigned his seat, saying briefly, 'Old man, my garments are dried, my hunger is appeased, thou art both wet and fasting.' So saying, he gathered together, and brought to a flame, the decaying brands which lay scattered on the ample hearth; took from the larger board a mess of pottage and seethed kid, placed it upon the small table at which he had himself supped, and, without waiting the Jew's thanks, went to the other side of the hall ;— whether from unwillingness to hold more close communication with the object of his benevolence, or from a wish to draw near to the upper end of the table, seemed uncertain.

Had there been painters in those days capable to execute such a subject, the Jew, as he bent his withered form, and expanded his chilled and trembling hands over the fire, would have formed no bad emblematical personification of the Winter season. Having dispelled the cold, he turned eagerly to the smoking mess which was placed before him, and ate with a haste and an apparent relish, that seemed to betoken long abstinence from food.

Meanwhile the Abbot and Cedric continued their discourse upon hunting; the Lady Rowena seemed engaged in conversation with one of her attendant females; and the haughty Templar, whose eye wandered from the Jew to the Saxon beauty, revolved in his mind thoughts which appeared deeply to interest him.

'I marvel, worthy Cedric,' said the Abbot, as their discourse proceeded, 'that, great as your predilection is for your own manly language, you do not receive the Norman-French into your favour, so far at least as the mystery of wood-craft and hunting is concerned. Surely no tongue is so rich in the various phrases which the field-sports demand, or furnishes means to the experienced woodman so well to express his jovial art.'

'Good Father Aymer,' said the Saxon, 'be it known to you, I care not for those over-sea refinements, without which I can well enough take my pleasure in the woods. I can wind my horn, though I call not the blast either a *recheate* or a *morte*—I can cheer my dogs on the prey, and I can flay and quarter the animal when it is brought down, without using the newfangled jargon of *curee*, *arber*, *nombles*, and all the babble of the fabulous Sir Tristrem.'*

---

* There was no language which the Normans more formally separated from that of common life than the terms of the chase. The objects of their pursuit, whether bird or animal, changed their name each year,

'The French,' said the Templar, raising his voice with the presumptuous and authoritative tone which he used upon all occasions, 'is not only the natural language of the chase, but that of love and of war, in which ladies should be won and enemies defied.'

'Pledge me in a cup of wine, Sir Templar,' said Cedric, 'and fill another to the Abbot, while I look back some thirty years to tell you another tale. As Cedric the Saxon then was, his plain English tale needed no garnish from French troubadours, when it was told in the ear of beauty; and the field of Northallerton, upon the day of the Holy Standard, could tell whether the Saxon war-cry was not heard as far within the ranks of the Scottish host as the *cri de guerre* of the boldest Norman baron. To the memory of the brave who fought there!— Pledge me, my guests.' He drank deep, and went on with increasing warmth. 'Ay, that was a day of cleaving of shields, when a hundred banners were bent forwards over the heads of the valiant, and blood flowed round like water, and death was held better than flight. A Saxon bard had called it a feast of the swords—a gathering of the eagles to the prey—the clashing of bills upon shield and

---

and there were a hundred conventional terms, to be ignorant of which was to be without one of the distinguishing marks of a gentleman. The reader may consult Dame Juliana Berners' book on the subject. The origin of this science was imputed to the celebrated Sir Tristrem, famous for his tragic intrigue with the beautiful Ysolte. As the Normans reserved the amusement of hunting strictly to themselves, the terms of this formal jargon were all taken from the French language.

helmet, the shouting of battle more joyful than the clamour of a bridal. But our bards are no more,' he said; 'our deeds are lost in those of another race —our language—our very name—is hastening to decay, and none mourns for it save one solitary old man—Cupbearer! knave, fill the goblets—To the strong in arms, Sir Templar, be their race or language what it will, who now bear them best in Palestine among the champions of the Cross!'

'It becomes not one wearing this badge to answer,' said Sir Brian de Bois-Guilbert; 'yet to whom, besides the sworn Champions of the Holy Sepulchre, can the palm be assigned among the champions of the Cross?'

'To the Knights Hospitallers,' said the Abbot; 'I have a brother of their order.'

'I impeach not their fame,' said the Templar; 'nevertheless——'

'I think, friend Cedric,' said Wamba, interfering, 'that had Richard of the Lion's Heart been wise enough to have taken a fool's advice, he might have staid at home with his merry Englishmen, and left the recovery of Jerusalem to those same Knights who had most to do with the loss of it.'

'Were there, then, none in the English army,' said the Lady Rowena, 'whose names are worthy to be mentioned with the Knights of the Temple, and of St. John?'

'Forgive me, lady,' replied De Bois-Guilbert; 'the English monarch did, indeed, bring to Palestine a host of gallant warriors, second only to those whose breasts have been the unceasing bulwark of that blessed land.'

'Second to NONE,' said the Pilgrim, who had stood near enough to hear, and had listened to this conversation with marked impatience. All turned toward the spot from whence this unexpected asseveration was heard. 'I say,' repeated the Pilgrim in a firm and strong voice, 'that the English chivalry were second to NONE who ever drew sword in defence of the Holy Land. I say besides, for I saw it, that King Richard himself, and five of his knights, held a tournament after the taking of St. John-de-Acre, as challengers against all comers. I say that, on that day, each knight ran three courses, and cast to the ground three antagonists. I add, that seven of these assailants were knights of the Temple—and Sir Brian de Bois-Guilbert well knows the truth of what I tell you.'

It is impossible for language to describe the bitter scowl of rage which rendered yet darker the swarthy countenance of the Templar. In the extremity of his resentment and confusion, his quivering fingers griped towards the handle of his sword, and perhaps only withdrew, from the consciousness that no act of violence could be safely executed in that place and presence. Cedric, whose feelings were all of a right onward and simple kind, and were seldom occupied by more than one object at once, omitted, in the joyous glee with which he heard of the glory of his countrymen, to remark the angry confusion of his guest; 'I would give thee this golden bracelet, Pilgrim,' he said, 'couldst thou tell me the names of those knights who upheld so gallantly the renown of merry England.'

'That will I do blithely,' replied the Pilgrim, 'and without guerdon; my oath, for a time, prohibits me from touching gold.'

'I will wear the bracelet for you, if you will, friend Palmer,' said Wamba.

'The first in honour as in arms, in renown as in place,' said the Pilgrim, 'was the brave Richard, King of England.'

'I forgive him,' said Cedric; 'I forgive him his descent from the tyrant Duke William.'

'The Earl of Leicester was the second,' continued the Pilgrim; 'Sir Thomas Multon of Gilsland was the third.'

'Of Saxon descent, he at least,' said Cedric, with exultation.

'Sir Foulk Doilly the fourth,' proceeded the Pilgrim.

'Saxon also, at least by the mother's side,' continued Cedric, who listened with the utmost eagerness, and forgot, in part at least, his hatred to the Normans, in the common triumph of the King of England and his islanders. 'And who was the fifth?' he demanded.

'The fifth was Sir Edwin Turneham.'

'Genuine Saxon, by the soul of Hengist!' shouted Cedric — 'And the sixth?' he continued with eagerness — 'how name you the sixth?'

'The sixth,' said the Palmer, after a pause, in which he seemed to recollect himself, 'was a young knight of lesser renown and lower rank, assumed into that honourable company, less to aid their enterprise than to make up their number — his name dwells not in my memory.'

'Sir Palmer,' said Sir Brian de Bois-Guilbert scornfully, 'this assumed forgetfulness, after so much has been remembered, comes too late to serve your purpose. I will myself tell the name of the knight before whose lance fortune and my horse's fault occasioned my falling—it was the Knight of Ivanhoe; nor was there one of the six that, for his years, had more renown in arms.— Yet this will I say, and loudly — that were he in England, and durst repeat, in this week's tournament, the challenge of St. John-de-Acre, I, mounted and armed as I now am, would give him every advantage of weapons, and abide the result.'

'Your challenge would be soon answered,' replied the Palmer, 'were your antagonist near you. As the matter is, disturb not the peaceful hall with vaunts of the issue of a conflict, which you well know cannot take place. If Ivanhoe ever returns from Palestine, I will be his surety that he meets you.'

'A goodly security!' said the Knight Templar; 'and what do you proffer as a pledge?'

'This reliquary,' said the Palmer, taking a small ivory box from his bosom, and crossing himself, 'containing a portion of the true cross, brought from the Monastery of Mount Carmel.'

The Prior of Jorvaulx crossed himself and repeated a pater noster, in which all devoutly joined, excepting the Jew, the Mahomedans, and the

Templar; the latter of whom, without vailing his bonnet, or testifying any reverence for the alleged sanctity of the relic, took from his neck a gold chain, which he flung on the board, saying — 'Let Prior Aymer hold my pledge and that of this nameless vagrant, in token that when the Knight of Ivanhoe comes within the four seas of Britain, he underlies the challenge of Brian de Bois-Guilbert, which, if he answer not, I will proclaim him as a coward on the walls of every Temple Court in Europe.'

'It will not need,' said the Lady Rowena, breaking silence; 'My voice shall be heard, if no other in this hall is raised in behalf of the absent Ivanhoe. I affirm he will meet fairly every honourable challenge. Could my weak warrant add security to the inestimable pledge of this holy pilgrim, I would pledge name and fame that Ivanhoe gives this proud knight the meeting he desires.'

A crowd of conflicting emotions seemed to have occupied Cedric, and kept him silent during this discussion. Gratified pride, resentment, embarrassment, chased each other over his broad and open brow, like the shadow of clouds drifting over a harvest-field; while his attendants, on whom the name of the sixth knight seemed to produce an effect almost electrical, hung in suspense upon their master's looks. But when Rowena spoke, the sound of her voice seemed to startle him from his silence.

'Lady,' said Cedric, 'this beseems not; were further pledge necessary, I myself, offended, and justly offended, as I am, would yet gage my honour for the honour of Ivanhoe. But the wager of battle is complete, even according to the fantastic fashions of Norman chivalry—Is it not, Father Aymer?'

'It is,' replied the Prior; 'and the blessed relic and rich chain will I bestow safely in the treasury of our convent, until the decision of this warlike challenge.'

Having thus spoken, he crossed himself again and again, and after many genuflections and muttered prayers, he delivered the reliquary to Brother Ambrose, his attendant monk, while he himself swept up with less ceremony, but perhaps with no less internal satisfaction, the golden chain, and bestowed it in a pouch lined with perfumed leather, which opened under his arm. 'And now, Sir Cedric,' he said, 'my ears are chiming vespers with the strength of your good wine—permit us another pledge to the welfare of the Lady Rowena, and indulge us with liberty to pass to our repose.'

'By the rood of Bromholme,' said the Saxon, 'you do but small credit to your fame, Sir Prior! Report speaks you a bonny monk, that would hear the matin chime ere he quitted his bowl; and, old as I am, I feared to have shame in encountering you. But, by my faith, a Saxon boy of twelve, in my time, would not so soon have relinquished his goblet.'

The Prior had his own reasons, however, for persevering in the course of temperance which he had adopted. He was not only a professional peacemaker, but from practice a hater of all feuds and brawls. It was not altogether from a love to his neighbour, or to himself, or from a mixture of both. On the present occasion, he had an instinctive apprehension of the fiery temper of the Saxon, and saw the danger that the reckless and presumptuous spirit, of which his companion had already given so many proofs, might at length produce some disagreeable explosion. He therefore gently insinuated the incapacity of the native of any other country to engage in the genial conflict of the bowl with the hardy and strong - headed Saxons; something he mentioned, but slightly, about his own holy character, and ended by pressing his proposal to depart to repose.

The grace-cup was accordingly served round, and the guests, after making deep obeisance to their landlord and to the Lady Rowena, arose and mingled in the hall, while the heads of the family, by separate doors, retired with their attendants.

'Unbelieving dog,' said the Templar to Isaac the Jew, as he passed him in the throng, 'dost thou bend thy course to the tournament?'

'I do so propose,' replied Isaac, bowing in all humility, 'if it please your reverend valour.'

'Ay,' said the Knight, 'to gnaw the bowels of our nobles with usury, and to gull women and boys with gauds and toys—I warrant thee store of shekels in thy Jewish scrip.'

'Not a shekel, not a silver penny, not a halfling—so help me the God of Abraham!' said the Jew, clasping his hands; 'I go but to seek the assistance of some brethren of my tribe to aid me

to pay the fine which the Exchequer of the Jews*
have imposed upon me—Father Jacob be my speed!
I am an impoverished wretch—the very gaberdine
I wear is borrowed from Reuben of Tadcaster.'

The Templar smiled sourly as he replied, ' Beshrew
thee for a false-hearted liar!' and passing onward,
as if disdaining farther conference, he communed
with his Moslem slaves in a language unknown
to the bystanders. The poor Israelite seemed so
staggered by the address of the military monk, that
the Templar had passed on to the extremity of the
hall ere he raised his head from the humble posture
which he had assumed, so far as to be sensible of
his departure. And when he did look around, it
was with the astonished air of one at whose feet a
thunderbolt has just burst, and who hears still the
astounding report ringing in his ears.

The Templar and Prior were shortly after
marshalled to their sleeping apartments by the
steward and the cupbearer, each attended by two
torch-bearers and two servants carrying refreshments, while servants of inferior condition indicated to their retinue and to the other guests their
respective places of repose.

---

* In those days the Jews were subjected to an Exchequer, specially
dedicated to that purpose, and which laid them under the most exorbitant
impositions.—L. T.

CHAPTER VI

To buy his favour I extend this friendship :
If he will take it, so ; if not, adieu;
And, for my love, I pray you wrong me not.
MERCHANT OF VENICE.

As the Palmer, lighted by a domestic with a
torch, past through the intricate combination of
apartments of this large and irregular mansion, the
cupbearer coming behind him whispered in his ear,
that if he had no objection to a cup of good mead
in his apartment, there were many domestics in
that family who would gladly hear the news he had
brought from the Holy Land, and particularly that
which concerned the Knight of Ivanhoe. Wamba
presently appeared to urge the same request, observing that a cup after midnight was worth three after
curfew. Without disputing a maxim urged by
such grave authority, the Palmer thanked them for
their courtesy, but observed that he had included
in his religious vow, an obligation never to speak in
the kitchen on matters which were prohibited in the
hall. 'That vow,' said Wamba to the cupbearer,
'would scarce suit a serving-man.'

The cupbearer shrugged up his shoulders in
displeasure. 'I thought to have lodged him in
the solere chamber,' said he; 'but since he is so

unsocial to Christians, e'en let him take the next stall to Isaac the Jew's.—Anwold,' said he to the torch-bearer, ' carry the Pilgrim to the southern cell.—I give you good-night,' he added, ' Sir Palmer, with small thanks for short courtesy.'

' Good-night, and Our Lady's benison,' said the Palmer, with composure ; and his guide moved forward.

In a small antechamber, into which several doors opened, and which was lighted by a small iron lamp, they met a second interruption from the waiting-maid of Rowena, who, saying in a tone of authority, that her mistress desired to speak with the Palmer, took the torch from the hand of Anwold, and, bidding him await her return, made a sign to the Palmer to follow. Apparently he did not think it proper to decline this invitation as he had done the former ; for, though his gesture indicated some surprise at the summons, he obeyed it without answer or remonstrance.

A short passage, and an ascent of seven steps, each of which was composed of a solid beam of oak, led him to the apartment of the Lady Rowena, the rude magnificence of which corresponded to the respect which was paid to her by the lord of the mansion. The walls were covered with embroidered hangings, on which different-coloured silks, inter-woven with gold and silver threads, had been employed with all the art of which the age was capable, to represent the sports of hunting and hawking. The bed was adorned with the same rich tapestry, and surrounded with curtains dyed

with purple. The seats had also their stained
coverings, and one, which was higher than the
rest, was accommodated with a footstool of ivory,
curiously carved.

No fewer than four silver candelabras, holding
great waxen torches, served to illuminate this apartment. Yet let not modern beauty envy the
magnificence of a Saxon princess. The walls of
the apartment were so ill finished and so full of
crevices, that the rich hangings shook to the night
blast, and, in despite of a sort of screen intended to
protect them from the wind, the flame of the torches
streamed sideways into the air, like the unfurled
pennon of a chieftain. Magnificence there was,
with some rude attempt at taste; but of comfort
there was little, and, being unknown, it was
unmissed.

The Lady Rowena, with three of her attendants
standing at her back, and arranging her hair ere
she lay down to rest, was seated in the sort of throne
already mentioned, and looked as if born to exact
general homage. The Pilgrim acknowledged her
claim to it by a low genuflection.

'Rise, Palmer,' said she graciously. 'The defender of the absent has a right to favourable
reception from all who value truth, and honour
manhood.' She then said to her train, 'Retire,
excepting only Elgitha; I would speak with this
holy Pilgrim.'

The maidens, without leaving the apartment,
retired to its further extremity, and sat down on a
small bench against the wall, where they remained

mute as statues, though at such a distance that
their whispers could not have interrupted the conversation of their mistress.

'Pilgrim,' said the lady, after a moment's pause,
during which she seemed uncertain how to address
him, 'you this night mentioned a name—I mean,'
she said, with a degree of effort, 'the name of
Ivanhoe, in the halls where by nature and kindred
it should have sounded most acceptably; and yet,
such is the perverse course of fate, that of many
whose hearts must have throbbed at the sound, I,
only, dare ask you where, and in what condition,
you left him of whom you spoke?—We heard,
that, having remained in Palestine, on account of
his impaired health, after the departure of the
English army, he had experienced the persecution
of the French faction, to whom the Templars are
known to be attached.'

'I know little of the Knight of Ivanhoe,' answered
the Palmer, with a troubled voice. 'I would I
knew him better, since you, lady, are interested
in his fate. He hath, I believe, surmounted the
persecution of his enemies in Palestine, and is
on the eve of returning to England, where you,
lady, must know better than I, what is his chance
of happiness.'

The Lady Rowena sighed deeply, and asked more
particularly when the Knight of Ivanhoe might be
expected in his native country, and whether he
would not be exposed to great dangers by the road.
On the first point, the Palmer professed ignorance;
on the second, he said that the voyage might be

safely made by the way of Venice and Genoa, and from thence through France to England. 'Ivanhoe,' he said, 'was so well acquainted with the language and manners of the French, that there was no fear of his incurring any hazard during that part of his travels.'

'Would to God,' said the Lady Rowena, 'he were here safely arrived, and able to bear arms in the approaching tournay, in which the chivalry of this land are expected to display their address and valour. Should Athelstane of Coningsburgh obtain the prize, Ivanhoe is like to hear evil tidings when he reaches England.—How looked he, stranger, when you last saw him ? Had disease laid her hand heavy upon his strength and comeliness ?'

'He was darker,' said the Palmer, 'and thinner, than when he came from Cyprus in the train of Cœur-de-Lion, and care seemed to sit heavy on his brow; but I approached not his presence, because he is unknown to me.'

'He will,' said the lady, 'I fear, find little in his native land to clear those clouds from his countenance. Thanks, good Pilgrim, for your information concerning the companion of my childhood.— Maidens,' she said, 'draw near—offer the sleeping cup to this holy man, whom I will no longer detain from repose.'

One of the maidens presented a silver cup, containing a rich mixture of wine and spice, which Rowena barely put to her lips. It was then offered to the Palmer, who, after a low obeisance, tasted a few drops.

"*Rise, Palmer,*" *said she graciously.*

'Accept this alms, friend,' continued the lady, offering a piece of gold, 'in acknowledgment of thy painful travail, and of the shrines thou hast visited.'

The Palmer received the boon with another low reverence, and followed Edwina out of the apartment.

In the anteroom he found his attendant Anwold, who, taking the torch from the hand of the waiting-maid, conducted him with more haste than ceremony to an exterior and ignoble part of the building, where a number of small apartments, or rather cells, served for sleeping-places to the lower order of domestics, and to strangers of mean degree.

'In which of these sleeps the Jew?' said the Pilgrim.

'The unbelieving dog,' answered Anwold, 'kennels in the cell next your holiness.—St. Dunstan, how it must be scraped and cleansed ere it be again fit for a Christian!'

'And where sleeps Gurth the swineherd?' said the stranger.

'Gurth,' replied the bondsman, 'sleeps in the cell on your right, as the Jew on that to your left; you serve to keep the child of circumcision separate from the abomination of his tribe. You might have occupied a more honourable place had you accepted of Oswald's invitation.'

'It is as well as it is,' said the Palmer; 'the company, even of a Jew, can hardly spread contamination through an oaken partition.'

So saying, he entered the cabin allotted to him,

and taking the torch from the domestic's hand, thanked him, and wished him good-night. Having shut the door of his cell, he placed the torch in a candlestick made of wood, and looked around his sleeping-apartment, the furniture of which was of the most simple kind. It consisted of a rude wooden stool, and still ruder hutch or bed-frame, stuffed with clean straw, and accommodated with two or three sheepskins by way of bed-clothes.

The Palmer, having extinguished his torch, threw himself, without taking off any part of his clothes, on this rude couch, and slept, or at least retained his recumbent posture, till the earliest sunbeams found their way through the little grated window, which served at once to admit both air and light to his uncomfortable cell. He then started up, and after repeating his matins, and adjusting his dress, he left it, and entered that of Isaac the Jew, lifting the latch as gently as he could.

The inmate was lying in troubled slumber upon a couch similar to that on which the Palmer himself had passed the night. Such parts of his dress as the Jew had laid aside on the preceding evening, were disposed carefully around his person, as if to prevent the hazard of their being carried off during his slumbers. There was a trouble on his brow amounting almost to agony. His hands and arms moved convulsively, as if struggling with the nightmare; and besides several ejaculations in Hebrew, the following were distinctly heard in the Norman-English, or mixed language of the country: 'For the sake of the God of Abraham, spare an

unhappy old man! I am poor, I am penniless—
should your irons wrench my limbs asunder, I
could not gratify you!'

The Palmer awaited not the end of the Jew's
vision, but stirred him with his pilgrim's staff. The
touch probably associated, as is usual, with some
of the apprehensions excited by his dream; for the
old man started up, his grey hair standing almost
erect upon his head, and huddling some part of his
garments about him, while he held the detached
pieces with the tenacious grasp of a falcon, he fixed
upon the Palmer his keen black eyes, expressive
of wild surprise and of bodily apprehension.

'Fear nothing from me, Isaac,' said the Palmer,
'I come as your friend.'

'The God of Israel requite you,' said the Jew,
greatly relieved; 'I dreamed—But Father Abraham
be praised, it was but a dream.' Then, collecting
himself, he added in his usual tone, 'And what
may it be your pleasure to want at so early an
hour with the poor Jew?'

'It is to tell you,' said the Palmer, 'that if
you leave not this mansion instantly, and travel
not with some haste, your journey may prove a
dangerous one.'

'Holy father!' said the Jew, 'whom could it
interest to endanger so poor a wretch as I am?'

'The purpose you can best guess,' said the Pilgrim;
'but rely on this, that when the Templar crossed
the hall yesternight, he spoke to his Mussulman
slaves in the Saracen language, which I well understand, and charged them this morning to watch the

journey of the Jew, to seize upon him when at a convenient distance from the mansion, and to conduct him to the castle of Philip de Malvoisin, or to that of Reginald Front-de-Bœuf.'

It is impossible to describe the extremity of terror which seized upon the Jew at this information, and seemed at once to overpower his whole faculties. His arms fell down to his sides, and his head drooped on his breast, his knees bent under his weight, every nerve and muscle of his frame seemed to collapse and lose its energy, and he sunk at the foot of the Palmer, not in the fashion of one who intentionally stoops, kneels, or prostrates himself to excite compassion, but like a man borne down on all sides by the pressure of some invisible force, which crushes him to the earth without the power of resistance.

'Holy God of Abraham!' was his first exclamation, folding and elevating his wrinkled hands, but without raising his grey head from the pavement; 'Oh, holy Moses! O, blessed Aaron! the dream is not dreamed for nought, and the vision cometh not in vain! I feel their irons already tear my sinews! I feel the rack pass over my body like the saws, and harrows, and axes of iron over the men of Rabbah, and of the cities of the children of Ammon!'

'Stand up, Isaac, and hearken to me,' said the Palmer, who viewed the extremity of his distress with a compassion in which contempt was largely mingled; 'you have cause for your terror, considering how your brethren have been used, in order to extort from them their hoards, both by princes and nobles; but stand up, I say, and I will point out to you the means of escape. Leave this mansion instantly, while its inmates sleep sound after the last night's revel. I will guide you by the secret paths of the forest, known as well to me as to any forester that ranges it, and I will not leave you till you are under safe-conduct of some chief or baron going to the tournament, whose good-will you have probably the means of securing.'

As the ears of Isaac received the hopes of escape which this speech intimated, he began gradually, and inch by inch, as it were, to raise himself up from the ground, until he fairly rested upon his knees, throwing back his long grey hair and beard, and fixing his keen black eyes upon the Palmer's face, with a look expressive at once of hope and fear, not unmingled with suspicion. But when he heard the concluding part of the sentence, his original terror appeared to revive in full force, and he dropt once more on his face, exclaiming, '*I* possess the means of securing good - will! alas! there is but one road to the favour of a Christian, and how can the poor Jew find it, whom extortions have already reduced to the misery of Lazarus?' Then, as if suspicion had overpowered his other feelings, he suddenly exclaimed, 'For the love of God, young man, betray me not—for the sake of the Great Father who made us all, Jew as well as Gentile, Israelite and Ishmaelite—do me no treason! I have not means to secure the good-will of a Christian beggar, were he rating it at a single penny.' As he spoke these last words, he raised himself, and grasped the Palmer's mantle with a look of the most earnest entreaty. The pilgrim extricated himself, as if there were contamination in the touch.

'Wert thou loaded with all the wealth of thy tribe,' he said, 'what interest have I to injure thee?—In this dress I am vowed to poverty, nor do I change it for aught save a horse and a coat of mail. Yet think not that I care for thy company, or propose myself advantage by it; remain here if thou wilt—Cedric the Saxon may protect thee.'

'Alas!' said the Jew, 'he will not let me travel in his train — Saxon or Norman will be equally ashamed of the poor Israelite; and to travel by myself through the domains of Philip de Malvoisin and Reginald Front-de-Bœuf—Good youth, I will go with you!—Let us haste—let us gird up our loins—let us flee!—Here is thy staff, why wilt thou tarry?'

'I tarry not,' said the Pilgrim, giving way to the urgency of his companion; 'but I must secure the means of leaving this place—follow me.'

He led the way to the adjoining cell, which, as the reader is apprised, was occupied by Gurth the swineherd. — 'Arise, Gurth,' said the Pilgrim, 'arise quickly. Undo the postern gate, and let out the Jew and me.'

Gurth, whose occupation, though now held so mean, gave him as much consequence in Saxon England as that of Eumæus in Ithaca, was offended at the familiar and commanding tone assumed by the Palmer. 'The Jew leaving Rotherwood,' said he, raising himself on his elbow, and looking superciliously at him without quitting his pallet, 'and travelling in company with the Palmer to boot——'

'I should as soon have dreamt,' said Wamba, who entered the apartment at the instant, 'of his stealing away with a gammon of bacon.'

'Nevertheless,' said Gurth, again laying down his head on the wooden log which served him for a pillow, 'both Jew and Gentile must be content to abide the opening of the great gate—we suffer no visitors to depart by stealth at these unseasonable hours.'

'Nevertheless,' said the Pilgrim, in a commanding tone, 'you will not, I think, refuse me that favour.'

So saying, he stooped over the bed of the recumbent swineherd, and whispered something in his ear in Saxon. Gurth started up as if electrified. The Pilgrim, raising his finger in an attitude as if to express caution, added, 'Gurth, beware—thou art wont to be prudent. I say, undo the postern—thou shalt know more anon.'

With hasty alacrity Gurth obeyed him, while Wamba and the Jew followed, both wondering at the sudden change in the swineherd's demeanour.

'My mule, my mule!' said the Jew, as soon as they stood without the postern.

'Fetch him his mule,' said the Pilgrim; 'and, hearest thou,—let me have another, that I may bear him company till he is beyond these parts—I

will return it safely to some of Cedric's train at
Ashby. And do thou'—he whispered the rest in
Gurth's ear.

'Willingly, most willingly shall it be done,'
said Gurth, and instantly departed to execute the
commission.

'I wish I knew,' said Wamba, when his comrade's back was turned, 'what you Palmers learn
in the Holy Land.'

'To say our orisons, fool,' answered the Pilgrim,
'to repent our sins, and to mortify ourselves with
fastings, vigils, and long prayers.'

'Something more potent than that,' answered
the Jester; 'for when would repentance or prayer
make Gurth do a courtesy, or fasting or vigil
persuade him to lend you a mule?—I trow you
might as well have told his favourite black boar
of thy vigils and penance, and wouldst have gotten
as civil an answer.'

'Go to,' said the Pilgrim, 'thou art but a
Saxon fool.'

'Thou sayst well,' said the Jester; 'had I
been born a Norman, as I think thou art, I would
have had luck on my side, and been next door to
a wise man.'

At this moment Gurth appeared on the opposite
side of the moat with the mules. The travellers
crossed the ditch upon a drawbridge of only two
planks breadth, the narrowness of which was
matched with the straitness of the postern, and
with a little wicket in the exterior palisade, which
gave access to the forest. No sooner had they

reached the mules, than the Jew, with hasty and trembling hands, secured behind the saddle a small bag of blue buckram, which he took from under his cloak, containing, as he muttered, 'a change of raiment—only a change of raiment.' Then getting upon the animal with more alacrity and haste than could have been anticipated from his years, he lost no time in so disposing of the skirts of his gaberdine as to conceal completely from observation the burden which he had thus deposited *en croupe*.

The Pilgrim mounted with more deliberation, reaching, as he departed, his hand to Gurth, who kissed it with the utmost possible veneration. The swineherd stood gazing after the travellers until they were lost under the boughs of the forest path, when he was disturbed from his reverie by the voice of Wamba.

'Knowest thou,' said the Jester, 'my good friend Gurth, that thou art strangely courteous and most unwontedly pious on this summer morning? I would I were a black Prior or a barefoot Palmer, to avail myself of thy unwonted zeal and courtesy— certes, I would make more out of it than a kiss of the hand.'

'Thou art no fool thus far, Wamba,' answered Gurth, 'though thou arguest from appearances, and the wisest of us can do no more—But it is time to look after my charge.'

So saying, he turned back to the mansion, attended by the Jester.

Meanwhile the travellers continued to press on their journey with a dispatch which argued the extremity of the Jew's fears, since persons at his age are seldom fond of rapid motion. The Palmer, to whom every path and outlet in the wood appeared to be familiar, led the way through the most devious paths, and more than once excited anew the suspicion of the Israelite, that he intended to betray him into some ambuscade of his enemies.

His doubts might have been indeed pardoned; for, except perhaps the flying fish, there was no race existing on the earth, in the air, or the waters, who were the object of such an unintermitting, general, and relentless persecution as the Jews of this period. Upon the slightest and most unreasonable pretences, as well as upon accusations the most absurd and groundless, their persons and property were exposed to every turn of popular fury; for Norman, Saxon, Dane, and Briton, however adverse these races were to each other, contended which should look with greatest detestation upon a people, whom it was accounted a point of religion to hate, to revile, to despise, to plunder, and to persecute. The kings of the Norman race, and the independent nobles, who followed their example in all acts of tyranny, maintained against this devoted people a persecution of a more regular, calculated, and self-interested kind. It is a well-known story of King John, that he confined a wealthy Jew in one of the royal castles, and daily caused one of his teeth to be torn out, until, when the jaw of the unhappy Israelite was half disfurnished, he consented to pay a large sum, which it was the tyrant's object to extort from him. The little ready money

which was in the country was chiefly in possession
of this persecuted people, and the nobility hesitated
not to follow the example of their sovereign, in
wringing it from them by every species of oppression, and even personal torture. Yet the passive
courage inspired by the love of gain, induced the
Jews to dare the various evils to which they were
subjected, in consideration of the immense profits
which they were enabled to realize in a country
naturally so wealthy as England. In spite of every
kind of discouragement, and even of the special
court of taxations already mentioned, called the
Jews' Exchequer, erected for the very purpose of
despoiling and distressing them, the Jews increased,
multiplied, and accumulated huge sums, which they
transferred from one hand to another by means of
bills of exchange—an invention for which commerce
is said to be indebted to them, and which enabled
them to transfer their wealth from land to land, that
when threatened with oppression in one country,
their treasure might be secured in another.

The obstinacy and avarice of the Jews being thus
in a measure placed in opposition to the fanaticism
and tyranny of those under whom they lived, seemed
to increase in proportion to the persecution with
which they were visited; and the immense wealth
they usually acquired in commerce, while it frequently placed them in danger, was at other times
used to extend their influence, and to secure to
them a certain degree of protection. On these
terms they lived; and their character, influenced
accordingly, was watchful, suspicious, and timid

yet obstinate, uncomplying, and skilful in evading the dangers to which they were exposed.

When the travellers had pushed on at a rapid rate through many devious paths, the Palmer at length broke silence.

' That large decayed oak,' he said, ' marks the boundaries over which Front-de-Bœuf claims authority—we are long since far from those of Malvoisin. There is now no fear of pursuit.'

' May the wheels of their chariots be taken off,' said the Jew, ' like those of the host of Pharaoh, that they may drive heavily!—But leave me not, good Pilgrim—Think but of that fierce and savage Templar, with his Saracen slaves—they will regard neither territory, nor manor, nor lordship.'

' Our road,' said the Palmer, ' should here separate; for it beseems not men of my character and thine to travel together longer than needs must be. Besides, what succour couldst thou have from me, a peaceful Pilgrim, against two armed heathens ? '

' O good youth,' answered the Jew, ' thou canst defend me, and I know thou wouldst. Poor as I am, I will requite it—not with money, for money, so help me my father Abraham, I have none — but—'

' Money and recompense,' said the Palmer, interrupting him, ' I have already said I require not of thee. Guide thee I can; and, it may be, even in some sort defend thee; since to protect a Jew against a Saracen, can scarce be accounted unworthy of a Christian. Therefore, Jew, I will see thee safe under some fitting escort. We are now not far from the town of Sheffield, where thou mayest easily find many of thy tribe with whom to take refuge.'

'The blessing of Jacob be upon thee, good youth!' said the Jew; 'in Sheffield I can harbour with my kinsman Zareth, and find some means of travelling forth with safety.'

'Be it so,' said the Palmer; 'at Sheffield then we part, and half-an-hour's riding will bring us in sight of that town.'

The half hour was spent in perfect silence on both parts; the Pilgrim perhaps disdaining to address the Jew, except in case of absolute necessity, and the Jew not presuming to force a conversation with a person whose journey to the Holy Sepulchre gave a sort of sanctity to his character. They paused on the top of a gently rising bank, and the Pilgrim, pointing to the town of Sheffield, which lay beneath them, repeated the words, 'Here, then, we part.'

'Not till you have had the poor Jew's thanks,' said Isaac; 'for I presume not to ask you to go with me to my kinsman Zareth's, who might aid me with some means of repaying your good offices.'

'I have already said,' answered the Pilgrim, 'that I desire no recompense. If, among the huge list of thy debtors, thou wilt, for my sake, spare the gyves and the dungeon to some unhappy Christian who stands in thy danger, I shall hold this morning's service to thee well bestowed.'

'Stay, stay,' said the Jew, laying hold of his garment; 'something would I do more than this, something for thyself.—God knows the Jew is poor —yes, Isaac is the beggar of his tribe—but forgive me should I guess what thou most lackest at this moment.'

'If thou wert to guess truly,' said the Palmer, 'it is what thou canst not supply, wert thou as wealthy as thou sayst thou art poor.'

'As I say?' echoed the Jew; 'O! believe it, I say but the truth; I am a plundered, indebted, distressed man. Hard hands have wrung from me my goods, my money, my ships, and all that I possessed—Yet I can tell thee what thou lackest, and, it may be, supply it too. Thy wish even now is for a horse and armour.'

The Palmer started, and turned suddenly towards the Jew:—'What fiend prompted that guess?' said he, hastily.

'No matter,' said the Jew, smiling, 'so that it be a true one—and, as I can guess thy want, so I can supply it.'

'But consider,' said the Palmer, 'my character, my dress, my vow.'

'I know you Christians,' replied the Jew, 'and that the noblest of you will take the staff and sandal in superstitious penance, and walk afoot to visit the graves of dead men.'

'Blaspheme not, Jew,' said the Pilgrim, sternly.

'Forgive me,' said the Jew; 'I spoke rashly. But there dropt words from you last night and this morning, that, like sparks from flint, showed the metal within; and in the bosom of that Palmer's gown, is hidden a knight's chain and spurs of gold.

They glanced as you stooped over my bed in the morning.'

The Pilgrim could not forbear smiling. 'Were thy garments searched by as curious an eye, Isaac,' said he, 'what discoveries might not be made?'

'No more of that,' said the Jew, changing colour; and drawing forth his writing materials in haste, as if to stop the conversation, he began to write upon a piece of paper which he supported on the top of his yellow cap, without dismounting from his mule. When he had finished, he delivered the scroll, which was in the Hebrew character, to the Pilgrim, saying, 'In the town of Leicester all men know the rich Jew, Kirjath Jairam of Lombardy; give him this scroll—he hath on sale six Milan harnesses, the worst would suit a crowned head —ten goodly steeds, the worst might mount a king, were he to do battle for his throne. Of these he will give thee thy choice, with every thing else that can furnish thee forth for the tournament: when it is over, thou wilt return them safely— unless thou shouldst have wherewith to pay their value to the owner.'

'But, Isaac,' said the Pilgrim, smiling, 'dost thou know that in these sports, the arms and steed of the knight who is unhorsed are forfeit to his victor? Now I may be unfortunate, and so lose what I cannot replace or repay.'

The Jew looked somewhat astounded at this possibility; but collecting his courage, he replied hastily, 'No—no—no—It is impossible—I will not think so. The blessing of Our Father will be upon thee. Thy lance will be powerful as the rod of Moses.'

So saying, he was turning his mule's head away, when the Palmer, in his turn, took hold of his gaberdine. 'Nay, but Isaac, thou knowest not all the risk. The steed may be slain, the armour injured—for I will spare neither horse nor man. Besides, those of thy tribe give nothing for nothing; something there must be paid for their use.'

The Jew twisted himself in the saddle, like a man in a fit of the colic; but his better feelings predominated over those which were most familiar to him. 'I care not,' he said, 'I care not—let me go. If there is damage, it will cost you nothing—if there is usage money, Kirjath Jairam will forgive it for the sake of his kinsman Isaac. Fare thee well!—Yet hark thee, good youth,' said he, turning about, 'thrust thyself not too forward into this vain hurly-burly—I speak not for endangering the steed, and coat of armour, but for the sake of thine own life and limbs.'

'Gramercy for thy caution,' said the Palmer, again smiling; 'I will use thy courtesy frankly, and it will go hard with me but I will requite it.'

They parted, and took different roads for the town of Sheffield.

CHAPTER VII

Knights, with a long retinue of their squires,
In gaudy liveries march and quaint attires;
One laced the helm, another held the lance,
A third the shining buckler did advance.
The courser paw'd the ground with restless feet,
And snorting foam'd and champ'd the golden bit.
The smiths and armourers on palfreys ride,
Files in their hands, and hammers at their side;
And nails for loosen'd spears, and thongs for shields provide.
The yeomen guard the streets in seemly bands;
And clowns come crowding on, with cudgels in their hands.
PALAMON AND ARCITE.

THE condition of the English nation was at this time sufficiently miserable. King Richard was absent a prisoner, and in the power of the perfidious and cruel Duke of Austria. Even the very place of his captivity was uncertain, and his fate but very imperfectly known to the generality of his subjects, who were, in the meantime, a prey to every species of subaltern oppression.

Prince John, in league with Philip of France, Cœur-de-Lion's mortal enemy, was using every species of influence with the Duke of Austria, to prolong the captivity of his brother Richard, to whom he stood indebted for so many favours. In the meantime, he was strengthening his own faction in the kingdom, of which he proposed to dispute

the succession, in case of the King's death, with
the legitimate heir, Arthur Duke of Brittany, son
of Geoffrey Plantagenet, the elder brother of John.
This usurpation, it is well known, he afterwards
effected. His own character being light, profligate,
and perfidious, John easily attached to his person
and faction, not only all who had reason to dread
the resentment of Richard for criminal proceedings
during his absence, but also the numerous class of
'lawless resolutes,' whom the crusades had turned
back on their country, accomplished in the vices of
the East, impoverished in substance, and hardened
in character, and who placed their hopes of harvest
in civil commotion.

To these causes of public distress and apprehension, must be added, the multitude of outlaws, who,
driven to despair by the oppression of the feudal
nobility, and the severe exercise of the forest laws,
banded together in large gangs, and, keeping possession of the forests and the wastes, set at defiance
the justice and magistracy of the country. The
nobles themselves, each fortified within his own
castle, and playing the petty sovereign over his
own dominions, were the leaders of bands scarce
less lawless and oppressive than those of the
avowed depredators. To maintain these retainers,
and to support the extravagance and magnificence
which their pride induced them to affect, the
nobility borrowed sums of money from the Jews
at the most usurious interest, which gnawed into
their estates like consuming cankers, scarce to be
cured unless when circumstances gave them an

opportunity of getting free, by exercising upon their creditors some act of unprincipled violence.

Under the various burdens imposed by this unhappy state of affairs, the people of England suffered deeply for the present, and had yet more dreadful cause to fear for the future. To augment their misery, a contagious disorder of a dangerous nature spread through the land; and, rendered more virulent by the uncleanness, the indifferent food, and the wretched lodging of the lower classes, swept off many whose fate the survivors were tempted to envy, as exempting them from the evils which were to come.

Yet amid these accumulated distresses, the poor as well as the rich, the vulgar as well as the noble, in the event of a tournament, which was the grand spectacle of that age, felt as much interested as the half-starved citizen of Madrid, who has not a real left to buy provisions for his family, feels in the issue of a bull-feast. Neither duty nor infirmity could keep youth or age from such exhibitions. The Passage of Arms, as it was called, which was to take place at Ashby, in the county of Leicester, as champions of the first renown were to take the field in the presence of Prince John himself, who was expected to grace the lists, had attracted universal attention, and an immense confluence of persons of all ranks hastened upon the appointed morning to the place of combat.

The scene was singularly romantic. On the verge of a wood, which approached to within a mile of the town of Ashby, was an extensive meadow, of the finest and most beautiful green turf, surrounded on one side by the forest, and fringed on the other by straggling oak-trees, some of which had grown to an immense size. The ground, as if fashioned on purpose for the martial display which was intended, sloped gradually down on all sides to a level bottom, which was enclosed for the lists with strong palisades, forming a space of a quarter of a mile in length, and about half as broad. The form of the enclosure was an oblong square, save that the corners were considerably rounded off, in order to afford more convenience for the spectators. The openings for the entry of the combatants were at the northern and southern extremities of the lists, accessible by strong wooden gates, each wide enough to admit two horsemen riding abreast. At each of these portals were stationed two heralds, attended by six trumpets, as many pursuivants, and a strong body of men-at-arms for maintaining order, and ascertaining the quality of the knights who proposed to engage in this martial game.

On a platform beyond the southern entrance, formed by a natural elevation of the ground, were pitched five magnificent pavilions, adorned with pennons of russet and black, the chosen colours of the five knights challengers. The cords of the tents were of the same colour. Before each pavilion was suspended the shield of the knight by whom it was occupied, and beside it stood his squire, quaintly disguised as a salvage or silvan man, or in some other fantastic dress, according to the taste of his master, and the character he was pleased to assume

during the game.* The central pavilion, as the
place of honour, had been assigned to Brian de Bois-
Guilbert, whose renown in all games of chivalry,
no less than his connexion with the knights who
had undertaken this Passage of Arms, had occasioned him to be eagerly received into the company
of the challengers, and even adopted as their chief
and leader, though he had so recently joined them.
On one side of his tent were pitched those of
Reginald Front-de-Bœuf and Philip de Malvoisin,
and on the other was the pavilion of Hugh de
Grantmesnil, a noble baron in the vicinity, whose
ancestor had been Lord High Steward of England
in the time of the Conqueror, and his son William
Rufus. Ralph de Vipont, a knight of St. John of
Jerusalem, who had some ancient possessions at a
place called Heather, near Ashby-de-la-Zouche,
occupied the fifth pavilion. From the entrance
into the lists, a gently sloping passage, ten yards
in breadth, led up to the platform on which the
tents were pitched. It was strongly secured by a
palisade on each side, as was the esplanade in front
of the pavilions, and the whole was guarded by
men-at-arms.

The northern access to the lists terminated in a
similar entrance of thirty feet in breadth, at the
extremity of which was a large enclosed space for
such knights as might be disposed to enter the lists
with the challengers, behind which were placed
tents containing refreshments of every kind for

---

* This sort of masquerade is supposed to have occasioned the introduction of supporters into the science of heraldry.

their accommodation, with armourers, farriers, and other attendants, in readiness to give their services wherever they might be necessary.

The exterior of the lists was in part occupied by temporary galleries, spread with tapestry and carpets, and accommodated with cushions for the convenience of those ladies and nobles who were expected to attend the tournament. A narrow space, betwixt these galleries and the lists, gave accommodation for yeomanry and spectators of a better degree than the mere vulgar, and might be compared to the pit of a theatre. The promiscuous multitude arranged themselves upon large banks of turf prepared for the purpose, which, aided by the natural elevation of the ground, enabled them to overlook the galleries, and obtain a fair view into the lists. Besides the accommodation which these stations afforded, many hundreds had perched themselves on the branches of the trees which surrounded the meadow; and even the steeple of a country church, at some distance, was crowded with spectators.

It only remains to notice respecting the general arrangement, that one gallery in the very centre of the eastern side of the lists, and consequently exactly opposite to the spot where the shock of the combat was to take place, was raised higher than the others, more richly decorated, and graced by a sort of throne and canopy, on which the royal arms were emblazoned. Squires, pages, and yeomen in rich liveries, waited around this place of honour, which was designed for Prince John and his attendants. Opposite to this royal gallery was another, elevated to the same height, on the western side of the lists; and more gaily, if less sumptuously decorated, than that destined for the Prince himself. A train of pages and of young maidens, the most beautiful who could be selected, gaily dressed in fancy habits of green and pink, surrounded a throne decorated in the same colours. Among pennons and flags bearing wounded hearts, burning hearts, bleeding hearts, bows and quivers, and all the commonplace emblems of the triumphs of Cupid, a blazoned inscription informed the spectators, that this seat of honour was designed for *La Royne de la Beaulté et des Amours.* But who was to represent the Queen of Beauty and of Love on the present occasion no one was prepared to guess.

Meanwhile, spectators of every description thronged forward to occupy their respective stations, and not without many quarrels concerning those which they were entitled to hold. Some of these were settled by the men-at-arms with brief ceremony; the shafts of their battle-axes, and pummels of their swords, being readily employed as arguments to convince the more refractory. Others, which involved the rival claims of more elevated persons, were determined by the heralds, or by the two marshals of the field, William de Wyvil, and Stephen de Martival, who, armed at all points, rode up and down the lists to enforce and preserve good order among the spectators.

Gradually the galleries became filled with knights

and nobles, in their robes of peace, whose long and rich-tinted mantles were contrasted with the gayer and more splendid habits of the ladies, who, in a greater proportion than even the men themselves, thronged to witness a sport, which one would have thought too bloody and dangerous to afford their sex much pleasure. The lower and interior space was soon filled by substantial yeomen and burghers, and such of the lesser gentry, as, from modesty, poverty, or dubious title, durst not assume any higher place. It was of course amongst these that the most frequent disputes for precedence occurred.

'Dog of an unbeliever,' said an old man, whose threadbare tunic bore witness to his poverty, as his sword, and dagger, and golden chain intimated his pretensions to rank, — 'whelp of a she-wolf! darest thou press upon a Christian, and a Norman gentleman of the blood of Montdidier?'

This rough expostulation was addressed to no other than our acquaintance Isaac, who, richly and even magnificently dressed in a gaberdine ornamented with lace and lined with fur, was endeavouring to make place in the foremost row beneath the gallery for his daughter, the beautiful Rebecca, who had joined him at Ashby, and who was now hanging on her father's arm, not a little terrified by the popular displeasure which seemed generally excited by her parent's presumption. But Isaac, though we have seen him sufficiently timid on other occasions, knew well that at present he had nothing to fear. It was not in places of general resort, or where their equals were assembled, that any avari-

cious or malevolent noble durst offer him injury.
At such meetings the Jews were under the protection of the general law; and if that proved a weak
assurance, it usually happened that there were
among the persons assembled some barons, who, for
their own interested motives, were ready to act as
their protectors.   On the present occasion, Isaac
felt more than usually confident, being aware that
Prince John was even then in the very act of
negotiating a large loan from the Jews of York, to
be secured upon certain jewels and lands.   Isaac's
own share in this transaction was considerable, and
he well knew that the Prince's eager desire to bring
it to a conclusion would ensure him his protection
in the dilemma in which he stood.

Emboldened by these considerations, the Jew
pursued his point, and jostled the Norman Christian,
without respect either to his descent, quality, or
religion.   The complaints of the old man, however, excited the indignation of the bystanders.
One of these, a stout well-set yeoman, arrayed in
Lincoln green, having twelve arrows stuck in his
belt, with a baldric and badge of silver, and a bow
of six feet length in his hand, turned short round,
and while his countenance, which his constant
exposure to weather had rendered brown as a hazel
nut, grew darker with anger, he advised the Jew
to remember that all the wealth he had acquired
by sucking the blood of his miserable victims had
but swelled him like a bloated spider, which might
be overlooked while he kept in a corner, but would
be crushed if it ventured into the light.   This

IVANHOE

intimation, delivered in Norman-English with a
firm voice and a stern aspect, made the Jew shrink
back; and he would have probably withdrawn himself altogether from a vicinity so dangerous, had
not the attention of every one been called to the
sudden entrance of Prince John, who at that
moment entered the lists, attended by a numerous
and gay train, consisting partly of laymen, partly
of churchmen, as light in their dress, and as gay
in their demeanour, as their companions. Among
the latter was the Prior of Jorvaulx, in the most
gallant trim which a dignitary of the church could
venture to exhibit. Fur and gold were not spared
in his garments; and the points of his boots, out-
heroding the preposterous fashion of the time,
turned up so very far, as to be attached, not to
his knees merely, but to his very girdle, and effectually prevented him from putting his foot into the
stirrup. This, however, was a slight inconvenience
to the gallant Abbot, who, perhaps, even rejoicing
in the opportunity to display his accomplished horsemanship before so many spectators, especially of the
fair sex, dispensed with the use of these supports
to a timid rider. The rest of Prince John's retinue
consisted of the favourite leaders of his mercenary
troops, some marauding barons and profligate attendants upon the court, with several Knights
Templars and Knights of St. John.

It may be here remarked, that the knights of
these two orders were accounted hostile to King
Richard, having adopted the side of Philip of France
in the long train of disputes which took place in

Palestine betwixt that monarch and the lion-hearted King of England. It was the well-known consequence of this discord that Richard's repeated victories had been rendered fruitless, his romantic attempts to besiege Jerusalem disappointed, and the fruit of all the glory which he had acquired had dwindled into an uncertain truce with the Sultan Saladin. With the same policy which had dictated the conduct of their brethren in the Holy Land, the Templars and Hospitallers in England and Normandy attached themselves to the faction of Prince John, having little reason to desire the return of Richard to England, or the succession of Arthur, his legitimate heir. For the opposite reason, Prince John hated and contemned the few Saxon families of consequence which subsisted in England, and omitted no opportunity of mortifying and affronting them; being conscious that his person and pretensions were disliked by them, as well as by the greater part of the English commons, who feared farther innovation upon their rights and liberties, from a sovereign of John's licentious and tyrannical disposition.

Attended by this gallant equipage, himself well mounted, and splendidly dressed in crimson and in gold, bearing upon his hand a falcon, and having his head covered by a rich fur bonnet, adorned with a circle of precious stones, from which his long curled hair ,escaped and overspread his shoulders, Prince John, upon a grey and high-mettled palfrey, caracoled within the lists at the head of his jovial party, laughing loud with his train, and eyeing with all the boldness of royal criticism the beauties who adorned the lofty galleries.

Those who remarked in the physiognomy of the Prince a dissolute audacity, mingled with extreme haughtiness and indifference to the feelings of others, could not yet deny to his countenance that sort of comeliness which belongs to an open set of features, well formed by nature, modelled by art to the usual rules of courtesy, yet so far frank and honest, that they seemed as if they disclaimed to conceal the natural workings of the soul. Such an expression is often mistaken for manly frankness, when in truth it arises from the reckless indifference of a libertine disposition, conscious of superiority of birth, of wealth, or of some other adventitious advantage, totally unconnected with personal merit. To those who did not think so deeply, and they were the greater number by a hundred to one, the splendour of Prince John's *rheno*, (*i.e.* fur tippet,) the richness of his cloak, lined with the most costly sables, his maroquin boots and golden spurs, together with the grace with which he managed his palfrey, were sufficient to merit clamorous applause.

In his joyous caracole round the lists, the attention of the Prince was called by the commotion, not yet subsided, which had attended the ambitious movement of Isaac towards the higher places of the assembly. The quick eye of Prince John instantly recognised the Jew, but was much more

agreeably attracted by the beautiful daughter of
Zion, who, terrified by the tumult, clung close to
the arm of her aged father.

The figure of Rebecca might indeed have compared with the proudest beauties of England, even
though it had been judged by as shrewd a connois-
seur as Prince John. Her form was exquisitely
symmetrical, and was shown to advantage by a
sort of Eastern dress, which she wore according
to the fashion of the females of her nation. Her
turban of yellow silk suited well with the darkness
of her complexion. The brilliancy of her eyes,
the superb arch of her eyebrows, her well-formed
aquiline nose, her teeth as white as pearl, and the
profusion of her sable tresses, which, each arranged
in its own little spiral of twisted curls, fell down
upon as much of a lovely neck and bosom as a
simarre of the richest Persian silk, exhibiting flowers
in their natural colours embossed upon a purple
ground, permitted to be visible—all these consti-
tuted a combination of loveliness, which yielded
not to the most beautiful of the maidens who
surrounded her. It is true, that of the golden
and pearl-studded clasps, which closed her vest
from the throat to the waist, the three upper-
most were left unfastened on account of the heat,
which something enlarged the prospect to which
we allude. A diamond necklace, with pendants of
inestimable value, were by this means also made
more conspicuous. The feather of an ostrich,
fastened in her turban by an agraffe set with
brilliants, was another distinction of the beautiful

Jewess, scoffed and sneered at by the proud dames who sat above her, but secretly envied by those who affected to deride them.

'By the bald scalp of Abraham,' said Prince John, 'yonder Jewess must be the very model of that perfection, whose charms drove frantic the wisest king that ever lived! What sayest thou, Prior Aymer?—By the Temple of that wise king, which our wiser brother Richard proved unable to recover, she is the very Bride of the Canticles!'

'The Rose of Sharon and the Lily of the Valley,' —answered the Prior, in a sort of snuffling tone; 'but your Grace must remember she is still but a Jewess.'

'Ay!' added Prince John, without heeding him, 'and there is my Mammon of unrighteousness too —the Marquis of Marks, the Baron of Byzants, contesting for place with penniless dogs, whose threadbare cloaks have not a single cross in their pouches to keep the devil from dancing there. By the body of St. Mark, my prince of supplies, with his lovely Jewess, shall have a place in the gallery! —What is she, Isaac? Thy wife or thy daughter, that Eastern houri that thou lockest under thy arm as thou wouldst thy treasure-casket?'

'My daughter Rebecca, so please your Grace,' answered Isaac, with a low congee, nothing embarrassed by the Prince's salutation, in which, however, there was at least as much mockery as courtesy.

'The wiser man thou,' said John, with a peal of laughter, in which his gay followers obsequiously

110

joined. ' But, daughter or wife, she should be preferred according to her beauty and thy merits.— Who sits above there ? ' he continued, bending his eye on the gallery. ' Saxon churls, lolling at their lazy length !—out upon them !—let them sit close, and make room for my prince of usurers and his lovely daughter. I 'll make the hinds know they must share the high places of the synagogue with those whom the synagogue properly belongs to.'

Those who occupied the gallery to whom this injurious and unpolite speech was addressed, were the family of Cedric the Saxon, with that of his ally and kinsman, Athelstane of Coningsburgh, a personage, who, on account of his descent from the last Saxon monarchs of England, was held in the highest respect by all the Saxon natives of the north of England. But with the blood of this ancient royal race, many of their infirmities had descended to Athelstane. He was comely in countenance, bulky and strong in person, and in the flower of his age—yet inanimate in expression, dull-eyed, heavy-browed, inactive and sluggish in all his motions, and so slow in resolution, that the soubriquet of one of his ancestors was conferred upon him, and he was very generally called Athelstane the Unready. His friends, and he had many, who, as well as Cedric, were passionately attached to him, contended that this sluggish temper arose not from want of courage, but from mere want of decision; others alleged that his hereditary vice of drunkenness had obscured his faculties, never of a very acute order, and that

111

the passive courage and meek good-nature which remained behind, were merely the dregs of a character that might have been deserving of praise, but of which all the valuable parts had flown off in the progress of a long course of brutal debauchery.

It was to this person, such as we have described him, that the Prince addressed his imperious command to make place for Isaac and Rebecca. Athelstane, utterly confounded at an order which the manners and feelings of the times rendered so injuriously insulting, unwilling to obey, yet undetermined how to resist, opposed only the *vis inertiæ* to the will of John; and, without stirring or making any motion whatever of obedience, opened his large grey eyes, and stared at the Prince with an astonishment which had in it something extremely ludicrous. But the impatient John regarded it in no such light.

'The Saxon porker,' he said, 'is either asleep or minds me not—Prick him with your lance, De Bracy,' speaking to a knight who rode near him, the leader of a band of Free Companions, or Condottieri; that is, of mercenaries belonging to no particular nation, but attached for the time to any prince by whom they were paid. There was a murmur even among the attendants of Prince John; but De Bracy, whose profession freed him from all scruples, extended his long lance over the space which separated the gallery from the lists, and would have executed the commands of the Prince before Athelstane the Unready had recovered presence of mind sufficient even to draw back his person from the weapon, had not Cedric, as prompt as his companion was tardy, unsheathed, with the speed of lightning, the short sword which he wore, and at a single blow severed the point of the lance from the handle. The blood rushed into the countenance of Prince John. He swore one of his deepest oaths, and was about to utter some threat corresponding in violence, when he was diverted from his purpose, partly by his own attendants, who gathered around him conjuring him to be patient, partly by a general exclamation of the crowd, uttered in loud applause of the spirited conduct of Cedric. The Prince rolled his eyes in indignation, as if to collect some safe and easy victim; and chancing to encounter the firm glance of the same archer whom we have already noticed, and who seemed to persist in his gesture of applause, in spite of the frowning aspect which the Prince bent upon him, he demanded his reason for clamouring thus.

'I always add my hollo,' said the yeoman, 'when I see a good shot, or a gallant blow.'

'Sayst thou?' answered the Prince; 'then thou canst hit the white thyself, I'll warrant.'

'A woodsman's mark, and at woodsman's distance, I can hit,' answered the yeoman.

'And Wat Tyrrel's mark, at a hundred yards,' said a voice from behind, but by whom uttered could not be discerned.

This allusion to the fate of William Rufus, his relative, at once incensed and alarmed Prince

John. He satisfied himself, however, with commanding the men-at-arms, who surrounded the lists, to keep an eye on the braggart, pointing to the yeoman.

'By St. Grizzel,' he added, 'we will try his own skill, who is so ready to give his voice to the feats of others!'

'I shall not fly the trial,' said the yeoman, with the composure which marked his whole deportment.

'Meanwhile, stand up, ye Saxon churls,' said the fiery Prince; 'for, by the light of Heaven, since I have said it, the Jew shall have his seat amongst ye!'

'By no means, an it please your Grace!—it is not fit for such as we to sit with the rulers of the land,' said the Jew; whose ambition for precedence, though it had led him to dispute place with the extenuated and impoverished descendant of the line of Montdidier, by no means stimulated him to an intrusion upon the privileges of the wealthy Saxons.

'Up, infidel dog, when I command you,' said Prince John, 'or I will have thy swarthy hide stript off, and tanned for horse-furniture.'

Thus urged, the Jew began to ascend the steep and narrow steps which led up to the gallery.

'Let me see,' said the Prince, 'who dare stop him,' fixing his eye on Cedric, whose attitude intimated his intention to hurl the Jew down headlong.

The catastrophe was prevented by the clown Wamba, who, springing betwixt his master and Isaac, and exclaiming, in answer to the Prince's

114

defiance, 'Marry, that will I!' opposed to the beard of the Jew a shield of brawn, which he plucked from beneath his cloak, and with which, doubtless, he had furnished himself, lest the tournament should have proved longer than his appetite could endure abstinence. Finding the abomination of his tribe opposed to his very nose, while the Jester, at the same time, flourished his wooden sword above his head, the Jew recoiled, missed his footing, and rolled down the steps,—an excellent jest to the spectators, who set up a loud laughter, in which Prince John and his attendants heartily joined.

'Deal me the prize, cousin Prince,' said Wamba; 'I have vanquished my foe in fair fight with sword and shield,' he added, brandishing the brawn in one hand and the wooden sword in the other.

'Who, and what art thou, noble champion?' said Prince John, still laughing.

'A fool by right of descent,' answered the Jester; 'I am Wamba, the son of Witless, who was the son of Weatherbrain, who was the son of an Alderman.'

'Make room for the Jew in front of the lower ring,' said Prince John, not unwilling perhaps to seize an apology to desist from his original purpose; 'to place the vanquished beside the victor were false heraldry.'

'Knave upon fool were worse,' answered the Jester, 'and Jew upon bacon worst of all.'

'Gramercy! good fellow,' cried Prince John, 'thou pleasest me—Here, Isaac, lend me a handful of byzants.'

IVANHOE

As the Jew, stunned by the request, afraid to refuse, and unwilling to comply, fumbled in the furred bag which hung by his girdle, and was perhaps endeavouring to ascertain how few coins might pass for a handful, the Prince stooped from his jennet and settled Isaac's doubts by snatching the pouch itself from his side; and flinging to Wamba a couple of the gold pieces which it contained, he pursued his career round the lists, leaving the Jew to the derision of those around him, and himself receiving as much applause from the spectators as if he had done some honest and honourable action.

CHAPTER VIII

At this the challenger with fierce defy
His trumpet sounds; the challenged makes reply:
With clangour rings the field, resounds the vaulted sky.
Their visors closed, their lances in the rest,
Or at the helmet pointed or the crest,
They vanish from the barrier, speed the race,
And spurring see decrease the middle space.

PALAMON AND ARCITE.

IN the midst of Prince John's cavalcade, he suddenly stopt, and appealing to the Prior of Jorvaulx, declared the principal business of the day had been forgotten.

'By my halidom,' said he, 'we have forgotten, Sir Prior, to name the fair Sovereign of Love and of Beauty, by whose white hand the palm is to be distributed. For my part, I am liberal in my ideas, and I care not if I give my vote for the black-eyed Rebecca.'

'Holy Virgin,' answered the Prior, turning up his eyes in horror, 'a Jewess!—We should deserve to be stoned out of the lists; and I am not yet old enough to be a martyr. Besides, I swear by my patron saint, that she is far inferior to the lovely Saxon, Rowena.'

'Saxon or Jew,' answered the Prince, 'Saxon or Jew, dog or hog, what matters it? I say, name Rebecca, were it only to mortify the Saxon churls.'

A murmur arose even among his own immediate attendants.

'This passes a jest, my lord,' said De Bracy; 'no knight here will lay lance in rest if such an insult is attempted.'

'It is the mere wantonness of insult,' said one of the oldest and most important of Prince John's followers, Waldemar Fitzurse, 'and if your Grace attempt it, cannot but prove ruinous to your projects.'

'I entertained you, sir,' said John, reining up his palfrey haughtily, 'for my follower, but not for my counsellor.'

'Those who follow your Grace in the paths which you tread,' said Waldemar, but speaking in a low voice, 'acquire the right of counsellors; for your interest and safety are not more deeply gaged than their own.'

From the tone in which this was spoken, John saw the necessity of acquiescence. 'I did but jest,' he said; 'and you turn upon me like so many adders! Name whom you will, in the fiend's name, and please yourselves.'

'Nay, nay,' said De Bracy, 'let the fair sovereign's throne remain unoccupied, until the conqueror shall be named, and then let him choose the lady by whom it shall be filled. It will add another grace to his triumph, and teach fair ladies to prize the love of valiant knights, who can exalt them to such distinction.'

'If Brian de Bois-Guilbert gain the prize,' said the Prior, 'I will gage my rosary that I name the Sovereign of Love and Beauty.'

'Bois-Guilbert,' answered De Bracy, 'is a good lance; but there are others around these lists, Sir Prior, who will not fear to encounter him.'

'Silence, sirs,' said Waldemar, 'and let the Prince assume his seat. The knights and spectators are alike impatient, the time advances, and highly fit it is that the sports should commence.'

Prince John, though not yet a monarch, had in Waldemar Fitzurse all the inconveniences of a favourite minister, who, in serving his sovereign, must always do so in his own way. The Prince acquiesced, however, although his disposition was precisely of that kind which is apt to be obstinate upon trifles, and, assuming his throne, and being surrounded by his followers, gave signal to the heralds to proclaim the laws of the tournament, which were briefly as follows:

First, the five challengers were to undertake all comers.

Secondly, any knight proposing to combat, might, if he pleased, select a special antagonist from among the challengers, by touching his shield. If he did so with the reverse of his lance, the trial of skill was made with what were called the arms of courtesy, that is, with lances at whose extremity a piece of round flat board was fixed, so that no danger was encountered, save from the shock of the horses and riders. But if the shield was touched with the sharp end of the lance, the combat was understood to be at *outrance*, that is, the knights were to fight with sharp weapons, as in actual battle.

Thirdly, when the knights present had accomplished their vow, by each of them breaking five lances, the Prince was to declare the victor in the first day's tourney, who should receive as prize a war-horse of exquisite beauty and matchless strength; and in addition to this reward of valour, it was now declared, he should have the peculiar honour of naming the Queen of Love and Beauty, by whom the prize should be given on the ensuing day.

Fourthly, it was announced, that, on the second day, there should be a general tournament, in which all the knights present, who were desirous to win praise, might take part; and being divided into two bands of equal numbers, might fight it out manfully, until the signal was given by Prince John to cease the combat. The elected Queen of Love and Beauty was then to crown the knight whom the Prince should adjudge to have borne himself best in this second day, with a coronet composed of thin gold plate, cut into the shape of a laurel crown. On this second day the knightly games ceased. But on that which was to follow, feats of archery, of bull-baiting, and other popular amusements, were to be practised, for the more immediate amusement of the populace. In this manner did Prince John endeavour to lay the foundation of a popularity, which he was perpetually throwing down by some inconsiderate act of wanton aggression upon the feelings and prejudices of the people.

The lists now presented a most splendid spectacle. The sloping galleries were crowded with all that was noble, great, wealthy, and beautiful in the northern and midland parts of England; and the

contrast of the various dresses of these dignified
spectators, rendered the view as gay as it was rich,
while the interior and lower space, filled with the
substantial burgesses and yeomen of merry England,
formed, in their more plain attire, a dark fringe, or
border, around this circle of brilliant embroidery,
relieving, and, at the same time, setting off its
splendour.

The heralds finished their proclamation with their
usual cry of ' Largesse, largesse, gallant knights ! '
and gold and silver pieces were showered on them
from the galleries, it being a high point of chivalry
to exhibit liberality towards those whom the age
accounted at once the secretaries and the historians
of honour. The bounty of the spectators was
acknowledged by the customary shouts of ' Love
of Ladies—Death of Champions—Honour to the
Generous—Glory to the Brave !' To which the more
humble spectators added their acclamations, and a
numerous band of trumpeters the flourish of their
martial instruments. When these sounds had
ceased, the heralds withdrew from the lists in gay
and glittering procession, and none remained within
them save the marshals of the field, who, armed
cap-a-pie, sat on horseback, motionless as statues,
at the opposite ends of the lists. Meantime, the
enclosed space at the northern extremity of the lists,
large as it was, was now completely crowded with
knights desirous to prove their skill against the
challengers, and, when viewed from the galleries, presented the appearance of a sea of waving plumage,
intermixed with glistening helmets, and tall lances,

to the extremities of which were, in many cases, attached small pennons of about a span's breadth, which, fluttering in the air as the breeze caught them, joined with the restless motion of the feathers to add liveliness to the scene.

At length the barriers were opened, and five knights, chosen by lot, advanced slowly into the area; a single champion riding in front, and the other four following in pairs. All were splendidly armed, and my Saxon authority (in the Wardour Manuscript) records at great length their devices, their colours, and the embroidery of their horse trappings. It is unnecessary to be particular on these subjects. To borrow lines from a contemporary poet, who has written but too little—

> ' The knights are dust,
>   And their good swords are rust,
>   Their souls are with the saints, we trust.' *

Their escutcheons have long mouldered from the walls of their castles. Their castles themselves are but green mounds and shattered ruins—the place that once knew them, knows them no more—nay, many a race since theirs has died out and been forgotten in the very land which they occupied, with all the authority of feudal proprietors and feudal lords. What, then, would it avail the reader

---

* These lines are part of an unpublished poem by Coleridge, whose Muse so often tantalizes with fragments which indicate her powers, while the manner in which she flings them from her betrays her caprice, yet whose unfinished sketches display more talent than the laboured masterpieces of others.

to know their names, or the evanescent symbols of their martial rank!

Now, however, no whit anticipating the oblivion which awaited their names and feats, the champions advanced through the lists, restraining their fiery steeds, and compelling them to move slowly, while, at the same time, they exhibited their paces, together with the grace and dexterity of the riders. As the procession entered the lists, the sound of a wild Barbaric music was heard from behind the tents of the challengers, where the performers were concealed. It was of Eastern origin, having been brought from the Holy Land; and the mixture of the cymbals and bells seemed to bid welcome at once, and defiance, to the knights as they advanced. With the eyes of an immense concourse of spectators fixed upon them, the five knights advanced up the platform upon which the tents of the challengers stood, and there separating themselves, each touched slightly, and with the reverse of his lance, the shield of the antagonist to whom he wished to oppose himself. The lower orders of spectators in general—nay, many of the higher class, and it is even said several of the ladies, were rather disappointed at the champions choosing the arms of courtesy. For the same sort of persons, who, in the present day, applaud most highly the deepest tragedies, were then interested in a tournament exactly in proportion to the danger incurred by the champions engaged.

Having intimated their more pacific purpose, the champions retreated to the extremity of the lists, where they remained drawn up in a line; while the challengers, sallying each from his pavilion, mounted their horses, and, headed by Brian de Bois-Guilbert, descended from the platform, and opposed themselves individually to the knights who had touched their respective shields.

At the flourish of clarions and trumpets, they started out against each other at full gallop; and such was the superior dexterity or good fortune of the challengers, that those opposed to Bois-Guilbert, Malvoisin, and Front-de-Bœuf, rolled on the ground. The antagonist of Grantmesnil, instead of bearing his lance-point fair against the crest or the shield of his enemy, swerved so much from the direct line as to break the weapon athwart the person of his opponent—a circumstance which was accounted more disgraceful than that of being actually unhorsed; because the latter might happen from accident, whereas the former evinced awkwardness and want of management of the weapon and of the horse. The fifth knight alone maintained the honour of his party, and parted fairly with the Knight of St. John, both splintering their lances without advantage on either side.

The shouts of the multitude, together with the acclamations of the heralds, and the clangour of the trumpets, announced the triumph of the victors and the defeat of the vanquished. The former retreated to their pavilions, and the latter, gathering themselves up as they could, withdrew from the lists in disgrace and dejection, to agree with their victors concerning the redemption of their arms and their

horses, which, according to the laws of the tournament, they had forfeited. The fifth of their number
alone tarried in the lists long enough to be greeted
by the applauses of the spectators, amongst whom
he retreated, to the aggravation, doubtless, of his
companions' mortification.

A second and a third party of knights took the
field; and although they had various success, yet,
upon the whole, the advantage decidedly remained with the challengers, not one of whom
lost his seat or swerved from his charge—misfor-
tunes which befell one or two of their antagonists
in each encounter. The spirits, therefore, of those
opposed to them, seemed to be considerably damped
by their continued success. Three knights only
appeared on the fourth entry, who, avoiding the
shields of Bois-Guilbert and Front-de-Bœuf, contented themselves with touching those of the three
other knights, who had not altogether manifested
the same strength and dexterity. This politic
selection did not alter the fortune of the field,
the challengers were still successful: one of their
antagonists was overthrown, and both the others
failed in the *attaint*,* that is, in striking the helmet
and shield of their antagonist firmly and strongly,
with the lance held in a direct line, so that the
weapon might break unless the champion was
overthrown.

After this fourth encounter, there was a consider-

---

* This term of chivalry, transferred to the law, gives the phrase of
being attainted of treason.

able pause; nor did it appear that any one was very desirous of renewing the contest. The spectators murmured among themselves; for, among the challengers, Malvoisin and Front-de-Bœuf were unpopular from their characters, and the others, except Grantmesnil, were disliked as strangers and foreigners.

But none shared the general feeling of dissatisfaction so keenly as Cedric the Saxon, who saw, in each advantage gained by the Norman challengers, a repeated triumph over the honour of England. His own education had taught him no skill in the games of chivalry, although, with the arms of his Saxon ancestors, he had manifested himself, on many occasions, a brave and determined soldier. He looked anxiously to Athelstane, who had learned the accomplishments of the age, as if desiring that he should make some personal effort to recover the victory which was passing into the hands of the Templar and his associates. But, though both stout of heart, and strong of person, Athelstane had a disposition too inert and unambitious to make the exertions which Cedric seemed to expect from him.

'The day is against England, my lord,' said Cedric, in a marked tone; 'are you not tempted to take the lance?'

'I shall tilt to-morrow,' answered Athelstane, 'in the *mêlée*; it is not worth while for me to arm myself to-day.'

Two things displeased Cedric in this speech. It contained the Norman word *mêlée*, (to express the

general conflict,) and it evinced some indifference
to the honour of the country; but it was spoken
by Athelstane, whom he held in such profound
respect, that he would not trust himself to canvass
his motives or his foibles. Moreover, he had no
time to make any remark, for Wamba thrust in
his word, observing, 'It was better, though scarce
easier, to be the best man among a hundred, than
the best man of two.'

Athelstane took the observation as a serious compliment; but Cedric, who better understood the
Jester's meaning, darted at him a severe and menacing look; and lucky it was for Wamba, perhaps,
that the time and place prevented his receiving,
notwithstanding his place and service, more sensible
marks of his master's resentment.

The pause in the tournament was still uninterrupted, excepting by the voices of the heralds exclaiming—'Love of ladies, splintering of lances!
stand forth, gallant knights, fair eyes look upon
your deeds!'

The music also of the challengers breathed from
time to time wild bursts expressive of triumph or
defiance, while the clowns grudged a holiday which
seemed to pass away in inactivity; and old knights
and nobles lamented in whispers the decay of martial spirit, spoke of the triumphs of their younger
days, but agreed that the land did not now supply
dames of such transcendent beauty as had animated
the jousts of former times. Prince John began to
talk to his attendants about making ready the
banquet, and the necessity of adjudging the prize

to Brian de Bois-Guilbert, who had, with a single spear, overthrown two knights, and foiled a third.

At length, as the Saracenic music of the challengers concluded one of those long and high flourishes with which they had broken the silence of the lists, it was answered by a solitary trumpet, which breathed a note of defiance from the northern extremity. All eyes were turned to see the new champion which these sounds announced, and no sooner were the barriers opened than he paced into the lists. As far as could be judged of a man sheathed in armour, the new adventurer did not greatly exceed the middle size, and seemed to be rather slender than strongly made. His suit of armour was formed of steel, richly inlaid with gold, and the device on his shield was a young oak-tree pulled up by the roots, with the Spanish word *Desdichado*, signifying Disinherited. He was mounted on a gallant black horse, and as he passed through the lists he gracefully saluted the Prince and the ladies by lowering his lance. The dexterity with which he managed his steed, and something of youthful grace which he displayed in his manner, won him the favour of the multitude, which some of the lower classes expressed by calling out, ' Touch Ralph de Vipont's shield—touch the Hospitaller's shield; he has the least sure seat, he is your cheapest bargain.'

The champion, moving onward amid these well-meant hints, ascended the platform by the sloping alley which led to it from the lists, and, to the astonishment of all present, riding straight up to the central pavilion, struck with the sharp end of his spear the shield of Brian de Bois-Guilbert until it rung again. All stood astonished at his presumption, but none more than the redoubted Knight whom he had thus defied to mortal combat, and who, little expecting so rude a challenge, was standing carelessly at the door of the pavilion.

'Have you confessed yourself, brother,' said the Templar, 'and have you heard mass this morning, that you peril your life so frankly?'

'I am fitter to meet death than thou art,' answered the Disinherited Knight; for by this name the stranger had recorded himself in the books of the tourney.

'Then take your place in the lists,' said Bois-Guilbert, 'and look your last upon the sun; for this night thou shalt sleep in paradise.'

'Gramercy for thy courtesy,' replied the Disinherited Knight, 'and to requite it, I advise thee to take a fresh horse and a new lance, for by my honour you will need both.'

Having expressed himself thus confidently, he reined his horse backward down the slope which he had ascended, and compelled him in the same manner to move backward through the lists, till he reached the northern extremity, where he remained stationary, in expectation of his antagonist. This feat of horsemanship again attracted the applause of the multitude.

However incensed at his adversary for the precautions which he recommended, Brian de Bois-Guilbert did not neglect his advice; for his honour was too nearly concerned, to permit his neglecting any means which might ensure victory over his presumptuous opponent. He changed his horse for a proved and fresh one of great strength and spirit. He chose a new and a tough spear, lest the wood of the former might have been strained in the previous encounters he had sustained. Lastly, he laid aside his shield, which had received some little damage, and received another from his squires. His first had only borne the general device of his rider, representing two knights riding upon one horse, an emblem expressive of the original humility and poverty of the Templars, qualities which they had since exchanged for the arrogance and wealth that finally occasioned their suppression. Bois-Guilbert's new shield bore a raven in full flight, holding in its claws a skull, and bearing the motto, *Gare le Corbeau.*

When the two champions stood opposed to each other at the two extremities of the lists, the public expectation was strained to the highest pitch. Few augured the possibility that the encounter could terminate well for the Disinherited Knight, yet his courage and gallantry secured the general good wishes of the spectators.

The trumpets had no sooner given the signal, than the champions vanished from their posts with the speed of lightning, and closed in the centre of the lists with the shock of a thunderbolt. The lances burst into shivers up to the very grasp, and it seemed at the moment that both knights had fallen, for the shock had made each horse recoil

backwards upon its haunches. The address of the
riders recovered their steeds by use of the bridle
and spur; and having glared on each other for an
instant with eyes which seemed to flash fire through
the bars of their visors, each made a demi-volte, and,
retiring to the extremity of the lists, received a
fresh lance from the attendants.

A loud shout from the spectators, waving of
scarfs and handkerchiefs, and general acclamations,
attested the interest taken by the spectators in this
encounter; the most equal, as well as the best per-
formed, which had graced the day. But no sooner
had the knights resumed their station, than the
clamour of applause was hushed into a silence, so
deep and so dead, that it seemed the multitude were
afraid even to breathe.

A few minutes' pause having been allowed, that
the combatants and their horses might recover
breath, Prince John with his truncheon signed to
the trumpets to sound the onset. The champions
a second time sprung from their stations, and closed
in the centre of the lists, with the same speed, the
same dexterity, the same violence, but not the same
equal fortune as before.

In this second encounter, the Templar aimed at
the centre of his antagonist's shield, and struck it
so fair and forcibly, that his spear went to shivers,
and the Disinherited Knight reeled in his saddle.
On the other hand, that champion had, in the
beginning of his career, directed the point of his
lance towards Bois-Guilbert's shield, but, changing
his aim almost in the moment of encounter, he

addressed it to the helmet, a mark more difficult to hit, but which, if attained, rendered the shock more irresistible. Fair and true he hit the Norman on the visor, where his lance's point kept hold of the bars. Yet, even at this disadvantage, the Templar sustained his high reputation ; and had not the girths of his saddle burst, he might not have been unhorsed. As it chanced, however, saddle, horse, and man, rolled on the ground under a cloud of dust.

To extricate himself from the stirrups and fallen steed, was to the Templar scarce the work of a moment; and, stung with madness, both at his disgrace and at the acclamations with which it was hailed by the spectators, he drew his sword and waved it in defiance of his conqueror. The Disinherited Knight sprung from his steed, and also unsheathed his sword. The marshals of the field, however, spurred their horses between them, and reminded them, that the laws of the tournament did not, on the present occasion, permit this species of encounter.

'We shall meet again, I trust,' said the Templar, casting a resentful glance at his antagonist; 'and where there are none to separate us.'

'If we do not,' said the Disinherited Knight, 'the fault shall not be mine. On foot or horseback, with spear, with axe, or with sword, I am alike ready to encounter thee.'

More and angrier words would have been exchanged, but the marshals, crossing their lances betwixt them, compelled them to separate. The Disinherited Knight returned to his first station, and Bois-Guilbert to his tent, where he remained for the rest of the day in an agony of despair.

Without alighting from his horse, the conqueror called for a bowl of wine, and opening the beaver, or lower part of his helmet, announced that he quaffed it, 'To all true English hearts, and to the confusion of foreign tyrants.' He then commanded his trumpet to sound a defiance to the challengers, and desired a herald to announce to them, that he should make no election, but was willing to encounter them in the order in which they pleased to advance against him.

The gigantic Front-de-Bœuf, armed in sable armour, was the first who took the field. He bore on a white shield a black bull's head, half defaced by the numerous encounters which he had undergone, and bearing the arrogant motto, *Cave, Adsum.* Over this champion the Disinherited Knight obtained a slight but decisive advantage. Both Knights broke their lances fairly, but Front-de-Bœuf, who lost a stirrup in the encounter, was adjudged to have the disadvantage.

In the stranger's third encounter with Sir Philip Malvoisin, he was equally successful; striking that baron so forcibly on the casque, that the laces of the helmet broke, and Malvoisin, only saved from falling by being unhelmeted, was declared vanquished like his companions.

In his fourth combat with De Grantmesnil, the Disinherited Knight showed as much courtesy as he had hitherto evinced courage and dexterity. De Grantmesnil's horse, which was young and violent, reared and plunged in the course of the career so as to disturb the rider's aim, and the stranger, declining to take the advantage which this accident afforded him, raised his lance, and passing his antagonist without touching him, wheeled his horse and rode back again to his own end of the lists, offering his antagonist, by a herald, the chance of a second encounter. This De Grantmesnil declined, avowing himself vanquished as much by the courtesy as by the address of his opponent.

Ralph de Vipont summed up the list of the stranger's triumphs, being hurled to the ground with such force, that the blood gushed from his nose and his mouth, and he was borne senseless from the lists.

The acclamations of thousands applauded the unanimous award of the Prince and marshals, announcing that day's honours to the Disinherited Knight.

CHAPTER IX

In the midst was seen
A lady of a more majestic mien,
By stature and by beauty mark'd their sovereign Queen.

*　　*　　*　　*　　*　　*

And as in beauty she surpass'd the choir,
So nobler than the rest was her attire;
A crown of ruddy gold enclosed her brow,
Plain without pomp, and rich without a show;
A branch of Agnus Castus in her hand,
She bore aloft her symbol of command.

THE FLOWER AND THE LEAF.

WILLIAM DE WYVIL and Stephen de Martival, the marshals of the field, were the first to offer their congratulations to the victor, praying him, at the same time, to suffer his helmet to be unlaced, or, at least, that he would raise his visor ere they conducted him to receive the prize of the day's tourney from the hands of Prince John. The Disinherited Knight, with all knightly courtesy, declined their request, alleging, that he could not at this time suffer his face to be seen, for reasons which he had assigned to the heralds when he entered the lists. The marshals were perfectly satisfied by this reply; for amidst the frequent and capricious vows by which knights were accustomed to bind themselves in the days of chivalry, there were none more common than those by which they engaged to

135

remain incognito for a certain space, or until some particular adventure was achieved. The marshals, therefore, pressed no farther into the mystery of the Disinherited Knight, but, announcing to Prince John the conqueror's desire to remain unknown, they requested permission to bring him before his Grace, in order that he might receive the reward of his valour.

John's curiosity was excited by the mystery observed by the stranger; and, being already displeased with the issue of the tournament, in which the challengers whom he favoured had been successively defeated by one knight, he answered haughtily to the marshals, 'By the light of Our Lady's brow, this same knight hath been disinherited as well of his courtesy as of his lands, since he desires to appear before us without uncovering his face. — Wot ye, my lords,' he said, turning round to his train, 'who this gallant can be, that bears himself thus proudly?'

'I cannot guess,' answered De Bracy, 'nor did I think there had been within the four seas that girth Britain a champion that could bear down these five knights in one day's jousting. By my faith, I shall never forget the force with which he shocked De Vipont. The poor Hospitaller was hurled from his saddle like a stone from a sling.'

'Boast not of that,' said a Knight of St. John, who was present; 'your Templar champion had no better luck. I saw your brave lance, Bois-Guilbert, roll thrice over, grasping his hands full of sand at every turn.'

De Bracy, being attached to the Templars, would have replied, but was prevented by Prince John. 'Silence, sirs!' he said; 'what unprofitable debate have we here?'

'The victor,' said De Wyvil, 'still waits the pleasure of your highness.'

'It is our pleasure,' answered John, 'that he do so wait until we learn whether there is not some one who can at least guess at his name and quality. Should he remain there till night-fall, he has had work enough to keep him warm.'

'Your Grace,' said Waldemar Fitzurse, 'will do less than due honour to the victor, if you compel him to wait till we tell your highness that which we cannot know; at least *I* can form no guess—unless he be one of the good lances who accompanied King Richard to Palestine, and who are now straggling homeward from the Holy Land.'

'It may be the Earl of Salisbury,' said De Bracy; 'he is about the same pitch.'

'Sir Thomas de Multon, the Knight of Gilsland, rather,' said Fitzurse; 'Salisbury is bigger in the bones.' A whisper arose among the train, but by whom first suggested could not be ascertained. 'It might be the King—it might be Richard Cœur-de-Lion himself!'

'Over God's forbode!' said Prince John, involuntarily turning at the same time as pale as death, and shrinking as if blighted by a flash of lightning; 'Waldemar!—De Bracy! brave knights and gentlemen, remember your promises, and stand truly by me!'

'Here is no danger impending,' said Waldemar Fitzurse; 'are you so little acquainted with the gigantic limbs of your father's son, as to think they can be held within the circumference of yonder suit of armour?—De Wyvil and Martival, you will best serve the Prince by bringing forward the victor to the throne, and ending an error that has conjured all the blood from his cheeks.—Look at him more closely,' he continued, 'your highness will see that he wants three inches of King Richard's height, and twice as much of his shoulder-breadth. The very horse he backs, could not have carried the ponderous weight of King Richard through a single course.'

While he was yet speaking, the marshals brought forward the Disinherited Knight to the foot of a wooden flight of steps, which formed the ascent from the lists to Prince John's throne. Still discomposed with the idea that his brother, so much injured, and to whom he was so much indebted, had suddenly arrived in his native kingdom, even the distinctions pointed out by Fitzurse did not altogether remove the Prince's apprehensions; and while, with a short and embarrassed eulogy upon his valour, he caused to be delivered to him the war-horse assigned as the prize, he trembled lest from the barred visor of the mailed form before him, an answer might be returned, in the deep and awful accents of Richard the Lion-hearted.

But the Disinherited Knight spoke not a word in reply to the compliment of the Prince, which he only acknowledged with a profound obeisance.

The horse was led into the lists by two grooms richly dressed, the animal itself being fully accoutred with the richest war-furniture; which, however, scarcely added to the value of the noble creature in the eyes of those who were judges. Laying one hand upon the pommel of the saddle, the Disinherited Knight vaulted at once upon the back of the steed without making use of the stirrup, and, brandishing aloft his lance, rode twice around the lists, exhibiting the points and paces of the horse with the skill of a perfect horseman.

The appearance of vanity, which might otherwise have been attributed to this display, was removed by the propriety shown in exhibiting to the best advantage the princely reward with which he had been just honoured, and the Knight was again greeted by the acclamations of all present.

In the meanwhile, the bustling Prior of Jorvaulx had reminded Prince John, in a whisper, that the victor must now display his good judgment, instead of his valour, by selecting from among the beauties who graced the galleries a lady, who should fill the throne of the Queen of Beauty and of Love, and deliver the prize of the tourney upon the ensuing day. The Prince accordingly made a sign with his truncheon, as the Knight passed him in his second career around the lists. The Knight turned towards the throne, and, sinking his lance, until the point was within a foot of the ground, remained motionless, as if expecting John's commands; while all admired the sudden dexterity with which he instantly reduced his fiery steed from a state of violent emotion and high excitation to the stillness of an equestrian statue.

'Sir Disinherited Knight,' said Prince John, 'since that is the only title by which we can address you, it is now your duty, as well as privilege, to name the fair lady, who, as Queen of Honour and of Love, is to preside over next day's festival. If, as a stranger in our land, you should require the aid of other judgment to guide your own, we can only say that Alicia, the daughter of our gallant knight Waldemar Fitzurse, has at our court been long held the first in beauty as in place. Nevertheless, it is your undoubted prerogative to confer on whom you please this crown, by the delivery of which to the lady of your choice, the election of to-morrow's Queen will be formal and complete.— Raise your lance.'

The Knight obeyed; and Prince John placed upon its point a coronet of green satin, having around its edge a circlet of gold, the upper edge of which was relieved by arrow-points and hearts placed interchangeably, like the strawberry leaves and balls upon a ducal crown.

In the broad hint which he dropped respecting the daughter of Waldemar Fitzurse, John had more than one motive, each the offspring of a mind, which was a strange mixture of carelessness and presumption with low artifice and cunning. He wished to banish from the minds of the chivalry around him his own indecent and unacceptable jest respecting the Jewess Rebecca; he was desirous of conciliating Alicia's father Waldemar, of whom he stood in awe, and who had more than once shown himself dissatisfied during the course of the day's proceedings. He had also a wish to establish himself in the good graces of the lady; for John was at least as licentious in his pleasures as profligate in his ambition. But besides all these reasons, he was desirous to raise up against the Disinherited Knight (towards whom he already entertained a strong dislike) a powerful enemy in the person of Waldemar Fitzurse, who was likely, he thought, highly to resent the injury done to his daughter, in case, as was not unlikely, the victor should make another choice.

And so indeed it proved. For the Disinherited Knight passed the gallery close to that of the Prince, in which the Lady Alicia was seated in the full pride of triumphant beauty, and, pacing forwards as slowly as he had hitherto rode swiftly around the lists, he seemed to exercise his right of examining the numerous fair faces which adorned that splendid circle.

It was worth while to see the different conduct of the beauties who underwent this examination, during the time it was proceeding. Some blushed, some assumed an air of pride and dignity, some looked straight forward, and essayed to seem utterly unconscious of what was going on, some drew back in alarm, which was perhaps affected, some endeavoured to forbear smiling, and there were two or three who laughed outright. There were also some who dropped their veils over their charms; but, as the Wardour Manuscript says these were fair ones of ten years' standing, it may be supposed that having had their full share of such vanities, they were willing to withdraw their claim, in order to give a fair chance to the rising beauties of the age.

At length the champion paused beneath the balcony in which the Lady Rowena was placed, and the expectation of the spectators was excited to the utmost.

It must be owned, that if an interest displayed in his success could have bribed the Disinherited Knight, the part of the lists before which he paused had merited his predilection. Cedric the Saxon, overjoyed at the discomfiture of the Templar, and still more so at the miscarriage of his two malevolent neighbours, Front - de - Bœuf and Malvoisin, had, with his body half stretched over the balcony, accompanied the victor in each course, not with his eyes only, but with his whole heart and soul. The Lady Rowena had watched the progress of the day with equal attention, though without openly betraying the same intense interest. Even the unmoved Athelstane had shown symptoms of shaking off his apathy, when, calling for a huge goblet of muscadine, he quaffed it to the health of the Disinherited Knight.

Another group, stationed under the gallery occupied by the Saxons, had shown no less interest in the fate of the day.

'Father Abraham!' said Isaac of York, when the first course was run betwixt the Templar and the Disinherited Knight, 'how fiercely that

Gentile rides! Ah, the good horse that was brought all the long way from Barbary, he takes no more care of him than if he were a wild ass's colt—and the noble armour, that was worth so many zecchins to Joseph Pareira, the armourer of Milan, besides seventy in the hundred of profits, he cares for it as little as if he had found it in the highways!'

'If he risks his own person and limbs, father,' said Rebecca, 'in doing such a dreadful battle, he can scarce be expected to spare his horse and armour.'

'Child!' replied Isaac, somewhat heated, 'thou knowest not what thou speakest—His neck and limbs are his own, but his horse and armour belong to——Holy Jacob! what was I about to say!—Nevertheless, it is a good youth—See, Rebecca! see, he is again about to go up to battle against the Philistine—Pray, child—pray for the safety of the good youth,—and of the speedy horse, and the rich armour.—God of my fathers!' he again exclaimed, 'he hath conquered, and the uncircumcised Philistine hath fallen before his lance,—even as Og the King of Bashan, and Sihon, King of the Amorites, fell before the sword of our fathers!—Surely he shall take their gold and their silver, and their war-horses, and their armour of brass and of steel, for a prey and for a spoil.'

The same anxiety did the worthy Jew display during every course that was run, seldom failing to hazard a hasty calculation concerning the value of the horse and armour which was forfeited to the champion upon each new success.   There had been therefore no small interest taken in the success of the Disinherited Knight, by those who occupied the part of the lists before which he now paused.

Whether from indecision or some other motive of hesitation, the champion of the day remained stationary for more than a minute, while the eyes of the silent audience were riveted upon his motions; and then, gradually and gracefully sinking the point of his lance, he deposited the coronet which it supported at the feet of the fair Rowena. The trumpets instantly sounded, while the heralds proclaimed the Lady Rowena the Queen of Beauty and of Love for the ensuing day, menacing with suitable penalties those who should be disobedient to her authority. They then repeated their cry of Largesse, to which Cedric, in the height of his joy, replied by an ample donative, and to which Athelstane, though less promptly, added one equally large.

There was some murmuring among the damsels of Norman descent, who were as much unused to see the preference given to a Saxon beauty, as the Norman nobles were to sustain defeat in the games of chivalry which they themselves had introduced. But these sounds of disaffection were drowned by the popular shout of 'Long live the Lady Rowena, the chosen and lawful Queen of Love and of Beauty!' To which many in the lower area added, 'Long live the Saxon Princess! long live the race of the immortal Alfred!'

However unacceptable these sounds might be to

Prince John, and to those around him, he saw himself nevertheless obliged to confirm the nomination of the victor, and accordingly calling to horse, he left his throne; and mounting his jennet, accompanied by his train, he again entered the lists. The Prince paused a moment beneath the gallery of the Lady Alicia, to whom he paid his compliments, observing, at the same time, to those around him—'By my halidome, sirs! if the Knight's feats in arms have shown that he hath limbs and sinews, his choice hath no less proved that his eyes are none of the clearest.'

It was on this occasion, as during his whole life, John's misfortune, not perfectly to understand the characters of those whom he wished to conciliate. Waldemar Fitzurse was rather offended than pleased at the Prince stating thus broadly an opinion, that his daughter had been slighted.

'I know no right of chivalry,' he said, 'more precious or inalienable than that of each free knight to choose his lady-love by his own judgment. My daughter courts distinction from no one; and in her own character, and in her own sphere, will never fail to receive the full proportion of that which is her due.'

Prince John replied not; but, spurring his horse, as if to give vent to his vexation, he made the animal bound forward to the gallery where Rowena was seated, with the crown still at her feet.

'Assume,' he said, 'fair lady, the mark of your sovereignty, to which none vows homage more

sincerely than ourself, John of Anjoù; and if it
please you to-day, with your noble sire and friends,
to grace our banquet in the Castle of Ashby, we
shall learn to know the empress to whose service
we devote to-morrow.'

Rowena remained silent, and Cedric answered for
her in his native Saxon.

'The Lady Rowena,' he said, 'possesses not the
language in which to reply to your courtesy, or to
sustain her part in your festival. I also, and the
noble Athelstane of Coningsburgh, speak only the
language, and practise only the manners, of our
fathers. We therefore decline with thanks your
Highness's courteous invitation to the banquet.
To-morrow, the Lady Rowena will take upon her
the state to which she has been called by the free
election of the victor Knight, confirmed by the
acclamations of the people.'

So saying, he lifted the coronet, and placed it
upon Rowena's head, in token of her acceptance of
the temporary authority assigned to her.

'What says he?' said Prince John, affecting not
to understand the Saxon language, in which, however, he was well skilled. The purport of Cedric's
speech was repeated to him in French. 'It is well,'
he said; 'to-morrow we will ourself conduct this
mute sovereign to her seat of dignity.—You, at
least, Sir Knight,' he added, turning to the victor,
who had remained near the gallery, 'will this day
share our banquet?'

The Knight, speaking for the first time, in a low
and hurried voice, excused himself by pleading

fatigue, and the necessity of preparing for to-morrow's encounter.

'It is well,' said Prince John, haughtily; 'although unused to such refusals, we will endeavour to digest our banquet as we may, though ungraced by the most successful in arms, and his elected Queen of Beauty.'

So saying, he prepared to leave the lists with his glittering train, and his turning his steed for that purpose, was the signal for the breaking up and dispersion of the spectators.

Yet, with the vindictive memory proper to offended pride, especially when combined with conscious want of desert, John had hardly proceeded three paces, ere again, turning around, he fixed an eye of stern resentment upon the yeoman who had displeased him in the early part of the day, and issued his commands to the men-at-arms who stood near—'On your life, suffer not that fellow to escape.'

The yeoman stood the angry glance of the Prince with the same unvaried steadiness which had marked his former deportment, saying, with a smile, 'I have no intention to leave Ashby until the day after to-morrow—I must see how Stafford-shire and Leicestershire can draw their bows—the forests of Needwood and Charnwood must rear good archers.'

'I,' said Prince John to his attendants, but not in direct reply,—'I will see how he can draw his own; and woe betide him unless his skill should prove some apology for his insolence!'

'It is full time,' said De Bracy, 'that the *outre-cuidance** of these peasants should be restrained by some striking example.'

Waldemar Fitzurse, who probably thought his patron was not taking the readiest road to popularity, shrugged up his shoulders and was silent. Prince John resumed his retreat from the lists, and the dispersion of the multitude became general.

In various routes, according to the different quarters from which they came, and in groups of various numbers, the spectators were seen retiring over the plain. By far the most numerous part streamed towards the town of Ashby, where many of the distinguished persons were lodged in the castle, and where others found accommodation in the town itself. Among these were most of the knights who had already appeared in the tournament, or who proposed to fight there the ensuing day, and who, as they rode slowly along, talking over the events of the day, were greeted with loud shouts by the populace. The same acclamations were bestowed upon Prince John, although he was indebted for them rather to the splendour of his appearance and train, than to the popularity of his character.

A more sincere and more general, as well as a better-merited acclamation, attended the victor of the day, until, anxious to withdraw himself from popular notice, he accepted the accommodation of one of those pavilions pitched at the extremities of

---

* Presumption, insolence.

the lists, the use of which was courteously tendered him by the marshals of the field. On his retiring to his tent, many who had lingered in the lists, to look upon and form conjectures concerning him, also dispersed.

The signs and sounds of a tumultuous concourse of men lately crowded together in one place, and agitated by the same passing events, were now exchanged for the distant hum of voices of different groups retreating in all directions, and these speedily died away in silence. No other sounds were heard save the voices of the menials who stripped the galleries of their cushions and tapestry, in order to put them in safety for the night, and wrangled among themselves for the half-used bottles of wine and relics of the refreshment which had been served round to the spectators.

Beyond the precincts of the lists more than one forge was erected; and these now began to glimmer through the twilight, announcing the toil of the armourers, which was to continue through the whole night, in order to repair or alter the suits of armour to be used again on the morrow.

A strong guard of men-at-arms, renewed at intervals, from two hours to two hours, surrounded the lists, and kept watch during the night.

CHAPTER X

Thus, like the sad presaging raven, that tolls
The sick man's passport in her hollow beak,
And in the shadow of the silent night
Doth shake contagion from her sable wings;
Vex'd and tormented, runs poor Barrabas,
With fatal curses towards these Christians.

JEW OF MALTA.

THE Disinherited Knight had no sooner reached his pavilion, than squires and pages in abundance tendered their services to disarm him, to bring fresh attire, and to offer him the refreshment of the bath. Their zeal on this occasion was perhaps sharpened by curiosity, since every one desired to know who the knight was that had gained so many laurels, yet had refused, even at the command of Prince John, to lift his visor or to name his name. But their officious inquisitiveness was not gratified. The Disinherited Knight refused all other assistance save that of his own squire, or rather yeoman—a clownish-looking man, who, wrapt in a cloak of dark-coloured felt, and having his head and face half-buried in a Norman bonnet made of black fur, seemed to affect the incognito as much as his master. All others being excluded from the tent, this attendant relieved his master from the more burdensome parts of his armour, and placed food and wine before him, which the exertions of the day rendered very acceptable.

The Knight had scarcely finished a hasty meal, ere his menial announced to him that five men, each leading a barbed steed, desired to speak with him. The Disinherited Knight had exchanged his armour for the long robe usually worn by those of his condition, which, being furnished with a hood, concealed the features, when such was the pleasure of the wearer, almost as completely as the visor of the helmet itself; but the twilight, which was now fast darkening, would of itself have rendered a disguise unnecessary, unless to persons to whom the face of an individual chanced to be particularly well known.

The Disinherited Knight, therefore, stept boldly forth to the front of his tent, and found in attendance the squires of the challengers, whom he easily knew by their russet and black dresses, each of whom led his master's charger, loaded with the armour in which he had that day fought.

'According to the laws of chivalry,' said the foremost of these men, 'I, Baldwin de Oyley, squire to the redoubted Knight Brian de Bois-Guilbert, make offer to you, styling yourself, for the present, the Disinherited Knight, of the horse and armour used by the said Brian de Bois-Guilbert in this day's Passage of Arms, leaving it with your nobleness to retain or to ransom the same, according to your pleasure; for such is the law of arms.'

The other squires repeated nearly the same formula, and then stood to await the decision of the Disinherited Knight.

'To you four, sirs,' replied the Knight, addressing those who had last spoken, 'and to your honourable and valiant masters, I have one common reply. Commend me to the noble knights, your masters, and say, I should do ill to deprive them of steeds and arms which can never be used by braver cavaliers.—I would I could here end my message to these gallant knights; but being, as I term myself, in truth and earnest, the Disinherited, I must be thus far bound to your masters, that they will, of their courtesy, be pleased to ransom their steeds and armour, since that which I wear I can hardly term mine own.'

'We stand commissioned, each of us,' answered the squire of Reginald Front-de-Bœuf, 'to offer a hundred zecchins in ransom of these horses and suits of armour.'

'It is sufficient,' said the Disinherited Knight. 'Half the sum my present necessities compel me to accept; of the remaining half, distribute one moiety among yourselves, sir squires, and divide the other half betwixt the heralds and the pursuivants, and minstrels, and attendants.'

The squires, with cap in hand, and low reverences, expressed their deep sense of a courtesy and generosity not often practised, at least upon a scale so extensive. The Disinherited Knight then addressed his discourse to Baldwin, the squire of Brian de Bois-Guilbert. 'From your master,' said he, 'I will accept neither arms nor ransom. Say to him in my name, that our strife is not ended— no, not till we have fought as well with swords as with lances—as well on foot as on horseback. To this mortal quarrel he has himself defied me, and I shall not forget the challenge.—Meantime, let him be assured, that I hold him not as one of his companions, with whom I can with pleasure exchange courtesies; but rather as one with whom I stand upon terms of mortal defiance.'

'My master,' answered Baldwin, 'knows how to requite scorn with scorn, and blows with blows, as well as courtesy with courtesy. Since you disdain to accept from him any share of the ransom at which you have rated the arms of the other knights, I must leave his armour and his horse here, being well assured that he will never deign to mount the one nor wear the other.'

'You have spoken well, good squire,' said the Disinherited Knight, 'well and boldly, as it beseemeth him to speak who answers for an absent master. Leave not, however, the horse and armour here. Restore them to thy master; or, if he scorns to accept them, retain them, good friend, for thine own use. So far as they are mine, I bestow them upon you freely.'

Baldwin made a deep obeisance, and retired with his companions; and the Disinherited Knight entered the pavilion.

'Thus far, Gurth,' said he, addressing his attendant, 'the reputation of English chivalry hath not suffered in my hands.'

'And I,' said Gurth, 'for a Saxon swineherd, have not ill played the personage of a Norman squire-at-arms.'

IVANHOE

'Yea, but,' answered the Disinherited Knight,
'thou hast ever kept me in anxiety lest thy clownish
bearing should discover thee.'

'Tush!' said Gurth, 'I fear discovery from none,
saving my playfellow, Wamba the Jester, of whom
I could never discover whether he were most knave
or fool. Yet I could scarce choose but laugh, when
my old master passed so near to me, dreaming all
the while that Gurth was keeping his porkers many
a mile off, in the thickets and swamps of Rotherwood. If I am discovered——'

'Enough,' said the Disinherited Knight, 'thou
knowest my promise.'

'Nay, for that matter,' said Gurth, 'I will never
fail my friend for fear of my skin-cutting. I have
a tough hide, that will bear knife or scourge as well
as any boar's hide in my herd.'

'Trust me, I will requite the risk you run for
my love, Gurth,' said the Knight. 'Meanwhile,
I pray you to accept these ten pieces of gold.'

'I am richer,' said Gurth, putting them into his
pouch, 'than ever was swineherd or bondsman.'

'Take this bag of gold to Ashby,' continued his
master, 'and find out Isaac the Jew of York, and
let him pay himself for the horse and arms with
which his credit supplied me.'

'Nay, by St. Dunstan,' replied Gurth, 'that I
will not do.'

'How, knave,' replied his master, 'wilt thou
not obey my commands?'

'So they be honest, reasonable, and Christian
commands,' replied Gurth; 'but this is none of

154

these. To suffer the Jew to pay himself would be dishonest, for it would be cheating my master; and unreasonable, for it were the part of a fool; and unchristian, since it would be plundering a believer to enrich an infidel.'

'See him contented, however, thou stubborn varlet,' said the Disinherited Knight.

'I will do so,' said Gurth, taking the bag under his cloak, and leaving the apartment; 'and it will go hard,' he muttered, 'but I content him with one-half of his own asking.' So saying, he departed, and left the Disinherited Knight to his own perplexed ruminations; which, upon more accounts than it is now possible to communicate to the reader, were of a nature peculiarly agitating and painful.

We must now change the scene to the village of Ashby, or rather to a country house in its vicinity belonging to a wealthy Israelite, with whom Isaac, his daughter, and retinue, had taken up their quarters; the Jews, it is well known, being as liberal in exercising the duties of hospitality and charity among their own people, as they were alleged to be reluctant and churlish in extending them to those whom they termed Gentiles, and whose treatment of them certainly merited little hospitality at their hand.

In an apartment, small indeed, but richly furnished with decorations of an Oriental taste, Rebecca was seated on a heap of embroidered cushions, which, piled along a low platform that surrounded the chamber, served, like the estrado of

the Spaniards, instead of chairs and stools. She
was watching the motions of her father with a look
of anxious and filial affection, while he paced the
apartment with a dejected mien and disordered
step; sometimes clasping his hands together—sometimes casting his eyes to the roof of the apartment,
as one who laboured under great mental tribula-
tion. ' O, Jacob !' he exclaimed—' O, all ye twelve
Holy Fathers of our tribe! what a losing venture
is this for one who hath duly kept every jot and
tittle of the law of Moses—Fifty zecchins wrenched
from me at one clutch, and by the talons of a
tyrant !'

' But, father,' said Rebecca, ' you seemed to give
the gold to Prince John willingly.'

' Willingly ? the blotch of Egypt upon him !—
Willingly, saidst thou ?—Ay, as willingly as when,
in the Gulf of Lyons, I flung over my merchandise
to lighten the ship, while she laboured in the tempest
—robed the seething billows in my choice silks—
perfumed their briny foam with myrrh and aloes—
enriched their caverns with gold and silver work !
And was not that an hour of unutterable misery,
though my own hands made the sacrifice ?'

' But it was a sacrifice which Heaven exacted
to save our lives,' answered Rebecca, ' and the God
of our fathers has since blessed your store and your
gettings.'

' Ay,' answered Isaac, ' but if the tyrant lays
hold on them as he did to-day, and compels me to
smile while he is robbing me ?—O, daughter, disinherited and wandering as we are, the worst evil

which befalls our race is, that when we are wronged
and plundered, all the world laughs around, and we
are compelled to suppress our sense of injury, and
to smile tamely, when we would revenge bravely.'

'Think not thus of it, my father,' said Rebecca;
'we also have advantages. These Gentiles, cruel
and oppressive as they are, are in some sort de-
pendent on the dispersed children of Zion, whom
they despise and persecute. Without the aid of
our wealth, they could neither furnish forth their
hosts in war, nor their triumphs in peace; and the
gold which we lend them returns with increase to
our coffers. We are like the herb which flourisheth
most when it is most trampled on. Even this day's
pageant had not proceeded without the consent of
the despised Jew, who furnished the means.'

'Daughter,' said Isaac, 'thou hast harped upon
another string of sorrow. The goodly steed and
the rich armour, equal to the full profit of my
adventure with our Kirjath Jairam of Leicester—
there is a dead loss too—ay, a loss which swallows
up the gains of a week; ay, of the space between
two Sabbaths—and yet it may end better than I
now think, for 'tis a good youth.'

'Assuredly,' said Rebecca, 'you shall not repent
you of requiting the good deed received of the
stranger knight.'

'I trust so, daughter,' said Isaac, 'and I trust
too in the rebuilding of Zion; but as well do I
hope with my own bodily eyes to see the walls
and battlements of the new Temple, as to see a
Christian, yea, the very best of Christians, repay

a debt to a Jew, unless under the awe of the judge and jailor.'

So saying, he resumed his discontented walk through the apartment; and Rebecca, perceiving that her attempts at consolation only served to awaken new subjects of complaint, wisely desisted from her unavailing efforts—a prudential line of conduct, and we recommend to all who set up for comforters and advisers, to follow it in the like circumstances.

The evening was now becoming dark, when a Jewish servant entered the apartment, and placed upon the table two silver lamps, fed with perfumed oil; the richest wines, and the most delicate re-freshments, were at the same time displayed by another Israelitish domestic on a small ebony table, inlaid with silver; for, in the interior of their houses, the Jews refused themselves no expensive indulgences. At the same time the servant informed Isaac, that a Nazarene (so they termed Christians, while conversing among themselves) desired to speak with him. He that would live by traffic, must hold himself at the disposal of every one claiming business with him. Isaac at once replaced on the table the untasted glass of Greek wine which he had just raised to his lips, and saying hastily to his daughter, ' Rebecca, veil thyself,' commanded the stranger to be admitted.

Just as Rebecca had dropped over her fine features a screen of silver gauze which reached to her feet, the door opened, and Gurth entered, wrapt in the ample folds of his Norman mantle. His

IVANHOE

appearance was rather suspicious than prepossess-
ing, especially as, instead of doffing his bonnet, he
pulled it still deeper over his rugged brow.

'Art thou Isaac the Jew of York?' said Gurth,
in Saxon.

'I am,' replied Isaac, in the same language,
(for his traffic had rendered every tongue spoken
in Britain familiar to him)—'and who art thou?'

'That is not to the purpose,' answered Gurth.

'As much as my name is to thee,' replied Isaac;
'for without knowing thine, how can I hold intercourse with thee?'

'Easily,' answered Gurth; 'I, being to pay
money, must know that I deliver it to the right
person; thou, who are to receive it, will not,
I think, care very greatly by whose hands it is
delivered.'

'O,' said the Jew, 'you are come to pay moneys?
—Holy Father Abraham! that altereth our relation to each other. And from whom dost thou
bring it?

'From the Disinherited Knight,' said Gurth,
'victor in this day's tournament. It is the price
of the armour supplied to him by Kirjath Jairam
of Leicester, on thy recommendation. The steed
is restored to thy stable. I desire to know the
amount of the sum which I am to pay for the
armour.'

'I said he was a good youth!' exclaimed Isaac
with joyful exultation. 'A cup of wine will do
thee no harm,' he added, filling and handing to
the swineherd a richer draught than Gurth had

ever before tasted. 'And how much money,' continued Isaac, 'hast thou brought with thee?'

'Holy Virgin!' said Gurth, setting down the cup, 'what nectar these unbelieving dogs drink, while true Christians are fain to quaff ale as muddy and thick as the draff we give to hogs!—What money have I brought with me?' continued the Saxon, when he had finished this uncivil ejaculation, 'even but a small sum; something in hand the whilst. What, Isaac! thou must bear a conscience, though it be a Jewish one.'

'Nay, but,' said Isaac, 'thy master has won goodly steeds and rich armours with the strength of his lance, and of his right hand—but 'tis a good youth—the Jew will take these in present payment, and render him back the surplus.'

'My master has disposed of them already,' said Gurth.

'Ah! that was wrong,' said the Jew, 'that was the part of a fool. No Christians here could buy so many horses and armour—no Jew except myself would give him half the values. But thou hast a hundred zecchins with thee in that bag,' said Isaac, prying under Gurth's cloak, 'it is a heavy one.'

'I have heads for cross-bow bolts in it,' said Gurth, readily.

'Well, then'—said Isaac, panting and hesitating between habitual love of gain and a new-born desire to be liberal in the present instance, 'if I should say that I would take eighty zecchins for the good steed and the rich armour, which leaves me not a guilder's profit, have you money to pay me?'

"A cup of wine will do thee no harm."

'Barely,' said Gurth, though the sum demanded was more reasonable than he expected, 'and it will leave my master nigh penniless. Nevertheless, if such be your least offer, I must be content.'

'Fill thyself another goblet of wine,' said the Jew. 'Ah! eighty zecchins is too little. It leaveth no profit for the usages of the moneys; and, besides, the good horse may have suffered wrong in this day's encounter. O, it was a hard and a dangerous meeting! man and steed rushing on each other like wild bulls of Bashan! The horse cannot but have had wrong.'

'And I say,' replied Gurth, 'he is sound, wind and limb; and you may see him now, in your stable. And I say, over and above, that seventy zecchins is enough for the armour, and I hope a Christian's word is as good as a Jew's. If you will not take seventy, I will carry this bag' (and he shook it till the contents jingled) 'back to my master.'

'Nay, nay!' said Isaac; 'lay down the talents —the shekels—the eighty zecchins, and thou shalt see I will consider thee liberally.'

Gurth at length complied; and telling out eighty zecchins upon the table, the Jew delivered out to him an acquittance for the horse and suit of armour. The Jew's hand trembled for joy as he wrapped up the first seventy pieces of gold. The last ten he told over with much deliberation, pausing, and saying something as he took each piece from the table, and dropt it into his purse. It seemed as if his avarice were struggling with his better nature, and compelling him to pouch zecchin after zecchin,

while his generosity urged him to restore some part
at least to his benefactor, or as a donation to his
agent. His whole speech ran nearly thus:

'Seventy-one—seventy-two; thy master is a
good youth—seventy-three, an excellent youth—
seventy-four—that piece had been clipt within the
ring—seventy-five—and that looketh light of weight
—seventy-six—when thy master wants money, let
him come to Isaac of York—seventy-seven—that
is, with reasonable security.' Here he made a considerable pause, and Gurth had good hope that the
last three pieces might escape the fate of their comrades; but the enumeration proceeded.—'Seventy-
eight—thou art a good fellow—seventy-nine—and
deservest something for thyself——'

Here the Jew paused again, and looked at the
last zecchin, intending, doubtless, to bestow it upon
Gurth. He weighed it upon the tip of his finger,
and made it ring by dropping it upon the table.
Had it rung too flat, or had it felt a hair's breadth
too light, generosity had carried the day; but, un-
happily for Gurth, the chime was full and true, the
zecchin plump, newly coined, and a grain above
weight. Isaac could not find in his heart to part
with it, so dropt it into his purse as if in absence of
mind, with the words, 'Eighty completes the tale,
and I trust thy master will reward thee handsomely.
—Surely,' he added, looking earnestly at the bag,
'thou hast more coins in that pouch?'

Gurth grinned, which was his nearest approach
to a laugh, as he replied, 'About the same quantity
which thou hast just told over so carefully.' He

then folded the quittance, and put it under his cap, adding,—'Peril of thy beard, Jew, see that this be full and ample!' He filled himself, unbidden, a third goblet of wine, and left the apartment without ceremony.

'Rebecca,' said the Jew, 'that Ishmaelite hath gone somewhat beyond me. Nevertheless his master is a good youth—ay, and I am well pleased that he hath gained shekels of gold and shekels of silver, even by the speed of his horse and by the strength of his lance, which, like that of Goliath the Philistine, might vie with a weaver's beam.'

As he turned to receive Rebecca's answer, he observed, that during his chaffering with Gurth, she had left the apartment unperceived.

In the meanwhile, Gurth had descended the stair, and, having reached the dark antechamber or hall, was puzzling about to discover the entrance, when a figure in white, shown by a small silver lamp which she held in her hand, beckoned him into a side apartment. Gurth had some reluctance to obey the summons. Rough and impetuous as a wild boar, where only earthly force was to be apprehended, he had all the characteristic terrors of a Saxon respecting fawns, forest-fiends, white women, and the whole of the superstitions which his ancestors had brought with them from the wilds of Germany. He remembered, moreover, that he was in the house of a Jew, a people who, besides the other unamiable qualities which popular report ascribed to them, were supposed to be profound necromancers and cabalists. Nevertheless, after a moment's pause, he obeyed the beckoning summons of the apparition, and followed her into the apartment which she indicated, where he found to his joyful surprise that his fair guide was the beautiful Jewess whom he had seen at the tournament, and a short time in her father's apartment.

She asked him the particulars of his transaction with Isaac, which he detailed accurately.

'My father did but jest with thee, good fellow,' said Rebecca; 'he owes thy master deeper kindness than these arms and steed could pay, were their value tenfold. What sum didst thou pay my father even now?'

'Eighty zecchins,' said Gurth, surprised at the question.

'In this purse,' said Rebecca, 'thou wilt find a hundred. Restore to thy master that which is his due, and enrich thyself with the remainder. Haste —begone—stay not to render thanks! and beware how you pass through this crowded town, where thou mayst easily lose both thy burden and thy life.—Reuben,' she added, clapping her hands together, 'light forth this stranger, and fail not to draw lock and bar behind him.'

Reuben, a dark-brow'd and black-bearded Israelite, obeyed her summons, with a torch in his hand; undid the outward door of the house, and conducting Gurth across a paved court, let him out through a wicket in the entrance - gate, which he closed behind him with such bolts and chains as would well have become that of a prison.

'By St. Dunstan,' said Gurth, as he stumbled up the dark avenue, 'this is no Jewess, but an angel from heaven! Ten zecchins from my brave young master—twenty from this pearl of Zion—Oh, happy day!—Such another, Gurth, will redeem thy bondage, and make thee a brother as free of thy guild as the best. And then do I lay down my swineherd's horn and staff, and take the freeman's sword and buckler, and follow my young master to the death, without hiding either my face or my name.'

CHAPTER XI

1st Outlaw. *Stand, sir, and throw us that you have about you;*
If not, we'll make you sit, and rifle you.
Speed. *Sir, we are undone! these are the villains*
That all the travellers do fear so much.
Val. *My friends,——*
1st Out. *That's not so, sir, we are your enemies.*
2nd Out. *Peace! we'll hear him.*
3rd Out. *Ay, by my beard, will we;*
For he's a proper man.

                                    Two Gentlemen of Verona.

THE nocturnal adventures of Gurth were not yet
concluded; indeed he himself became partly of that
mind, when, after passing one or two straggling
houses which stood in the outskirts of the village,
he found himself in a deep lane, running between
two banks overgrown with hazel and holly, while
here and there a dwarf oak flung its arms altogether
across the path. The lane was moreover much
rutted and broken up by the carriages which had
recently transported articles of various kinds to
the tournament; and it was dark, for the banks
and bushes intercepted the light of the harvest
moon.

From the village were heard the distant sounds
of revelry, mixed occasionally with loud laughter,
sometimes broken by screams, and sometimes by
wild strains of distant music. All these sounds,

intimating the disorderly state of the town, crowded with military nobles and their dissolute attendants, gave Gurth some uneasiness. 'The Jewess was right,' he said to himself. 'By heaven and St. Dunstan, I would I were safe at my journey's end with all this treasure! Here are such numbers, I will not say of arrant thieves, but of errant knights and errant squires, errant monks and errant minstrels, errant jugglers and errant jesters, that a man with a single merk would be in danger, much more a poor swineherd with a whole bagful of zecchins. Would I were out of the shade of these infernal bushes, that I might at least see any of St. Nicholas's clerks before they spring on my shoulders.'

Gurth accordingly hastened his pace, in order to gain the open common to which the lane led, but was not so fortunate as to accomplish his object. Just as he had attained the upper end of the lane, where the underwood was thickest, four men sprung upon him, even as his fears anticipated, two from each side of the road, and seized him so fast, that resistance, if at first practicable, would have been now too late.—'Surrender your charge,' said one of them; 'we are the deliverers of the common-wealth, who ease every man of his burden.'

'You should not ease me of mine so lightly,' muttered Gurth, whose surly honesty could not be tamed even by the pressure of immediate violence, —'had I it but in my power to give three strokes in its defence.'

'We shall see that presently,' said the robber;

and, speaking to his companions, he added, 'bring along the knave. I see he would have his head broken, as well as his purse cut, and so be let blood in two veins at once.'

Gurth was hurried along agreeably to this mandate, and having been dragged somewhat roughly over the bank, on the left-hand side of the lane, found himself in a straggling thicket, which lay betwixt it and the open common. He was compelled to follow his rough conductors into the very depth of this cover, where they stopt unexpectedly in an irregular open space, free in a great measure from trees, and on which, therefore, the beams of the moon fell without much interruption from boughs and leaves. Here his captors were joined by two other persons, apparently belonging to the gang. They had short swords by their sides, and quarter-staves in their hands, and Gurth could now observe that all six wore visors, which rendered their occupation a matter of no question, even had their former proceedings left it in doubt.

'What money hast thou, churl?' said one of the thieves.

'Thirty zecchins of my own property,' answered Gurth, doggedly.

'A forfeit—a forfeit,' shouted the robbers; 'a Saxon hath thirty zecchins, and returns sober from a village! An undeniable and unredeemable forfeit of all he hath about him.'

'I hoarded it to purchase my freedom,' said Gurth.

'Thou art an ass,' replied one of the thieves;

'three quarts of double ale had rendered thee as free as thy master, ay, and freer too, if he be a Saxon like thyself.'

'A sad truth,' replied Gurth; 'but if these same thirty zecchins will buy my freedom from you, unloose my hands, and I will pay them to you.'

'Hold,' said one who seemed to exercise some authority over the others; 'this bag which thou bearest, as I can feel through thy cloak, contains more coin than thou hast told us of.'

'It is the good knight my master's,' answered Gurth, 'of which, assuredly, I would not have spoken a word, had you been satisfied with working your will upon mine own property.'

'Thou art an honest fellow,' replied the robber, 'I warrant thee; and we worship not St. Nicholas so devoutly but what thy thirty zecchins may yet escape, if thou deal uprightly with us. Meantime render up thy trust for the time.' So saying, he took from Gurth's breast the large leathern pouch, in which the purse given him by Rebecca, was enclosed, as well as the rest of the zecchins, and then continued his interrogation. — 'Who is thy master?'

'The Disinherited Knight,' said Gurth.

'Whose good lance,' replied the robber, 'won the prize in to-day's tourney? What is his name and lineage?'

'It is his pleasure,' answered Gurth, 'that they be concealed; and from me, assuredly, you will learn nought of them.'

'What is thine own name and lineage?'

'To tell that,' said Gurth, 'might reveal my master's.'

'Thou art a saucy groom,' said the robber, 'but of that anon. How comes thy master by this gold? is it of his inheritance, or by what means hath it accrued to him?'

'By his good lance,' answered Gurth.—'These bags contain the ransom of four good horses, and four good suits of armour.'

'How much is there?' demanded the robber.

'Two hundred zecchins.'

'Only two hundred zecchins!' said the bandit; 'your master hath dealt liberally by the vanquished, and put them to a cheap ransom. Name those who paid the gold.'

Gurth did so.

'The armour and horse of the Templar Brian de Bois-Guilbert, at what ransom were they held? —Thou seest thou canst not deceive me.'

'My master,' replied Gurth, 'will take nought from the Templar save his life's-blood. They are on terms of mortal defiance, and cannot hold courteous intercourse together.'

'Indeed!'— repeated the robber, and paused after he had said the word. 'And what wert thou now doing at Ashby with such a charge in thy custody?'

'I went thither to render to Isaac the Jew of York,' replied Gurth, 'the price of a suit of armour with which he fitted my master for this tournament.'

'And how much didst thou pay to Isaac?—

Methinks, to judge by weight, there is still two hundred zecchins in this pouch.'

'I paid to Isaac,' said the Saxon, 'eighty zecchins, and he restored me a hundred in lieu thereof.'

'How! what!' exclaimed all the robbers at once; 'darest thou trifle with us, that thou tellest such improbable lies?'

'What I tell you,' said Gurth, 'is as true as the moon is in heaven. You will find the just sum in a silken purse within the leathern pouch, and separate from the rest of the gold.'

'Bethink thee, man,' said the Captain; 'thou speakest of a Jew—of an Israelite,—as unapt to restore gold, as the dry sand of his deserts to return the cup of water which the pilgrim spills upon them.'

'There is no more mercy in them,' said another of the banditti, 'than in an unbribed sheriff's officer.'

'It is, however, as I say,' said Gurth.

'Strike a light instantly,' said the Captain; 'I will examine this said purse; and if it be as this fellow says, the Jew's bounty is little less miraculous than the stream which relieved his fathers in the wilderness.'

A light was procured accordingly, and the robber proceeded to examine the purse. The others crowded around him, and even two who had hold of Gurth relaxed their grasp while they stretched their necks to see the issue of the search. Availing himself of their negligence, by a sudden exertion of strength and activity, Gurth shook himself free of their hold, and might have escaped, could he have resolved to leave his master's property behind him. But such was no part of his intention. He wrenched a quarter-staff from one of the fellows, struck down the Captain, who was altogether unaware of his purpose, and had wellnigh repossessed himself of the pouch and treasure. The thieves, however, were too nimble for him, and again secured both the bag and the trusty Gurth.

'Knave!' said the Captain, getting up, 'thou hast broken my head; and with other men of our sort thou wouldst fare the worse for thy insolence. But thou shalt know thy fate instantly. First let us speak of thy master; the knight's matters must go before the squire's, according to the due order of chivalry. Stand thou fast in the meantime — if thou stir again, thou shalt have that will make thee quiet for thy life — Comrades!' he then said, addressing his gang, 'this purse is embroidered with Hebrew characters, and I well believe the yeoman's tale is true. The errant knight, his master, must needs pass us toll-free. He is too like ourselves for us to make booty of him, since dogs should not worry dogs where wolves and foxes are to be found in abundance.'

'Like us?' answered one of the gang; 'I should like to hear how that is made good.'

'Why, thou fool,' answered the Captain, 'is he not poor and disinherited as we are?—Doth he not win his substance at the sword's point as we do?— Hath he not beaten Front-de-Bœuf and Malvoisin,

172

even as we would beat them if we could? Is he
not the enemy to life and death of Brian de Bois-
Guilbert, whom we have so much reason to fear?
And were all this otherwise, wouldst thou have
us show a worse conscience than an unbeliever,
a Hebrew Jew?'

'Nay, that were a shame,' muttered the other
fellow; 'and yet, when I served in the band of
stout old Gandelyn, we had no such scruples of
conscience. And this insolent peasant,—he too,
I warrant me, is to be dismissed scatheless?'

'Not if *thou* canst scathe him,' replied the
Captain. — 'Here, fellow,' continued he, addressing Gurth, 'canst thou use the staff, that thou
starts to it so readily?'

'I think,' said Gurth, 'thou shouldst be best able
to reply to that question.'

'Nay, by my troth, thou gavest me a round
knock,' replied the Captain; 'do as much for this
fellow, and thou shalt pass scot-free; and if thou
dost not—why, by my faith, as thou art such a
sturdy knave, I think I must pay thy ransom
myself.—Take thy staff, Miller,' he added, 'and
keep thy head; and do you others let the fellow
go, and give him a staff—there is light enough
to lay on load by.'

The two champions being alike armed with
quarter-staves, stepped forward into the centre
of the open space, in order to have the full benefit
of the moonlight; the thieves in the meantime
laughing, and crying to their comrade, 'Miller!
beware thy toll-dish.' The Miller, on the other

hand, holding his quarter-staff by the middle, and making it flourish round his head after the fashion which the French call *faire le moulinet*, exclaimed boastfully, 'Come on, churl, an thou darest: thou shalt feel the strength of a miller's thumb!'

'If thou be'st a miller,' answered Gurth, undauntedly, making his weapon play around his head with equal dexterity, 'thou art doubly a thief, and I, as a true man, bid thee defiance.'

So saying, the two champions closed together, and for a few minutes they displayed great equality in strength, courage, and skill, intercepting and returning the blows of their adversary with the most rapid dexterity, while, from the continued clatter of their weapons, a person at a distance might have supposed that there were at least six persons engaged on each side. Less obstinate, and even less dangerous combats, have been described in good heroic verse; but that of Gurth and the Miller must remain unsung, for want of a sacred poet to do justice to its eventful progress. Yet, though quarter-staff play be out of date, what we can in prose we will do for these bold champions.

Long they fought equally, until the Miller began to lose temper at finding himself so stoutly opposed, and at hearing the laughter of his companions, who, as usual in such cases, enjoyed his vexation. This was not a state of mind favourable to the noble game of quarter-staff, in which, as in ordinary cudgel-playing, the utmost coolness is requisite; and it gave Gurth, whose temper was steady, though surly, the opportunity of acquiring a decided advantage, in availing himself of which he displayed great mastery.

The Miller pressed furiously forward, dealing blows with either end of his weapon alternately, and striving to come to half-staff distance, while Gurth defended himself against the attack, keeping his hands about a yard asunder, and covering himself by shifting his weapon with great celerity, so as to protect his head and body. Thus did he maintain the defensive, making his eye, foot, and hand keep true time, until, observing his antagonist to lose wind, he darted the staff at his face with his left hand; and, as the Miller endeavoured to parry the thrust, he slid his right hand down to his left, and with the full swing of the weapon struck his opponent on the left side of the head, who instantly measured his length upon the green sward.

'Well and yeomanly done!' shouted the robbers; 'fair play and Old England for ever! The Saxon hath saved both his purse and his hide, and the Miller has met his match.'

'Thou mayst go thy ways, my friend,' said the Captain, addressing Gurth, in special confirmation of the general voice, 'and I will cause two of my comrades to guide thee by the best way to thy master's pavilion, and to guard thee from night-walkers that might have less tender consciences than ours; for there is many one of them upon the amble in such a night as this. Take heed, however,' he added sternly; 'remember thou hast refused to tell thy name—ask not after ours, nor endeavour to discover who or what we are; for, if thou makest such an attempt, thou wilt come by worse fortune than has yet befallen thee.'

Gurth thanked the Captain for his courtesy, and promised to attend to his recommendation. Two of the outlaws, taking up their quarter-staves, and desiring Gurth to follow close in the rear, walked roundly forward along a by-path, which traversed the thicket and the broken ground adjacent to it. On the very verge of the thicket two men spoke to his conductors, and receiving an answer in a whisper, withdrew into the wood, and suffered them to pass unmolested. This circumstance induced Gurth to believe both that the gang was strong in numbers, and that they kept regular guards around their place of rendezvous.

When they arrived on the open heath, where Gurth might have had some trouble in finding his road, the thieves guided him straight forward to the top of a little eminence, whence he could see, spread beneath him in the moonlight, the palisades of the lists, the glimmering pavilions pitched at either end, with the pennons which adorned them fluttering in the moonbeam, and from which could be heard the hum of the song with which the sentinels were beguiling their night-watch.

Here the thieves stopt.

'We go with you no farther,' said they; 'it were not safe that we should do so.—Remember the warning you have received—keep secret what has this night befallen you, and you will have no room to repent it—neglect what is now told you, and the Tower of London shall not protect you against our revenge.'

'Good night to you, kind sirs,' said Gurth; 'I shall remember your orders, and trust that there is no offence in wishing you a safer and an honester trade.'

Thus they parted, the outlaws returning in the direction from whence they had come, and Gurth proceeding to the tent of his master, to whom, notwithstanding the injunction he had received, he communicated the whole adventures of the evening.

The Disinherited Knight was filled with astonishment, no less at the generosity of Rebecca, by which, however, he resolved he would not profit, than that of the robbers, to whose profession such a quality seemed totally foreign. His course of reflections upon these singular circumstances was, however, interrupted by the necessity for taking repose, which the fatigue of the preceding day, and the propriety of refreshing himself for the morrow's encounter, rendered alike indispensable.

The knight, therefore, stretched himself for repose upon a rich couch with which the tent was provided; and the faithful Gurth, extending his hardy limbs upon a bear-skin which formed a sort of carpet to the pavilion, laid himself across the opening of the tent, so that no one could enter without awakening him.

CHAPTER XII

The heralds left their pricking up and down
Now ringen trumpets loud and clarion.
There is no more to say, but east and west,
In go the speares sadly in the rest,
In goth the sharp spur into the side,
There see men who can just and who can ride;
There shiver shaftes upon shieldes thick,
He feeleth through the heart-spone the prick;
Up springen speares, twenty feet in height,
Out go the swordes to the silver bright;
The helms they to-hewn and to-shred;
Out burst the blood with stern streames red.

CHAUCER.

MORNING arose in unclouded splendour, and ere the sun was much above the horizon, the idlest or the most eager of the spectators appeared on the common, moving to the lists as to a general centre, in order to secure a favourable situation for viewing the continuation of the expected games.

The marshals and their attendants appeared next on the field, together with the heralds, for the purpose of receiving the names of the knights who intended to just, with the side which each chose to espouse. This was a necessary precaution, in order to secure equality betwixt the two bodies who should be opposed to each other.

According to due formality, the Disinherited Knight was to be considered as leader of the one body, while Brian de Bois-Guilbert, who had been rated as having done second-best in the preceding day, was named first champion of the other band. Those who had concurred in the challenge adhered to his party, of course, excepting only Ralph de Vipont, whom his fall had rendered unfit so soon to put on his armour. There was no want of distinguished and noble candidates to fill up the ranks on either side.

In fact, although the general tournament, in which all knights fought at once, was more dangerous than single encounters, they were, nevertheless, more frequented and practised by the chivalry of the age. Many knights, who had not sufficient confidence in their own skill to defy a single adversary of high reputation, were, nevertheless, desirous of displaying their valour in the general combat, where they might meet others with whom they were more upon an equality. On the present occasion, about fifty knights were inscribed as desirous of combating upon each side, when the marshals declared that no more could be admitted, to the disappointment of several who were too late in preferring their claim to be included.

About the hour of ten o'clock, the whole plain was crowded with horsemen, horsewomen, and foot-passengers, hastening to the tournament; and shortly after, a grand flourish of trumpets announced Prince John and his retinue, attended by many of those knights who meant to take share in the game, as well as others who had no such intention.

About the same time arrived Cedric the Saxon, with the Lady Rowena, unattended, however, by Athelstane. This Saxon lord had arrayed his tall and strong person in armour, in order to take his place among the combatants; and, considerably to the surprise of Cedric, had chosen to enlist himself on the part of the Knight Templar. The Saxon, indeed, had remonstrated strongly with his friend upon the injudicious choice he had made of his party; but he had only received that sort of answer usually given by those who are more obstinate in following their own course, than strong in justifying it.

His best, if not his only reason, for adhering to the party of Brian de Bois-Guilbert, Athelstane had the prudence to keep to himself. Though his apathy of disposition prevented his taking any means to recommend himself to the Lady Rowena, he was, nevertheless, by no means insensible to her charms, and considered his union with her as a matter already fixed beyond doubt, by the assent of Cedric and her other friends. It had therefore been with smothered displeasure that the proud though indolent Lord of Coningsburgh beheld the victor of the preceding day select Rowena as the object of that honour which it became his privilege to confer. In order to punish him for a preference which seemed to interfere with his own suit, Athelstane, confident of his strength, and to whom his flatterers, at least, ascribed great skill in arms, had determined not only to deprive the Disinherited Knight of his powerful succour, but, if an opportunity should occur, to make him feel the weight of his battle-axe.

De Bracy, and other knights attached to Prince John, in obedience to a hint from him, had joined the party of the challengers, John being desirous to secure, if possible, the victory to that side. On the other hand, many other knights, both English and Norman, natives and strangers, took part against the challengers, the more readily that the opposite band was to be led by so distinguished a champion as the Disinherited Knight had approved himself.

As soon as Prince John observed that the destined Queen of the day had arrived upon the field, assuming that air of courtesy which sat well upon him when he was pleased to exhibit it, he rode forward to meet her, doffed his bonnet, and, alighting from his horse, assisted the Lady Rowena from her saddle, while his followers uncovered at the same time, and one of the most distinguished dismounted to hold her palfrey.

'It is thus,' said Prince John, 'that we set the dutiful example of loyalty to the Queen of Love and Beauty, and are ourselves her guide to the throne which she must this day occupy.—Ladies,' he said, 'attend your Queen, as you wish in your turn to be distinguished by like honours.'

So saying, the Prince marshalled Rowena to the seat of honour opposite his own, while the fairest and most distinguished ladies present crowded after her to obtain places as near as possible to their temporary sovereign.

No sooner was Rowena seated, than a burst of

music, half-drowned by the shouts of the multitude, greeted her new dignity. Meantime, the sun shone fierce and bright upon the polished arms of the knights of either side, who crowded the opposite extremities of the lists, and held eager conference together concerning the best mode of arranging their line of battle, and supporting the conflict.

The heralds then proclaimed silence until the laws of the tourney should be rehearsed. These were calculated in some degree to abate the dangers of the day; a precaution the more necessary, as the conflict was to be maintained with sharp swords and pointed lances.

The champions were therefore prohibited to thrust with the sword, and were confined to striking. A knight, it was announced, might use a mace or battle-axe at pleasure, but the dagger was a prohibited weapon. A knight unhorsed might renew the fight on foot with any other on the opposite side in the same predicament; but mounted horsemen were in that case forbidden to assail him. When any knight could force his antagonist to the extremity of the lists, so as to touch the palisade with his person or arms, such opponent was obliged to yield himself vanquished, and his armour and horse were placed at the disposal of the conqueror. A knight thus overcome was not permitted to take farther share in the combat. If any combatant was struck down, and unable to recover his feet, his squire or page might enter the lists, and drag his master out of the press; but in that case the knight was adjudged vanquished, and his arms and horse declared forfeited. The combat was to cease as soon as Prince John should throw down his leading staff, or truncheon; another precaution usually taken to prevent the unnecessary effusion of blood by the too long endurance of a sport so desperate. Any knight breaking the rules of the tournament, or otherwise transgressing the rules of honourable chivalry, was liable to be stript of his arms, and, having his shield reversed to be placed in that posture astride upon the bars of the palisade, and exposed to public derision, in punishment of his unknightly conduct. Having announced these precautions, the heralds concluded with an exhortation to each good knight to do his duty, and to merit favour from the Queen of Beauty and of Love.

This proclamation having been made, the heralds withdrew to their stations. The knights, entering at either end of the lists in long procession, arranged themselves in a double file, precisely opposite to each other, the leader of each party being in the centre of the foremost rank, a post which he did not occupy until each had carefully marshalled the ranks of his party, and stationed every one in his place.

It was a goodly, and at the same time an anxious, sight, to behold so many gallant champions, mounted bravely, and armed richly, stand ready prepared for an encounter so formidable, seated on their war-saddles like so many pillars of iron, and awaiting the signal of encounter with the same ardour as their generous steeds, which, by neighing and pawing the ground, gave signal of their impatience.

IVANHOE

As yet the knights held their long lances upright, their bright points glancing to the sun, and the streamers with which they were decorated fluttering over the plumage of the helmets. Thus they remained while the marshals of the field surveyed their ranks with the utmost exactness, lest either party had more or fewer than the appointed number. The tale was found exactly complete. The marshals then withdrew from the lists, and William de Wyvil, with a voice of thunder, pronounced the signal words — *Laissez aller !* The trumpets sounded as he spoke—the spears of the champions were at once lowered and placed in the rests—the spurs were dashed into the flanks of the horses, and the two foremost ranks of either party rushed upon each other in full gallop, and met in the middle of the lists with a shock, the sound of which was heard at a mile's distance. The rear rank of each party advanced at a slower pace to sustain the defeated, and follow up the success of the victors of their party.

The consequences of the encounter were not instantly seen, for the dust raised by the trampling of so many steeds darkened the air, and it was a minute ere the anxious spectators could see the fate of the encounter. When the fight became visible, half the knights on each side were dismounted, some by the dexterity of their adversary's lance, —some by the superior weight and strength of opponents, which had borne down both horse and man,—some lay stretched on earth as if never more to rise,—some had already gained their feet, and were closing hand to hand with those of their antagonists who were in the same predicament,— and several on both sides, who had received wounds by which they were disabled, were stopping their blood with their scarfs, and endeavouring to extricate themselves from the tumult. The mounted knights, whose lances had been almost all broken by the fury of the encounter, were now closely engaged with their swords, shouting their war-cries, and exchanging buffets, as if honour and life depended on the issue of the combat.

The tumult was presently increased by the advance of the second rank on either side, which, acting as a reserve, now rushed on to aid their companions. The followers of Brian de Bois-Guilbert shouted—'*Ha! Beau-seant! Beau-seant!** —For the Temple—For the Temple!' The opposite party shouted in answer—'*Desdichado! Desdichado!*' —which watchword they took from the motto upon their leader's shield.

The champions thus encountering each other with the utmost fury, and with alternate success, the tide of battle seemed to flow now toward the southern, now toward the northern extremity of the lists, as the one or the other party prevailed. Meantime the clang of the blows, and the shouts of the combatants, mixed fearfully with the sound of the trumpets, and drowned the groans of those who

---

* *Beau-seant* was the name of the Templars' banner, which was half black, half white, to intimate, it is said, that they were candid and fair towards Christians, but black and terrible towards infidels.

fell, and lay rolling defenceless beneath the feet of the horses. The splendid armour of the combatants was now defaced with dust and blood, and gave way at every stroke of the sword and battle-axe. The gay plumage, shorn from the crests, drifted upon the breeze like snow-flakes. All that was beautiful and graceful in the martial array had disappeared, and what was now visible was only calculated to awake terror or compassion.

Yet such is the force of habit, that not only the vulgar spectators, who are naturally attracted by sights of horror, but even the ladies of distinction, who crowded the galleries, saw the conflict with a thrilling interest certainly, but without a wish to withdraw their eyes from a sight so terrible. Here and there, indeed, a fair cheek might turn pale, or a faint scream might be heard, as a lover, a brother, or a husband, was struck from his horse. But, in general, the ladies around encouraged the combatants, not only by clapping their hands and waving their veils and kerchiefs, but even by exclaiming, 'Brave lance! Good sword!' when any successful thrust or blow took place under their observation.

Such being the interest taken by the fair sex in this bloody game, that of the men is the more easily understood. It showed itself in loud acclamations upon every change of fortune, while all eyes were so riveted on the lists, that the spectators seemed as if they themselves had dealt and received the blows which were there so freely bestowed. And between every pause was heard the voice of the heralds, exclaiming, 'Fight on, brave knights!

Man dies, but glory lives!—Fight on—death is better than defeat!—Fight on, brave knights!—for bright eyes behold your deeds!'

Amid the varied fortunes of the combat, the eyes of all endeavoured to discover the leaders of each band, who, mingling in the thick of the fight, encouraged their companions both by voice and example. Both displayed great feats of gallantry, nor did either Bois-Guilbert or the Disinherited Knight find in the ranks opposed to them a champion who could be termed their unquestioned match. They repeatedly endeavoured to single out each other, spurred by mutual animosity, and aware that the fall of either leader might be considered as decisive of victory. Such, however, was the crowd and confusion, that, during the earlier part of the conflict, their efforts to meet were unavailing, and they were repeatedly separated by the eagerness of their followers, each of whom was anxious to win honour, by measuring his strength against the leader of the opposite party.

But when the field became thin by the numbers on either side who had yielded themselves vanquished, had been compelled to the extremity of the lists, or been otherwise rendered incapable of continuing the strife, the Templar and the Disinherited Knight at length encountered hand to hand, with all the fury that mortal animosity, joined to rivalry of honour, could inspire. Such was the address of each in parrying and striking, that the spectators broke forth into a unanimous and involuntary shout, expressive of their delight and admiration.

But at this moment the party of the Disinherited Knight had the worst; the gigantic arm of Front-de-Bœuf on the one flank, and the ponderous strength of Athelstane on the other, bearing down and dispersing those immediately exposed to them. Finding themselves freed from their immediate antagonists, it seems to have occurred to both these knights at the same instant, that they would render the most decisive advantage to their party, by aiding the Templar in his contest with his rival. Turning their horses, therefore, at the same moment, the Norman spurred against the Disinherited Knight on the one side, and the Saxon on the other. It was utterly impossible that the object of this unequal and unexpected assault could have sustained it, had he not been warned by a general cry from the spectators, who could not but take interest in one exposed to such disadvantage.

‘ Beware ! beware ! Sir Disinherited ! ’ was shouted so universally, that the knight became aware of his danger ; and, striking a full blow at the Templar, he reined back his steed in the same moment, so as to escape the charge of Athelstane and Front-de-Bœuf. These knights, therefore, their aim being thus eluded, rushed from opposite sides betwixt the object of their attack and the Templar, almost running their horses against each other ere they could stop their career. Recovering their horses, however, and wheeling them round, the whole three pursued their united purpose of bearing to the earth the Disinherited Knight.

Nothing could have saved him, except the remarkable strength and activity of the noble horse which he had won on the preceding day.

This stood him in the more stead, as the horse of Bois-Guilbert was wounded, and those of Front-de-Bœuf and Athelstane were both tired with the weight of their gigantic masters, clad in complete armour, and with the preceding exertions of the day. The masterly horsemanship of the Disinherited Knight, and the activity of the noble animal which he mounted, enabled him for a few minutes to keep at sword's point his three antagonists, turning and wheeling with the agility of a hawk upon the wing, keeping his enemies as far separate as he could, and rushing now against the one, now against the other, dealing sweeping blows with his sword, without waiting to receive those which were aimed at him in return.

But although the lists rang with the applauses of his dexterity, it was evident that he must at last be overpowered; and the nobles around Prince John implored him with one voice to throw down his warder, and to save so brave a knight from the disgrace of being overcome by odds.

'Not I, by the light of Heaven!' answered Prince John; 'this same springal, who conceals his name, and despises our proffered hospitality, hath already gained one prize, and may now afford to let others have their turn.' As he spoke thus, an unexpected incident changed the fortune of the day.

There was among the ranks of the Disinherited Knight a champion in black armour, mounted on a black horse, large of size, tall, and to all appearance powerful and strong, like the rider by whom he was mounted. This knight, who bore on his shield no device of any kind, had hitherto evinced very little interest in the event of the fight, beating off with seeming ease those combatants who attacked him, but neither pursuing his advantages, nor himself assailing any one. In short, he had hitherto acted the part rather of a spectator than of a party in the tournament, a circumstance which procured him among the spectators the name of *Le Noir Faineant*, or the Black Sluggard.

At once this knight seemed to throw aside his apathy, when he discovered the leader of his party so hard bestead; for, setting spurs to his horse, which was quite fresh, he came to his assistance like a thunderbolt, exclaiming, in a voice like a trumpet-call, '*Desdichado*, to the rescue!' It was high time; for, while the Disinherited Knight was pressing upon the Templar, Front-de-Bœuf had got nigh to him with his uplifted sword; but ere the blow could descend, the Sable Knight dealt a stroke on his head, which, glancing from the polished helmet, lighted with violence scarcely abated on the *chamfron* of the steed, and Front-de-Bœuf rolled on the ground, both horse and man equally stunned by the fury of the blow. *Le Noir Faineant* then turned his horse upon Athelstane of Coningsburgh; and his own sword having been broken in his encounter with Front-de-Bœuf, he

wrenched from the hand of the bulky Saxon the
battle-axe which he wielded, and, like one familiar
with the use of the weapon, bestowed him such a
blow upon the crest, that Athelstane also lay senseless on the field. Having achieved this double
feat, for which he was the more highly applauded
that it was totally unexpected from him, the knight
seemed to resume the sluggishness of his character,
returning calmly to the northern extremity of the
lists, leaving his leader to cope as he best could
with Brian de Bois-Guilbert. This was no longer
matter of so much difficulty as formerly. The
Templar's horse had bled much, and gave way
under the shock of the Disinherited Knight's
charge. Brian de Bois-Guilbert rolled on the field,
encumbered with the stirrup, from which he was
unable to draw his foot. His antagonist sprung
from horseback, waved his fatal sword over the
head of his adversary, and commanded him to yield
himself; when Prince John, more moved by the
Templar's dangerous situation than he had been
by that of his rival, saved him the mortification of
confessing himself vanquished, by casting down his
warder, and putting an end to the conflict.

It was, indeed, only the relics and embers of the
fight which continued to burn; for of the few
knights who still continued in the lists, the greater
part had, by tacit consent, forborne the conflict for
some time, leaving it to be determined by the strife
of the leaders.

The squires, who had found it a matter of danger
and difficulty to attend their masters during the

engagement, now thronged into the lists to pay their dutiful attendance to the wounded, who were removed with the utmost care and attention to the neighbouring pavilions, or to the quarters prepared for them in the adjoining village.

Thus ended the memorable field of Ashby-de-la-Zouche, one of the most gallantly contested tournaments of that age; for although only four knights, including one who was smothered by the heat of his armour, had died upon the field, yet upwards of thirty were desperately wounded, four or five of whom never recovered. Several more were disabled for life; and those who escaped best carried the marks of the conflict to the grave with them. Hence it is always mentioned in the old records, as the Gentle and Joyous Passage of Arms of Ashby.

It being now the duty of Prince John to name the knight who had done best, he determined that the honour of the day remained with the knight whom the popular voice had termed *Le Noir Faineant*. It was pointed out to the Prince, in impeachment of this decree, that the victory had been in fact won by the Disinherited Knight, who, in the course of the day, had overcome six champions with his own hand, and who had finally unhorsed and struck down the leader of the opposite party. But Prince John adhered to his own opinion, on the ground that the Disinherited Knight and his party had lost the day, but for the powerful assistance of the Knight of the Black Armour, to whom, therefore, he persisted in awarding the prize.

To the surprise of all present, however, the knight thus preferred was nowhere to be found. He had left the lists immediately when the conflict ceased, and had been observed by some spectators to move down one of the forest glades with the same slow pace and listless and indifferent manner which had procured him the epithet of the Black Sluggard. After he had been summoned twice by sound of trumpet, and proclamation of the heralds, it became necessary to name another to receive the honours which had been assigned to him. Prince John had now no further excuse for resisting the claim of the Disinherited Knight, whom, therefore, he named the champion of the day.

Through a field slippery with blood, and encumbered with broken armour and the bodies of slain and wounded horses, the marshals of the lists again conducted the victor to the foot of Prince John's throne.

'Disinherited Knight,' said Prince John, 'since by that title only you will consent to be known to us, we a second time award to you the honours of this tournament, and announce to you your right to claim and receive from the hands of the Queen of Love and Beauty, the Chaplet of Honour which your valour has justly deserved.' The Knight bowed low and gracefully, but returned no answer.

While the trumpets sounded, while the heralds strained their voices in proclaiming honour to the brave and glory to the victor—while ladies waved their silken kerchiefs and embroidered veils, and while all ranks joined in a clamorous shout of exultation, the marshals conducted the Disinherited Knight across the lists to the foot of that throne of honour which was occupied by the Lady Rowena.

On the lower step of this throne the champion was made to kneel down. Indeed his whole action since the fight had ended, seemed rather to have been upon the impulse of those around him than from his own free will; and it was observed that he tottered as they guided him the second time across the lists. Rowena, descending from her station with a graceful and dignified step, was about to place the chaplet which she held in her hand upon the helmet of the champion, when the marshals exclaimed with one voice, 'It must not be thus — his head must be bare.' The knight muttered faintly a few words, which were lost in the hollow of his helmet, but their purport seemed to be a desire that his casque might not be removed.

Whether from love of form, or from curiosity, the marshals paid no attention to his expressions of reluctance, but unhelmed him by cutting the laces of his casque, and undoing the fastening of his gorget. When the helmet was removed, the well-formed, yet sun-burnt features of a young man of twenty-five were seen, amidst a profusion of short fair hair. His countenance was as pale as death, and marked in one or two places with streaks of blood.

Rowena had no sooner beheld him than she uttered a faint shriek; but at once summoning up the energy of her disposition, and compelling herself, as it were, to proceed, while her frame yet trembled with the violence of sudden emotion, she placed upon the drooping head of the victor the splendid chaplet which was the destined reward of the day, and pronounced, in a clear and distinct tone, these words: ' I bestow on thee this chaplet, Sir Knight, as the meed of valour assigned to this day's victor': Here she paused a moment, and then firmly added, ' And upon brows more worthy could a wreath of chivalry never be placed!'

The knight stooped his head, and kissed the hand of the lovely Sovereign by whom his valour had been rewarded; and then, sinking yet farther forward, lay prostrate at her feet.

There was a general consternation. Cedric, who had been struck mute by the sudden appearance of his banished son, now rushed forward, as if to separate him from Rowena. But this had been already accomplished by the marshals of the field, who, guessing the cause of Ivanhoe's swoon, had hastened to undo his armour, and found that the head of a lance had penetrated his breastplate, and inflicted a wound in his side.

CHAPTER XIII

' Heroes, approach !'   Atrides thus aloud,
' Stand forth distinguish'd from the circling crowd,
Ye who by skill or manly force may claim,
Your rivals to surpass and merit fame.
This cow, worth twenty oxen, is decreed,
For him who farthest sends the winged reed.'

ILIAD.

THE name of Ivanhoe was no sooner pronounced
than it flew from mouth to mouth, with all the
celerity with which eagerness could convey and
curiosity receive it. It was not long ere it reached
the circle of the Prince, whose brow darkened as he
heard the news. Looking around him, however,
with an air of scorn, 'My lords,' said he, 'and
especially you, Sir Prior, what think ye of the
doctrine the learned tell us, concerning innate
attractions and antipathies? Methinks that I
felt the presence of my brother's minion, even
when I least guessed whom yonder suit of armour
enclosed.'

'Front-de-Bœuf must prepare to restore his fief
of Ivanhoe,' said De Bracy, who, having discharged
his part honourably in the tournament, had laid his
shield and helmet aside, and again mingled with
the Prince's retinue.

'Ay,' answered Waldemar Fitzurse, 'this gallant

There was a general consternation.

is likely to reclaim the castle and manor which Richard assigned to him, and which your Highness's generosity has since given to Front-de-Bœuf.'

'Front-de-Bœuf,' replied John, 'is a man more willing to swallow three manors such as Ivanhoe, than to disgorge one of them. For the rest, sirs, I hope none here will deny my right to confer the fiefs of the crown upon the faithful followers who are around me, and ready to perform the usual military service, in the room of those who have wandered to foreign countries, and can neither render homage nor service when called upon.'

The audience were too much interested in the question not to pronounce the Prince's assumed right altogether indubitable. 'A generous Prince! —a most noble Lord, who thus takes upon himself the task of rewarding his faithful followers!'

Such were the words which burst from the train, expectants all of them of similar grants at the expense of King Richard's followers and favourites, if indeed they had not as yet received such. Prior Aymer also assented to the general proposition, observing, however, 'That the blessed Jerusalem could not indeed be termed a foreign country. She was *communis mater*—the mother of all Christians. But he saw not,' he declared, 'how the Knight of Ivanhoe could plead any advantage from this, since he' (the Prior) 'was assured that the crusaders, under Richard, had never proceeded much farther than Askalon, which, as all the world knew, was a town of the Philistines, and entitled to none of the privileges of the Holy City.'

Waldemar, whose curiosity had led him towards the place where Ivanhoe had fallen to the ground, now returned. 'The gallant,' said he, 'is likely to give your Highness little disturbance, and to leave Front-de-Bœuf in the quiet possession of his gains—he is severely wounded.'

'Whatever becomes of him,' said Prince John, 'he is victor of the day; and were he tenfold our enemy, or the devoted friend of our brother, which is perhaps the same, his wounds must be looked to —our own physician shall attend him.'

A stern smile curled the Prince's lip as he spoke. Waldemar Fitzurse hastened to reply, that Ivanhoe was already removed from the lists, and in the custody of his friends.

'I was somewhat afflicted,' he said, 'to see the grief of the Queen of Love and Beauty, whose sovereignty of a day this event has changed into mourning. I am not a man to be moved by a woman's lament for her lover, but this same Lady Rowena suppressed her sorrow with such dignity of manner, that it could only be discovered by her folded hands, and her tearless eye, which trembled as it remained fixed on the lifeless form before her.'

'Who is this Lady Rowena,' said Prince John, 'of whom we have heard so much?'

'A Saxon heiress of large possessions,' replied the Prior Aymer; 'a rose of loveliness, and a jewel of wealth; the fairest among a thousand, a bundle of myrrh, and a cluster of camphire.'

'We shall cheer her sorrows,' said Prince John, 'and amend her blood, by wedding her to a Norman.

She seems a minor, and must therefore be at our royal disposal in marriage.—How sayst thou, De Bracy? What thinkst thou of gaining fair lands and livings, by wedding a Saxon, after the fashion of the followers of the Conqueror?'

'If the lands are to my liking, my lord,' answered De Bracy, 'it will be hard to displease me with a bride; and deeply will I hold myself bound to your highness for a good deed, which will fulfil all promises made in favour of your servant and vassal.'

'We will not forget it,' said Prince John; 'and that we may instantly go to work, command our seneschal presently to order the attendance of the Lady Rowena and her company—that is, the rude churl her guardian, and the Saxon ox whom the Black Knight struck down in the tournament, upon this evening's banquet.—De Bigot,' he added to his seneschal, 'thou wilt word this our second summons so courteously, as to gratify the pride of these Saxons, and make it impossible for them again to refuse; although, by the bones of Becket, courtesy to them is casting pearls before swine.'

Prince John had proceeded thus far, and was about to give the signal for retiring from the lists, when a small billet was put into his hand.

'From whence?' said Prince John, looking at the person by whom it was delivered.

'From foreign parts, my lord, but from whence I know not,' replied his attendant. 'A Frenchman brought it hither, who said, he had ridden night and day to put it into the hands of your highness.'

199

The Prince looked narrowly at the superscription, and then at the seal, placed so as to secure the flox-silk with which the billet was surrounded, and which bore the impression of three fleurs-de-lis. John then opened the billet with apparent agitation, which visibly and greatly increased when he had perused the contents, which were expressed in these words—

'*Take heed to yourself, for the Devil is unchained!*'

The Prince turned as pale as death, looked first on the earth, and then up to heaven, like a man who has received news that sentence of execution has been passed upon him. Recovering from the first effects of his surprise, he took Waldemar Fitzurse and De Bracy aside, and put the billet into their hands successively. 'It means,' he added, in a faltering voice, 'that my brother Richard has obtained his freedom.'

'This may be a false alarm, or a forged letter,' said De Bracy.

'It is France's own hand and seal,' replied Prince John.

'It is time, then,' said Fitzurse, 'to draw our party to a head, either at York, or some other centrical place. A few days later, and it will be indeed too late. Your highness must break short this present mummery.'

'The yeomen and commons,' said De Bracy, 'must not be dismissed discontented, for lack of their share in the sports.'

'The day,' said Waldemar, 'is not yet very far

spent—let the archers shoot a few rounds at the target, and the prize be adjudged. This will be an abundant fulfilment of the Prince's promises, so far as this herd of Saxon serfs is concerned.'

'I thank thee, Waldemar,' said the Prince; 'thou remindest me, too, that I have a debt to pay to that insolent peasant who yesterday insulted our person. Our banquet also shall go forward to-night as we proposed. Were this my last hour of power, it should be an hour sacred to revenge and to pleasure —let new cares come with to-morrow's new day.'

The sound of the trumpets soon recalled those spectators who had already begun to leave the field; and proclamation was made that Prince John, suddenly called by high and peremptory public duties, held himself obliged to discontinue the entertainments of to-morrow's festival : Nevertheless, that, unwilling so many good yeoman should depart without a trial of skill, he was pleased to appoint them, before leaving the ground, presently to execute the competition of archery intended for the morrow. To the best archer a prize was to be awarded, being a bugle-horn, mounted with silver, and a silken baldric richly ornamented with a medallion of St. Hubert, the patron of silvan sport.

More than thirty yeomen at first presented themselves as competitors, several of whom were rangers and under-keepers in the royal forests of Needwood and Charnwood. When, however, the archers understood with whom they were to be matched, upwards of twenty withdrew themselves from the contest, unwilling to encounter the dishonour of almost certain defeat. For in those days the skill of each celebrated marksman was as well known for many miles round him, as the qualities of a horse trained at Newmarket are familiar to those who frequent that well-known meeting.

The diminished list of competitors for silvan fame still amounted to eight. Prince John stepped from his royal seat to view more nearly the persons of these chosen yeomen, several of whom wore the royal livery. Having satisfied his curiosity by this investigation, he looked for the object of his resentment, whom he observed standing on the same spot, and with the same composed countenance which he had exhibited upon the preceding day.

'Fellow,' said Prince John, 'I guessed by thy insolent babble thou wert no true lover of the long-bow, and I see thou darest not adventure thy skill among such merry-men as stand yonder.'

'Under favour, sir,' replied the yeoman, 'I have another reason for refraining to shoot, besides the fearing discomfiture and disgrace.'

'And what is thy other reason?' said Prince John, who, for some cause which perhaps he could not himself have explained, felt a painful curiosity respecting this individual.

'Because,' replied the woodsman, 'I know not if these yeomen and I are used to shoot at the same marks; and because, moreover, I know not how your Grace might relish the winning of a third prize by one who has unwittingly fallen under your displeasure.'

Prince John coloured as he put the question, 'What is thy name, yeoman?'

'Locksley,' answered the yeoman.

'Then, Locksley,' said Prince John, 'thou shalt shoot in thy turn, when these yeomen have displayed their skill. If thou carriest the prize, I will add to it twenty nobles; but if thou losest it, thou shalt be stript of thy Lincoln green, and scourged out of the lists with bowstrings, for a wordy and insolent braggart.'

'And how if I refuse to shoot on such a wager?' said the yeoman.—'Your Grace's power, supported, as it is, by so many men-at-arms, may indeed easily strip and scourge me, but cannot compel me to bend or to draw my bow.'

'If thou refusest my fair proffer,' said the Prince, 'the Provost of the lists shall cut thy bowstring, break thy bow and arrows, and expel thee from the presence as a faint-hearted craven.'

'This is no fair chance you put on me, proud Prince,' said the yeoman, 'to compel me to peril myself against the best archers of Leicester and Staffordshire, under the penalty of infamy if they should overshoot me. Nevertheless, I will obey your pleasure.'

'Look to him close, men-at-arms,' said Prince John, 'his heart is sinking; I am jealous lest he attempt to escape the trial.—And do you, good fellows, shoot boldly round; a buck and a butt of wine are ready for your refreshment in yonder tent, when the prize is won.'

A target was placed at the upper end of the

southern avenue which led to the lists. The contending archers took their station in turn, at the bottom of the southern access; the distance between that station and the mark allowing full distance for what was called a shot at rovers. The archers, having previously determined by lot their order of precedence, were to shoot each three shafts in succession. The sports were regulated by an officer of inferior rank, termed the Provost of the Games; for the high rank of the marshals of the lists would have been held degraded, had they condescended to superintend the sports of the yeomanry.

One by one the archers, stepping forward, delivered their shafts yeomanlike and bravely. Of twenty-four arrows, shot in succession, ten were fixed in the target, and the others ranged so near it, that, considering the distance of the mark, it was accounted good archery. Of the ten shafts which hit the target, two within the inner ring were shot by Hubert, a forester in the service of Malvoisin, who was accordingly pronounced victorious.

' Now, Locksley,' said Prince John to the bold yeoman, with a bitter smile, ' wilt thou try conclusions with Hubert, or wilt thou yield up bow, baldric, and quiver, to the Provost of the sports ? '

' Sith it be no better,' said Locksley, ' I am content to try my fortune; on condition that when I have shot two shafts at yonder mark of Hubert's, he shall be bound to shoot one at that which I shall propose.'

' That is but fair,' answered Prince John, ' and it shall not be refused thee.—If thou dost beat this braggart, Hubert, I will fill the bugle with silver pennies for thee.'

'A man can do but his best,' answered Hubert; 'but my grandsire drew a good long bow at Hastings, and I trust not to dishonour his memory.'

The former target was now removed, and a fresh one of the same size placed in its room. Hubert, who, as victor in the first trial of skill, had the right to shoot first, took his aim with great deliberation, long measuring the distance with his eye, while he held in his hand his bended bow, with the arrow placed on the string. At length he made a step forward, and raising the bow at the full stretch of his left arm, till the centre or grasping-place was nigh level with his face, he drew his bowstring to his ear. The arrow whistled through the air, and lighted within the inner ring of the target, but not exactly in the centre.

'You have not allowed for the wind, Hubert,' said his antagonist, bending his bow, 'or that had been a better shot.'

So saying, and without showing the least anxiety to pause upon his aim, Locksley stept to the appointed station, and shot his arrow as carelessly in appearance as if he had not even looked at the mark. He was speaking almost at the instant that the shaft left the bowstring, yet it alighted in the target two inches nearer to the white spot which marked the centre than that of Hubert.

'By the light of heaven!' said Prince John to Hubert, 'an thou suffer that runagate knave to overcome thee, thou art worthy of the gallows!'

Hubert had but one set speech for all occasions. 'An your highness were to hang me,' he said, 'a man can but do his best. Nevertheless, my grandsire drew a good bow——'

'The foul fiend on thy grandsire and all his generation!' interrupted John; 'shoot, knave, and shoot thy best, or it shall be the worse for thee!'

Thus exhorted, Hubert resumed his place, and not neglecting the caution which he had received from his adversary, he made the necessary allowance for a very light air of wind, which had just arisen, and shot so successfully that his arrow alighted in the very centre of the target.

'A Hubert! a Hubert!' shouted the populace, more interested in a known person than in a stranger. 'In the clout!—in the clout!—a Hubert for ever!'

'Thou canst not mend that shot, Locksley,' said the Prince, with an insulting smile.

'I will notch his shaft for him, however,' replied Locksley.

And letting fly his arrow with a little more precaution than before, it lighted right upon that of his competitor, which it split to shivers. The people who stood around were so astonished at his wonderful dexterity, that they could not even give vent to their surprise in their usual clamour. 'This must be the devil, and no man of flesh and blood,' whispered the yeomen to each other; 'such archery was never seen since a bow was first bent in Britain.'

'And now,' said Locksley, 'I will crave your

Grace's permission to plant such a mark as is used in the North Country; and welcome every brave yeoman who shall try a shot at it to win a smile from the bonny lass he loves best.'

He then turned to leave the lists. 'Let your guards attend me,' he said, 'if you please—I go but to cut a rod from the next willow-bush.'

Prince John made a signal that some attendants should follow him in case of his escape : but the cry of 'Shame! shame!' which burst from the multitude, induced him to alter his ungenerous purpose.

Locksley returned almost instantly with a willow wand about six feet in length, perfectly straight, and rather thicker than a man's thumb. He began to peel this with great composure, observing at the same time, that to ask a good woodsman to shoot at a target so broad as had hitherto been used, was to put shame upon his skill. 'For his own part,' he said, 'and in the land where he was bred, men would as soon take for their mark King Arthur's round-table, which held sixty knights around it. A child of seven years old,' he said, 'might hit yonder target with a headless shaft; but,' added he, walking deliberately to the other end of the lists, and sticking the willow wand upright in the ground, 'he that hits that rod at five-score yards, I call him an archer fit to bear both bow and quiver before a king, an it were the stout King Richard himself.'

'My grandsire,' said Hubert, 'drew a good bow at the battle of Hastings, and never shot at such a mark in his life—and neither will I. If this yeoman can cleave that rod, I give him the bucklers—or rather, I yield to the devil that is in his jerkin, and not to any human skill; a man can but do his best, and I will not shoot where I am sure to miss. I might as well shoot at the edge of our parson's whittle, or at a wheat straw, or at a sunbeam, as at a twinkling white streak, which I can hardly see.'

'Cowardly dog!' said Prince John. — 'Sirrah Locksley, do thou shoot; but, if thou hittest such a mark, I will say thou art the first man ever did so. Howe'er it be, thou shalt not crow over us with a mere show of superior skill.'

'I will do my best, as Hubert says,' answered Locksley; 'no man can do more.'

So saying, he again bent his bow, but on the present occasion looked with attention to his weapon, and changed the string, which he thought was no longer truly round, having been a little frayed by the two former shots. He then took his aim with some deliberation, and the multitude awaited the event in breathless silence. The archer vindicated their opinion of his skill: his arrow split the willow rod against which it was aimed. A jubilee of acclamations followed; and even Prince John, in admiration of Locksley's skill, lost for an instant his dislike to his person. 'These twenty nobles,' he said, 'which, with the bugle, thou hast fairly won, are thine own; we will make them fifty, if thou wilt take livery and service with us as a yeoman of our body guard, and be near to our person. For never did so strong a hand bend a bow, or so true an eye direct a shaft.'

'Pardon me, noble Prince,' said Locksley; 'but I have vowed, that if ever I take service, it should be with your royal brother King Richard. These twenty nobles I leave to Hubert, who has this day drawn as brave a bow as his grandsire did at Hastings. Had his modesty not refused the trial, he would have hit the wand as well as I.'

Hubert shook his head as he received with reluctance the bounty of the stranger; and Locksley, anxious to escape further observation, mixed with the crowd, and was seen no more.

The victorious archer would not perhaps have escaped John's attention so easily, had not that Prince had other subjects of anxious and more important meditation pressing upon his mind at that instant. He called upon his chamberlain as he gave the signal for retiring from the lists, and commanded him instantly to gallop to Ashby, and seek out Isaac the Jew. 'Tell the dog,' he said, 'to send me, before sun-down, two thousand crowns. He knows the security; but thou mayst show him this ring for a token. The rest of the money must be paid at York within six days. If he neglects, I will have the unbelieving villain's head. Look that thou pass him not on the way; for the circumcised slave was displaying his stolen finery amongst us.'

So saying, the Prince resumed his horse, and returned to Ashby, the whole crowd breaking up and dispersing upon his retreat.

CHAPTER XIV

In rough magnificence array'd,
When ancient Chivalry display'd
The pomp of her heroic games,
And crested chiefs and tissued dames
Assembled, at the clarion's call,
In some proud castle's high-arch'd hall.

WARTON.

PRINCE JOHN held his high festival in the Castle of Ashby. This was not the same building of which the stately ruins still interest the traveller, and which was erected at a later period by the Lord Hastings, High Chamberlain of England, one of the first victims of the tyranny of Richard the Third, and yet better known as one of Shakspeare's characters than by his historical fame. The castle and town of Ashby, at this time, belonged to Roger de Quincy, Earl of Winchester, who, during the period of our history, was absent in the Holy Land. Prince John, in the meanwhile, occupied his castle, and disposed of his domains without scruple; and seeking at present to dazzle men's eyes by his hospitality and magnificence, had given orders for great preparations, in order to render the banquet as splendid as possible.

The purveyors of the Prince, who exercised on this and other occasions the full authority of royalty, had swept the country of all that could be collected which was esteemed fit for their master's table. Guests also were invited in great numbers; and in the necessity in which he then found himself of courting popularity, Prince John had extended his invitation to a few distinguished Saxon and Danish families, as well as to the Norman nobility and gentry of the neighbourhood. However despised and degraded on ordinary occasions, the great numbers of the Anglo-Saxons must necessarily render them formidable in the civil commotions which seemed approaching, and it was an obvious point of policy to secure popularity with their leaders.

It was accordingly the Prince's intention, which he for some time maintained, to treat these unwonted guests with a courtesy to which they had been little accustomed. But although no man with less scruple made his ordinary habits and feelings bend to his interest, it was the misfortune of this Prince, that his levity and petulance were perpetually breaking out, and undoing all that had been gained by his previous dissimulation.

Of this fickle temper he gave a memorable example in Ireland, when sent thither by his father, Henry the Second, with the purpose of buying golden opinions of the inhabitants of that new and important acquisition to the English crown. Upon this occasion the Irish chieftains contended which should first offer to the young Prince their loyal homage and the kiss of peace. But, instead of receiving their salutations with courtesy, John and his petulant attendants could not resist the temptation of pulling the long beards of the Irish chieftains; a conduct which, as might have been expected, was highly resented by these insulted dignitaries, and produced fatal consequences to the English domination in Ireland. It is necessary to keep these inconsistencies of John's character in view, that the reader may understand his conduct during the present evening.

In execution of the resolution which he had formed during his cooler moments, Prince John received Cedric and Athelstane with distinguished courtesy, and expressed his disappointment, without resentment, when the indisposition of Rowena was alleged by the former as a reason for her not attending upon his gracious summons. Cedric and Athelstane were both dressed in the ancient Saxon garb, which, although not unhandsome in itself, and in the present instance composed of costly materials, was so remote in shape and appearance from that of the other guests, that Prince John took great credit to himself with Waldemar Fitzurse for refraining from laughter at a sight which the fashion of the day rendered ridiculous. Yet, in the eye of sober judgment, the short close tunic and long mantle of the Saxons was a more graceful, as well as a more convenient dress, than the garb of the Normans, whose under garment was a long doublet, so loose as to resemble a shirt or waggoner's frock, covered by a cloak of scanty dimensions, neither fit to defend the wearer from cold or from rain, and the only purpose of which appeared to be to display as much fur, embroidery, and jewellery work, as the ingenuity of the tailor could contrive to lay upon it. The Emperor Charlemagne, in whose reign they were first introduced, seems to have been very sensible of the inconveniences arising from the fashion of this garment. 'In Heaven's name,' said he, 'to what purpose serve these abridged cloaks? If we are in bed they are no cover, on horseback they are no protection from the wind and rain, and when seated, they do not guard our legs from the damp or the frost.'

Nevertheless, spite of this imperial objurgation, the short cloaks continued in fashion down to the time of which we treat, and particularly among the princes of the House of Anjoù. They were therefore in universal use among Prince John's courtiers; and the long mantle, which formed the upper garment of the Saxons, was held in proportional derision.

The guests were seated at a table which groaned under the quantity of good cheer. The numerous cooks who attended on the Prince's progress, having exerted all their art in varying the forms in which the ordinary provisions were served up, had succeeded almost as well as the modern professors of the culinary art in rendering them perfectly unlike their natural appearance. Besides these dishes of domestic origin, there were various delicacies brought from foreign parts, and a quantity of rich pastry, as well as of the simnel-bread and wastle cakes, which were only used at the tables of the highest nobility. The banquet was crowned with the richest wines, both foreign and domestic.

But, though luxurious, the Norman nobles were not, generally speaking, an intemperate race. While indulging themselves in the pleasures of the table, they aimed at delicacy, but avoided excess, and were apt to attribute gluttony and drunkenness to the vanquished Saxons, as vices peculiar to their inferior station. Prince John, indeed, and those who courted his pleasure by imitating his foibles, were apt to indulge to excess in the pleasures of the trencher and the goblet; and indeed it is well known that his death was occasioned by a surfeit upon peaches and new ale. His conduct, however, was an exception to the general manners of his countrymen.

With sly gravity, interrupted only by private signs to each other, the Norman knights and nobles beheld the ruder demeanour of Athelstane and Cedric at a banquet, to the form and fashion of which they were unaccustomed. And while their manners were thus the subject of sarcastic observation, the untaught Saxons unwittingly transgressed several of the arbitrary rules established for the regulation of society. Now, it is well known, that a man may with more impunity be guilty of an actual breach either of real good breeding or of good morals, than appear ignorant of the most minute point of fashionable etiquette. Thus Cedric, who dried his hands with a towel, instead of suffering the moisture to exhale by waving them gracefully in the air, incurred more ridicule than his companion Athelstane, when he swallowed to his own single share the whole of a large pasty composed of the most exquisite foreign delicacies, and termed at that time a *Karum-pie*. When, however, it was discovered, by a serious cross-examination, that the Thane of Coningsburgh (or Franklin, as the Normans termed him) had no idea what he had been devouring, and that he had taken the contents of the Karum-pie for larks and pigeons, whereas they were in fact beccaficoes and nightingales, his ignorance brought him in for an ample share of the ridicule which would have been more justly bestowed on his gluttony.

The long feast had at length its end; and, while the goblet circulated freely, men talked of the feats of the preceding tournament, — of the unknown victor in the archery games, of the Black Knight, whose self-denial had induced him to withdraw from the honours he had won,—and of the gallant Ivanhoe, who had so dearly bought the honours of the day. The topics were treated with military frankness, and the jest and laugh went round the hall. The brow of Prince John alone was over-clouded during these discussions; some overpowering care seemed agitating his mind, and it was only when he received occasional hints from his attendants, that he seemed to take interest in what was passing around him. On such occasions he would start up, quaff a cup of wine as if to raise his spirits, and then mingle in the conversation by some observation made abruptly or at random.

'We drink this beaker,' said he, 'to the health

of Wilfred of Ivanhoe, champion of this Passage
of Arms, and grieve that his wound renders him
absent from our board—Let all fill to the pledge,
and especially Cedric of Rotherwood, the worthy
father of a son so promising.'

'No, my lord,' replied Cedric, standing up, and
placing on the table his untasted cup, 'I yield not
the name of son to the disobedient youth, who at
once despises my commands, and relinquishes the
manners and customs of his fathers.'

''Tis impossible,' cried Prince John, with well-
feigned astonishment, 'that so gallant a knight
should be an unworthy or disobedient son!'

'Yet, my lord,' answered Cedric, 'so it is with
this Wilfred. He left my homely dwelling to
mingle with the gay nobility of your brother's court,
where he learned to do those tricks of horsemanship which you prize so highly. He left it contrary
to my wish and command; and in the days of
Alfred that would have been termed disobedience—
ay, and a crime severely punishable.'

'Alas!' replied Prince John, with a deep sigh
of affected sympathy, 'since your son was a follower of my unhappy brother, it need not be en-
quired where or from whom he learned the lesson
of filial disobedience.'

Thus spake Prince John, wilfully forgetting,
that of all the sons of Henry the Second, though
no one was free from the charge, he himself had
been most distinguished for rebellion and ingrati-
tude to his father.

'I think,' said he, after a moment's pause, 'that

my brother proposed to confer upon his favourite the rich manor of Ivanhoe.'

'He did endow him with it,' answered Cedric; 'nor is it my least quarrel with my son, that he stooped to hold, as a feudal vassal, the very domains which his fathers possessed in free and independent right.'

'We shall then have your willing sanction, good Cedric,' said Prince John, 'to confer this fief upon a person whose dignity will not be diminished by holding land of the British crown.—Sir Reginald Front-de-Bœuf,' he said, turning towards that Baron, 'I trust you will so keep the goodly Barony of Ivanhoe, that Sir Wilfred shall not incur his father's farther displeasure by again entering upon that fief.'

'By St. Anthony!' answered the black-brow'd giant, 'I will consent that your highness shall hold me a Saxon, if either Cedric or Wilfred, or the best that ever bore English blood, shall wrench from me the gift with which your highness has graced me.'

'Whoever shall call thee Saxon, Sir Baron,' replied Cedric, offended at a mode of expression by which the Normans frequently expressed their habitual contempt of the English, 'will do thee an honour as great as it is undeserved.'

Front-de-Bœuf would have replied, but Prince John's petulance and levity got the start.

'Assuredly,' said he, 'my lords, the noble Cedric speaks truth; and his race may claim precedence over us as much in the length of their pedigrees as in the longitude of their cloaks.'

'They go before us indeed in the field—as deer before dogs,' said Malvoisin.

'And with good right may they go before us—forget not,' said the Prior Aymer, 'the superior decency and decorum of their manners.'

'Their singular abstemiousness and temperance,' said De Bracy, forgetting the plan which promised him a Saxon bride.

'Together with the courage and conduct,' said Brian de Bois-Guilbert, 'by which they distinguished themselves at Hastings and elsewhere.'

While, with smooth and smiling cheek, the courtiers, each in turn, followed their Prince's example, and aimed a shaft of ridicule at Cedric, the face of the Saxon became inflamed with passion, and he glanced his eyes fiercely from one to another, as if the quick succession of so many injuries had prevented his replying to them in turn ; or, like a baited bull, who, surrounded by his tormentors, is at a loss to choose from among them the immediate object of his revenge. At length he spoke, in a voice half choked with passion ; and, addressing himself to Prince John as the head and front of the offence which he had received, 'Whatever,' he said, 'have been the follies and vices of our race, a Saxon would have been held *nidering*,'* (the most

---

* There was nothing accounted so ignominious among the Saxons as to merit this disgraceful epithet. Even William the Conqueror, hated as he was by them, continued to draw a considerable army of Anglo-Saxons to his standard, by threatening to stigmatize those who staid at home, as *nidering*. Bartholinus, I think, mentions a similar phrase which had like influence on the Danes.—L. T.

emphatic term for abject worthlessness,) 'who should in his own hall, and while his own wine-cup passed, have treated, or suffered to be treated, an unoffending guest as your highness has this day beheld me used; and whatever was the misfortune of our fathers on the field of Hastings, those may at least be silent,' here he looked at Front-de-Bœuf and the Templar, 'who have within these few hours once and again lost saddle and stirrup before the lance of a Saxon.'

'By my faith, a biting jest!' said Prince John. 'How like you it, sirs?—Our Saxon subjects rise in spirit and courage; become shrewd in wit, and bold in bearing, in these unsettled times — What say ye, my lords?—By this good light, I hold it best to take our galleys, and return to Normandy in time.'

'For fear of the Saxons?' said De Bracy, laughing; 'we should need no weapon but our hunting spears to bring these boars to bay.'

'A truce with your raillery, Sir Knights,' said Fitzurse;—'and it were well,' he added, addressing the Prince, 'that your highness should assure the worthy Cedric there is no insult intended him by jests, which must sound but harshly in the ear of a stranger.'

'Insult?' answered Prince John, resuming his courtesy of demeanour; 'I trust it will not be thought that I could mean, or permit any, to be offered in my presence. Here! I fill my cup to Cedric himself, since he refuses to pledge his son's health.'

IVANHOE

The cup went round amid the well-dissembled applause of the courtiers, which, however, failed to make the impression on the mind of the Saxon that had been designed. He was not naturally acute of perception, but those too much undervalued his understanding who deemed that this flattering compliment would obliterate the sense of the prior insult. He was silent, however, when the royal pledge again passed round, 'To Sir Athelstane of Coningsburgh.'

The knight made his obeisance, and showed his sense of the honour by draining a huge goblet in answer to it.

'And now, sirs,' said Prince John, who began to be warmed with the wine which he had drank, 'having done justice to our Saxon guests, we will pray of them some requital to our courtesy.— Worthy Thane,' he continued, addressing Cedric, 'may we pray you to name to us some Norman whose mention may least sully your mouth, and to wash down with a goblet of wine all bitterness which the sound may leave behind it?'

Fitzurse arose while Prince John spoke, and gliding behind the seat of the Saxon, whispered to him not to omit the opportunity of putting an end to unkindness betwixt the two races, by naming Prince John. The Saxon replied not to this politic insinuation, but, rising up, and filling his cup to the brim, he addressed Prince John in these words: 'Your highness has required that I should name a Norman deserving to be remembered at our banquet. This, perchance, is a hard task, since it

calls on the slave to sing the praises of the master—
upon the vanquished, while pressed by all the evils
of conquest, to sing the praises of the conqueror.
Yet I *will* name a Norman—the first in arms and
in place—the best and the noblest of his race. And
the lips that shall refuse to pledge me to his well-
earned fame, I term false and dishonoured, and will
so maintain them with my life.—I quaff this goblet
to the health of Richard the Lion-hearted!'

Prince John, who had expected that his own
name would have closed the Saxon's speech, started
when that of his injured brother was so unexpectedly introduced. He raised mechanically the
wine-cup to his lips, then instantly set it down, to
view the demeanour of the company at this unexpected proposal, which many of them felt it as
unsafe to oppose as to comply with. Some of them,
ancient and experienced courtiers, closely imitated
the example of the Prince himself, raising the
goblet to their lips, and again replacing it before
them. There were many who, with a more generous feeling, exclaimed, 'Long live King Richard!
and may he be speedily restored to us!' And some
few, among whom were Front-de-Bœuf and the
Templar, in sullen disdain suffered their goblets
to stand untasted before them. But no man
ventured directly to gainsay a pledge filled to the
health of the reigning monarch.

Having enjoyed his triumph for about a minute,
Cedric said to his companion, 'Up, noble Athelstane! we have remained here long enough, since
we have requited the hospitable courtesy of Prince

John's banquet. Those who wish to know further of our rude Saxon manners must henceforth seek us in the homes of our fathers, since we have seen enough of royal banquets, and enough of Norman courtesy.'

So saying, he arose and left the banqueting room, followed by Athelstane, and by several other guests, who, partaking of the Saxon lineage, held themselves insulted by the sarcasms of Prince John and his courtiers.

'By the bones of St. Thomas,' said Prince John, as they retreated, 'the Saxon churls have borne off the best of the day, and have retreated with triumph!'

'*Conclamatum est, poculatum est,*' said Prior Aymer; 'we have drunk and we have shouted,— it were time we left our wine flagons.'

'The monk hath some fair penitent to shrive to-night, that he is in such a hurry to depart,' said De Bracy.

'Not so, Sir Knight,' replied the Abbot; 'but I must move several miles forward this evening upon my homeward journey.'

'They are breaking up,' said the Prince in a whisper to Fitzurse; 'their fears anticipate the event, and this coward Prior is the first to shrink from me.'

'Fear not, my lord,' said Waldemar; 'I will show him such reasons as shall induce him to join us when we hold our meeting at York.—Sir Prior,' he said, 'I must speak with you in private, before you mount your palfrey.'

The other guests were now fast dispersing, with the exception of those immediately attached to Prince John's faction, and his retinue.

'This, then, is the result of your advice,' said the Prince, turning an angry countenance upon Fitzurse; 'that I should be bearded at my own board by a drunken Saxon churl, and that, on the mere sound of my brother's name, men should fall off from me as if I had the leprosy?'

'Have patience, sir,' replied his counsellor; 'I might retort your accusation, and blame the inconsiderate levity which foiled my design, and misled your own better judgment. But this is no time for recrimination. De Bracy and I will instantly go among these shuffling cowards, and convince them they have gone too far to recede.'

'It will be in vain,' said Prince John, pacing the apartment with disordered steps, and expressing himself with an agitation to which the wine he had drank partly contributed—'It will be in vain —they have seen the handwriting on the wall— they have marked the paw of the lion in the sand —they have heard his approaching roar shake the wood—nothing will reanimate their courage.'

'Would to God,' said Fitzurse to De Bracy, 'that aught could reanimate his own! His brother's very name is an ague to him. Unhappy are the counsellors of a Prince, who wants fortitude and perseverance alike in good and in evil!'

CHAPTER XV

And yet he thinks,—ha, ha, ha, ha,—he thinks
I am the tool and servant of his will.
Well, let it be; through all the maze of trouble
His plots and base oppression must create,
I'll shape myself a way to higher things,
And who will say 'tis wrong?

BASIL, A TRAGEDY.

No spider ever took more pains to repair the shattered meshes of his web, than did Waldemar Fitzurse to reunite and combine the scattered members of Prince John's cabal. Few of these were attached to him from inclination, and none from personal regard. It was therefore necessary, that Fitzurse should open to them new prospects of advantage, and remind them of those which they at present enjoyed. To the young and wild nobles, he held out the prospect of unpunished license and uncontrolled revelry; to the ambitious, that of power, and to the covetous, that of increased wealth and extended domains. The leaders of the mercenaries received a donation in gold; an argument the most persuasive to their minds, and without which all others would have proved in vain. Promises were still more liberally distributed than money by this active agent; and, in fine, nothing was left undone that could determine the wavering,

224

or animate the disheartened. The return of King Richard he spoke of as an event altogether beyond the reach of probability; yet, when he observed, from the doubtful looks and uncertain answers which he received, that this was the apprehension by which the minds of his accomplices were most haunted, he boldly treated that event, should it really take place, as one which ought not to alter their political calculations.

'If Richard returns,' said Fitzurse, 'he returns to enrich his needy and impoverished crusaders at the expense of those who did not follow him to the Holy Land. He returns to call to a fearful reckoning, those who, during his absence, have done aught that can be construed offence or encroachment upon either the laws of the land or the privileges of the crown. He returns to avenge upon the Orders of the Temple and the Hospital, the preference which they showed to Philip of France during the wars in the Holy Land. He returns, in fine, to punish as a rebel every adherent of his brother Prince John. Are ye afraid of his power?' continued the artful confident of that Prince; 'we acknowledge him a strong and valiant knight; but these are not the days of King Arthur, when a champion could encounter an army. If Richard indeed comes back, it must be alone,—unfollowed—unfriended. The bones of his gallant army have whitened the sands of Palestine. The few of his followers who have returned have straggled hither like this Wilfred of Ivanhoe, beggared and broken men.—And what talk ye of Richard's right of birth?' he proceeded, in answer to those who objected scruples on that head. 'Is Richard's title of primogeniture more decidedly certain than that of Duke Robert of Normandy, the Conqueror's eldest son? And yet William the Red, and Henry, his second and third brothers, were successively preferred to him by the voice of the nation. Robert had every merit which can be pleaded for Richard; he was a bold knight, a good leader, generous to his friends and to the church, and, to crown the whole, a crusader and a conqueror of the Holy Sepulchre; and yet he died a blind and miserable prisoner in the Castle of Cardiff, because he opposed himself to the will of the people, who chose that he should not rule over them. It is our right,' he said, 'to choose from the blood royal the prince who is best qualified to hold the supreme power—that is,' said he, correcting himself, 'him whose election will best promote the interests of the nobility. In personal qualifications,' he added, 'it was possible that Prince John might be inferior to his brother Richard; but when it was considered that the latter returned with the sword of vengeance in his hand, while the former held out rewards, immunities, privileges, wealth, and honours, it could not be doubted which was the king whom in wisdom the nobility were called on to support.'

These, and many more arguments, some adapted to the peculiar circumstances of those whom he addressed, had the expected weight with the nobles of Prince John's faction. Most of them consented to attend the proposed meeting at York, for the purpose of making general arrangements for placing the crown upon the head of Prince John.

It was late at night, when, worn out and exhausted with his various exertions, however gratified with the result, Fitzurse, returning to the Castle of Ashby, met with De Bracy, who had exchanged his banqueting garments for a short green kirtle, with hose of the same cloth and colour, a leathern cap or head-piece, a short sword, a horn slung over his shoulder, a long bow in his hand, and a bundle of arrows stuck in his belt. Had Fitzurse met this figure in an outer apartment, he would have passed him without notice, as one of the yeomen of the guard; but finding him in the inner hall, he looked at him with more attention, and recognised the Norman knight in the dress of an English yeoman.

'What mummery is this, De Bracy?' said Fitzurse, somewhat angrily; 'is this a time for Christmas gambols and quaint maskings, when the fate of our master, Prince John, is on the very verge of decision? Why hast thou not been, like me, among these heartless cravens, whom the very name of King Richard terrifies, as it is said to do the children of the Saracens?'

'I have been attending to mine own business,' answered De Bracy calmly, 'as you, Fitzurse, have been minding yours.'

'I minding mine own business!' echoed Waldemar; 'I have been engaged in that of Prince John, our joint patron.'

'As if thou hadst any other reason for that,

Waldemar,' said De Bracy, 'than the promotion of thine own individual interest? Come, Fitzurse, we know each other — ambition is thy pursuit, pleasure is mine, and they become our different ages. Of Prince John thou thinkest as I do; that he is too weak to be a determined monarch, too tyrannical to be an easy monarch, too insolent and presumptuous to be a popular monarch, and too fickle and timid to be long a monarch of any kind. But he is a monarch by whom Fitzurse and De Bracy hope to rise and thrive; and therefore you aid him with your policy, and I with the lances of my Free Companions.'

'A hopeful auxiliary,' said Fitzurse, impatiently; 'playing the fool in the very moment of utter necessity.—What on earth dost thou purpose by this absurd disguise at a moment so urgent?'

'To get me a wife,' answered De Bracy, coolly, 'after the manner of the tribe of Benjamin.'

'The tribe of Benjamin?' said Fitzurse; 'I comprehend thee not.'

'Wert thou not in presence yester-even,' said De Bracy, 'when we heard the Prior Aymer tell us a tale in reply to the romance which was sung by the Minstrel?—He told how, long since in Palestine, a deadly feud arose between the tribe of Benjamin and the rest of the Israelitish nation; and how they cut to pieces wellnigh all the chivalry of that tribe; and how they swore by our blessed Lady, that they would not permit those who remained to marry in their lineage; and how they became grieved for their vow, and sent to consult his holiness the Pope how they might be absolved from it; and how, by the advice of the Holy Father, the youth of the tribe of Benjamin carried off from a superb tournament all the ladies who were there present, and thus won them wives without the consent either of their brides or their brides' families.'

'I have heard the story,' said Fitzurse, 'though either the Prior or thou hast made some singular alterations in date and circumstances.'

'I tell thee,' said De Bracy, 'that I mean to purvey me a wife after the fashion of the tribe of Benjamin; which is as much as to say, that in this same equipment I will fall upon that herd of Saxon bullocks, who have this night left the castle, and carry off from them the lovely Rowena.'

'Art thou mad, De Bracy?' said Fitzurse. 'Bethink thee that, though the men be Saxons, they are rich and powerful, and regarded with the more respect by their countrymen, that wealth and honour are but the lot of few of Saxon descent.'

'And should belong to none,' said De Bracy; 'the work of the Conquest should be completed.'

'This is no time for it at least,' said Fitzurse; 'the approaching crisis renders the favour of the multitude indispensable, and Prince John cannot refuse justice to any one who injures their favourites.'

'Let him grant it, if he dare,' said De Bracy; 'he will soon see the difference betwixt the support of such a lusty lot of spears as mine, and that of a heartless mob of Saxon churls. Yet I mean no immediate discovery of myself. Seem I not in this garb as bold a forester as ever blew horn? The blame of the violence shall rest with the outlaws of the Yorkshire forests. I have sure spies on the Saxons' motions—To-night they sleep in the convent of Saint Wittol, or Withold, or whatever they call that churl of a Saxon Saint at Burton-on-Trent. Next day's march brings them within our reach, and, falcon-ways, we swoop on them at once. Presently after I will appear in mine own shape, play the courteous knight, rescue the unfortunate and afflicted fair one from the hands of the rude ravishers, conduct her to Front-de-Bœuf's Castle, or to Normandy, if it should be necessary, and produce her not again to her kindred until she be the bride and dame of Maurice de Bracy.'

'A marvellously sage plan,' said Fitzurse, 'and, as I think, not entirely of thine own device.—Come, be frank, De Bracy, who aided thee in the invention? and who is to assist in the execution? for, as I think, thine own band lies as far off as York.'

'Marry, if thou must needs know,' said De Bracy, 'it was the Templar Brian de Bois-Guilbert that shaped out the enterprise, which the adventure of the men of Benjamin suggested to me. He is to aid me in the onslaught, and he and his followers will personate the outlaws, from whom my valorous arm is, after changing my garb, to rescue the lady.'

'By my halidome,' said Fitzurse, 'the plan was worthy of your united wisdom! and thy prudence, De Bracy, is most especially manifested in the project of leaving the lady in the hands of thy worthy confederate. Thou mayst, I think, succeed in taking her from her Saxon friends, but how thou wilt rescue her afterwards from the clutches of Bois-Guilbert seems considerably more doubtful —He is a falcon well accustomed to pounce on a partridge, and to hold his prey fast.'

'He is a Templar,' said De Bracy, ' and cannot therefore rival me in my plan of wedding this heiress;—and to attempt aught dishonourable against the intended bride of De Bracy—By Heaven! were he a whole Chapter of his Order in his single person, he dared not do me such an injury!'

'Then since nought that I can say,' said Fitzurse, ' will put this folly from thy imagination, (for well I know the obstinacy of thy disposition,) at least waste as little time as possible—let not thy folly be lasting as well as untimely.'

'I tell thee,' answered De Bracy, 'that it will be the work of a few hours, and I shall be at York at the head of my daring and valorous fellows, as ready to support any bold design as thy policy can be to form one.—But I hear my comrades assembling, and the steeds stamping and neighing in the outer court.—Farewell.—I go, like a true knight, to win the smiles of beauty.'

'Like a true knight?' repeated Fitzurse, looking after him; ' like a fool, I should say, or like a child, who will leave the most serious and needful occupation, to chase the down of the thistle that drives past him.—But it is with such tools that I must work;—and for whose advantage?—For that of a

Prince as unwise as he is profligate, and as likely to be an ungrateful master as he has already proved a rebellious son and an unnatural brother. But he—he, too, is but one of the tools with which I labour; and, proud as he is, should he presume to separate his interest from mine, this is a secret which he shall soon learn.'

The meditations of the statesman were here interrupted by the voice of the Prince from an interior apartment, calling out, 'Noble Waldemar Fitzurse!' and, with bonnet doffed, the future Chancellor (for to such high preferment did the wily Norman aspire) hastened to receive the orders of the future sovereign.

CHAPTER XVI

Far in a wild, unknown to public view,
From youth to age a reverend hermit grew;
The moss his bed, the cave his humble cell,
His food the fruits, his drink the crystal well;
Remote from man, with God he pass'd his days,
Prayer all his business—all his pleasure praise.

PARNELL.

THE reader cannot have forgotten that the event of the tournament was decided by the exertions of an unknown knight, whom, on account of the passive and indifferent conduct which he had manifested on the former part of the day, the spectators had entitled, *Le Noir Faineant.* This knight had left the field abruptly when the victory was achieved; and when he was called upon to receive the reward of his valour, he was nowhere to be found. In the meantime, while summoned by heralds and by trumpets, the knight was holding his course northward, avoiding all frequented paths, and taking the shortest road through the woodlands. He paused for the night at a small hostelry lying out of the ordinary route, where, however, he obtained from a wandering minstrel news of the event of the tourney.

On the next morning the knight departed early, with the intention of making a long journey; the

233

condition of his horse, which he had carefully spared during the preceding morning, being such as enabled him to travel far without the necessity of much repose. Yet his purpose was baffled by the devious paths through which he rode, so that when evening closed upon him, he only found himself on the frontiers of the West Riding of Yorkshire. By this time both horse and man required refreshment, and it became necessary, moreover, to look out for some place in which they might spend the night, which was now fast approaching.

The place where the traveller found himself seemed unpropitious for obtaining either shelter or refreshment, and he was likely to be reduced to the usual expedient of knights-errant, who, on such occasions, turned their horses to graze, and laid themselves down to meditate on their lady-mistress, with an oak-tree for a canopy. But the Black Knight either had no mistress to meditate upon, or, being as indifferent in love as he seemed to be in war, was not sufficiently occupied by passionate reflections upon her beauty and cruelty, to be able to parry the effects of fatigue and hunger, and suffer love to act as a substitute for the solid comforts of a bed and supper. He felt dissatisfied, therefore, when, looking around, he found himself deeply involved in woods, through which indeed there were many open glades, and some paths, but such as seemed only formed by the numerous herds of cattle which grazed in the forest, or by the animals of chase, and the hunters who made prey of them.

The sun, by which the knight had chiefly

directed his course, had now sunk behind the
Derbyshire hills on his left, and every effort
which he might make to pursue his journey was
as likely to lead him out of his road as to advance
him on his route. After having in vain endeavoured to select the most beaten path, in hopes
it might lead to the cottage of some herdsman,
or the silvan lodge of a forester, and having repeatedly found himself totally unable to determine on a choice, the knight resolved to trust
to the sagacity of his horse; experience having,
on former occasions, made him acquainted with
the wonderful talent possessed by these animals
for extricating themselves and their riders on such
emergencies.

The good steed, grievously fatigued with so long
a day's journey under a rider cased in mail, had no
sooner found, by the slackened reins, that he was
abandoned to his own guidance, than he seemed
to assume new strength and spirit; and whereas
formerly he had scarce replied to the spur, otherwise than by a groan, he now, as if proud of the
confidence reposed in him, pricked up his ears,
and assumed, of his own accord, a more lively
motion. The path which the animal adopted
rather turned off from the course pursued by
the knight during the day; but as the horse
seemed confident in his choice, the rider abandoned himself to his discretion.

He was justified by the event; for the footpath
soon after appeared a little wider and more worn,
and the tinkle of a small bell gave the knight to

understand that he was in the vicinity of some chapel or hermitage.

Accordingly, he soon reached an open plat of turf, on the opposite side of which, a rock, rising abruptly from a gently sloping plain, offered its grey and weatherbeaten front to the traveller. Ivy mantled its sides in some places, and in others oaks and holly bushes, whose roots found nourishment in the cliffs of the crag, waved over the precipices below, like the plumage of the warrior over his steel helmet, giving grace to that whose chief expression was terror. At the bottom of the rock, and leaning, as it were, against it, was constructed a rude hut, built chiefly of the trunks of trees felled in the neighbouring forest, and secured against the weather by having its crevices stuffed with moss mingled with clay. The stem of a young fir-tree lopped of its branches, with a piece of wood tied across near the top, was planted upright by the door, as a rude emblem of the holy cross. At a little distance on the right hand, a fountain of the purest water trickled out of the rock, and was received in a hollow stone, which labour had formed into a rustic basin. Escaping from thence, the stream murmured down the descent by a channel which its course had long worn, and so wandered through the little plain to lose itself in the neighbouring wood.

Beside this fountain were the ruins of a very small chapel, of which the roof had partly fallen in. The building, when entire, had never been above

At the bottom of the rock . . . was constructed
a rude hut . . .

sixteen feet long by twelve feet in breadth, and the
roof, low in proportion, rested upon four concentric
arches which sprung from the four corners of the
building, each supported upon a short and heavy
pillar. The ribs of two of these arches remained,
though the roof had fallen down betwixt them ;
over the others it remained entire. The entrance
to this ancient place of devotion was under a very
low round arch, ornamented by several courses of
that zig-zag moulding, resembling shark's teeth,
which appears so often in the more ancient Saxon
architecture. A belfry rose above the porch on
four small pillars, within which hung the green and
weatherbeaten bell, the feeble sounds of which had
been some time before heard by the Black Knight.

The whole peaceful and quiet scene lay glimmering in twilight before the eyes of the traveller,
giving him good assurance of lodging for the night ;
since it was a special duty of those hermits who
dwelt in the woods, to exercise hospitality towards
benighted or bewildered passengers.

Accordingly, the knight took no time to consider
minutely the particulars which we have detailed,
but thanking Saint Julian (the patron of travellers)
who had sent him good harbourage, he leaped from
his horse and assailed the door of the hermitage
with the but of his lance, in order to arouse
attention and gain admittance.

It was some time before he obtained any answer,
and the reply, when made, was unpropitious.

'Pass on, whosoever thou art,' was the answer
given by a deep hoarse voice from within the hut,

'and disturb not the servant of God and St. Dunstan in his evening devotions.'

'Worthy father,' answered the knight, 'here is a poor wanderer bewildered in these woods, who gives thee the opportunity of exercising thy charity and hospitality.'

'Good brother,' replied the inhabitant of the hermitage, 'it has pleased Our Lady and St. Dunstan to destine me for the object of those virtues, instead of the exercise thereof. I have no provisions here which even a dog would share with me, and a horse of any tenderness of nurture would despise my couch—pass therefore on thy way, and God speed thee.'

'But how,' replied the knight, 'is it possible for me to find my way through such a wood as this, when darkness is coming on? I pray you, reverend father, as you are a Christian, to undo your door, and at least point out to me my road.'

'And I pray you, good Christian brother,' replied the anchorite, 'to disturb me no more. You have already interrupted one *pater*, two *aves*, and a *credo*, which I, miserable sinner that I am, should, according to my vow, have said before moonrise.'

'The road—the road!' vociferated the knight, 'give me directions for the road, if I am to expect no more from thee.'

'The road,' replied the hermit, 'is easy to hit. The path from the wood leads to a morass, and from thence to a ford, which, as the rains have abated, may now be passable. When thou hast crossed the ford, thou wilt take care of thy footing

up the left bank, as it is somewhat precipitous; and
the path, which hangs over the river, has lately, as
I learn, (for I seldom leave the duties of my chapel),
given way in sundry places. Thou wilt then keep
straight forward——'

'A broken path—a precipice—a ford, and a
morass!' said the knight, interrupting him,—'Sir
Hermit, if you were the holiest that ever wore
beard or told bead, you shall scarce prevail on me
to hold this road to-night. I tell thee, that thou,
who livest by the charity of the country—ill deserved, as I doubt it is—hast no right to refuse
shelter to the wayfarer when in distress. Either
open the door quickly, or, by the rood, I will beat
it down and make entry for myself.'

'Friend wayfarer,' replied the hermit, 'be not
importunate; if thou puttest me to use the carnal
weapon in mine own defence, it will be e'en the
worse for you.'

At this moment a distant noise of barking and
growling, which the traveller had for some time
heard, became extremely loud and furious, and
made the knight suppose that the hermit, alarmed
by his threat of making forcible entry, had called
the dogs who made this clamour to aid him in his
defence, out of some inner recess in which they had
been kennelled. Incensed at this preparation on
the hermit's part for making good his inhospitable
purpose, the knight struck the door so furiously
with his foot, that posts as well as staples shook
with violence.

The anchorite, not caring again to expose his door

to a similar shock, now called out aloud, 'Patience, patience—spare thy strength, good traveller, and I will presently undo the door, though, it may be, my doing so will be little to thy pleasure.'

The door accordingly was opened ; and the hermit, a large, strong-built man, in his sackcloth gown and hood, girt with a rope of rushes, stood before the knight. He had in one hand a lighted torch, or link, and in the other a baton of crab-tree, so thick and heavy, that it might well be termed a club. Two large shaggy dogs, half greyhound half mastiff, stood ready to rush upon the traveller as soon as the door should be opened. But when the torch glanced upon the lofty crest and golden spurs of the knight, who stood without, the hermit, altering probably his original intentions, repressed the rage of his auxiliaries, and, changing his tone to a sort of churlish courtesy, invited the knight to enter his hut, making excuse for his unwillingness to open his lodge after sunset, by alleging the multitude of robbers and outlaws who were abroad, and who gave no honour to Our Lady or St. Dunstan, nor to those holy men who spent life in their service.

'The poverty of your cell, good father,' said the knight, looking around him, and seeing nothing but a bed of leaves, a crucifix rudely carved in oak, a missal, with a rough-hewn table and two stools, and one or two clumsy articles of furniture—'the poverty of your cell should seem a sufficient defence against any risk of thieves, not to mention the aid of two trusty dogs, large and strong enough, I think, to pull down a stag, and of course, to match with most men.'

'The good keeper of the forest,' said the hermit, 'hath allowed me the use of these animals, to protect my solitude until the times shall mend.'

Having said this, he fixed his torch in a twisted branch of iron which served for a candlestick; and, placing the oaken trivet before the embers of the fire, which he refreshed with some dry wood, he placed a stool upon one side of the table, and beckoned to the knight to do the same upon the other.

They sat down, and gazed with great gravity at each other, each thinking in his heart that he had seldom seen a stronger or more athletic figure than was placed opposite to him.

'Reverend hermit,' said the knight, after looking long and fixedly at his host, 'were it not to interrupt your devout meditations, I would pray to know three things of your holiness; first, where I am to put my horse?—secondly, what I can have for supper?—thirdly, where I am to take up my couch for the night?'

'I will reply to you,' said the hermit, 'with my finger, it being against my rule to speak by words where signs can answer the purpose.' So saying, he pointed successively to two corners of the hut. 'Your stable,' said he, 'is there—your bed there; and,' reaching down a platter with two handfuls of parched pease upon it from the neighbouring shelf, and placing it upon the table, he added, 'your supper is here.'

The knight shrugged his shoulders, and leaving

the hut, brought in his horse, (which in the interim he had fastened to a tree,) unsaddled him with much attention, and spread upon the steed's weary back his own mantle.

The hermit was apparently somewhat moved to compassion by the anxiety as well as address which the stranger displayed in tending his horse; for, muttering something about provender left for the keeper's palfrey, he dragged out of a recess a bundle of forage, which he spread before the knight's charger, and immediately afterwards shook down a quantity of dried fern in the corner which he had assigned for the rider's couch. The knight returned him thanks for his courtesy; and, this duty done, both resumed their seats by the table, whereon stood the trencher of pease placed between them. The hermit, after a long grace, which had once been Latin, but of which original language few traces remained, excepting here and there the long rolling termination of some word or phrase, set example to his guest, by modestly putting into a very large mouth, furnished with teeth which might have ranked with those of a boar both in sharpness and whiteness, some three or four dried pease, a miserable grist as it seemed for so large and able a mill.

The knight, in order to follow so laudable an example, laid aside his helmet, his corslet, and the greater part of his armour, and showed to the hermit a head thick-curled with yellow hair, high features, blue eyes remarkably bright and sparkling, a mouth well formed, having an upper lip clothed with mustachoes darker than his hair, and bearing

altogether the look of a bold, daring, and enter-
prising man, with which his strong form well
corresponded.

The hermit, as if wishing to answer to the confidence of his guest, threw back his cowl, and
showed a round bullet head belonging to a man
in the prime of life. His close-shaven crown, surrounded by a circle of stiff curled black hair, had
something the appearance of a parish pinfold begirt
by its high hedge. The features expressed nothing
of monastic austerity, or of ascetic privations; on
the contrary, it was a bold bluff countenance, with
broad black eyebrows, a well-turned forehead, and
cheeks as round and vermilion as those of a
trumpeter, from which descended a long and curly
black beard. Such a visage, joined to the brawny
form of the holy man, spoke rather of sirloins and
haunches, than of pease and pulse. This incon-
gruity did not escape the guest. After he had with
great difficulty accomplished the mastication of a
mouthful of the dried pease, he found it absolutely
necessary to request his pious entertainer to furnish
him with some liquor; who replied to his request
by placing before him a large can of the purest
water from the fountain.

'It is from the well of St Dunstan,' said he,
'in which, betwixt sun and sun, he baptized five
hundred heathen Danes and Britons—blessed be
his name!' And applying his black beard to the
pitcher, he took a draught much more moderate in
quantity than his encomium seemed to warrant.

'It seems to me, reverend father,' said the knight,

'that the small morsels which you eat, together with this holy, but somewhat thin beverage, have thriven with you marvellously. You appear a man more fit to win the ram at a wrestling match, or the ring at a bout at quarter-staff, or the bucklers at a sword-play, than to linger out your time in this desolate wilderness, saying masses, and living upon parched pease and cold water.'

'Sir Knight,' answered the hermit, 'your thoughts, like those of the ignorant laity, are according to the flesh. It has pleased Our Lady and my patron saint to bless the pittance to which I restrain myself, even as the pulse and water was blessed to the children Shadrach, Meshech, and Abednego, who drank the same rather than defile themselves with the wine and meats which were appointed them by the King of the Saracens.'

'Holy father,' said the knight, 'upon whose countenance it hath pleased Heaven to work such a miracle, permit a sinful layman to crave thy name?'

'Thou mayst call me,' answered the hermit, 'the Clerk of Copmanhurst, for so I am termed in these parts—They add, it is true, the epithet holy, but I stand not upon that, as being unworthy of such addition.—And now, valiant knight, may I pray ye for the name of my honourable guest?'

'Truly,' said the knight, 'Holy Clerk of Copmanhurst, men call me in these parts the Black Knight,—many, sir, add to it the epithet of Sluggard, whereby I am no way ambitious to be distinguished.'

The hermit could scarcely forbear from smiling at his guest's reply.

'I see,' said he, 'Sir Sluggish Knight, that thou art a man of prudence and of counsel; and moreover, I see that my poor monastic fare likes thee not, accustomed, perhaps, as thou hast been, to the license of courts and of camps, and the luxuries of cities; and now I bethink me, Sir Sluggard, that when the charitable keeper of this forest-walk left these dogs for my protection, and also those bundles of forage, he left me also some food, which, being unfit for my use, the very recollection of it had escaped me amid my more weighty meditations.'

'I dare be sworn he did so,' said the knight; 'I was convinced that there was better food in the cell, Holy Clerk, since you first doffed your cowl.— Your keeper is ever a jovial fellow; and none who beheld thy grinders contending with these pease, and thy throat flooded with this ungenial element, could see thee doomed to such horse-provender and horse-beverage,' (pointing to the provisions upon the table,) 'and refrain from mending thy cheer. Let us see the keeper's bounty, therefore, without delay.'

The hermit cast a wistful look upon the knight, in which there was a sort of comic expression of hesitation, as if uncertain how far he should act prudently in trusting his guest. There was, however, as much of bold frankness in the knight's countenance as was possible to be expressed by features. His smile, too, had something in it irresistibly comic, and gave an assurance of faith and loyalty, with which his host could not refrain from sympathizing.

After exchanging a mute glance or two, the hermit went to the further side of the hut, and opened a hutch, which was concealed with great care and some ingenuity. Out of the recesses of a dark closet, into which this aperture gave admittance, he brought a large pasty baked in a pewter platter of unusual dimensions. This mighty dish he placed before his guest, who, using his poniard to cut it open, lost no time in making himself acquainted with its contents.

'How long is it since the good keeper has been here?' said the knight to his host, after having swallowed several hasty morsels of this reinforcement to the hermit's good cheer.

'About two months,' answered the father hastily.

'By the true Lord,' answered the knight, 'every thing in your hermitage is miraculous, Holy Clerk! for I would have been sworn that the fat buck which furnished this venison had been running on foot within the week.'

The hermit was somewhat discountenanced by this observation; and, moreover, he made but a poor figure while gazing on the diminution of the pasty, on which his guest was making desperate inroads; a warfare in which his previous profession of abstinence left him no pretext for joining.

'I have been in Palestine, Sir Clerk,' said the knight, stopping short of a sudden, 'and I bethink me it is a custom there that every host who enter-

246

tains a guest shall assure him of the wholesomeness of his food, by partaking of it along with him. Far be it from me to suspect so holy a man of aught inhospitable; nevertheless I will be highly bound to you would you comply with this Eastern custom.'

'To ease your unnecessary scruples, Sir Knight, I will for once depart from my rule,' replied the hermit. And as there were no forks in those days, his clutches were instantly in the bowels of the pasty.

The ice of ceremony being once broken, it seemed matter of rivalry between the guest and the entertainer which should display the best appetite; and although the former had probably fasted longest, yet the hermit fairly surpassed him.

'Holy Clerk,' said the Knight, when his hunger was appeased, 'I would gage my good horse yonder against a zecchin, that that same honest keeper to whom we are obliged for the venison has left thee a stoup of wine, or a runlet of canary, or some such trifle, by way of ally to this noble pasty. This would be a circumstance, doubtless, totally unworthy to dwell in the memory of so rigid an anchorite; yet, I think, were you to search yonder crypt once more, you would find that I am right in my conjecture.'

The hermit only replied by a grin; and returning to the hutch, he produced a leathern bottle, which might contain about four quarts. He also brought forth two large drinking cups, made out of the horn of the urus, and hooped with silver. Having made this goodly provision for washing down the supper, he seemed to think no farther ceremonious scruple necessary on his part; but filling both cups, and saying, in the Saxon fashion, ' *Waes hael,* Sir Sluggish Knight!' he emptied his own at a draught.

' *Drink hael,* Holy Clerk of Copmanhurst!' answered the warrior, and did his host reason in a similar brimmer.

'Holy Clerk,' said the stranger, after the first cup was thus swallowed, 'I cannot but marvel that a man possessed of such thews and sinews as thine, and who therewithal shows the talent of so goodly a trencher-man, should think of abiding by himself in this wilderness. In my judgment, you are fitter to keep a castle or a fort, eating of the fat and drinking of the strong, than to live here upon pulse and water, or even upon the charity of the keeper. At least, were I as thou, I should find myself both disport and plenty out of the king's deer. There is many a goodly herd in these forests, and a buck will never be missed that goes to the use of Saint Dunstan's chaplain.'

'Sir Sluggish Knight,' replied the Clerk, 'these are dangerous words, and I pray you to forbear them. I am true hermit to the king and law, and were I to spoil my liege's game, I should be sure of the prison, and, an my gown saved me not, were in some peril of hanging.'

'Nevertheless, were I as thou,' said the knight, 'I would take my walk by moonlight, when foresters and keepers were warm in bed, and ever and anon,—as I pattered my prayers,—I would let

fly a shaft among the herds of dun deer that feed in
the glades—Resolve me, Holy Clerk, hast thou
never practised such a pastime?'

'Friend Sluggard,' answered the hermit, 'thou
hast seen all that can concern thee of my house-
keeping, and something more than he deserves who
takes up his quarters by violence. Credit me, it is
better to enjoy the good which God sends thee,
than to be impertinently curious how it comes.
Fill thy cup, and welcome; and do not, I pray thee,
by further impertinent enquiries, put me to show
that thou couldst hardly have made good thy
lodging had I been earnest to oppose thee.'

'By my faith,' said the knight, 'thou makest
me more curious than ever! Thou art the most
mysterious hermit I ever met; and I will know
more of thee ere we part. As for thy threats,
know, holy man, thou speakest to one whose trade
it is to find out danger wherever it is to be met
with.'

'Sir Sluggish Knight, I drink to thee,' said the
hermit; 'respecting thy valour much, but deeming
wondrous slightly of thy discretion. If thou wilt
take equal arms with me, I will give thee, in all
friendship and brotherly love, such sufficing penance
and complete absolution, that thou shalt not for
the next twelve months sin the sin of excess of
curiosity.'

The knight pledged him, and desired him to name
his weapons.

'There is none,' replied the hermit, 'from the
scissors of Delilah, and the tenpenny nail of Jael,

to the scimitar of Goliath, at which I am not a match for thee—But, if I am to make the election, what sayst thou, good friend, to these trinkets?'

Thus speaking, he opened another hutch, and took out from it a couple of broadswords and bucklers, such as were used by the yeomanry of the period. The knight, who watched his motions, observed that this second place of concealment was furnished with two or three good long-bows, a crossbow, a bundle of bolts for the latter, and half-a-dozen sheaves of arrows for the former. A harp, and other matters of a very uncanonical appearance, were also visible when this dark recess was opened.

'I promise thee, brother Clerk,' said he, 'I will ask thee no more offensive questions. The contents of that cupboard are an answer to all my enquiries; and I see a weapon there' (here he stooped and took out the harp) 'on which I would more gladly prove my skill with thee, than at the sword and buckler.'

'I hope, Sir Knight,' said the hermit, 'thou hast given no good reason for thy surname of the Sluggard. I do promise thee I suspect thee grievously. Nevertheless, thou art my guest, and I will not put thy manhood to the proof without thine own free will. Sit thee down, then, and fill thy cup; let us drink, sing, and be merry. If thou knowest ever a good lay, thou shalt be welcome to a nook of pasty at Copmanhurst so long as I serve the chapel of St. Dunstan, which, please God, shall be till I change my grey covering for one of green turf. But come, fill a flagon, for it will crave some time to tune the harp; and nought pitches the voice and sharpens the ear like a cup of wine. For my part, I love to feel the grape at my very finger-ends before they make the harp-strings tinkle.' *

---

* THE JOLLY HERMIT.—All readers, however slightly acquainted with black letter, must recognise in the Clerk of Copmanhurst, Friar Tuck, the buxom Confessor of Robin Hood's gang, the Curtal Friar of Fountain's Abbey.

CHAPTER XVII

At eve, within yon studious nook,
I ope my brass-embossed book,
Portray'd with many a holy deed
Of martyrs crown'd with heavenly meed;
Then, as my taper waxes dim,
Chant, ere I sleep, my measured hymn.
*   *   *   *   *
Who but would cast his pomp away,
To take my staff and amice grey,
And to the world's tumultuous stage,
Prefer the peaceful HERMITAGE?

WARTON.

NOTWITHSTANDING the prescription of the genial
hermit, with which his guest willingly complied,
he found it no easy matter to bring the harp to
harmony.

'Methinks, holy father,' said he, 'the instrument
wants one string, and the rest have been somewhat
misused.'

'Ay, mark'st thou that?' replied the hermit;
'that shows thee a master of the craft. Wine and
wassail,' he added, gravely casting up his eyes—
'all the fault of wine and wassail!—I told Allan-a-
Dale, the northern minstrel, that he would damage
the harp if he touched it after the seventh cup, but
he would not be controlled—Friend, I drink to thy
successful performance.'

So saying, he took off his cup with much gravity,

at the same time shaking his head at the intemperance of the Scottish harper.

The knight, in the meantime, had brought the strings into some order, and after a short prelude, asked his host whether he would choose a *sirvente* in the language of *oc*, or a *lai* in the language of *oui*, or a *virelai*, or a ballad in the vulgar English.*

'A ballad, a ballad,' said the hermit, 'against all the *ocs* and *ouis* of France. Downright English am I, Sir Knight, and downright English was my patron St. Dunstan, and scorned *oc* and *oui*, as he would have scorned the parings of the devil's hoof—downright English alone shall be sung in this cell.'

'I will assay, then,' said the knight, 'a ballad composed by a Saxon glee-man, whom I knew in Holy Land.'

It speedily appeared, that if the knight was not a complete master of the minstrel art, his taste for it had at least been cultivated under the best instructors. Art had taught him to soften the faults of a voice which had little compass, and was naturally rough rather than mellow, and, in short, had done all that culture can do in supplying natural deficiencies. His performance, therefore, might have been termed very respectable by abler judges than the hermit, especially as the knight threw into the notes now a degree of spirit, and now of plaintive enthusiasm, which gave force and energy to the verses which he sung.

---

* See Note C. Minstrelsy.

IVANHOE

THE CRUSADER'S RETURN

1

High deeds achieved of knightly fame,
From Palestine the champion came;
The cross upon his shoulders borne,
Battle and blast had dimm'd and torn.
Each dint upon his batter'd shield
Was token of a foughten field;
And thus, beneath his lady's bower,
He sung, as fell the twilight hour :—

2

'Joy to the fair!—thy knight behold,
Return'd from yonder land of gold;
No wealth he brings, nor wealth can need,
Save his good arms and battle-steed;
His spurs, to dash against a foe,
His lance and sword to lay him low;
Such all the trophies of his toil,
Such—and the hope of Tekla's smile!

3

'Joy to the fair! whose constant knight
Her favour fired to feats of might;
Unnoted shall she not remain,
Where meet the bright and noble train;
Minstrel shall sing and herald tell—
"Mark yonder maid of beauty well,
'Tis she for whose bright eyes was won
The listed field at Askalon!

4

'"Note well her smile!—it edged the blade
Which fifty wives to widows made,
When, vain his strength and Mahound's spell,
Iconium's turban'd Soldan fell.

Seest thou her locks, whose sunny glow
Half shows, half shades, her neck of snow?
Twines not of them one golden thread,
But for its sake a Paynim bled."

5

' Joy to the fair!—my name unknown,
Each deed, and all its praise thine own ;
Then, oh! unbar this churlish gate,
The night dew falls, the hour is late.
Inured to Syria's glowing breath,
I feel the north breeze chill as death ;
Let grateful love quell maiden shame,
And grant him bliss who brings thee fame.'

During this performance, the hermit demeaned himself much like a first-rate critic of the present day at a new opera. He reclined back upon his seat, with his eyes half shut ; now, folding his hands and twisting his thumbs, he seemed absorbed in attention, and anon, balancing his expanded palms, he gently flourished them in time to the music. At one or two favourite cadences, he threw in a little assistance of his own. where the knight's voice seemed unable to carry the air so high as his worshipful taste approved. When the song was ended, the anchorite emphatically declared it a good one, and well sung.

' And yet,' said he, ' I think my Saxon countrymen had herded long enough with the Normans, to fall into the tone of their melancholy ditties. What took the honest knight from home ? or what could he expect but to find his mistress agreeably engaged with a rival on his return, and his serenade,

as they call it, as little regarded as the caterwauling
of a cat in the gutter? Nevertheless, Sir Knight,
I drink this cup to thee, to the success of all true
lovers—I fear you are none,' he added, on observing
that the knight (whose brain began to be heated
with these repeated draughts) qualified his flagon
from the water pitcher.

'Why,' said the knight, 'did you not tell me
that this water was from the well of your blessed
patron, St. Dunstan?'

'Ay, truly,' said the hermit, 'and many a hundred
of pagans did he baptize there, but I never heard
that he drank any of it. Every thing should be put
to its proper use in this world. St. Dunstan knew,
as well as any one, the prerogatives of a jovial
friar.'

And so saying, he reached the harp, and entertained his guest with the following characteristic
song, to a sort of derry-down chorus, appropriate
to an old English ditty. *

THE BAREFOOTED FRIAR

1

I'll give thee, good fellow, a twelvemonth or twain,
To search Europe through, from Byzantium to Spain;
But ne'er shall you find, should you search till you tire,
So happy a man as the Barefooted Friar.

---

* It may be proper to remind the reader, that the chorus of 'derry-
down' is supposed to be as ancient, not only as the times of the
Heptarchy, but as those of the Druids, and to have furnished the chorus
to the hymns of those venerable persons when they went to the wood
to gather mistletoe.

2

Your knight for his lady pricks forth in career,
And is brought home at even-song prick'd through with a spear;
I confess him in haste—for his lady desires
No comfort on earth save the Barefooted Friar's.

3

Your monarch?—Pshaw! many a prince has been known
To barter his robes for our cowl and our gown,
But which of us e'er felt the idle desire
To exchange for a crown the grey hood of a Friar!

4

The Friar has walk'd out, and where'er he has gone,
The land and its fatness is mark'd for his own;
He can roam where he lists, he can stop when he tires,
For every man's house is the Barefooted Friar's.

5

He's expected at noon, and no wight till he comes
May profane the great chair, or the porridge of plums;
For the best of the cheer, and the seat by the fire,
Is the undenied right of the Barefooted Friar.

6

He's expected at night, and the pasty's made hot,
They broach the brown ale, and they fill the black pot,
And the goodwife would wish the goodman in the mire,
Ere he lack'd a soft pillow, the Barefooted Friar.

7

Long flourish the sandal, the cord, and the cope,
The dread of the devil and trust of the Pope;
For to gather life's roses, unscathed by the briar,
Is granted alone to the Barefooted Friar.

'By my troth,' said the knight, 'thou hast
sung well and lustily, and in high praise of thine
order. And, talking of the devil, Holy Clerk, are

you not afraid that he may pay you a visit during some of your uncanonical pastimes?'

'I uncanonical!' answered the hermit; 'I scorn the charge—I scorn it with my heels!—I serve the duty of my chapel duly and truly—Two masses daily, morning and evening, primes, noons, and vespers, *aves, credos, paters*——'

'Excepting moonlight nights, when the venison is in season,' said his guest.

'*Exceptis excipiendis*,' replied the hermit, 'as our old abbot taught me to say, when impertinent laymen should ask me if I kept every punctilio of mine order.'

'True, holy father,' said the knight; 'but the devil is apt to keep an eye on such exceptions; he goes about, thou knowest, like a roaring lion.'

'Let him roar here if he dares,' said the friar; 'a touch of my cord will make him roar as loud as the tongs of St. Dunstan himself did. I never feared man, and I as little fear the devil and his imps. Saint Dunstan, Saint Dubric, Saint Winibald, Saint Winifred, Saint Swibert, Saint Willick, not forgetting Saint Thomas a Kent, and my own poor merits to speed, I defy every devil of them, come cut and long tail.—But to let you into a secret, I never speak upon such subjects, my friend, until after morning vespers.'

He changed the conversation; fast and furious grew the mirth of the parties, and many a song was exchanged betwixt them, when their revels were interrupted by a loud knocking at the door of the hermitage.

IVANHOE

The occasion of this interruption we can only explain by resuming the adventures of another set of our characters; for, like old Ariosto, we do not pique ourselves upon continuing uniformly to keep company with any one personage of our drama.

CHAPTER XVIII

Away ! our journey lies through dell and dingle,
Where the blithe fawn trips by its timid mother,
Where the broad oak, with intercepting boughs,
Chequers the sunbeam in the green-sward alley—
Up and away !—for lovely paths are these
To tread, when the glad Sun is on his throne :
Less pleasant, and less safe, when Cynthia's lamp
With doubtful glimmer lights the dreary forest.

ETTRICK FOREST.

WHEN Cedric the Saxon saw his son drop down
senseless in the lists at Ashby, his first impulse
was to order him into the custody and care of his
own attendants, but the words choked in his throat.
He could not bring himself to acknowledge, in
presence of such an assembly, the son whom he
had renounced and disinherited. He ordered, however, Oswald to keep an eye upon him; and directed
that officer, with two of his serfs, to convey Ivanhoe
to Ashby as soon as the crowd had dispersed.
Oswald, however, was anticipated in this good office.
The crowd dispersed, indeed, but the knight was
nowhere to be seen.

It was in vain that Cedric's cupbearer looked
around for his young master—he saw the bloody
spot on which he had lately sunk down, but himself
he saw no longer; it seemed as if the fairies had
conveyed him from the spot. Perhaps Oswald (for

the Saxons were very superstitious) might have
adopted some such hypothesis, to account for
Ivanhoe's disappearance, had he not suddenly cast
his eye upon a person attired like a squire, in
whom he recognised the features of his fellow-
servant Gurth. Anxious concerning his master's
fate, and in despair at his sudden disappearance,
the translated swineherd was searching for him
everywhere, and had neglected, in doing so, the
concealment on which his own safety depended.
Oswald deemed it his duty to secure Gurth, as a
fugitive of whose fate his master was to judge.

Renewing his enquiries concerning the fate of
Ivanhoe, the only information which the cupbearer
could collect from the bystanders was, that the
knight had been raised with care by certain well-
attired grooms, and placed in a litter belonging
to a lady among the spectators, which had immediately transported him out of the press. Oswald,
on receiving this intelligence, resolved to return to
his master for farther instructions, carrying along
with him Gurth, whom he considered in some sort
as a deserter from the service of Cedric.

The Saxon had been under very intense and
agonizing apprehensions concerning his son; for
Nature had asserted her rights, in spite of the
patriotic stoicism which laboured to disown her.
But no sooner was he informed that Ivanhoe was
in careful, and probably in friendly hands, than the
paternal anxiety which had been excited by the
dubiety of his fate, gave way anew to the feeling of
injured pride and resentment, at what he termed

Wilfred's filial disobedience. 'Let him wander his way,' said he—'let those leech his wounds for whose sake he encountered them. He is fitter to do the juggling tricks of the Norman chivalry than to maintain the fame and honour of his English ancestry with the glaive and brown-bill, the good old weapons of his country.'

'If to maintain the honour of ancestry,' said Rowena, who was present, 'it is sufficient to be wise in council and brave in execution — to be boldest among the bold, and gentlest among the gentle, I know no voice, save his father's——'

'Be silent, Lady Rowena!—on this subject only I hear you not. Prepare yourself for the Prince's festival: we have been summoned thither with unwonted circumstance of honour and of courtesy, such as the haughty Normans have rarely used to our race since the fatal day of Hastings. Thither will I go, were it only to show these proud Normans how little the fate of a son, who could defeat their bravest, can affect a Saxon.'

'Thither,' said Rowena, 'do I NOT go; and I pray you to beware, lest what you mean for courage and constancy, shall be accounted hardness of heart.'

'Remain at home, then, ungrateful lady,' answered Cedric; 'thine is the hard heart, which can sacrifice the weal of an oppressed people to an idle and unauthorized attachment. I seek the noble Athelstane, and with him attend the banquet of John of Anjoù.'

He went accordingly to the banquet, of which

we have already mentioned the principal events. Immediately upon retiring from the castle, the Saxon thanes, with their attendants, took horse; and it was during the bustle which attended their doing so, that Cedric, for the first time, cast his eyes upon the deserter Gurth. The noble Saxon had returned from the banquet, as we have seen, in no very placid humour, and wanted but a pretext for wreaking his anger upon some one. 'The gyves!' he said, 'the gyves!— Oswald — Hundibert!—Dogs and villains!—why leave ye the knave unfettered?'

Without daring to remonstrate, the companions of Gurth bound him with a halter, as the readiest cord which occurred. He submitted to the operation without remonstrance, except that, darting a reproachful look at his master, he said, 'This comes of loving your flesh and blood better than mine own.'

'To horse, and forward!' said Cedric.

'It is indeed full time,' said the noble Athelstane; 'for, if we ride not the faster, the worthy Abbot Waltheoff's preparations for a rere-supper * will be altogether spoiled.'

The travellers, however, used such speed as to reach the convent of St. Withold's before the apprehended evil took place. The Abbot, himself of ancient Saxon descent, received the noble Saxons with the profuse and exuberant hospitality of their

---

* A rere-supper was a night-meal, and sometimes signified a collation, which was given at a late hour, after the regular supper had made its appearance.—L. T.

nation, wherein they indulged to a late, or rather an early hour; nor did they take leave of their reverend host the next morning until they had shared with him a sumptuous refection.

As the cavalcade left the court of the monastery, an incident happened somewhat alarming to the Saxons, who, of all people of Europe, were most addicted to a superstitious observance of omens, and to whose opinions can be traced most of those notions upon such subjects, still to be found among our popular antiquities. For the Normans being a mixed race, and better informed according to the information of the times, had lost most of the superstitious prejudices which their ancestors had brought from Scandinavia, and piqued themselves upon thinking freely on such topics.

In the present instance, the apprehension of impending evil was inspired by no less respectable a prophet than a large lean black dog, which, sitting upright, howled most piteously as the foremost riders left the gate, and presently afterwards, barking wildly, and jumping to and fro, seemed bent upon attaching itself to the party.

'I like not that music, father Cedric,' said Athelstane; for by this title of respect he was accustomed to address him.

'Nor I either, uncle,' said Wamba; 'I greatly fear we shall have to pay the piper.'

'In my mind,' said Athelstane, upon whose memory the Abbot's good ale (for Burton was already famous for that genial liquor) had made a favourable impression,—'in my mind we had

better turn back, and abide with the Abbot until
the afternoon. It is unlucky to travel where your
path is crossed by a monk, a hare, or a howling
dog, until you have eaten your next meal.'

'Away!' said Cedric, impatiently; 'the day
is already too short for our journey. For the dog,
I know it to be the cur of the runaway slave Gurth,
a useless fugitive like its master.'

So saying, and rising at the same time in his
stirrups, impatient at the interruption of his journey,
he launched his javelin at poor Fangs—for Fangs
it was, who, having traced his master thus far
upon his stolen expedition, had here lost him,
and was now, in his uncouth way, rejoicing at his
reappearance. The javelin inflicted a wound upon
the animal's shoulder, and narrowly missed pinning
him to the earth; and Fangs fled howling from
the presence of the enraged thane. Gurth's heart
swelled within him; for he felt this meditated
slaughter of his faithful adherent in a degree much
deeper than the harsh treatment he had himself
received. Having in vain attempted to raise his
hand to his eyes, he said to Wamba, who, seeing
his master's ill humour, had prudently retreated to
the rear, 'I pray thee, do me the kindness to wipe
my eyes with the skirt of thy mantle; the dust
offends me, and these bonds will not let me help
myself one way or another.'

Wamba did him the service he required, and
they rode side by side for some time, during which
Gurth maintained a moody silence. At length he
could repress his feelings no longer.

'Friend Wamba,' said he, 'of all those who are fools enough to serve Cedric, thou alone hast dexterity enough to make thy folly acceptable to him. Go to him, therefore, and tell him that neither for love nor fear will Gurth serve him longer. He may strike the head from me—he may scourge me — he may load me with irons — but henceforth he shall never compel me either to love or to obey him. Go to him, then, and tell him that Gurth the son of Beowulph renounces his service.'

'Assuredly,' said Wamba, 'fool as I am, I shall not do your fool's errand. Cedric hath another javelin stuck into his girdle, and thou knowest he does not always miss his mark.'

'I care not,' replied Gurth, 'how soon he makes a mark of me. Yesterday he left Wilfred, my young master, in his blood. To-day he has striven to kill before my face the only other living creature that ever showed me kindness. By St. Edmund, St. Dunstan, St. Withold, St. Edward the Confessor, and every other Saxon saint in the calendar,' (for Cedric never swore by any that was not of Saxon lineage, and all his household had the same limited devotion,) 'I will never forgive him !'

'To my thinking now,' said the Jester, who was frequently wont to act as peace-maker in the family, 'our master did not propose to hurt Fangs, but only to affright him. For, if you observed, he rose in his stirrups, as thereby meaning to overcast the mark ; and so he would have done, but Fangs happening to bound up at the very moment, received a scratch, which I will be bound to heal with a penny's breadth of tar.'

'If I thought so,' said Gurth—'if I could but think so—but no—I saw the javelin was well aimed —I heard it whizz through the air with all the wrathful malevolence of him who cast it, and it quivered after it had pitched in the ground, as if with regret for having missed its mark. By the hog dear to St. Anthony, I renounce him!'

And the indignant swineherd resumed his sullen silence, which no efforts of the Jester could again induce him to break.

Meanwhile Cedric and Athelstane, the leaders of the troop, conversed together on the state of the land, on the dissensions of the royal family, on the feuds and quarrels among the Norman nobles, and on the chance which there was that the oppressed Saxons might be able to free themselves from the yoke of the Normans, or at least to elevate themselves into national consequence and independence, during the civil convulsions which were likely to ensue. On this subject Cedric was all animation. The restoration of the independence of his race was the idol of his heart, to which he had willingly sacrificed domestic happiness and the interests of his own son. But, in order to achieve this great revolution in favour of the native English, it was necessary that they should be united among themselves, and act under an acknowledged head. The necessity of choosing their chief from the Saxon blood-royal was not only evident in itself, but had been made a solemn condition by those whom Cedric had intrusted with his secret plans and hopes. Athelstane had this quality at least; and though he had few mental accomplishments or talents to recommend him as a leader, he had still a goodly person, was no coward, had been accustomed to martial exercises, and seemed willing to defer to the advice of counsellors more wise than himself. Above all, he was known to be liberal and hospitable, and believed to be good-natured. But whatever pretensions Athelstane had to be considered as head of the Saxon confederacy, many of that nation were disposed to prefer to his the title of the Lady Rowena, who drew her descent from Alfred, and whose father having been a chief renowned for wisdom, courage, and generosity, his memory was highly honoured by his oppressed countrymen.

It would have been no difficult thing for Cedric, had he been so disposed, to have placed himself at the head of a third party, as formidable at least as any of the others. To counterbalance their royal descent, he had courage, activity, energy, and, above all, that devoted attachment to the cause which had procured him the epithet of THE SAXON, and his birth was inferior to none, excepting only that of Athelstane and his ward. These qualities, however, were unalloyed by the slightest shade of selfishness; and, instead of dividing yet farther his weakened nation by forming a faction of his own, it was a leading part of Cedric's plan to extinguish that which already existed, by promoting a marriage betwixt Rowena and Athelstane. An obstacle occurred to this his favourite project, in the mutual attachment of his ward and his son; and hence the original cause of the banishment of Wilfred from the house of his father.

This stern measure Cedric had adopted, in hopes that, during Wilfred's absence, Rowena might relinquish her preference, but in this hope he was disappointed; a disappointment which might be attributed in part to the mode in which his ward had been educated. Cedric, to whom the name of Alfred was as that of a deity, had treated the sole remaining scion of that great monarch with a degree of observance, such as, perhaps, was in those days scarce paid to an acknowledged princess. Rowena's will had been in almost all cases a law to his household; and Cedric himself, as if determined that her sovereignty should be fully acknowledged within that little circle at least, seemed to take a pride in acting as the first of her subjects. Thus trained in the exercise not only of free will, but despotic authority, Rowena was, by her previous education, disposed both to resist and to resent any attempt to control her affections, or dispose of her hand contrary to her inclinations, and to assert her independence in a case in which even those females who have been trained up to obedience and subjection, are not infrequently apt to dispute the authority of guardians and parents. The opinions which she felt strongly, she avowed boldly; and Cedric, who could not free himself from his habitual deference to her opinions, felt totally at a loss how to enforce his authority of guardian.

It was in vain that he attempted to dazzle her

with the prospect of a visionary throne. Rowena, who possessed strong sense, neither considered his plan as practicable, nor as desirable, so far as she was concerned, could it have been achieved. Without attempting to conceal her avowed preference of Wilfred of Ivanhoe, she declared that, were that favoured knight out of question, she would rather take refuge in a convent, than share a throne with Athelstane, whom, having always despised, she now began, on account of the trouble she received on his account, thoroughly to detest.

Nevertheless, Cedric, whose opinion of women's constancy was far from strong, persisted in using every means in his power to bring about the proposed match, in which he conceived he was rendering an important service to the Saxon cause. The sudden and romantic appearance of his son in the lists at Ashby, he had justly regarded as almost a death's blow to his hopes. His paternal affection, it is true, had for an instant gained the victory over pride and patriotism ; but both had returned in full force, and under their joint operation, he was now bent upon making a determined effort for the union of Athelstane and Rowena, together with expediting those other measures which seemed necessary to forward the restoration of Saxon independence.

On this last subject, he was now labouring with Athelstane, not without having reason, every now and then, to lament, like Hotspur, that he should have moved such a dish of skimmed milk to so honourable an action. Athelstane, it is true, was

vain enough, and loved to have his ears tickled
with tales of his high descent, and of his right by
inheritance to homage and sovereignty.   But his
petty vanity was sufficiently gratified by receiving
this homage at the hands of his immediate attendants, and of the Saxons who approached him.   If
he had the courage to encounter danger, he at least
hated the trouble of going to seek it; and while he
agreed in the general principles laid down by Cedric
concerning the claim of the Saxons to independence,
and was still more easily convinced of his own title
to reign over them when that independence should
be attained, yet when the means of asserting these
rights came to be discussed, he was still 'Athelstane
the Unready,' slow, irresolute, procrastinating, and
unenterprising.   The warm and impassioned ex-
hortations of Cedric had as little effect upon his
impassive temper, as red-hot balls alighting in the
water, which produce a little sound and smoke, and
are instantly extinguished.

If, leaving this task, which might be compared
to spurring a tired jade, or to hammering upon cold
iron, Cedric fell back to his ward Rowena, he received little more satisfaction from conferring with
her.   For, as his presence interrupted the discourse
between the lady and her favourite attendant upon
the gallantry and fate of Wilfred, Elgitha failed
not to revenge both her mistress and herself, by
recurring to the overthrow of Athelstane in the
lists, the most disagreeable subject which could
greet the ears of Cedric.   To this sturdy Saxon,
therefore, the day's journey was fraught with all

manner of displeasure and discomfort; so that he more than once internally cursed the tournament, and him who had proclaimed it, together with his own folly in ever thinking of going thither.

At noon, upon the motion of Athelstane, the travellers paused in a woodland shade, by a fountain, to repose their horses and partake of some provisions, with which the hospitable Abbot had loaded a sumpter mule. Their repast was a pretty long one; and these several interruptions rendered it impossible for them to hope to reach Rotherwood without travelling all night, a conviction which induced them to proceed on their way at a more hasty pace than they had hitherto used.

CHAPTER XIX

A train of armed men, some noble dame
Escorting, (so their scatter'd words discover'd,
As unperceived I hung upon their rear,)
Are close at hand, and mean to pass the night
Within the castle.

ORRA, A TRAGEDY.

THE travellers had now reached the verge of the
wooded country, and were about to plunge into
its recesses, held dangerous at that time from the
number of outlaws whom oppression and poverty
had driven to despair, and who occupied the forests
in such large bands as could easily bid defiance
to the feeble police of the period. From these
rovers, however, notwithstanding the lateness of
the hour, Cedric and Athelstane accounted themselves secure, as they had in attendance ten
servants, besides Wamba and Gurth, whose aid
could not be counted upon, the one being a jester
and the other a captive. It may be added, that in
travelling thus late through the forest, Cedric and
Athelstane relied on their descent and character,
as well as their courage. The outlaws, whom the
severity of the forest laws had reduced to this
roving and desperate mode of life, were chiefly
peasants and yeomen of Saxon descent, and were

273

generally supposed to respect the persons and property of their countrymen.

As the travellers journeyed on their way, they were alarmed by repeated cries for assistance; and when they rode up to the place from whence they came, they were surprised to find a horse-litter placed upon the ground, beside which sat a young woman, richly dressed in the Jewish fashion, while an old man, whose yellow cap proclaimed him to belong to the same nation, walked up and down with gestures expressive of the deepest despair, and wrung his hands, as if affected by some strange disaster.

To the enquiries of Athelstane and Cedric, the old Jew could for some time only answer by invoking the protection of all the patriarchs of the Old Testament successively against the sons of Ishmael, who were coming to smite them, hip and thigh, with the edge of the sword. When he began to come to himself out of this agony of terror, Isaac of York (for it was our old friend) was at length able to explain, that he had hired a body-guard of six men at Ashby, together with mules for carrying the litter of a sick friend. This party had undertaken to escort him as far as Doncaster. They had come thus far in safety; but having received information from a wood-cutter that there was a strong band of outlaws lying in wait in the woods before them, Isaac's mercenaries had not only taken flight, but had carried off with them the horses which bore the litter, and left the Jew and his daughter without the means either of defence or of retreat.

to be plundered, and probably murdered, by the banditti, whom they expected every moment would bring down upon them. 'Would it but please your valours,' added Isaac, in a tone of deep humiliation, 'to permit the poor Jews to travel under your safe-guard, I swear by the tables of our law, that never has favour been conferred upon a child of Israel since the days of our captivity, which shall be more gratefully acknowledged.'

'Dog of a Jew!' said Athelstane, whose memory was of that petty kind which stores up trifles of all kinds, but particularly trifling offences, 'dost not remember how thou didst beard us in the gallery at the tilt-yard? Fight or flee, or compound with the outlaws as thou dost list, ask neither aid nor company from us; and if they rob only such as thee, who rob all the world, I, for mine own share, shall hold them right honest folk.'

Cedric did not assent to the severe proposal of his companion. 'We shall do better,' said he, 'to leave them two of our attendants and two horses to convey them back to the next village. It will diminish our strength but little; and with your good sword, noble Athelstane, and the aid of those who remain, it will be light work for us to face twenty of those runagates.'

Rowena, somewhat alarmed by the mention of outlaws in force, and so near them, strongly seconded the proposal of her guardian. But Rebecca, suddenly quitting her dejected posture, and making her way through the attendants to the palfrey of the Saxon lady, knelt down, and, after the

Oriental fashion in addressing superiors, kissed the hem of Rowena's garment. Then rising, and throwing back her veil, she implored her in the great name of the God whom they both worshipped, and by that revelation of the Law upon Mount Sinai, in which they both believed, that she would have compassion upon them, and suffer them to go forward under their safeguard. 'It is not for myself that I pray this favour,' said Rebecca; 'nor is it even for that poor old man. I know, that to wrong and to spoil our nation is a light fault, if not a merit, with the Christians; and what is it to us whether it be done in the city, in the desert, or in the field? But it is in the name of one dear to many, and dear even to you, that I beseech you to let this sick person be transported with care and tenderness under your protection. For, if evil chance him, the last moment of your life would be embittered with regret for denying that which I ask of you.'

The noble and solemn air with which Rebecca made this appeal, gave it double weight with the fair Saxon.

'The man is old and feeble,' she said to her guardian, 'the maiden young and beautiful, their friend sick and in peril of his life—Jews though they be, we cannot as Christians leave them in this extremity. Let them unload two of the sumpter-mules, and put the baggage behind two of the serfs. The mules may transport the litter, and we have led horses for the old man and his daughter.'

Cedric readily assented to what she proposed, and Athelstane only added the condition, 'that they should travel in the rear of the whole party, where Wamba,' he said, ' might attend them with his shield of boar's brawn.'

' I have left my shield in the tilt-yard,' answered the Jester, ' as has been the fate of many a better knight than myself.'

Athelstane coloured deeply, for such had been his own fate on the last day of the tournament; while Rowena, who was pleased in the same pro-portion, as if to make amends for the brutal jest of her unfeeling suitor, requested Rebecca to ride by her side.

' It were not fit I should do so,' answered Rebecca, with proud humility, ' where my society might be held a disgrace to my protectress.'

By this time the change of baggage was hastily achieved; for the single word ' outlaws ' rendered every one sufficiently alert, and the approach of twilight made the sound yet more impressive. Amid the bustle, Gurth was taken from horseback, in the course of which removal he prevailed upon the Jester to slack the cord with which his arms were bound. It was so negligently refastened, perhaps intentionally, on the part of Wamba, that Gurth found no difficulty in freeing his arms altogether from bondage, and then, gliding into the thicket, he made his escape from the party.

The bustle had been considerable, and it was some time before Gurth was missed; for, as he was to be placed for the rest of the journey behind a servant, every one supposed that some other of his companions had him under his custody, and when it began to be whispered among them that Gurth had actually disappeared, they were under such immediate expectation of an attack from the outlaws, that it was not held convenient to pay much attention to the circumstance.

The path upon which the party travelled was now so narrow, as not to admit, with any sort of convenience, above two riders abreast, and began to descend into a dingle, traversed by a brook whose banks were broken, swampy, and overgrown with dwarf willows. Cedric and Athelstane, who were at the head of their retinue, saw the risk of being attacked at this pass; but neither of them having had much practice in war, no better mode of preventing the danger occurred to them than that they should hasten through the defile as fast as possible. Advancing, therefore, without much order, they had just crossed the brook with a part of their followers, when they were assailed in front, flank, and rear at once, with an impetuosity to which, in their confused and ill-prepared condition, it was impossible to offer effectual resistance. The shout of 'A white dragon! — a white dragon! — Saint George for merry England!' war-cries adopted by the assailants, as belonging to their assumed character of Saxon outlaws, was heard on every side, and on every side enemies appeared with a rapidity of advance and attack which seemed to multiply their numbers.

Both the Saxon chiefs were made prisoners at the same moment, and each under circumstances expressive of his character. Cedric, the instant that an enemy appeared, launched at him his remaining javelin, which, taking better effect than that which he had hurled at Fangs, nailed the man against an oak-tree that happened to be close behind him. Thus far successful, Cedric spurred his horse against a second, drawing his sword at the same time, and striking with such inconsiderate fury, that his weapon encountered a thick branch which hung over him, and he was disarmed by the violence of his own blow. He was instantly made prisoner, and pulled from his horse by two or three of the banditti who crowded around him. Athelstane shared his captivity, his bridle having been seized, and he himself forcibly dismounted, long before he could draw his weapon, or assume any posture of effectual defence.

The attendants, embarrassed with baggage, surprised and terrified at the fate of their masters, fell an easy prey to the assailants; while the Lady Rowena, in the centre of the cavalcade, and the Jew and his daughter in the rear, experienced the same misfortune.

Of all the train none escaped except Wamba, who showed upon the occasion much more courage than those who pretended to greater sense. He possessed himself of a sword belonging to one of the domestics, who was just drawing it with a tardy and irresolute hand, laid it about him like a lion, drove back several who approached him, and made a brave though ineffectual attempt to succour his master. Finding himself overpowered, the Jester at length threw himself from his horse, plunged into the thicket, and, favoured by the general confusion, escaped from the scene of action.

Yet the valiant Jester, as soon as he found himself safe, hesitated more than once whether he should not turn back and share the captivity of a master to whom he was sincerely attached.

' I have heard men talk of the blessings of freedom,' he said to himself, ' but I wish any wise man would teach me what use to make of it now that I have it.'

As he pronounced these words aloud, a voice very near him called out, in a low and cautious tone, ' Wamba!' and, at the same time, a dog, which he recognised to be Fangs, jumped up and fawned upon him. ' Gurth!' answered Wamba, with the same caution, and the swineherd immediately stood before him.

' What is the matter?' said he eagerly; ' what mean these cries, and that clashing of swords?'

' Only a trick of the times,' said Wamba; ' they are all prisoners.'

' Who are prisoners?' exclaimed Gurth, impatiently.

' My lord, and my lady, and Athelstane, and Hundibert, and Oswald.'

' In the name of God!' said Gurth, ' how came they prisoners?—and to whom?'

' Our master was too ready to fight,' said the Jester; ' and Athelstane was not ready enough, and no other person was ready at all. And they are prisoners to green cassocks, and black visors. And they lie all tumbled about on the green, like

the crab-apples that you shake down to your swine.
And I would laugh at it,' said the honest Jester,
'if I could for weeping.' And he shed tears of
unfeigned sorrow.

Gurth's countenance kindled — 'Wamba,' he
said, 'thou hast a weapon, and thy heart was ever
stronger than thy brain,—we are only two—but a
sudden attack from men of resolution will do much
—follow me!'

'Whither?—and for what purpose?' said the
Jester.

'To rescue Cedric.'

'But you have renounced his service but now,'
said Wamba.

'That,' said Gurth, 'was but while he was fortunate—follow me!'

As the Jester was about to obey, a third person
suddenly made his appearance, and commanded
them both to halt. From his dress and arms,
Wamba would have conjectured him to be one of
those outlaws who had just assailed his master; but,
besides that he wore no mask, the glittering baldric
across his shoulder, with the rich bugle-horn which
it supported, as well as the calm and commanding
expression of his voice and manner, made him, notwithstanding the twilight, recognise Locksley the
yeoman, who had been victorious, under such dis-
advantageous circumstances, in the contest for the
prize of archery.

'What is the meaning of all this,' said he, 'or
who is it that rifle, and ransom, and make prisoners,
in these forests?'

'You may look at their cassocks close by,' said Wamba, 'and see whether they be thy children's coats or no—for they are as like thine own, as one green pea-cod is to another.'

'I will learn that presently,' answered Locksley; 'and I charge ye, on peril of your lives, not to stir from the place where ye stand, until I have returned. Obey me, and it shall be the better for you and your masters.—Yet stay, I must render myself as like these men as possible.'

So saying, he unbuckled his baldric with the bugle, took a feather from his cap, and gave them to Wamba; then drew a vizard from his pouch, and, repeating his charges to them to stand fast, went to execute his purposes of reconnoitring.

'Shall we stand fast, Gurth?' said Wamba; 'or shall we e'en give him leg-bail? In my foolish mind, he had all the equipage of a thief too much in readiness, to be himself a true man.'

'Let him be the devil,' said Gurth, 'an he will. We can be no worse of waiting his return. If he belong to that party, he must already have given them the alarm, and it will avail nothing either to fight or fly. Besides, I have late experience, that arrant thieves are not the worst men in the world to have to deal with.'

The yeoman returned in the course of a few minutes.

'Friend Gurth,' he said, 'I have mingled among yon men, and have learnt to whom they belong, and whither they are bound. There is, I think, no chance that they will proceed to any actual violence against their prisoners. For three men to attempt them at this moment, were little else than madness; for they are good men of war, and have, as such, placed sentinels to give the alarm when any one approaches. But I trust soon to gather such a force, as may act in defiance of all their precautions; you are both servants, and, as I think, faithful servants, of Cedric the Saxon, the friend of the rights of Englishmen. He shall not want English hands to help him in this extremity. Come then with me, until I gather more aid.'

So saying, he walked through the wood at a great pace, followed by the jester and the swineherd. It was not consistent with Wamba's humour to travel long in silence.

'I think,' said he, looking at the baldric and bugle which he still carried, 'that I saw the arrow shot which won this gay prize, and that not so long since as Christmas.'

'And I,' said Gurth, 'could take it on my halidome, that I have heard the voice of the good yeoman who won it, by night as well as by day, and that the moon is not three days older since I did so.'

'Mine honest friends,' replied the yeoman, 'who, or what I am, is little to the present purpose; should I free your master, you will have reason to think me the best friend you have ever had in your lives. And whether I am known by one name or another—or whether I can draw a bow as well or better than a cow-keeper, or whether it is my pleasure to walk in sunshine or by moonlight, are matters which, as they do not concern you, so neither need ye busy yourselves respecting them.'

'Our heads are in the lion's mouth,' said Wamba, in a whisper to Gurth, 'get them out how we can.'

'Hush—be silent,' said Gurth. 'Offend him not by thy folly, and I trust sincerely that all will go well.'

CHAPTER XX

When autumn nights were long and drear,
  And forest walks were dark and dim,
How sweetly on the pilgrim's ear
  Was wont to steal the hermit's hymn !

Devotion borrows Music's tone,
  And Music took Devotion's wing;
And, like the bird that hails the sun,
  They soar to heaven, and soaring sing.
                    THE HERMIT OF ST. CLEMENT'S WELL.

IT was after three hours' good walking that the
servants of Cedric, with their mysterious guide,
arrived at a small opening in the forest, in the
centre of which grew an oak-tree of enormous
magnitude, throwing its twisted branches in every
direction. Beneath this tree four or five yeomen lay
stretched on the ground, while another, as sentinel,
walked to and fro in the moonlight shade.

Upon hearing the sound of feet approaching, the
watch instantly gave the alarm, and the sleepers as
suddenly started up and bent their bows. Six
arrows placed on the string were pointed towards
the quarter from which the travellers approached,
when their guide, being recognised, was welcomed
with every token of respect and attachment, and
all signs and fears of a rough reception at once
subsided.

285

'Where is the Miller?' was his first question.

'On the road towards Rotherham.'

'With how many?' demanded the leader, for such he seemed to be.

'With six men, and good hope of booty, if it please St. Nicholas.'

'Devoutly spoken,' said Locksley; 'and where is Allan-a-Dale?'

'Walked up towards the Watling-street, to watch for the Prior of Jorvaulx.'

'That is well thought on also,' replied the Captain;—'and where is the Friar?'

'In his cell.'

'Thither will I go,' said Locksley. 'Disperse and seek your companions. Collect what force you can, for there's game afoot that must be hunted hard, and will turn to bay. Meet me here by daybreak. — And, stay,' he added, 'I have forgotten what is most necessary of the whole— Two of you take the road quickly towards Torquilstone, the Castle of Front-de-Bœuf. A set of gallants, who have been masquerading in such guise as our own, are carrying a band of prisoners thither — Watch them closely, for even if they reach the castle before we collect our force, our honour is concerned to punish them, and we will find means to do so. Keep a close watch on them therefore; and dispatch one of your comrades, the lightest of foot, to bring the news of the yeomen thereabout.'

They promised implicit obedience, and departed with alacrity on their different errands. In the

286

meanwhile, their leader and his two companions, who now looked upon him with great respect, as well as some fear, pursued their way to the Chapel of Copmanhurst.

When they had reached the little moonlight glade, having in front the reverend, though ruinous chapel, and the rude hermitage, so well suited to ascetic devotion, Wamba whispered to Gurth, 'If this be the habitation of a thief, it makes good the old proverb, The nearer the church the farther from God.—And by my cockscomb,' he added, 'I think it be even so—Hearken but to the black sanctus which they are singing in the hermitage!'

In fact the anchorite and his guest were performing, at the full extent of their very powerful lungs, an old drinking song, of which this was the burden:—

> 'Come, trowl the brown bowl to me,
>   Bully boy, bully boy,
> Come, trowl the brown bowl to me:
>   Ho! jolly Jenkin, I spy a knave in drinking,
> Come, trowl the brown bowl to me.'

'Now, that is not ill sung,' said Wamba, who had thrown in a few of his own flourishes to help out the chorus. 'But who, in the saint's name, ever expected to have heard such a jolly chant come from out a hermit's cell at midnight!'

'Marry, that should I,' said Gurth, 'for the jolly Clerk of Copmanhurst is a known man, and kills half the deer that are stolen in this walk. Men say that the keeper has complained to his official, and that he will be stripped of his cowl and cope altogether, if he keep not better order.'

While they were thus speaking, Locksley's loud and repeated knocks had at length disturbed the anchorite and his guest. 'By my beads,' said the hermit, stopping short in a grand flourish, 'here come more benighted guests. I would not for my cowl that they found us in this goodly exercise. All men have their enemies, good Sir Sluggard; and there be those malignant enough to construe the hospitable refreshment which I have been offering to you, a weary traveller, for the matter of three short hours, into sheer drunkenness and debauchery, vices alike alien to my profession and my disposition.'

'Base calumniators!' replied the knight; 'I would I had the chastising of them. Nevertheless, Holy Clerk, it is true that all have their enemies; and there be those in this very land whom I would rather speak to through the bars of my helmet than barefaced.'

'Get thine iron pot on thy head then, friend Sluggard, as quickly as thy nature will permit,' said the hermit, 'while I remove these pewter flagons, whose late contents run strangely in mine own pate; and to drown the clatter—for, in faith, I feel somewhat unsteady—strike into the tune which thou hearest me sing; it is no matter for the words—I scarce know them myself.'

So saying, he struck up a thundering *De profundis clamavi*, under cover of which he removed the apparatus of their banquet; while the knight, laughing heartily, and arming himself all the while, assisted his host with his voice from time to time as his mirth permitted.

'What devil's matins are you after at this hour?' said a voice from without.

'Heaven forgive you, Sir Traveller!' said the hermit, whose own noise, and perhaps his nocturnal potations, prevented from recognising accents which were tolerably familiar to him—'Wend on your way, in the name of God and Saint Dunstan, and disturb not the devotions of me and my holy brother.'

'Mad priest,' answered the voice from without, 'open to Locksley!'

'All's safe—all's right,' said the hermit to his companion.

'But who is he?' said the Black Knight; 'it imports me much to know.'

'Who is he?' answered the hermit; 'I tell thee he is a friend.'

'But what friend?' answered the knight; 'for he may be friend to thee and none of mine?'

'What friend?' replied the hermit; 'that, now, is one of the questions that is more easily asked than answered. What friend?—why, he is, now that I bethink me a little, the very same honest keeper I told thee of a while since.'

'Ay, as honest a keeper as thou art a pious hermit,' replied the knight, 'I doubt it not. But undo the door to him before he beat it from its hinges.'

The dogs, in the meantime, which had made a

dreadful baying at the commencement of the disturbance, seemed now to recognise the voice of
him who stood without; for, totally changing their
manner, they scratched and whined at the door,
as if interceding for his admission. The hermit
speedily unbolted his portal, and admitted Locksley,
with his two companions.

'Why, hermit,' was the yeoman's first question
as soon as he beheld the knight, 'what boon
companion hast thou here?'

'A brother of our order,' replied the friar,
shaking his head; 'we have been at our orisons
all night.'

'He is a monk of the church militant, I think,'
answered Locksley; 'and there be more of them
abroad. I tell thee, friar, thou must lay down
the rosary and take up the quarter-staff; we shall
need every one of our merry men, whether clerk
or layman.— But,' he added, taking him a step
aside, 'art thou mad? to give admittance to a
knight thou dost not know? Hast thou forgot
our articles?'

'Not know him!' replied the friar, boldly, 'I
know him as well as the beggar knows his dish.'

'And what is his name, then?' demanded
Locksley.

'His name,' said the hermit — 'his name is Sir
Anthony of Scrabelstone—as if I would drink with
a man, and did not know his name!'

'Thou hast been drinking more than enough,
friar,' said the woodsman, 'and, I fear, prating
more than enough too.'

'Good yeoman,' said the knight, coming forward,
'be not wroth with my merry host. He did but
afford me the hospitality which I would have
compelled from him if he had refused it.'

'Thou compel!' said the friar; 'wait but till
I have changed this grey gown for a green cassock,
and if I make not a quarter-staff ring twelve
upon thy pate, I am neither true clerk nor good
woodsman.'

While he spoke thus, he stript off his gown, and
appeared in a close black buckram doublet and
drawers, over which he speedily did on a cassock
of green, and hose of the same colour. 'I pray
thee truss my points,' said he to Wamba, 'and
thou shalt have a cup of sack for thy labour.'

'Gramercy for thy sack,' said Wamba; 'but
think'st thou it is lawful for me to aid you to
transmew thyself from a holy hermit into a sinful
forester?'

'Never fear,' said the hermit; 'I will but confess
the sins of my green cloak to my greyfriar's frock,
and all shall be well again.'

'Amen!' answered the Jester; 'a broadcloth
penitent should have a sackcloth confessor, and
your frock may absolve my motley doublet into
the bargain.'

So saying, he accommodated the friar with his
assistance in tying the endless number of points, as
the laces which attached the hose to the doublet
were then termed.

While they were thus employed, Locksley led
the knight a little apart, and addressed him thus:—

' Deny it not, Sir Knight—you are he who decided the victory to the advantage of the English against the strangers on the second day of the tournament at Ashby.'

' And what follows if you guess truly, good yeoman?' replied the knight.

' I should in that case hold you,' replied the yeoman, ' a friend to the weaker party.'

' Such is the duty of a true knight at least,' replied the Black Champion; ' and I would not willingly that there were reason to think otherwise of me.'

' But for my purpose,' said the yeoman, ' thou shouldst be as well a good Englishman as a good knight; for that, which I have to speak of, concerns, indeed, the duty of every honest man, but is more especially that of a true-born native of England.'

' You can speak to no one,' replied the knight, ' to whom England, and the life of every Englishman, can be dearer than to me.'

' I would willingly believe so,' said the woodsman, ' for never had this country such need to be supported by those who love her. Hear me, and I will tell thee of an enterprise, in which, if thou be'st really that which thou seemest, thou mayst take an honourable part. A band of villains, in the disguise of better men than themselves, have made themselves master of the person of a noble Englishman, called Cedric the Saxon, together with his ward, and his friend Athelstane of Coningsburgh, and have transported them to a castle in this forest, called Torquilstone. I ask of thee, as a good knight and a good Englishman, wilt thou aid in their rescue?'

'I am bound by my vow to do so,' replied the knight; 'but I would willingly know who you are, who request my assistance in their behalf?'

'I am,' said the forester, 'a nameless man; but I am the friend of my country, and of my country's friends — With this account of me you must for the present remain satisfied, the more especially since you yourself desire to continue unknown. Believe, however, that my word, when pledged, is as inviolate as if I wore golden spurs.'

'I willingly believe it,' said the knight; 'I have been accustomed to study men's countenances, and I can read in thine honesty and resolution. I will, therefore, ask thee no further questions, but aid thee in setting at freedom these oppressed captives; which done, I trust we shall part better acquainted, and well satisfied with each other.'

'So,' said Wamba to Gurth,—for the friar being now fully equipped, the Jester, having approached to the other side of the hut, had heard the conclusion of the conversation,—'So we have got a new ally?—I trust the valour of the knight will be truer metal than the religion of the hermit, or the honesty of the yeoman; for this Locksley looks like a born deer-stealer, and the priest like a lusty hypocrite.'

'Hold thy peace, Wamba,' said Gurth; 'it

may all be as thou dost guess; but were the horned devil to rise and proffer me his assistance to set at liberty Cedric and the Lady Rowena, I fear I should hardly have religion enough to refuse the foul fiend's offer, and bid him get behind me.'

The friar was now completely accoutred as a yeoman, with sword and buckler, bow and quiver, and a strong partisan over his shoulder. He left his cell at the head of the party, and, having carefully locked the door, deposited the key under the threshold.

'Art thou in condition to do good service, friar,' said Locksley, 'or does the brown bowl still run in thy head?'

'Not more than a draught of St. Dunstan's fountain will allay,' answered the priest; 'something there is of a whizzing in my brain, and of instability in my legs, but you shall presently see both pass away.'

So saying, he stepped to the stone basin, in which the waters of the fountain as they fell formed bubbles which danced in the white moonlight, and took so long a draught as if he had meant to exhaust the spring.

'When didst thou drink as deep a draught of water before, Holy Clerk of Copmanhurst?' said the Black Knight.

'Never since my wine-butt leaked, and let out its liquor by an illegal vent,' replied the friar, 'and so left me nothing to drink but my patron's bounty here.'

Then plunging his hands and head into the fountain, he washed from them all marks of the midnight revel.

Thus refreshed and sobered, the jolly priest twirled his heavy partisan round his head with three fingers, as if he had been balancing a reed, exclaiming at the same time, ' Where be those false ravishers, who carry off wenches against their will ? May the foul fiend fly off with me, if I am not man enough for a dozen of them.'

' Swearest thou, Holy Clerk ? ' said the Black Knight.

' Clerk me no Clerks,' replied the transformed priest; ' by Saint George and the Dragon, I am no longer a shaveling than while my frock is on my back—When I am cased in my green cassock, I will drink, swear, and woo a lass, with any blithe forester in the West Riding.'

' Come on, Jack Priest,' said Locksley, ' and be silent; thou art as noisy as a whole convent on a holy eve, when the Father Abbot has gone to bed. — Come on you, too, my masters, tarry not to talk of it—I say, come on, we must collect all our forces, and few enough we shall have, if we are to storm the Castle of Reginald Front-de-Bœuf.'

' What ! is it Front-de-Bœuf,' said the Black Knight, ' who has stopt on the king's highway the king's liege subjects ?—Is he turned thief and oppressor ? '

' Oppressor he ever was,' said Locksley.

' And for thief,' said the priest, ' I doubt if

ever he were even half so honest a man as many a thief of my acquaintance.'

'Move on, priest, and be silent,' said the yeoman; 'it were better you led the way to the place of rendezvous, than say what should be left unsaid, both in decency and prudence.'

CHAPTER XXI

Alas, how many hours and years have past,
Since human forms have round this table sate,
Or lamp, or taper, on its surface gleam'd !
Methinks, I hear the sound of time long pass'd
Still murmuring o'er us, in the lofty void
Of these dark arches, like the ling'ring voices
Of those who long within their graves have slept.

ORRA, A TRAGEDY.

WHILE these measures were taking in behalf of
Cedric and his companions, the armed men by whom
the latter had been seized, hurried their captives
along towards the place of security, where they
intended to imprison them. But darkness came
on fast, and the paths of the wood seemed but imperfectly known to the marauders. They were
compelled to make several long halts, and once or
twice to return on their road to resume the direction which they wished to pursue. The summer
morn had dawned upon them ere they could travel
in full assurance that they held the right path. But
confidence returned with light, and the cavalcade
now moved rapidly forward. Meanwhile, the following dialogue took place between the two leaders of
the banditti.

' It is time thou shouldst leave us, Sir Maurice,'
said the Templar to De Bracy, ' in order to prepare

297

the second part of thy mystery. Thou art next, thou knowest, to act the Knight Deliverer.'

'I have thought better of it,' said De Bracy; 'I will not leave thee till the prize is fairly deposited in Front-de-Bœuf's castle. There will I appear before the Lady Rowena in mine own shape, and trust that she will set down to the vehemence of my passion the violence of which I have been guilty.'

'And what has made thee change thy plan, De Bracy?' replied the Knight Templar.

'That concerns thee nothing,' answered his companion.

'I would hope, however, Sir Knight,' said the Templar, 'that this alteration of measures arises from no suspicion of my honourable meaning, such as Fitzurse endeavoured to instil into thee?'

'My thoughts are my own,' answered De Bracy; 'the fiend laughs, they say, when one thief robs another; and we know, that were he to spit fire and brimstone instead, it would never prevent a Templar from following his bent.'

'Or the leader of a Free Company,' answered the Templar, 'from dreading at the hands of a comrade and friend, the injustice he does to all mankind.'

'This is unprofitable and perilous recrimination,' answered De Bracy; 'suffice it to say, I know the morals of the Temple-Order, and I will not give thee the power of cheating me out of the fair prey for which I have run such risks.'

'Psha,' replied the Templar, 'what hast thou to fear?—Thou knowest the vows of our order.'

'Right well,' said De Bracy, 'and also how they are kept. Come, Sir Templar, the laws of gallantry have a liberal interpretation in Palestine, and this is a case in which I will trust nothing to your conscience.'

'Hear the truth, then,' said the Templar; 'I care not for your blue-eyed beauty. There is in that train one who will make me a better mate.'

'What! wouldst thou stoop to the waiting-damsel?' said De Bracy.

'No, Sir Knight,' said the Templar, haughtily. 'To the waiting-woman will I not stoop. I have a prize among the captives as lovely as thine own.'

'By the mass, thou meanest the fair Jewess!' said De Bracy.

'And if I do,' said Bois-Guilbert, 'who shall gainsay me?'

'No one that I know,' said De Bracy, 'unless it be your vow of celibacy, or a check of conscience for an intrigue with a Jewess.'

'For my vow,' said the Templar, 'our Grand Master hath granted me a dispensation. And for my conscience, a man that has slain three hundred Saracens, need not reckon up every little failing, like a village girl at her first confession upon Good Friday eve.'

'Thou knowest best thine own privileges,' said De Bracy. 'Yet, I would have sworn thy thought had been more on the old usurer's money bags, than on the black eyes of the daughter.'

'I can admire both,' answered the Templar: 'besides, the old Jew is but half-prize. I must share his spoils with Front-de-Bœuf, who will not lend us the use of his castle for nothing. I must have something that I can term exclusively my own by this foray of ours, and I have fixed on the lovely Jewess as my peculiar prize. But, now thou knowest my drift, thou wilt resume thine own original plan, wilt thou not ? — Thou hast nothing, thou seest, to fear from my interference.'

'No,' replied De Bracy, 'I will remain beside my prize. What thou sayst is passing true, but I like not the privileges acquired by the dispensation of the Grand Master, and the merit acquired by the slaughter of three hundred Saracens. You have too good a right to a free pardon, to render you very scrupulous about peccadilloes.'

While this dialogue was proceeding, Cedric was endeavouring to wring out of those who guarded him an avowal of their character and purpose. 'You should be Englishmen,' said he ; 'and yet, sacred Heaven ! you prey upon your countrymen as if you were very Normans. You should be my neighbours, and, if so, my friends ; for which of my English neighbours have reason to be otherwise ? I tell ye, yeomen, that even those among ye who have been branded with outlawry have had from me protection ; for I have pitied their miseries, and curst the oppression of their tyrannic nobles. What, then, would you have of me ? or in what can this violence serve ye ?—Ye are worse than brute beasts in your actions, and will you imitate them in their very dumbness ? '

It was in vain that Cedric expostulated with his

guards, who had too many good reasons for their silence to be induced to break it either by his wrath or his expostulations. They continued to hurry him along, travelling at a very rapid rate, until, at the end of an avenue of huge trees, arose Torquilstone, now the hoary and ancient castle of Reginald Front-de-Bœuf. It was a fortress of no great size, consisting of a donjon, or large and high square tower, surrounded by buildings of inferior height, which were encircled by an inner courtyard. Around the exterior wall was a deep moat, supplied with water from a neighbouring rivulet. Front-de-Bœuf, whose character placed him often at feud with his enemies, had made considerable additions to the strength of his castle, by building towers upon the outward wall, so as to flank it at every angle. The access, as usual in castles of the period, lay through an arched barbican, or outwork, which was terminated and defended by a small turret at each corner.

Cedric no sooner saw the turrets of Front-de-Bœuf's castle raise their grey and moss-grown battlements, glimmering in the morning sun above the woods by which they were surrounded, than he instantly augured more truly concerning the cause of his misfortune.

'I did injustice,' he said, 'to the thieves and outlaws of these woods, when I supposed such banditti to belong to their bands; I might as justly have confounded the foxes of these brakes with the ravening wolves of France. Tell me, dogs—is it my life or my wealth that your master aims at? Is

it too much that two Saxons, myself and the noble
Athelstane, should hold land in the country which
was once the patrimony of our race?—Put us then
to death, and complete your tyranny by taking our
lives, as you began with our liberties. If the Saxon
Cedric cannot rescue England, he is willing to die
for her. Tell your tyrannical master, I do only
beseech him to dismiss the Lady Rowena in honour
and safety. She is a woman, and he need not dread
her; and with us will die all who dare fight in her
cause.'

The attendants remained as mute to this address
as to the former, and they now stood before the
gate of the castle. De Bracy winded his horn
three times, and the archers and cross-bow men,
who had manned the wall upon seeing their approach, hastened to lower the drawbridge, and
admit them. The prisoners were compelled by
their guards to alight, and were conducted to an
apartment where a hasty repast was offered them,
of which none but Athelstane felt any inclination
to partake. Neither had the descendant of the
Confessor much time to do justice to the good
cheer placed before them, for their guards gave
him and Cedric to understand that they were to
be imprisoned in a chamber apart from Rowena.
Resistance was vain; and they were compelled to
follow to a large room, which, rising on clumsy
Saxon pillars, resembled those refectories and
chapter-houses which may be still seen in the
most ancient parts of our most ancient monasteries.

The Lady Rowena was next separated from her

train, and conducted, with courtesy, indeed, but still without consulting her inclination, to a distant apartment. The same alarming distinction was conferred on Rebecca, in spite of her father's entreaties, who offered even money, in this extremity of distress, that she might be permitted to abide with him. 'Base unbeliever,' answered one of his guards, 'when thou hast seen thy lair, thou wilt not wish thy daughter to partake it.' And, without farther discussion, the old Jew was forcibly dragged off in a different direction from the other prisoners. The domestics, after being carefully searched and disarmed, were confined in another part of the castle; and Rowena was refused even the comfort she might have derived from the attendance of her handmaiden Elgitha.

The apartment in which the Saxon chiefs were confined, for to them we turn our first attention, although at present used as a sort of guard-room, had formerly been the great hall of the castle. It was now abandoned to meaner purposes, because the present lord, among other additions to the convenience, security, and beauty of his baronial residence, had erected a new and noble hall, whose vaulted roof was supported by lighter and more elegant pillars, and fitted up with that higher degree of ornament, which the Normans had already introduced into architecture.

Cedric paced the apartment, filled with indignant reflections on the past and on the present, while the apathy of his companion served, instead of patience and philosophy, to defend him against every thing save the inconvenience of the present moment; and so little did he feel even this last, that he was only from time to time roused to a reply by Cedric's animated and impassioned appeal to him.

'Yes,' said Cedric, half speaking to himself, and half addressing himself to Athelstane, 'it was in this very hall that my father feasted with Torquil Wolfganger, when he entertained the valiant and unfortunate Harold, then advancing against the Norwegians, who had united themselves to the rebel Tosti. It was in this hall that Harold returned the magnanimous answer to the ambassador of his rebel brother. Oft have I heard my father kindle as he told the tale. The envoy of Tosti was admitted, when this ample room could scarce contain the crowd of the noble Saxon leaders, who were quaffing the blood-red wine around their monarch.'

'I hope,' said Athelstane, somewhat moved by this part of his friend's discourse, 'they will not forget to send us some wine and refections at noon —we had scarce a breathing-space allowed to break our fast, and I never have the benefit of my food when I eat immediately after dismounting from horseback, though the leeches recommend that practice.'

Cedric went on with his story without noticing this interjectional observation of his friend.

'The envoy of Tosti,' he said, 'moved up the hall, undismayed by the frowning countenances of all around him, until he made his obeisance before the throne of King Harold.

IVANHOE

' " What terms," he said, " Lord King, hath thy brother Tosti to hope, if he should lay down his arms, and crave peace at thy hands ? "

' " A brother's love," cried the generous Harold, " and the fair earldom of Northumberland."

' " But should Tosti accept these terms," continued the envoy, " what lands shall be assigned to his faithful ally, Hardrada, King of Norway ? "

' " Seven feet of English ground," answered Harold, fiercely, " or, as Hardrada is said to be a giant, perhaps we may allow him twelve inches more."

' The hall rung with acclamations, and cup and horn was filled to the Norwegian, who should be speedily in possession of his English territory.'

' I could have pledged him with all my soul,' said Athelstane, ' for my tongue cleaves to my palate.'

' The baffled envoy,' continued Cedric, pursuing with animation his tale, though it interested not the listener, ' retreated, to carry to Tosti and his ally the ominous answer of his injured brother. It was then that the distant towers of York, and the bloody streams of the Derwent,* beheld that direful conflict, in which, after displaying the most undaunted valour, the King of Norway, and Tosti, both fell, with ten thousand of their bravest followers. Who would have thought that upon the proud day when this battle was won, the very gale which waved the Saxon banners in triumph, was filling the Norman sails, and impelling them to the

* See Note D.   Battle of Stamford.

fatal shores of Sussex?—Who would have thought
that Harold, within a few brief days, would himself
possess no more of his kingdom, than the share
which he allotted in his wrath to the Norwegian
invader?—Who would have thought that you, noble
Athelstane—that you, descended of Harold's blood,
and that I, whose father was not the worst defender
of the Saxon crown, should be prisoners to a vile
Norman, in the very hall in which our ancestors
held such high festival?'

'It is sad enough,' replied Athelstane; 'but I
trust they will hold us to a moderate ransom—At
any rate it cannot be their purpose to starve us
outright; and yet, although it is high noon, I see
no preparations for serving dinner. Look up at the
window, noble Cedric, and judge by the sunbeams
if it is not on the verge of noon.'

'It may be so,' answered Cedric; 'but I cannot
look on that stained lattice without its awakening
other reflections than those which concern the passing moment, or its privations. When that window
was wrought, my noble friend, our hardy fathers
knew not the art of making glass, or of staining it
—The pride of Wolfganger's father brought an
artist from Normandy to adorn his hall with this
new species of emblazonment, that breaks the
golden light of God's blessed day into so many
fantastic hues. The foreigner came here poor,
beggarly, cringing, and subservient, ready to doff
his cap to the meanest native of the household. He
returned pampered and proud, to tell his rapacious
countrymen of the wealth and the simplicity of the

Saxon nobles—a folly, oh, Athelstane, foreboded of old, as well as foreseen, by those descendants of Hengist and his hardy tribes, who retained the simplicity of their manners. We made these strangers our bosom friends, our confidential servants; we borrowed their artists and their arts, and despised the honest simplicity and hardihood with which our brave ancestors supported themselves, and we became enervated by Norman arts long ere we fell under Norman arms. Far better was our homely diet, eaten in peace and liberty, than the luxurious dainties, the love of which hath delivered us as bondsmen to the foreign conqueror!'

'I should,' replied Athelstane, 'hold very humble diet a luxury at present; and it astonishes me, noble Cedric, that you can bear so truly in mind the memory of past deeds, when it appeareth you forget the very hour of dinner.'

'It is time lost,' muttered Cedric apart and impatiently, 'to speak to him of aught else but that which concerns his appetite! The soul of Hardicanute hath taken possession of him, and he hath no pleasure save to fill, to swill, and to call for more. —Alas!' said he, looking at Athelstane with compassion, 'that so dull a spirit should be lodged in so goodly a form! Alas! that such an enterprise as the regeneration of England should turn on a hinge so imperfect! Wedded to Rowena, indeed, her nobler and more generous soul may yet awake the better nature which is torpid within him. Yet how should this be, while Rowena, Athelstane, and I myself, remain the prisoners of this brutal marauder, and have been made so perhaps from a sense of the dangers which our liberty might bring to the usurped power of his nation?'

While the Saxon was plunged in these painful reflections, the door of their prison opened, and gave entrance to a sewer, holding his white rod of office. This important person advanced into the chamber with a grave pace, followed by four attendants, bearing in a table covered with dishes, the sight and smell of which seemed to be an instant compensation to Athelstane for all the inconvenience he had undergone. The persons who attended on the feast were masked and cloaked.

'What mummery is this?' said Cedric; 'think you that we are ignorant whose prisoners we are, when we are in the castle of your master? Tell him,' he continued, willing to use this opportunity to open a negotiation for his freedom,—'Tell your master, Reginald Front-de-Bœuf, that we know no reason he can have for withholding our liberty, excepting his unlawful desire to enrich himself at our expense. Tell him that we yield to his rapacity, as in similar circumstances we should do to that of a literal robber. Let him name the ransom at which he rates our liberty, and it shall be paid, providing the exaction is suited to our means.'

The sewer made no answer, but bowed his head.

'And tell Sir Reginald Front-de-Bœuf,' said Athelstane, 'that I send him my mortal defiance, and challenge him to combat with me, on foot or horseback, at any secure place, within eight days after our liberation; which, if he be a true knight, he will not, under these circumstances, venture to refuse or to delay.'

' I shall deliver to the knight your defiance,' answered the sewer; 'meanwhile I leave you to your food.'

.The challenge of Athelstane was delivered with no good grace; for a large mouthful, which required the exercise of both jaws at once, added to a natural hesitation, considerably damped the effect of the bold defiance it contained. Still, however, his speech was hailed by Cedric as an incontestable token of reviving spirit in his companion, whose previous indifference had begun, notwithstanding his respect for Athelstane's descent, to wear out his patience. But he now cordially shook hands with him in token of his approbation, and was somewhat grieved when Athelstane observed, 'that he would fight a dozen such men as Front-de-Bœuf, if, by so doing, he could hasten his departure from a dungeon where they put so much garlic into their pottage.' Notwithstanding this intimation of a relapse into the apathy of sensuality, Cedric placed himself opposite to Athelstane, and soon showed, that if the distresses of his country could banish the recollection of food while the table was uncovered, yet no sooner were the victuals put there, than he proved that the appetite of his Saxon ancestors had descended to him along with their other qualities.

The captives had not long enjoyed their refreshment, however, ere their attention was disturbed even from this most serious occupation by the blast of a horn winded before the gate. It was repeated three times, with as much violence as if it had been blown before an enchanted castle by the destined knight, at whose summons halls and towers, barbican and battlement, were to roll off like a morning vapour. The Saxons started from the table, and hastened to the window. But their curiosity was disappointed; for these outlets only looked upon the court of the castle, and the sound came from beyond its precincts. The summons, however, seemed of importance, for a considerable degree of bustle instantly took place in the castle.

CHAPTER XXII

LEAVING the Saxon chiefs to return to their banquet as soon as their ungratified curiosity should permit them to attend to the calls of their half-satiated appetite, we have to look in upon the yet more severe imprisonment of Isaac of York. The poor Jew had been hastily thrust into a dungeon-vault of the castle, the floor of which was deep beneath the level of the ground, and very damp, being lower than even the moat itself. The only light was received through one or two loop-holes far above the reach of the captive's hand. These apertures admitted, even at mid-day, only a dim and uncertain light, which was changed for utter darkness long before the rest of the castle had lost the blessing of day. Chains and shackles, which had been the portion of former captives, from whom active exertions to escape had been apprehended, hung rusted and empty on the walls of the prison, and in the rings of one of those sets of fetters there remained two mouldering bones, which seemed to have been once those of the human leg, as if some

311

prisoner had been left not only to perish there, but to be consumed to a skeleton.

At one end of this ghastly apartment was a large fire-grate, over the top of which were stretched some transverse iron bars, half devoured with rust.

The whole appearance of the dungeon might have appalled a stouter heart than that of Isaac, who, nevertheless, was more composed under the imminent pressure of danger, than he had seemed to be while affected by terrors, of which the cause was as yet remote and contingent. The lovers of the chase say that the hare feels more agony during the pursuit of the greyhounds, than when she is struggling in their fangs.* And thus it is probable, that the Jews, by the very frequency of their fear on all occasions, had their minds in some degree prepared for every effort of tyranny which could be practised upon them; so that no aggression, when it had taken place, could bring with it that surprise which is the most disabling quality of terror. Neither was it the first time that Isaac had been placed in circumstances so dangerous. He had therefore experience to guide him, as well as hope, that he might again, as formerly, be delivered as a prey from the fowler. Above all, he had upon his side the unyielding obstinacy of his nation, and that unbending resolution, with which Israelites have been frequently known to submit to the uttermost evils which power and violence can inflict upon

---

* *Nota Bene.*—We by no means warrant the accuracy of this piece of natural history, which we give on the authority of the Wardour MS.

L. T.

them, rather than gratify their oppressors by granting their demands.

In this humour of passive resistance, and with his garment collected beneath him to keep his limbs from the wet pavement, Isaac sat in a corner of his dungeon, where his folded hands, his dishevelled hair and beard, his furred cloak and high cap, seen by the wiry and broken light, would have afforded a study for Rembrandt, had that celebrated painter existed at the period. The Jew remained, without altering his position, for nearly three hours, at the expiry of which steps were heard on the dungeon stair. The bolts screamed as they were withdrawn —the hinges creaked as the wicket opened, and Reginald Front-de-Bœuf, followed by the two Saracen slaves of the Templar, entered the prison.

Front-de-Bœuf, a tall and strong man, whose life had been spent in public war or in private feuds and broils, and who had hesitated at no means of extending his feudal power, had features corresponding to his character, and which strongly expressed the fiercer and more malignant passions of the mind. The scars with which his visage was seamed, would, on features of a different cast, have excited the sympathy and veneration due to the marks of honourable valour ; but, in the peculiar case of Front-de-Bœuf, they only added to the ferocity of his countenance, and to the dread which his presence inspired. This formidable baron was clad in a leathern doublet, fitted close to his body, which was frayed and soiled with the stains of his armour. He had no weapon, excepting a poniard at his belt, which served to counterbalance the weight of the bunch of rusty keys that hung at his right side.

The black slaves who attended Front-de-Bœuf were stripped of their gorgeous apparel, and attired in jerkins and trowsers of coarse linen, their sleeves being tucked up above the elbow, like those of butchers when about to exercise their function in the slaughter-house. Each had in his hand a small pannier; and, when they entered the dungeon, they stopt at the door until Front-de-Bœuf himself carefully locked and double-locked it. Having taken this precaution, he advanced slowly up the apartment towards the Jew, upon whom he kept his eye fixed, as if he wished to paralyze him with his glance, as some animals are said to fascinate their prey. It seemed indeed as if the sullen and malignant eye of Front-de-Bœuf possessed some portion of that supposed power over his unfortunate prisoner. The Jew sate with his mouth a-gape, and his eyes fixed on the savage baron with such earnestness of terror, that his frame seemed literally to shrink together, and to diminish in size while encountering the fierce Norman's fixed and baleful gaze. The unhappy Isaac was deprived not only of the power of rising to make the obeisance which his terror dictated, but he could not even doff his cap, or utter any word of supplication; so strongly was he agitated by the conviction that tortures and death were impending over him.

On the other hand, the stately form of the Norman appeared to dilate in magnitude, like that

of the eagle, which ruffles up its plumage when
about to pounce on its defenceless prey. He paused
within three steps of the corner in which the unfortunate Jew had now, as it were, coiled himself
up into the smallest possible space, and made a
sign for one of the slaves to approach. The black
satellite came forward accordingly, and, producing
from his basket a large pair of scales and several
weights, he laid them at the feet of Front-de-Bœuf,
and again retired to the respectful distance, at which
his companion had already taken his station.

The motions of these men were slow and solemn,
as if there impended over their souls some precon-
ception of horror and of cruelty. Front-de-Bœuf
himself opened the scene by thus addressing his ill-
fated captive.

'Most accursed dog of an accursed race,' he said,
awaking with his deep and sullen voice the sullen
echoes of his dungeon vault, 'seest thou these
scales?'

The unhappy Jew returned a feeble affirmative.

'In these very scales shalt thou weigh me out,'
said the relentless Baron, 'a thousand silver pounds,
after the just measure and weight of the Tower of
London.'

'Holy Abraham!' returned the Jew, finding
voice through the very extremity of his danger,
'heard man ever such a demand? — Who ever
heard, even in a minstrel's tale, of such a sum as
a thousand pounds of silver?—What human sight
was ever blessed with the vision of such a mass of
treasure?—Not within the walls of York, ransack

my house and that of all my tribe, wilt thou find the tithe of that huge sum of silver that thou speakest of.'

' I am reasonable,' answered Front-de-Bœuf, ' and if silver be scant, I refuse not gold. At the rate of a mark of gold for each six pounds of silver, thou shalt free thy unbelieving carcass from such punishment as thy heart has never even conceived.'

' Have mercy on me, noble knight!' exclaimed Isaac; ' I am old, and poor, and helpless. It were unworthy to triumph over me—It is a poor deed to crush a worm.'

' Old thou mayest be,' replied the knight; ' more shame to their folly who have suffered thee to grow grey in usury and knavery—Feeble thou mayst be, for when had a Jew either heart or hand—But rich it is well known thou art.'

' I swear to you, noble knight,' said the Jew, ' by all which I believe, and by all which we believe in common——'

' Perjure not thyself,' said the Norman, interrupting him, ' and let not thine obstinacy seal thy doom, until thou hast seen and well considered the fate that awaits thee. Think not I speak to thee only to excite thy terror, and practise on the base cowardice thou hast derived from thy tribe. I swear to thee by that which thou dost NOT believe, by the gospel which our church teaches, and by the keys which are given her to bind and to loose, that my purpose is deep and peremptory. This dungeon is no place for trifling. Prisoners ten thousand times more distinguished than thou have died within these walls, and their fate hath never been known! But for thee is reserved a long and lingering death, to which theirs were luxury.'

He again made a signal for the slaves to approach, and spoke to them apart, in their own language; for he also had been in Palestine, where, perhaps, he had learnt his lesson of cruelty. The Saracens produced from their baskets a quantity of charcoal, a pair of bellows, and a flask of oil. While the one struck a light with a flint and steel, the other disposed the charcoal in the large rusty grate which we have already mentioned, and exercised the bellows until the fuel came to a red glow.

'Seest thou, Isaac,' said Front-de-Bœuf, 'the range of iron bars above that glowing charcoal? *— on that warm couch thou shalt lie, stripped of thy clothes as if thou wert to rest on a bed of down. One of these slaves shall maintain the fire beneath thee, while the other shall anoint thy wretched limbs with oil, lest the roast should burn.—Now, choose betwixt such a scorching bed and the payment of a thousand pounds of silver; for, by the head of my father, thou hast no other option.'

'It is impossible,' exclaimed the miserable Jew —'it is impossible that your purpose can be real! The good God of nature never made a heart capable of exercising such cruelty!'

'Trust not to that, Isaac,' said Front-de-Bœuf, 'it were a fatal error. Dost thou think that I, who

---

* See Note E. The range of iron bars above that glowing charcoal.

have seen a town sacked, in which thousands of my Christian countrymen perished by sword, by flood, and by fire, will blench from my purpose for the outcries or screams of one single wretched Jew?— or thinkest thou that these swarthy slaves, who have neither law, country, nor conscience, but their master's will—who use the poison, or the stake, or the poniard, or the cord, at his slightest wink— thinkest thou that *they* will have mercy, who do not even understand the language in which it is asked?—Be wise, old man; discharge thyself of a portion of thy superfluous wealth; repay to the hands of a Christian a part of what thou hast acquired by the usury thou hast practised on those of his religion. Thy cunning may soon swell out once more thy shrivelled purse, but neither leech nor medicine can restore thy scorched hide and flesh wert thou once stretched on these bars. Tell down thy ransom, I say, and rejoice that at such rate thou canst redeem thee from a dungeon, the secrets of which few have returned to tell. I waste no more words with thee—choose between thy dross and thy flesh and blood, and as thou choosest, so shall it be.'

'So may Abraham, Jacob, and all the fathers of our people assist me,' said Isaac, 'I cannot make the choice, because I have not the means of satisfying your exorbitant demand!'

'Seize him and strip him, slaves,' said the knight, 'and let the fathers of his race assist him if they can.'

The assistants, taking their directions more from

the Baron's eye and his hand than his tongue, once more stepped forward, laid hands on the unfortunate Isaac, plucked him up from the ground, and, holding him between them, waited the hard-hearted Baron's farther signal. The unhappy Jew eyed their countenances and that of Front-de-Bœuf, in hope of discovering some symptoms of relenting; but that of the Baron exhibited the same cold, half-sullen, half-sarcastic smile which had been the prelude to his cruelty; and the savage eyes of the Saracens, rolling gloomily under their dark brows, acquiring a yet more sinister expression by the whiteness of the circle which surrounds the pupil, evinced rather the secret pleasure which they expected from the approaching scene, than any reluctance to be its directors or agents. The Jew then looked at the glowing furnace, over which he was presently to be stretched, and seeing no chance of his tormentor's relenting, his resolution gave way.

'I will pay,' he said, 'the thousand pounds of silver—That is,' he added, after a moment's pause, 'I will pay it with the help of my brethren; for I must beg as a mendicant at the door of our synagogue ere I make up so unheard-of a sum.— When and where must it be delivered?'

'Here,' replied Front-de-Bœuf, 'here it must be delivered—weighed it must be—weighed and told down on this very dungeon floor.—Thinkest thou I will part with thee until thy ransom is secure?'

'And what is to be my surety,' said the Jew, 'that I shall be at liberty after this ransom is paid?'

'The word of a Norman noble, thou pawn-broking slave,' answered Front-de-Bœuf; 'the faith of a Norman nobleman, more pure than the gold and silver of thee and all thy tribe.'

'I crave pardon, noble lord,' said Isaac timidly, 'but wherefore should I rely wholly on the word of one who will trust nothing to mine?'

'Because thou canst not help it, Jew,' said the knight, sternly. 'Wert thou now in thy treasure-chamber at York, and were I craving a loan of thy shekels, it would be thine to dictate the time of payment, and the pledge of security. This is *my* treasure-chamber. Here I have thee at advantage, nor will I again deign to repeat the terms on which I grant thee liberty.'

The Jew groaned deeply.—'Grant me,' he said, 'at least with my own liberty, that of the companions with whom I travel. They scorned me as a Jew, yet they pitied my desolation, and because they tarried to aid me by the way, a share of my evil hath come upon them; moreover, they may contribute in some sort to my ransom.'

'If thou meanest yonder Saxon churls,' said Front-de-Bœuf, 'their ransom will depend upon other terms than thine. Mind thine own concerns, Jew, I warn thee, and meddle not with those of others.'

'I am, then,' said Isaac, 'only to be set at liberty, together with mine wounded friend?'

'Shall I twice recommend it,' said Front-de-Bœuf, 'to a son of Israel, to meddle with his own concerns, and leave those of others alone?—Since thou hast made thy choice, it remains but that thou payest down thy ransom, and that at a short day.'

'Yet hear me,' said the Jew—'for the sake of that very wealth which thou wouldst obtain at the expense of thy——' Here he stopt short, afraid of irritating the savage Norman. But Front-de-Bœuf only laughed, and himself filled up the blank at which the Jew had hesitated. 'At the expense of my conscience, thou wouldst say, Isaac; speak it out—I tell thee, I am reasonable. I can bear the reproaches of a loser, even when that loser is a Jew. Thou wert not so patient, Isaac, when thou didst invoke justice against Jacques Fitzdotterel, for calling thee a usurious blood-sucker, when thy exactions had devoured his patrimony.'

'I swear by the Talmud,' said the Jew, 'that your valour has been misled in that matter. Fitzdotterel drew his poniard upon me in mine own chamber, because I craved him for mine own silver. The term of payment was due at the Passover.'

'I care not what he did,' said Front-de-Bœuf; 'the question is, when shall I have mine own?— when shall I have the shekels, Isaac?'

'Let my daughter Rebecca go forth to York,' answered Isaac, 'with your safe conduct, noble knight, and so soon as man and horse can return, the treasure——' Here he groaned deeply, but added, after the pause of a few seconds,—'The treasure shall be told down on this very floor.'

'Thy daughter!' said Front-de-Bœuf, as if surprised.—'By heavens, Isaac, I would I had known of this. I deemed that yonder black-browed girl had been thy concubine, and I gave her to be a handmaiden to Sir Brian de Bois-Guilbert, after the fashion of patriarchs and heroes of the days of old, who set us in these matters a wholesome example.'

The yell which Isaac raised at this unfeeling communication made the very vault to ring, and astounded the two Saracens so much that they let go their hold of the Jew. He availed himself of his enlargement to throw himself on the pavement, and clasp the knees of Front-de-Bœuf.

'Take all that you have asked,' said he, 'Sir Knight—take ten times more—reduce me to ruin and to beggary, if thou wilt,—nay, pierce me with thy poniard, broil me on that furnace, but spare my daughter, deliver her in safety and honour!— As thou art born of woman, spare the honour of a helpless maiden—She is the image of my deceased Rachael, she is the last of six pledges of her love —Will you deprive a widowed husband of his sole remaining comfort?—Will you reduce a father to wish that his only living child were laid beside her dead mother, in the tomb of our fathers?'

'I would,' said the Norman, somewhat relenting, 'that I had known of this before. I thought your race had loved nothing save their money-bags.'

'Think not so vilely of us, Jews though we be,' said Isaac, eager to improve the moment of apparent sympathy; 'the hunted fox, the tortured wild-cat, loves its young—the despised and persecuted race of Abraham love their children!'

'Be it so,' said Front-de-Bœuf; 'I will believe it in future, Isaac, for thy very sake—but it aids us not now, I cannot help what has happened, or what is to follow; my word is passed to my comrade in arms, nor would I break it for ten Jews and Jewesses to boot. Besides, why shouldst thou think evil is to come to the girl, even if she became Bois-Guilbert's booty?'

'There will, there must!' exclaimed Isaac, wringing his hands in agony; 'when did Templars breathe aught but cruelty to men, and dishonour to women!'

'Dog of an infidel,' said Front-de-Bœuf, with sparkling eyes, and not sorry, perhaps, to seize a pretext for working himself into a passion, 'blaspheme not the Holy Order of the Temple of Zion, but take thought instead to pay me the ransom thou hast promised, or woe betide thy Jewish throat!'

'Robber and villain!' said the Jew, retorting the insults of his oppressor with passion, which, however impotent, he now found it impossible to bridle, 'I will pay thee nothing—not one silver penny will I pay thee, unless my daughter is delivered to me in safety and honour?'

'Art thou in thy senses, Israelite?' said the Norman, sternly—'has thy flesh and blood a charm against heated iron and scalding oil?'

'I care not!' said the Jew, rendered desperate by paternal affection; 'do thy worst. My daughter is my flesh and blood, dearer to me a thousand times than those limbs which thy cruelty threatens. No silver will I give thee, unless I were to pour it molten down thy avaricious throat—no, not a silver penny will I give thee, Nazarene, were it to save thee from the deep damnation thy whole life has merited! Take my life if thou wilt, and say, the Jew, amidst his tortures, knew how to disappoint the Christian.'

'We shall see that,' said Front-de-Bœuf; 'for by the blessed rood, which is the abomination of thy accursed tribe, thou shalt feel the extremities of fire and steel!—Strip him, slaves, and chain him down upon the bars.'

In spite of the feeble struggles of the old man, the Saracens had already torn from him his upper garment, and were proceeding totally to disrobe him, when the sound of a bugle, twice winded without the castle, penetrated even to the recesses of the dungeon, and immediately after loud voices were heard calling for Sir Reginald Front-de-Bœuf. Unwilling to be found engaged in his hellish occupation, the savage Baron gave the slaves a signal to restore Isaac's garment, and, quitting the dungeon with his attendants, he left the Jew to thank God for his own deliverance, or to lament over his daughter's captivity, and probable fate, as his personal or parental feelings might prove strongest.

CHAPTER XXIII

Nay, if the gentle spirit of moving words
Can no way change you to a milder form,
I'll woo you, like a soldier, at arms' end,
And love you 'gainst the nature of love, force you.
TWO GENTLEMEN OF VERONA.

THE apartment to which the Lady Rowena had been introduced was fitted up with some rude attempts at ornament and magnificence, and her being placed there might be considered as a peculiar mark of respect not offered to the other prisoners. But the wife of Front-de-Bœuf, for whom it had been originally furnished, was long dead, and decay and neglect had impaired the few ornaments with which her taste had adorned it. The tapestry hung down from the walls in many places, and in others was tarnished and faded under the effects of the sun, or tattered and decayed by age. Desolate, however, as it was, this was the apartment of the castle which had been judged most fitting for the accommodation of the Saxon heiress; and here she was left to meditate upon her fate, until the actors in this nefarious drama had arranged the several parts which each of them was to perform. This had been settled in a council held by Front-de-Bœuf, De Bracy, and the Templar, in which, after a long and warm debate concerning the several advantages which each insisted upon deriving from his peculiar share in this audacious enterprise, they had at length determined the fate of their unhappy prisoners.

It was about the hour of noon, therefore, when De Bracy, for whose advantage the expedition had been first planned, appeared to prosecute his views upon the hand and possessions of the Lady Rowena.

The interval had not entirely been bestowed in holding council with his confederates, for De Bracy had found leisure to decorate his person with all the foppery of the times. His green cassock and vizard were now flung aside. His long luxuriant hair was trained to flow in quaint tresses down his richly furred cloak. His beard was closely shaved, his doublet reached to the middle of his leg, and the girdle which secured it, and at the same time supported his ponderous sword, was embroidered and embossed with gold work. We have already noticed the extravagant fashion of the shoes at this period, and the points of Maurice de Bracy's might have challenged the prize of extravagance with the gayest, being turned up and twisted like the horns of a ram. Such was the dress of a gallant of the period; and, in the present instance, that effect was aided by the handsome person and good demeanour of the wearer, whose manners partook alike of the grace of a courtier, and the frankness of a soldier.

He saluted Rowena by doffing his velvet bonnet,

garnished with a golden brooch, representing St. Michael trampling down the Prince of Evil. With this, he gently motioned the lady to a seat; and, as she still retained her standing posture, the knight ungloved his right hand, and motioned to conduct her thither. But Rowena declined, by her gesture, the proffered compliment, and replied, 'If I be in the presence of my jailor, Sir Knight — nor will circumstances allow me to think otherwise—it best becomes his prisoner to remain standing till she learns her doom.'

'Alas! fair Rowena,' returned De Bracy, 'you are in presence of your captive, not your jailor; and it is from your fair eyes that De Bracy must receive that doom which you fondly expect from him.'

'I know you not, sir,' said the lady, drawing herself up with all the pride of offended rank and beauty; 'I know you not—and the insolent familiarity with which you apply to me the jargon of a troubadour, forms no apology for the violence of a robber.'

'To thyself, fair maid,' answered De Bracy, in his former tone—' to thine own charms be ascribed whate'er I have done which passed the respect due to her, whom I have chosen queen of my heart, and loadstar of my eyes.'

'I repeat to you, Sir Knight, that I know you not, and that no man wearing chain and spurs ought thus to intrude himself upon the presence of an unprotected lady.'

'That I am unknown to you,' said De Bracy,

'is indeed my misfortune; yet let me hope that De Bracy's name has not been always unspoken, when minstrels or heralds have praised deeds of chivalry, whether in the lists or in the battle-field.'

'To heralds and to minstrels, then, leave thy praise, Sir Knight,' replied Rowena, 'more suiting for their mouths than for thine own; and tell me which of them shall record in song, or in book of tourney, the memorable conquest of this night, a conquest obtained over an old man, followed by a few timid hinds; and its booty, an unfortunate maiden, transported against her will to the castle of a robber?'

'You are unjust, Lady Rowena,' said the knight, biting his lips in some confusion, and speaking in a tone more natural to him than that of affected gallantry, which he had at first adopted; 'yourself free from passion, you can allow no excuse for the frenzy of another, although caused by your own beauty.'

'I pray you, Sir Knight,' said Rowena, 'to cease a language so commonly used by strolling minstrels, that it becomes not the mouth of knights or nobles. Certes, you constrain me to sit down, since you enter upon such commonplace terms, of which each vile crowder hath a stock that might last from hence to Christmas.'

'Proud damsel,' said De Bracy, incensed at finding his gallant style procured him nothing but contempt—'proud damsel, thou shalt be as proudly encountered. Know then, that I have supported

IVANHOE

my pretensions to your hand in the way that best
suited thy character. It is meeter for thy humour
to be wooed with bow and bill, than in set terms,
and in courtly language.'

'Courtesy of tongue,' said Rowena, 'when it is
used to veil churlishness of deed, is but a knight's
girdle around the breast of a base clown. I wonder
not that the restraint appears to gall you—more
it were for your honour to have retained the dress
and language of an outlaw, than to veil the deeds
of one under an affectation of gentle language and
demeanour.'

'You counsel well, lady,' said the Norman;
'and in the bold language which best justifies bold
action, I tell thee, thou shalt never leave this castle,
or thou shalt leave it as Maurice de Bracy's wife.
I am not wont to be baffled in my enterprises, nor
needs a Norman noble scrupulously to vindicate his
conduct to the Saxon maiden whom he distin-
guishes by the offer of his hand. Thou art proud,
Rowena, and thou art the fitter to be my wife.
By what other means couldst thou be raised
to high honour and to princely place, saving
by my alliance? How else wouldst thou escape
from the mean precincts of a country grange,
where Saxons herd with the swine which form
their wealth, to take thy seat, honoured as thou
shouldst be, and shalt be, amid all in England
that is distinguished by beauty, or dignified by
power?'

'Sir Knight,' replied Rowena, 'the grange which
you contemn hath been my shelter from infancy;

329

and, trust me, when I leave it—should that day ever arrive—it shall be with one who has not learnt to despise the dwelling and manners in which I have been brought up.'

'I guess your meaning, lady,' said De Bracy, 'though you may think it lies too obscure for my apprehension. But dream not, that Richard Cœur de Lion will ever resume his throne, far less that Wilfred of Ivanhoe, his minion, will ever lead thee to his footstool, to be there welcomed as the bride of a favourite. Another suitor might feel jealousy while he touched this string; but my firm purpose cannot be changed by a passion so childish and so hopeless. Know, lady, that this rival is in my power, and that it rests but with me to betray the secret of his being within the castle to Front-de-Bœuf, whose jealousy will be more fatal than mine.'

'Wilfred here?' said Rowena, in disdain; 'that is as true as that Front-de-Bœuf is his rival.'

De Bracy looked at her steadily for an instant. 'Wert thou really ignorant of this?' said he; 'didst thou not know that Wilfred of Ivanhoe travelled in the litter of the Jew?—a meet conveyance for the crusader, whose doughty arm was to reconquer the Holy Sepulchre!' And he laughed scornfully.

'And if he is here,' said Rowena, compelling herself to a tone of indifference, though trembling with an agony of apprehension which she could not suppress, 'in what is he the rival of Front-de-Bœuf? or what has he to fear beyond a short imprisonment, and an honourable ransom, according to the use of chivalry?'

'Rowena,' said De Bracy, 'art thou, too, deceived by the common error of thy sex, who think there can be no rivalry but that respecting their own charms? Knowest thou not there is a jealousy of ambition and of wealth, as well as of love; and that this our host, Front-de-Bœuf, will push from his road him who opposes his claim to the fair barony of Ivanhoe, as readily, eagerly, and unscrupulously, as if he were preferred to him by some blue-eyed damsel? But smile on my suit, lady, and the wounded champion shall have nothing to fear from Front-de-Bœuf, whom else thou mayst mourn for, as in the hands of one who has never shown compassion.'

'Save him, for the love of Heaven!' said Rowena, her firmness giving way under terror for her lover's impending fate.

'I can—I will—it is my purpose,' said De Bracy; 'for, when Rowena consents to be the bride of De Bracy, who is it shall dare to put forth a violent hand upon her kinsman—the son of her guardian—the companion of her youth? But it is thy love must buy his protection. I am not romantic fool enough to further the fortune, or avert the fate, of one who is likely to be a successful obstacle between me and my wishes. Use thine influence with me in his behalf, and he is safe,— refuse to employ it, Wilfred dies, and thou thyself art not the nearer to freedom.'

'Thy language,' answered Rowena, 'hath in its

IVANHOE

indifferent bluntness something which cannot be reconciled with the horrors it seems to express. I believe not that thy purpose is so wicked, or thy power so great.'

'Flatter thyself, then, with that belief,' said De Bracy, 'until time shall prove it false. Thy lover lies wounded in this castle—thy preferred lover. He is a bar betwixt Front-de-Bœuf and that which Front-de-Bœuf loves better than either ambition or beauty. What will it cost beyond the blow of a poniard, or the thrust of a javelin, to silence his opposition for ever? Nay, were Front-de-Bœuf afraid to justify a deed so open, let the leech but give his patient a wrong draught—let the chamberlain, or the nurse who tends him, but pluck the pillow from his head, and Wilfred, in his present condition, is sped without the effusion of blood. Cedric also——'

'And Cedric also,' said Rowena, repeating his words; 'my noble—my generous guardian! I deserved the evil I have encountered, for forgetting his fate even in that of his son!'

'Cedric's fate also depends upon thy determination,' said De Bracy; 'and I leave thee to form it.'

Hitherto, Rowena had sustained her part in this trying scene with undismayed courage, but it was because she had not considered the danger as serious and imminent. Her disposition was naturally that which physiognomists consider as proper to fair complexions, mild, timid, and gentle; but it had been tempered, and, as it were, hardened, by

332

the circumstances of her education. Accustomed
to see the will of all, even of Cedric himself,
(sufficiently arbitrary with others,) give way before
her wishes, she had acquired that sort of courage
and self-confidence which arises from the habitual
and constant deference of the circle in which we
move. She could scarce conceive the possibility of
her will being opposed, far less that of its being
treated with total disregard.

Her haughtiness and habit of domination was,
therefore, a fictitious character, induced over that
which was natural to her, and it deserted her when
her eyes were opened to the extent of her own
danger, as well as that of her lover and her guardian;
and when she found her will, the slightest expression of which was wont to command respect and
attention, now placed in opposition to that of a
man of a strong, fierce, and determined mind, who
possessed the advantage over her, and was resolved
to use it, she quailed before him.

After casting her eyes around, as if to look for
the aid which was nowhere to be found, and after
a few broken interjections, she raised her hands to
heaven, and burst into a passion of uncontrolled
vexation and sorrow. It was impossible to see so
beautiful a creature in such extremity without feeling for her, and De Bracy was not unmoved, though
he was yet more embarrassed than touched. He
had, in truth, gone too far to recede; and yet, in
Rowena's present condition, she could not be acted
on either by argument or threats. He paced the
apartment to and fro, now vainly exhorting the

terrified maiden to compose herself, now hesitating concerning his own line of conduct.

If, thought he, I should be moved by the tears and sorrow of this disconsolate damsel, what should I reap but the loss of those fair hopes for which I have encountered so much risk, and the ridicule of Prince John and his jovial comrades? ' And yet,' he said to himself, ' I feel myself ill framed for the part which I am playing. I cannot look on so fair a face while it is disturbed with agony, or on those eyes when they are drowned in tears. I would she had retained her original haughtiness of disposition, or that I had a larger share of Front-de-Bœuf's thrice-tempered hardness of heart!'

Agitated by these thoughts, he could only bid the unfortunate Rowena be comforted, and assure her, that as yet she had no reason for the excess of despair to which she was now giving way. But in this task of consolation De Bracy was interrupted by the horn, ' hoarse-winded blowing far and keen,' which had at the same time alarmed the other inmates of the castle, and interrupted their several plans of avarice and of license. Of them all, perhaps, De Bracy least regretted the interruption; for his conference with the Lady Rowena had arrived at a point, where he found it equally difficult to prosecute or to resign his enterprise.

And here we cannot but think it necessary to offer some better proof than the incidents of an idle tale, to vindicate the melancholy representation of manners which has been just laid before the reader. It is grievous to think that those valiant barons, to whose stand against the crown the liberties of England were indebted for their existence, should themselves have been such dreadful oppressors, and capable of excesses contrary not only to the laws of England, but to those of nature and humanity. But, alas! we have only to extract from the industrious Henry one of those numerous passages which he has collected from contemporary historians, to prove that fiction itself can hardly reach the dark reality of the horrors of the period.

The description given by the author of the Saxon Chronicle of the cruelties exercised in the reign of King Stephen by the great barons and lords of castles, who were all Normans, affords a strong proof of the excesses of which they were capable when their passions were inflamed. 'They grievously oppressed the poor people by building castles; and when they were built, they filled them with wicked men, or rather devils, who seized both men and women who they imagined had any money, threw them into prison, and put them to more cruel tortures than the martyrs ever endured. They suffocated some in mud, and suspended others by the feet, or the head, or the thumbs, kindling fires below them. They squeezed the heads of some with knotted cords till they pierced their brains, while they threw others into dungeons swarming with serpents, snakes, and toads.' But it would be cruel to put the reader to the pain of perusing the remainder of this description.*

---

* Henry's Hist. edit. 1805, vol. vii. p. 346.

As another instance of these bitter fruits of conquest, and perhaps the strongest that can be quoted, we may mention, that the Princess Matilda, though a daughter of the King of Scotland, and afterwards both Queen of England, niece to Edgar Atheling, and mother to the Empress of Germany, the daughter, the wife, and the mother of monarchs, was obliged, during her early residence for education in England, to assume the veil of a nun, as the only means of escaping the licentious pursuit of the Norman nobles. This excuse she stated before a great council of the clergy of England, as the sole reason for her having taken the religious habit. The assembled clergy admitted the validity of the plea, and the notoriety of the circumstances upon which it was founded; giving thus an indubitable and most remarkable testimony to the existence of that disgraceful license by which that age was stained. It was a matter of public knowledge, they said, that after the conquest of King William, his Norman followers, elated by so great a victory, acknowledged no law but their own wicked pleasure, and not only despoiled the conquered Saxons of their lands and their goods, but invaded the honour of their wives and of their daughters with the most unbridled license; and hence it was then common for matrons and maidens of noble families to assume the veil, and take shelter in convents, not as called thither by the vocation of God, but solely to preserve their honour from the unbridled wickedness of man.

Such and so licentious were the times, as

announced by the public declaration of the assembled
clergy, recorded by Eadmer ; and we need add
nothing more to vindicate the probability of the
scenes which we have detailed, and are about to
detail, upon the more apocryphal authority of the
Wardour MS.

END OF VOLUME I

NOTES

CHAPTER I

Note A, p. 13.—THE RANGER OF THE FOREST, THAT CUTS THE FORECLAWS OFF OUR DOGS

A MOST sensible grievance of those aggrieved times were the Forest Laws. These oppressive enactments were the produce of the Norman Conquest, for the Saxon laws of the chase were mild and humane; while those of William, enthusiastically attached to the exercise and its rights, were to the last degree tyrannical. The formation of the New Forest, bears evidence to his passion for hunting, where he reduced many a happy village to the condition of that one commemorated by my friend, Mr. William Stewart Rose:

> 'Amongst the ruins of the church,
> The midnight raven found a perch,
> A melancholy place;
> The ruthless Conqueror cast down,
> Woe worth the deed, that little town,
> To lengthen out his chase.'

The disabling dogs, which might be necessary for keeping flocks and herds, from running at the deer, was called *lawing*, and was in general use. The Charter of the Forest designed to lessen those evils, declares that inquisition, or view, for lawing dogs, shall be made every third year, and shall be then done by the view and testimony of lawful men, not otherwise; and they whose dogs shall be then found unlawed, shall give three shillings for mercy, and for the future no man's ox shall be taken for lawing. Such lawing also shall be done by the assize commonly used, and which is, that three claws shall be cut off without the ball of the right foot. See on this subject the Historical Essay on the Magna Charta of King John, (a most beautiful volume), by Richard Thomson.

IVANHOE

CHAPTER II

Note B, p. 22.—Negro Slaves

The severe accuracy of some critics has objected to the complexion of the slaves of Brian de Bois-Guilbert, as being totally out of costume and propriety. I remember the same objection being made to a set of sable functionaries, whom my friend, Mat Lewis, introduced as the guards and mischief-doing satellites of the wicked Baron, in his Castle Spectre. Mat treated the objection with great contempt, and averred in reply, that he made the slaves black in order to obtain a striking effect of contrast, and that, could he have derived a similar advantage from making his heroine blue, blue she should have been.

I do not pretend to plead the immunities of my order so highly as this; but neither will I allow that the author of a modern antique romance is obliged to confine himself to the introduction of those manners only which can be proved to have absolutely existed in the times he is depicting, so that he restrain himself to such as are plausible and natural, and contain no obvious anachronism. In this point of view, what can be more natural, than that the Templars, who, we know, copied closely the luxuries of the Asiatic warriors with whom they fought, should use the service of the enslaved Africans, whom the fate of war transferred to new masters? I am sure, if there are no precise proofs of their having done so, there is nothing, on the other hand, that can entitle us positively to conclude that they never did. Besides, there is an instance in romance.

John of Rampayne, an excellent juggler and minstrel, undertook to effect the escape of one Audulf de Bracy, by presenting himself in disguise at the court of the king, where he was confined. For this purpose, ' he stained his hair and his whole body entirely as black as jet, so that nothing was white but 'his teeth,' and succeeded in imposing himself on the king, as an Ethiopian minstrel. He effected, by stratagem, the escape of the prisoner. Negroes, therefore, must have been known in England in the dark ages.*

CHAPTER XVII

Note C, p. 253.—Minstrelsy

The realm of France, it is well known, was divided betwixt the Norman and Teutonic race, who spoke the language in

---

* Dissertation on Romance and Minstrelsy, prefixed to Ritson's Ancient Metrical Romances, p. clxxxvii.

NOTES

which the word Yes is pronounced as *oui*, and the inhabitants of the southern regions, whose speech bearing some affinity to the Italian, pronounced the same word *oc*. The poets of the former race were called *Minstrels*, and their poems *Lays*: those of the latter were termed *Troubadours*, and their compositions called *sirventes*, and other names. Richard, a professed admirer of the joyous science in all its branches, could imitate either the minstrel or troubadour. It is less likely that he should have been able to compose or sing an English ballad; yet so much do we wish to assimilate Him of the Lion Heart to the band of warriors whom he led, that the anachronism, if there be one, may readily be forgiven.

CHAPTER XXI

Note D, p. 305.—Battle of Stamford

A great topographical blunder occurred here in former editions. The bloody battle alluded to in the text, fought and won by King Harold, over his brother the rebellious Tosti, and an auxiliary force of Danes or Norsemen, was said, in the text, and a corresponding note, to have taken place at Stamford, in Leicestershire, and upon the river Welland. This is a mistake, into which the author has been led by trusting to his memory, and so confounding two places of the same name. The Stamford, Strangford, or Staneford, at which the battle really was fought, is a ford upon the river Derwent, at the distance of about seven miles from York, and situated in that large and opulent county. A long wooden bridge over the Derwent, the site of which, with one remaining buttress, is still shown to the curious traveller, was furiously contested. One Norwegian long defended it by his single arm, and was at length pierced with a spear thrust through the planks of the bridge from a boat beneath.

The neighbourhood of Stamford, on the Derwent, contains some memorials of the battle. Horseshoes, swords, and the heads of halberds, or bills, are often found there; one place is called the 'Danes' well,' another the 'Battle flats.' From a tradition that the weapon with which the Norwegian champion was slain, resembled a pear, or, as others say, that the trough or boat in which the soldier floated under the bridge to strike the blow, had such a shape, the country people usually begin a great market, which is held at Stamford, with an entertainment called the Pear-pie feast, which after all may be a corruption of the Spear-pie feast. For more particulars, Drake's History of York

IVANHOE

may be referred to. The author's mistake was pointed out to him, in the most obliging manner, by Robert Belt, Esq. of Bossal House. The battle was fought in 1066.

CHAPTER XXII

Note E, p. 317. — THE RANGE OF IRON BARS ABOVE THAT GLOWING CHARCOAL

This horrid species of torture may remind the reader of that to which the Spaniards subjected Guatimozin, in order to extort a discovery of his concealed wealth. But, in fact, an instance of similar barbarity is to be found nearer home, and occurs in the annals of Queen Mary's time, containing so many other examples of atrocity. Every reader must recollect, that after the fall of the Catholic Church, and the Presbyterian Church Government had been established by law, the rank, and especially the wealth, of the Bishops, Abbots, Priors, and so forth, were no longer vested in ecclesiastics, but in lay impropriators of the church revenues, or, as the Scottish lawyers called them, *titulars* of the temporalities of the benefice, though having no claim to the spiritual character of their predecessors in office.

Of these laymen, who were thus invested with ecclesiastical revenues, some were men of high birth and rank, like the famous Lord James Stewart, the Prior of St. Andrews, who did not fail to keep for their own use the rents, lands, and revenues of the church. But if, on the other hand, the titulars were men of inferior importance, who had been inducted into the office by the interest of some powerful person, it was generally understood that the new Abbot should grant for his patron's benefit such leases and conveyances of the church lands and tithes as might afford their protector the lion's share of the booty. This was the origin of those who were wittily termed Tulchan * Bishops, being a sort of imaginary prelate, whose image was set up to enable his patron and principal to plunder the benefice under his name.

There were other cases, however, in which men who had got grants of these secularised benefices, were desirous of retaining them for their own use, without having the influence sufficient to establish their purpose ; and these became frequently unable to

---

* A *Tulchan* is a calf's skin stuffed, and placed before a cow who has lost its calf, to induce the animal to part with her milk. The resemblance between such a Tulchan and a Bishop named to transmit the temporalities of a benefice to some powerful patron, is easily understood.

NOTES

protect themselves, however unwilling to submit to the exactions of the feudal tyrant of the district.

Bannatyne, secretary to John Knox, recounts a singular course of oppression practised on one of those titular abbots, by the Earl of Cassilis in Ayrshire, whose extent of feudal influence was so wide that he was usually termed the King of Carrick. We give the fact as it occurs in Bannatyne's Journal, only premising that the Journalist held his master's opinions, both with respect to the Earl of Cassilis as an opposer of the king's party, and as being a detester of the practice of granting church revenues to titulars, instead of their being devoted to pious uses, such as the support of the clergy, expense of schools, and the relief of the national poor. He mingles in the narrative, therefore, a well-deserved feeling of execration against the tyrant who employed the torture, with a tone of ridicule towards the patient, as if, after all, it had not been ill bestowed on such an equivocal and amphibious character as a titular abbot. He entitles his narrative,

THE EARL OF CASSILIS'. TYRANNY AGAINST A QUICK
(*i.e.* LIVING) MAN

'Master Allan Stewart, friend to Captain James Stewart of Cardonall, by means of the Queen's corrupted court, obtained the Abbey of Crossraguel. The said Earl thinking himself greater than any king in those quarters, determined to have that whole benefice (as he hath divers others) to pay at his pleasure; and because he could not find sic security as his insatiable appetite required, this shift was devised. The said Mr. Allan being in company with the Laird of Bargany, (also a Kennedy,) was, by the Earl and his friends, enticed to leave the safeguard which he had with the Laird, and come to make good cheer with the said Earl. The simplicity of the imprudent man was suddenly abused; and so he passed his time with them certain days, which he did in Maybole with Thomas Kennedie, uncle to the said Earl: after which the said Mr. Allan passed, with quiet company, to visit the place and bounds of Crossraguel, [his abbacy,] of which the said Earl being surely advertised, determined to put in practice the tyranny which long before he had conceaved. And so, as king of the country, apprehended the said Mr. Allan, and carried him to the house of Denure, where for a season he was honourably treated, (gif a prisoner can think any entertainment pleasing;) but after that certain days were spent, and that the Earl could not obtain the feus of Crossraguel according to his awin appetite, he determined to prove gif a collation could work that which neither dinner nor supper could do for a long time. And so the

343

IVANHOE

said Mr. Allan was carried to a secret chamber: with him passed
the honourable Earl, his worshipful brother, and such as were
appointed to be servants at that banquet. In the chamber there
was a grit iron chimlay, under it a fire; other grit provision was
not seen. The first course was,—"My Lord Abbot," (said the
Earl,) "it will please you confess here, that with your own consent
you remain in my company, because ye durst not commit yourself
to the hands of others." The Abbot answered, "Would you, my
lord, that I should make a manifest lie for your pleasure? The
truth is, my lord, it is against my will that I am here; neither
yet have I any pleasure in your company." "But ye shall remain
with me, nevertheless, at this time," said the Earl. "I am not
able to resist your will and pleasure," said the Abbot, "in this
place." "Ye must then obey me," said the Earl,—and with that
were presented unto him certain letters to subscribe, amongst
which there was a five years' tack, and a nineteen years' tack, and
a charter of feu of all the lands of Crossraguel, with all the clauses
necessary for the Earl to haste him to hell. For gif adultery,
sacrilege, oppression, barbarous cruelty, and theft heaped upon
theft, deserve hell, the great King of Carrick can no more escape
hell for ever, than the imprudent Abbot escaped the fire for a
season as follows.

' After that the Earl spied repugnance, and saw that he could
not come to his purpose by fair means, he commanded his cooks
to prepare the banquet: and so first they flayed the sheep, that
is, they took off the Abbot's cloathes even to his skin, and next
they bound him to the chimney—his legs to the one end, and his
arms to the other; and so they began to beet [i.e. feed] the fire
sometimes to his buttocks, sometimes to his legs, sometimes to
his shoulders and arms; and that the roast might not burn, but
that it might rest in soppe, they spared not flambing with oil,
(basting as a cook bastes roasted meat); Lord, look thou to sic
cruelty! And that the crying of the miserable man should not
be heard, they closed his mouth that the voice might be stopped.
It may be suspected that some partisan of the King's [Darnley's]
murder was there. In that torment they held the poor man,
till that often he cried for God's sake to dispatch him; for he
had as meikle gold in his awin purse as would buy powder enough
to shorten his pain. The famous King of Carrick and his cooks
perceiving the roast to be aneuch, commanded it to be tane fra
the fire, and the Earl himself began the grace in this manner:—
" Benedicite, Jesus Maria, you are the most obstinate man that ever
I saw; gif I had known that ye had been so stubborn, I would not
for a thousand crowns have handled you so; I never did so to

344

man before you." And yet he returned to the same practice within two days, and ceased not till that he obtained his formost purpose, that is, that he had got all his pieces subscryvit alsweill as ane half-roasted hand could do it. The Earl thinking himself sure enough so long as he had the half-roasted Abbot in his awin keeping, and yet being ashamed of his presence by reason of his former cruelty, left the place of Denure in the hands of certain of his servants, and the half-roasted Abbot to be kept there as prisoner. The Laird of Bargany, out of whose company the said Abbot had been enticed, understanding, (not the extremity,) but the retaining of the man, sent to the court, and raised letters of deliverance of the person of the man according to the order, which being disobeyed, the said Earl for his contempt was denounced rebel, and put to the horne. But yet hope was there none, neither to the afflicted to be delivered, neither yet to the purchaser [*i.e.* procurer] of the letters to obtain any comfort thereby; for in that time God was despised, and the lawful authority was contemned in Scotland, in hope of the sudden return and regiment of that cruel murderer of her awin husband, of whose lords the said Earl was called one; and yet, oftener than once, he was solemnly sworn to the King and to his Regent.'

The Journalist then recites the complaint of the injured Allan Stewart, Commendator of Crossraguel, to the Regent and Privy Council, averring his having been carried, partly by flattery, partly by force, to the black vault of Denure, a strong fortalice, built on a rock overhanging the Irish channel, where its ruins are still visible. Here he stated he had been required to execute leases and conveyances of the whole churches and parsonages belonging to the Abbey of Crossraguel, which he utterly refused as an unreasonable demand, and the more so that he had already conveyed them to John Stewart of Cardonall, by whose interest he had been made Commendator. The complainant proceeds to state, that he was, after many menaces, stript, bound, and his limbs exposed to fire in the manner already described, till, compelled by excess of agony, he subscribed the charter and leases presented to him, of the contents of which he was totally ignorant. A few days afterwards, being again required to execute a ratification of these deeds before a notary and witnesses, and refusing to do so, he was once more subjected to the same torture, until his agony was so excessive that he exclaimed, 'Fye on you, why do you not strike your whingers into me, or blow me up with a barrel of powder, rather than torture me thus unmercifully?' upon which the Earl commanded Alexander Richard, one of his

345

attendants, to stop the patient's mouth with a napkin, which was done accordingly. Thus he was once more compelled to submit to their tyranny. The petition concluded with stating, that the Earl, under pretence of the deeds thus iniquitously obtained, had taken possession of the whole place and living of Crossraguel, and enjoyed the profits thereof for three years.

The doom of the Regent and Council shows singularly the total interruption of justice at this calamitous period, even in the most clamant cases of oppression. The Council declined interference with the course of the ordinary justice of the county, (which was completely under the said Earl of Cassilis' control,) and only enacted, that he should forbear molestation of the unfortunate Commendator, under the surety of two thousand pounds Scots. The Earl was appointed also to keep the peace towards the celebrated George Buchanan, who had a pension out of the same Abbacy, to a similar extent, and under the like penalty.

The consequences are thus described by the Journalist already quoted.

'The said Laird of Bargany perceiving that the ordiner justice could neither help the oppressed, nor yet the afflicted, applied his mind to the next remedy, and in the end, by his servants, took the house of Denure, where the poor Abbot was kept prisoner. The bruit flew fra Carrick to Galloway, and so suddenly assembled herd and hyre-man that pertained to the band of the Kennedies; and so within a few hours was the house of Denure environed again. The master of Cassilis was the frackast [*i.e.* the readiest or boldest] and would not stay, but in his heat would lay fire to the dungeon, with no small boasting that all enemies within the house should die.

'He was required and admonished by those that were within to be more moderate, and not to hazard himself so foolishly. But no admonition would help, till that the wind of an hacquebute blasted his shoulder, and then ceased he from further pursuit in fury. The Laird of Bargany had before purchest [obtained] of the authorities, letters, charging all faithfull subjects to the King's Majesty, to assist him against that cruel tyrant and man-sworn traitor, the Earl of Cassilis; which letters, with his private writings, he published, and shortly found sic concurrence of Kyle and Cunynghame with his other friends, that the Carrick company drew back fra the house: and so the other approached, furnished the house with more men, delivered the said Mr. Allan, and carried him to Ayr, where, publicly at the market cross of the said town, he declared how cruelly he was entreated, and how the murdered King suffered not sic torment as he did, excepting

NOTES

only he escaped the death : and, therefore, publickly did revoke all things that were done in that extremity, and especially he revoked the subscription of the three writings, to wit, of a fyve yeir tack and nineteen year tack, and of a charter of feu. And so the house remained, and remains (till this day, the 7th of February, 1571,) in the custody of the said Laird of Bargany and of his servants. And so cruelty was disappointed of proffeit present, and shall be eternallie punished, unless he earnestly repent. And this far for the cruelty committed, to give occasion unto others, and to such as hate the monstrous dealing of degenerate nobility, to look more diligently upon their behaviours, and to paint them forth unto the world, that they themselves may be ashamed of their own beastliness, and that the world may be advertised and admonished to abhor, detest, and avoid the company of all sic tyrants, who are not worthy of the society of men, but ought to be sent suddenly to the devil, with whom they must burn without end, for their contempt of God, and cruelty committed against his creatures. Let Cassilis and his brother be the first to be the example unto others. Amen. Amen.' *

This extract has been somewhat amended or modernized in orthography, to render it more intelligible to the general reader. I have to add, that the Kennedies of Bargany, who interfered in behalf of the oppressed Abbot, were themselves a younger branch of the Cassilis family, but held different politics, and were powerful enough in this, and other instances, to bid them defiance.

The ultimate issue of this affair does not appear; but as the house of Cassilis are still in possession of the greater part of the feus and leases which belonged to Crossraguel Abbey, it is probable the talons of the King of Carrick were strong enough, in those disorderly times, to retain the prey which they had so mercilessly fixed upon.

I may also add, that it appears by some papers in my possession, that the officers or Country Keepers on the border, were accustomed to torment their prisoners by binding them to the iron bars of their chimneys, to extort confession.

---

* Bannatyne's Journal.

GLOSSARY

agraffe, *a clasp or hook,* 109.

alsweill, *as well,* 347.

amice, *a loose flowing garment worn by religious orders, made of or lined with gray fur,* 252.

an, *if.*

ane, *one.*

aneuch, *enough.*

arber, *the pluck (heart, liver and lungs) of the deer,* 66.

arrets, *decrees,* 31.

attaint, the, *see* p. 125.

Auchinleck Manuscripts, *a collection made by Sir Alexander Boswell of Auchinleck (1775-1822), some of which were printed by him at his private press in Auchinleck House, Ayrshire,* xlv.

awin, *own,* 345.

baith, *both,* xxii.

bandeau, *a narrow band,* 10.

banderole, *a streamer,* 21.

Bannatyne Manuscript, *a manuscript preserving much ancient Scottish poetry, compiled during the pestilence of 1568 by George Bannatyne (1545-1608), a native of Forfarshire,* xlv.

Beau-seant, *the banner of the Templars, see* p. 185.

beccafico, *a bird of the warbler species,* 215.

beet, *add fuel,* 346.

black sanctus, *a burlesque of the Sanctus of the Missal,* 287.

bow-hand, *left hand,* i.e. *not quite right,* 54.

brown-bill, *battle-axe,* 262.

bzyant, *a Byzantine gold coin,* 110.

caracoled, *pranced,* 107.

cave, adsum, *beware, I am here,* 133.

chaffering, *bargaining,* 163.

chamfrom, *plated head-piece of a horse,* 21.

chimlay, *chimney,* 346.

clipt within the ring, *the mediæval method of sweating the coinage,* 162.

cnichts, *originally military attendants, sometimes free, sometimes bondsmen; the Saxon word became, as 'knight,' the synonym for the Norman chevalier,* 43.

cockle-shell, *the badge of a pilgrim from the Holy Land,* 51.

crowder, *fiddler, minstrel,* 328.

curee, *the portion of the deer given to the hounds,* 66.

curtal friar, *a lower order of friar, wearing a short gown,* 251.

demi-volte, *a half-turn on horseback,* 131.

desdichado, *disinherited,* 128.

donjon, *central tower of a castle,* 301.

drink hael, *I drink your health,* 248.

enow, *enough.*

epopeia, *the history or fable on which an epic is founded,* xxx.

estrado, *raised platform or dais,* 155.

349

IVANHOE

Exchequer of the Jews, *an office for exacting tribute from the Jews,* 75, 91.

feu, *land held in return for feudal services,* 345.

fra, *from.*

frackast, *readiest, boldest,* 348.

franklin, *Saxon gentleman.*

Free Companions, *mercenaries.*

freedom of the Rules, *freedom granted to a Scots advocate to plead in the English courts,* xxvii.

fusty bandias, ... strike pantnere, '*thirsty bandits . . . . strike [open] the bottle,*' xxiii-iv.

gaberdine, *a long loose felt cloak, worn distinctively by Jews,* 104.

gaged, *pledged,* 118.

gare le corbeau, *beware the raven,* 130.

gauds, *trinkets,* 74.

gif, *if.*

glaive, *sword,* 262.

gorget, *throat armour,* 194.

gramercy, *great thanks,* 96.

grange, *farm-house,* 329.

guilder, *a coin worth 2s. 4d.,* 160.

hacquebute, *an ancient musquet,* 348.

halfling, *half of a silver penny,* 74.

halidom, *honour, faith;* lit. *something holy or sacred,* 117.

heart-spone, *the breast-bone,* 178.

hership, *pillage,* 45.

High Jinks, *see Guy Mannering,* ii. 83.

hog dear to St. Anthony, *St. Anthony was the patron saint of swineherds,* 267.

Holy Standard, day of the, *the battle of Northallerton, in which the English defeated the Scots (22nd August 1138); so named because the*

English carried into battle a mast bearing on its summit the consecrated host, and the banners of three saints, 67.

hyreman, *a hired servant,* 348.

karum-pie, *a pasty of delicacies,* 215.

kye, *cows,* xxii.

laird, *lord of the manor,* 345.

lawing, *mutilation of dogs to prevent their chasing deer,* 341.

leg-bail, to give, *to run away,* 282.

le noir faineant, *the black sluggard.* 190.

lere, *learn,* xxii.

Mahound, *Mahomet,* 31.

mansworn, *perjured,* 348.

mark, merk, *a coin worth* 13s. 4d., 110, 167.

maroquin, *morocco leather,* 108.

meikle, *much,* 346.

morat, *a drink made of honey flavoured with the juice of mulberries,* 47.

morte, *the hunters' call at the death of the stag,* 66.

muscadine, *a sweet wine made from muscat grapes,* 142.

Nazarene, *a Christian,* 158.

nidering, *lowest of the low; a Saxon epithet of the deepest contempt,* 218.

nombles, *the testicles of the deer,* 66.

Oldbuck of Monkbarns, *see The Antiquary.*

ordiner, *ordinary.*

outrecuidance, *presumption, insolence,* 148.

over God's forbode, *God forbid,* 137.

partisan, *a pike or halbert,* 294.

350

GLOSSARY

paynim, *a heathen*, 255.

pigment, *a sweet and rich liquor, composed of wine highly spiced, and sweetened with honey*, 47.

pinfold, *a fold or enclosure for animals*, 243.

prime, *the office said at the first hour after sunrise*, 258.

proffeit, *profit*, 349.

purchaser, *procurer*, 347 ; purchest, *obtained*, 348.

put to the horne, *outlawed ; the formal sentence of outlawry being formerly preceded by the blast of a horn*, 347.

real, *a Spanish coin worth* 2½d., 99.

recheate, *the hunters' call to the hounds*, 66.

reeve, *steward*, xix.

regiment, *rule, government*, 347.

rere-supper, *a night-meal ; sometimes a collation given at a late hour, after the regular supper*, 263.

rheno, *fur tippet*, 108.

runagate, *vagabond*, 275.

runlet, *a small barrel*, 247.

St. Nicholas's clerks, *robbers ; worshippers of St. Nicholas, the patron saint of thieves*, 167, 286.

sewer, *servitor, butler*, 308.

shaveling, *a contemptuous term for a monk*, 295.

simarre, *woman's loose light robe*, 109.

simnel-bread, *a cake of the finest white bread ;* tech. *a cake offered as a gift on Simnel (or Mothering) Sunday in Mid-Lent*, 213.

sith, *since*, 204.

soldan, *sultan*, 254.

soppe, *sap, gravy*, 346.

springal, *youth*, 189.

tack, *lease*, 346.

tane, *taken*.

Termagaunt, *an imaginary tempestuous deity supposed by the Crusaders to have been worshipped by the Saracens*, 63.

titulars, *lay impropriators of church revenues*, 344.

to-hewn and to-shred, *hack and cut in pieces*, 178.

trowl, *push*.

truss my points, *tie the laces of my dress*, 291.

tulchan bishop, *see* p. 344.

urus, *a wild bull*, 247.

waes hael, *be in health*, 248.

Wardour, Sir Arthur, *see The Antiquary*.

warlock, *wizard*, xxxiv.

wassail, *spiced ale or wine*, 252.

wastle cakes, *cakes of the finest white bread*, 213.

Watling-Street, *the travellers'* (wadla) *street ; one of the great Roman roads, which, beginning at Dover, passed through London, thence to Chester and north to Scotland*, 286.

Wat Tyrrel, *the archer who slew William Rufus, Aug. 2, 1100*, 113.

whinger, *a cutlass*, 347.

whittle, *a small clasp-knife*, 208.

zecchin, *a Byzantine gold coin worth about* 9s. 4d.

351

This book designed by
William B. Taylor
is a production of
Heron Books, London

Printed on wood free paper
and bound by Hazell Watson & Viney Ltd.
Aylesbury, Bucks

Printed and bound in England